W. ROYAL STOKES

Backwards Over

A Novel in Three Parts

Part 1: Rufus Has Been on the Lam

Hannah Books

Backwards Over, a trilogy of novels, is a work of fiction. The characters constituting the work's *dramatis personae* and the incidents that flesh out their stories are creations of the author's imagination. Although locales, walks of life, occupations, lifestyles, types of personalities, and the sorts of circumstances that the author is familiar with are drawn from and utilized in outline, any resemblance to actual persons or events is coincidental and unintentional.

Hannah Books
wroyalstokes.com

Printed in the United States of America

First Printing, 2015

ISBN 978-0692277140

Cover Design by Clare Connolly
Author Photo by Neale Stokes

For

Erika Hartmann Stokes
Sutton Royal Stokes
Neale Hartmann Stokes

"If you don't live it, it won't come out of your horn."
Charlie Parker

"Le coeur a ses raisons que la raison ne connaît point."
Blaise Pascal

Chapter 1

This ain't no Hahvahd Squay-yer!

James Clifton Harsh had a shop for rebuilding Volkswagens. Of course, that was only his specialty. He knew most all cars, and sometimes combined different makes in strange ways. For instance, he had spent a year one time—in his spare time, that is, for he always had many projects in progress—replacing the air-cooled rear-end engine of a Corvair sedan with a water-cooled Model-A Ford engine. He was quite proud of the finished product and drove it as his main car for a couple of months before selling it for a handsome price to an Austin collector of offbeat and antique vehicles.

What he would do was pick up the cheapest Volkswagen Beetles or busses he could find, combing the Sunday classified ads for ten and fifteen-year-old models; some of the Beetles had that tiny window in the rear. Sometimes they would be on their second or third engines, the total mileage often at the 300,000 mark, the bodies battered and assaulted, fenders not matching in color. He seldom paid more than fifty or a hundred dollars for these decrepit wrecks and more often than not had to tow them back to his shop.

And since many of his finds were tireless or perhaps even missing one or more wheels, Harsh had built a low flatbed trailer with runways and equipped it with a hand-operated winch. The design of this rig had been inspired by one of a similar nature used by the police in Barcelona. In fact, he had seen his own Beetle hauled off before his very eyes on one such device because he had refused to heed warning signs and parked it with its passenger-side wheels on the sidewalk in an alley around the corner from the hotel where he had checked in fifteen minutes before. He had reasoned that the signs forbidding parking need not be taken seriously since twenty or so other vehicles were ignoring them and not one of these had been ticketed. It was the sidewalk factor, it was later pointed out to him by the clerk handing him a receipt for the rather minimal fine, that had distinguished his offense from that of the other cars, trucks, and busses parked in the alley. "In Barcelona don't never park on no sidewalk," he was advised.

There were always ten or so of these hulks strewn about the yard of Harsh's shop in various stages of decomposition, some disemboweled, others missing fenders, hoods, roofs, a few on their sides or upturned. And scattered here and there were axles, doors, engine blocks, bumpers, and many smaller parts such as generators and fuel pumps.

Inside the shed—for it was hardly more than that—were work tables covered with more parts as well as tools of every description, even a hand saw and other carpentry accessories, for example, a miter box, and all of these tools seemed to have been left where they had last been used, which was actually the case since nothing was ever put away in the shop. In fact, Harsh would say, by way of explaining the utter disorder of the premises, "There ain't no place to *put* anything away!"

Over in one corner were four engines, two of which were mounted on low stands, and in the very center of the shed was a Beetle, its empty engine compartment gaping up at a chain hoist suspended from a girder, which itself was attached at either end to two legs, the five massive pieces of metal forming an eight-foot high sawhorse. To the rear of the car, on a tarpaulin, was the car's engine.

The body of the VW was in excellent shape. Indeed, but for that small rear window it could have been this year's model, so glistening was its newly painted surface. The interior was immaculate and of a style that could well have been of custom design and careful, handcrafted execution. In fact, this was one of the shop's specialties, Harsh being an accomplished upholsterer. This talent, along with his expertise in body work, enabled him to refashion both the interior and exterior of his creations. For it must be understood that Jim Harsh created anew, he did not repair the old, and he did this from the assembled bodies, chassis, engines, and parts that lay about him. He always made it very clear, before accepting a contract, that he had to be "given a certain amount of rein."

Of late, he had avoided engine work, leaving that to his assistant, the master mechanic Boswell, known to all as Boz. Jim had found that he much preferred the creative possibilities of wielding the needle, the paint brush, and the paint gun and applying the necessary raw materials to the body and the interior. Oh, the design of all major alterations, such as the conversion of the Corvair, was left to him. He would lend Boz a hand for a half hour now and then if a task required his help, and he was always available for consultation and problem solving. But the truth was that long hours over an engine had begun in the past year or so to bore him.

On this particular August morning of 1968 at Sea Horse Bodies & Innards, two persons were in the shed. One was seated on a wooden box the faded stenciled letters on the side of which indicated that it had once served as container for Wenatchee Apples. Gaunt of physique and close cropped of hair, this individual could have served as stand-in for Humphrey Bogart in scenes in *High Sierra* that required only a background profile shot. He was shirtless, his denim overalls were spotted with grease and dirt, and his high-top work shoes were decorated with a rainbow assortment of paint splashes. Hunched over the engine, he was involved in an apparently difficult task, for both hands held tools and it was not possible to discern whether the tools were in motion or at rest.

Seated on one of the engines in the corner was a man with a Fu Man Chu moustache, widow's peak, and blond hair of shoulder length. He was smoking a stub of a cigar. Now breaking the several-minute silence that had succeeded the exchange of "Good morning," he asked, "Boz, do you think Harsh will be back today?"

The mechanic raised his head only to that point at which his eyes met those of his interlocutor.

"Fer sure today," he drawled, "mos' lakly purty soon."

"But I thought he went to Dallas yesterday."

"That's right he did, but he said he'd git on the road by nine this mornin' so's he could be here fer lunch. And I *needs him* on this fucker! Takes more hands than I got, thas fer sure, and you has made it knowd that you wants to drive it outa here today."

"And he's going to get here by twelve? Hell, Dallas is almost two-hundred miles from Austin! How's he—?"

"Fer Jimbo iz a two-an'-half, three-hour run." He returned his eyes to the engine, leaning down and gripping the tools tightly.

"That's really hoofing it with a trailer. Those damn things start swaying when you get past fifty or so."

"You're talkin' horse trailers 'r Airstream 'r somethin'," Boz corrected him, looking up again. "That thar rig's gonna be empty onna return trip, and the way Jimbo builded it iz real low down an' balanced and the air doan git up agin it lak no house trailer. No, you can't hardly notice it back there and you can cruise real nice 'roun' seventy-five per. Yessiree, ol' Jimbo, he be pullin' up real soon. He know you gonna raise hell iffen we don't get this baby outa here by nightfall."

"*Damn right!* And I'm going to sit here and make sure you do!"

"You soun' a little pissed off there, Mister Oliver," Boz mumbled, straining to tighten a bolt on the engine head.

"Well, I tell you, Boz, it's not so much the wait for this bloody job to get done as it is learning last night that the bus Harsh sold to my good friend Joe Lewis turned out to be on the stolen car list and the pigs impounded it." Oliver dropped his cigar and ground it into the dirt with his right loafer.

Boz put the two wrenches on the tarp and sat up

straight.

"There!" He sighed in evident relief, surveying the completed task. "Got thet back on there okay." He turned toward Oliver. "Yeah, I heerd about it," he said.

"What? You know about it?"

Boz nodded.

"Does Harsh?"

"Yep."

"When—?"

"Yestiday, jes afore Jimbo took off, Perfesser Lewis done phoned 'im."

"Well, what the hell does Harsh intend to do about it?"

"Ask *'im!* Ah doan speak fer no man."

"I certainly shall, as soon as he walks through that door."

"You know, Jimbo dint steal no bus, he pay hard cash fer it, like as how he always do."

"*Christ all mighty!*" Oliver exploded, suddenly getting to his feet and nearly losing his balance in the act. "*What are his sources?*"

"He bought that bus offin a student o'er at the college. The youngster boughten it new and only had it six month or so afore he run it offin the road one night."

"Probably one of my students," Oliver said with a laugh.

"You *teach* over there?"

"Yes."

"I thought you was a post gra-jew-ate er somethin'."

"I'm that too."

Boz suddenly slashed at the air in front of his face. "*Git* th' *fuck outa here!*" he said, swatting this time at his right ear. "God *damn* these *fuckin' Tex-ass hoss flies!*" His hand now quickly gestured toward the shed's wide door. "*Hey*, here come the man now!"

The roar of an engine that had been souped up with a dual carburetor and a head exhaust system had somewhat muffled Boz's announcement, and the blast of a two-tone Italian tourist-bus air horn punctuated the termination of the engine's sound.

"The sea horse has beached!" a voice shouted from the shed's yard.

The man who strode through the door was of impressively handsome appearance despite his ragged attire—bleached gray and much-patched cut-off jeans, a tee shirt that was missing one sleeve and had a large rent in the armpit of the other, a dirt-smudged once-white baseball cap, and, incongruously, a pair of red-trimmed flip flops of so new a look that they well could have been purchased that morning. His eyes were perhaps his most prominent feature, for they were singularly large and seemed to be always upon you. When, in discomfort from his penetrating stare, one deflected one's gaze and moved a few paces away, his eyes remained concentrated as before, much as in the case of some painted portraits the eyes of which follow one around a room. As if this did not cause disquiet enough, Harsh's eyes gave the impression that they were being consciously held open wider than was normal.

And Jim Harsh's movements were nearly always darting, both when his entire body was in motion and when he shifted the position of a limb or even flexed a muscle. When he raised his Zippo lighter to a Gauloises hanging from his lips, an act that occurred like clockwork every ten or fifteen minutes, it was almost as though he had suffered a sudden pain in his lower jaw and was reacting, involuntarily, to the sensation. It was really only when seated that he could keep still and even then the hand holding the cigarette would tremble while resting on a knee.

Once inside the shed, Jim was the first to speak. His slow, Texan-accented, yet distinctively enunciated, manner of speaking had more of the broad A in it than one would perhaps expect, on occasion lending to his delivery a somewhat ludicrous flavor. Some meeting him for the first time would wonder at his mocking imitation of a prep school-nurtured product of an Ivy League institution, but the fact was that Jim, with a Yale undergraduate degree, had spent three years, from 1959 to 1962, completing all the requirements except the dissertation for a Harvard doctorate in English literature.

"I was walking down the street this morning in Dallas and this little girl—couldn't have been more than four years old—says, *'Hey there Mister Hippie Man!' Hippie* Man! So I yells back—." Harsh was smiling down at Boz as he began his anecdote but broke off, startled, when he heard Oliver's anger-filled voice. His eyes not yet adapted to the penumbra, Jim blinked and scanned the corner in the rear whence came the voice.

"Harsh, what the fuck's going on with the Lewis bus?"

"The Louis bus. Now what in the name of my crazy Aunt Sally is the 'Louis bus'?"

"*No, no!*" Oliver hastened to correct him, pointedly exaggerating the apostrophe, "The Lewis-*iz* bus!"

"Oh, you mean Joe Lewis's and Jane Phillips' bus!"

He approached Oliver, pulling from a hip pocket a leather cigarette case and, flipping it open with his index finger, extended it to him.

"Here, calm the nerves with one o' Uncle Jimbo's

nails, man. In fact, let me buy you a suds."

He turned to an ancient, hip-high Dr. Pepper soft drink cooler, punched its coin return button three times, opened the hinged lid, and re-deposited the three disgorged nickels one by one. As each dropped into the coin box, he slid along under the imprisoning bars to the opening now provided a slender, blue-labeled brown bottle.

"Ale," he said, as he levered off the caps by means of the cooler's opener, handing one bottle to Oliver, taking another to Boz. "Yeah," he called over his shoulder to Oliver. "Well, I'm going over there as soon as we get your engine in. I don't know what happened but I'll make it good for them. First time that's happened in a year or so."

"You mean it's a regular thing!" Oliver cut him off.

"Like I mean it happens once a year or so, like I said!" Jim shot back. "If you call that regular—well, I wouldn't care to get mine regular like that, if you know what I mean, babe."

"I see you're still drinking this German brand, Jim," said Oliver, putting the bottle to his lips and evidently warming to the shop's proprietor upon being assured that he intended to resolve the matter of the Lewis vehicle.

Harsh put the side of his left thong against another apple box and, walking sideways, slid it over next to Boz. Between gulps of their ales, the two spoke in low tones as they looked over the engine at their feet.

The cold ale had done much to alleviate the stress caused by Oliver's outburst. Fact was, it was a desert-hot day of a summer not much blessed with rain, none for almost a month, and in the shop the only relief from the oppressive heat came from two fans of the kind one sees in old-fashioned hotels or barbershops, that is, mounted on tall metal spars in round stands. These fans were kept on when the shop was occupied but only at the lowest speed lest they stir up a minor dust storm in the shed. They had been purchased at an auction of the furnishings, kitchenware, and linens of a large downtown Austin hotel which was now in the final stages of demolition.

"I'm going to have another one of these," Harsh said, rising. "How about you, Oliver? By the way, stick around, man. You can watch us do a transplant, maybe learn something useful—for a change."

"Still slamming academe, I see," Oliver responded with a smile.

Jim returned with three more bottles of ale and a pair of rubber surgical gloves. He pulled the gloves on and sat down on the apple box. "Here's your brew, Oliver. I ain't got time to bring it over there."

About two hours later, the three were rolling north on Route 35 in Oliver's Beetle, Jim at the wheel, Boz to his right, Oliver leaning forward from the middle of the back seat. Harsh had insisted upon handling this test drive ("It's *routine*, man!" he had informed the car's owner.), eliciting from Oliver a promise that he would drive them back to the shop if other transportation failed to materialize.

Oliver had been transfixed watching the two install the rebuilt engine in his car. After they had lowered the engine into its compartment, Harsh remained, surgeon-like, nearly immobile except for that part of his arms from the elbows, his hands and wrists moving rapidly with socket wrenches and other tools. Every ten or so minutes he would pause to light with his Zippo one of his aromatic "nails," only to place it with trembling hand in an aluminum pie pan to the left of his flip flops and forget about it as it burnt to an ash. Boz acted as nurse to this surgeon, fetching tools from all around the shop, the location of which Jim would bellow to him if Boz could not find one or another item, Jim seeming to know precisely where all in his domain resided.

Once the engine was installed and had been started up, Jim backed the Beetle out of the shed and left it there to idle in the shade of a giant oak tree. Returning to the two standing on the tool-scattered tarp, Jim gave them the thumbs-up sign and continued toward the Dr. Pepper cooler, returning with three more opened bottles of the German ale.

"I challenge you," he announced, handing bottles to Boz and Oliver and raising his own to his lips. Harsh won, his gullet seeming not to move as he virtually poured the twelve ounces of cold beverage down his throat.

"I learned that from a German tugboat operator," he informed them, wiping away the tears that had formed in his eyes. "Only, that sonovabich could do that to a fuckin' *liter!* Come on, let's take a test drive over to Joe and Jane's."

As they waited in the left lane, preparing to turn onto 38th Street, a loud whistle came from a pickup truck to their right. Only a few feet from them, its hefty driver, shaved of head and of regular-army drill-cadre cast, grinned mockingly in the direction of Oliver in the back seat, raised a sixteen ounce can of beer to his mouth in toast, gunned his engine, and roared off. Harsh smiled and gave him the peace sign. Boz, declining to acknowledge the episode, had fixed his gaze upon two teen-aged girls on the sidewalk, one of whom smiled and waved. Oliver, more than a little red in the face, whether from the heat or rage or a combination thereof, had been thumbing his nose at the now departed driver of the pickup.

"*Stupid fucking redneck!*" he yelled, causing Boz to raise his hands to his ears and Harsh to burst out laughing.

"*Come on,* Ollie!" Jim shouted over his shoulder, "*you're* in *Tex-*ass! *This* ain't no *Hahvahd Squay-yer!*"

Several blocks short of Guadalupe Street, Oliver commenced to tell them the history of a group of abandoned sanitarium-like buildings that occupied an entire block on their left. It had been constructed, he informed them, around the turn of the century as a hospital and rest home for the widows of Civil War veterans.

"Two or three years ago," Oliver continued, "only three of these superannuated survivors remained housed there and because of the considerable expense of maintaining the facility, a virtual Spandau Prison, these three ancient crones were moved, along with their wedding dresses and photograph albums, their memories and their hacking coughs, to a private nursing home in the suburbs. One of them, at something like a hundred and fifteen, died within a week, another lived for a half year or so, and I think she was about a hundred and five. The remaining one was the second, and much younger, wife of a Confederate colonel who went to his eternal reward in his mid-sixties upon suffering a heart attack, it is said, while screwing her on their wedding night around the turn of the century. She would have been around twenty-five at the time. Anyway, this old lady is still with us at ninety-three or so, still drinking her two ounces of cognac three times a day, still talking about the Baltimore fire of

1904, paranoid out of her skull about 'those colored people calling me on the telephone all the time.'"

Oliver said he didn't know the legal details, could only conjecture that the original grant prevented the use of the Confederate Ladies Home for any other purpose than that for which it was established nearly seventy years ago, perhaps until the last known widow of a Texan Civil War veteran was deceased.

"Wow, what a story!" Jim exclaimed, and Boz nodded in affirmation, glancing to his left at Oliver, who had been leaning forward between the two all the while as he recounted what little he knew of the home's history and present circumstances.

"I always wondered about that place," Jim added. "I bet that would be some kind of trip to get in there with a sixteen-millimeter camera and wander around for a while, then get someone to do a musical score for background. Wow!"

"You probably couldn't get permission to do that," Oliver said, "but maybe the caretaker could be bribed. I've seen an old black dude mowing the grass and clipping the hedge. Maybe he stays there—yeah, I've seen a light on at night."

By this time the VW had traveled south on Guadalupe for a few blocks and then turned right into a street quite unlike any they had so far traversed. It had more the appearance of the interior of an amusement park fun house than of a street of lived-in houses. Varicolored school busses, vans, and walk-in bread and milk delivery trucks lined both sides of this rather narrow street and overflowed the driveways of the houses. Some of the vehicles dated back to the early 1950s. There were several Volkswagen Beetles and busses, a dozen or so motorcycles, some of these last named on the lawns, and many bicycles, some of them on racks on the rear ends or roofs of the busses. Here and there were driveway-bound wheel-less cars resting on cinder blocks.

Some of the houses sported flags, an American (but of only forty-eight stars) here, two Viet Cong there, and a lone Confederate draped over the hood of a Ford pickup. Many of the houses' windows framed posters that faced out. There was one of W.C. Fields in top hat peering cannily over a hand of cards, a Jane Fonda reclining on a beach, several Bogarts, a Paul Newman, and a Robert Vaughn. Some of the three-story houses had porticoes that had been painted in garish reds and blues and greens, one color here, another there, and in one case each of the four columns supporting the second-story porch had been assigned a different psychedelic hue.

Harsh brought the car to a stop at the terminus of the dead-end street.

"Hope somebody's at home," he said, looking across Boz and shaking a cigarette out of the leather case. "Lookee!" he mimicked the Hollywood version of a Chinese immigrant's accent. "Someone at window!"

"It's Jane," Oliver said, reaching over Boz's shoulder and out of the car's window for the door handle. "I think that means to come on in."

The three of them piled out of the Volkswagen and moved slowly across what could only by a considerable application of imagination be described as a lawn, for the space that served as apron to the turn-of-century structure was nearly covered with foot-high weeds. Here and there, washed-out dirt flecked with unhealthy looking crab grass peeked through the taller growth.

Upon entering the house, the three seemed to be

relieved of an almost physical burden. They glanced fleetingly at the dark woodwork and the ponderous Victorian furnishings in the front hall, faint smiles appearing on the faces of Jim and Oliver, Boz merely winking his right eye.

"I always gets a feeling like I has just stepped into one o' them ol' fashion movie parlors," the latter whispered.

"Yeah, it's almost like it was air conditioned," Jim said. "Almost like a blast of cold air had hit you."

"Coolest place in town," Oliver added.

"Shut the god damned door, would you *please!*" boomed a deep male voice from a room on the left. "Before you flood the place with *bloody Tex-ass heat!*"

"*Hey,* that sounds like my man *Joe Edwards Lewis!*" Harsh cried out, making his way between the other two toward the double sliding doors.

A rumbling sound accompanied the leftward motion of one of the doors and a tall, slim, and long-bearded man stood grinning at the trio standing before him. The mismatch of the man's hair, which fell in a ponytail onto his back, and his beard was striking. The former was of a rich brown and, except for a high widow's peak at his part on the right, was still full. His handlebar mustache and mutton chops were of a similarly unblemished brown, but his beard was flecked with gray throughout its first three inches and then became completely so as it settled onto his chest. Also notable were the figure and posture of this man of about forty years, for Joe Lewis carried his slender six-foot, one-inch height with the erect carriage of a military officer and his abdomen was of a flatness that made one wonder what prevented his beltless jeans from falling to his ankles. He wore a white T-shirt and was shod in blue flip flops.

Standing a step or two to Joe's rear was a strikingly handsome woman of trim build in her early-twenties and about a half-foot shorter than her companion. She was barefoot, dressed in cut-off jeans and a University of Toronto sweatshirt with its sleeves bunched up past her elbows, and was holding a Siamese cat in her arms. Her full black hair fell six inches or so below her shoulders. She came forward and addressed the newcomers.

"Jim, Boz, Oliver! How nice to see you! We were just having our tea and a smoke. Would you like to join us?" Her diction was very slightly clipped in the manner of a public-school-educated Britisher.

"Well, now, I think that would be just a dandy way to start the day or the afternoon or whatever it is. I haven't slept for thirty hours or so and can't seem to put it together what time of day it is. Especially here in the coolness of your sanctuary. I mean, why not? Want Boz to roll some weed?" Having blurted this out with breakneck rapidity, Harsh turned to Boz and was about to speak when Joe interrupted.

"Thanks, but we want to use our new hookah," he said, gesturing to the rear with a nod of his head.

Jim leaned to the right to better see the huge telephone-cable spool that served as the room's lone table. The water pipe sat in the middle of it.

"Does it draw well?" Oliver asked.

"Oh, for sure you'll see some interesting pictures, my friend. Let's find out. I just now took it out of the box it arrived in and filled it with water," said Joe, gesturing to the cardboard and paper packing materials on the floor. "We've got some mighty potent shit here that supposedly came from Colombia." He pointed to a clear plastic bottle with screw cap beside the hookah. "Take me but a minute to load 'er up."

"What'd thet lid set you back, Perfesser?" asked Boz.

"Twenty clams, Boz," said Joe, motioning the three to join him at the spool where he was lowering himself onto a cushion on the floor. "How's that tea doing, babe?"

Joe reached under the spool and produced the *New York Times Magazine,* which he opened and laid before him and upon which he placed the water pipe. Then he unscrewed the cap of the bottle and deftly shook the finely ground marijuana into the hookah's bowl, gently patting it down with his index finger. Moving the bottle, its cap, and the hookah to one side, he lifted the magazine and formed it into a narrow trough held in a steep slope over the bottle and coaxed the few spilled grains to roll down into the bottle.

"It's like watching a chemist at work," said Harsh softly.

"A *mad* chemist!" said Oliver, chuckling.

"Yes, and you are my guinea pigs—or better still, my rhesus monkeys—and I am very curious to see what sort of strange transformations you undergo after sampling my potion."

"*Joe!*" Harsh called from across the table, "did I ever tell you about when I was at Harvard a couple of those little rhesus monkeys escaped from some lab in New York and one day people were walking down Sixth Avenue or somewhere downtown and they looked down at one of those grates in the sidewalk and these tiny little fingers were curled around the bars?"

"One can only assume that they came to the city on business," Joe muttered as he returned the magazine to its place beneath the spool. "*Monkey* business!"

"Well, I'm glad everybody is enjoying himself," said

Jane as she came into the room carrying in front of her a large tray laden with tea pot, cups and saucers, a jar of honey, small pitcher of milk, and bowl of lemon wedges. "I daren't inquire what the joke was."

"A very innocent sort of jest, my dear," said Joe absently as he put to his lips the mouthpiece at the end of the hookah's foot-and-a half-long hose and tentatively drew upon it. "I do think we is in bizness."

As Jane, seated on the cushion to his right, took orders for the steaming beverage, Joe looked around him. Despite its high ceiling, the room's orientation was to its lower regions. The only furnishings that were higher than thigh level were the sound system's cater-cornered speakers, which hung from the ceiling, and the posters. One of these depicted a wooden Indian and was captioned, "What this country needs is a good five-cent joint," and on the opposite wall was Allen Ginsberg in sandwich boards calling for the legalization of marijuana. Another was of a stunning brunette standing in water holding up her skirt. Four cushions made of fifty-pound flour sacks and spaced two feet apart made it comfortable to sit and browse among the hundred or so books and several stacks of magazines and newspapers, as well as to operate the controls of the turntable, reel-to-reel tape recorder, and other sound equipment, all of which occupied the two long cement-block-supported boards that served as shelves against one wall.

Oliver, across the spool to Joe's left, had been staring intently at his host's profile for the several minutes it took Jane to distribute the coffee and tea. "One wants to enter this room sitting," he said.

"You read my mind, my friend, I was just thinking along those very lines."

"Well, as you know, we do call it our 'sitting room'," said Jane.

"I seem to be fresh out of matches here at the table. Can someone provided me with some fire so we can get this show on the road ? Or do I have to get my tired old body to its feet and fetch a box from the galley?"

"Honestly, honey, you'd think you were eighty years old!" said Jane, laughing.

"It's this god-awful Tex-ass heat that slows me down, my dear," waving away Jim's Zippo lighter and accepting the box of matches Boz was offering him.

"Come on, Joe," said Jim, "a southern boy like you? If a Yankee like Ollie here can take it, you sure as hell ought to be able to."

"Well, it does puzzle me that one-hundred-plus heat doesn't bother you nawthenahs. Like Jane here, she doesn't seem to notice it, even though where she hails from it rarely gets into the eighties."

All fell silent as Joe held the thumbnail-struck wooden match to the hookah's bowl and drew several short, rapid breaths. Assured by the red glow of the bowl's contents that it was well lighted, he inhaled deeply, eyes closed, and passed the mouthpiece to Jane. No one spoke until each had had a turn at the pipe. It was Oliver who broke the silence. His eyes were fixed upon the wall behind Joe and Jane.

"I've been looking at that picture for all this time and I didn't figure it out until this very moment," he said slowly.

Joe and Jane turned and looked at the wall behind them. Jim and Boz had only to raise their eyes in order to determine which of the posters Oliver was referring to.

"What do you mean?" Jane asked.

"The Wingate Paine?" added Joe.

"The girl there. I knew this teaching assistant in music, a violinist, who had that same photo on the wall of her office and she told me the girl didn't have any pants on. I thought she meant underneath her skirt, that she was using her imagination, letting the photo do some kind of head trip on her. But now I see what she meant."

"I sure wouldn't mind her doing a head trip on me," Jim muttered.

"Oliver, I'm surprised at you!" Jane said in a mocking way. "I thought you, of all people, would immediately catch on."

Joe slapped the flat of his hand on the surface of the spool. "*Come on,* Ollie, are you telling me it's taken you a *god damned year* to see what Wingate Paine is doing with the water and the lady's pussy?"

"Yeah, I see it now, but I always thought the dress was only about halfway up her thighs. That's her bush there, and she sure as hell doesn't have underwear on. It's the reflection on the water that creates the illusion that her legs bend there, like that's her knees there at the water's surface."

"Is that thing out?" Joe asked.

"Nozur," Boz slurred. "Izdoinjuzfine."

"This is very fast shit," Jim observed, looking across at Joe. "I completely forget what we were talking about. I mean, I followed all of that about the photo, and I have to admit that it took me quite a while of staring at that scene to realize that the girl's—" he caught Jane's eyes "—shall we say, *private parts* are exposed—."

"Most delicately expressed," Joe interposed wryly. "Pussies is s'pos'd be private." He reached under the edge of the spool and caressed Jane's thigh and she squeezed his hand.

"—but I haven't the foggiest notion what we were talking about before that," Jim continued."

"I think it concerned matches, Jim," said Jane, smiling.

"Oh, right, yeah, that's what we—." Jim took the mouthpiece from Oliver and inhaled, suddenly lurching forward upon removing it but keeping his lips tightly compressed.

"Don't *lose it*, Jimbo!" Boz admonished him. "It be *too good* to lose."

A single "ding" from the kitchen caused all to abruptly sit up straight.

"Oh, Joe, my *scones!*" said Jane, starting to rise.

"I'll get them, babe, keep your seat." Joe was on his feet before the last word was spoken. "I have a craving for *caffé con latte,*" he called back over his shoulder as he headed for the kitchen, a hint of mirth in his voice.

"He found an old espresso pot he had in Italy six or seven years ago and he's dying to use it," Jane explained. "No telling what else he's up to though. He's quite unpredictable."

Oliver had gotten to his feet and was stretching. "Jane, would it be okay to put some music on?"

"Sure, just start the tape. Joe got it ready to go just before you arrived."

Oliver lowered himself to a cushion at the shelves, examined the controls of the sound system, and pushed the play button. The room was immediately filled with heavy guitar chords, which introduced up-tempo two-handed picking. Oliver returned to his cushion at the spool and, along with the others, remained silent during the opening selection, which was strong with Flamenco flavor yet also contained elements of blues, folk, and country, even a jazz lick here and there.

"That Fahey can sure pick that guitar!" said Oliver, the first to speak after the number had concluded.

The smiles of the three across the spool from her alerted Jane to the return of Joe and she glanced up at him as he leaned over to place a silver tray on the spool. He had donned a black swallow-tailed coat and upon his head was a top hat.

"Now here we have Miss Jane's special scones and various delicious choices of things to put upon them, and also the makings of several styles of *caffé Italiano.*"

Joe studied the tray. On it were several jars of honey, a bottle of Blackstrap Molasses, a dish of butter, a three-sectioned server containing jams, a bowl of brown sugar, a small glass pitcher of foamed whipped cream, a stainless steel pitcher of heated milk, a large espresso pot, five Italian-bar-style cups, silver spoons and knives, and an empty wicker basket.

"You'll notice that the lone deviation from Italian service is the absence of white sugar, a poisonous substance that we recently eliminated from our diet. Anyone care for cappuccino?"

"What's thet like, Perfesser?" Boz inquired and, pointing to the pot, added, "and 'splain me how that *dee*-vice work, woodja?"

"Cappuccino is half coffee and half steamed milk," Joe explained, "and you put a lot of sugar in it, or honey, if you prefer." He picked up the pot and poured into two cups.

"I'm going to provide you with your very first experience, one might say your *virgin* experience, of cappuccino, Boz." He looked up and fixed his eyes upon the three men. "Now there's an interesting circumstance for your analysis, gentlemen, to wit, at what point during a virgin experience does one cease being a virgin?" Having filled the two cups halfway, Joe held the pot up and pointed first to its lower compartment, then to its upper section. "The cold water starts here and upon boiling rises in a pipe and through the coffee into this part whence it is poured. I'll take it apart for you after it cools down, Boz, so that you can examine its finer points in detail at your leisure." He spooned brown sugar into the cups, topped them off with a generous helping of the foamed milk, and handed one of them across the table to Boz.

"I wish I had you on film explaining that, Joe," Jim said. "In fact, why don't we work up a skit of that and you packing the water pipe and doing that. I'll bring my sixteen millimeter and some lights over. What say?"

"Agreed—except for one demur, friend."

"What's that?"

"It will have to be improvised. I can't read lines or rehearse or anything. Has to be as spontaneous as we can make it. Why don't you sneak in here in the middle of the night with all of your equipment and I'll come down to see what the hell is going on and—."

"Yes, that would be *perfect!*" Jane interrupted, giggling. "You know, Joe *always* puts on his cutaway and stovepipe hat when he gets up in the middle of the night."

"Yes, that's true," Joe agreed, "and since it's usually because I can't sleep, the first thing I do is put on a pot of espresso—and pack the pipe. Nothing like the combination of caffeine and Columbian shit to put you into a special kind of dreamland. Now I don't recommend that if you want to *sleep*—but for a most rewarding hallucinatory session, be my guest." He broke off into choking laughter, nearly falling onto Jane as he gripped the edge of the spool and pushed himself to a kneeling position. "*I forgot your scones!*"

"Oh, honey, they'll be burnt to a crisp!"

"No worry, I took them out of the oven. I'm not *completely* wiped away, babe."

"I'll get them, honey. I forgot ice and glasses," she said, her hand on his arm.

"What's your pleasure, Jim, Oliver?" said Joe, sitting back down upon the cushion.

"Think I'll wait on that ice and have me a tall cold one, Joe, of tea, that is," Oliver replied.

"*É possibile fare per mi un cappuccino con ghiaccio, Giusèppe?*"

"*Si, con piacere, Giacomo, appena che Giovanna retorna.*"*

"Oh, I just remembered what we were talking about before—those rhesus monkeys," said Jim."

"Ah, yes, the infamous *Macacae mulattae,*" replied Joe, turning to take the bucket of ice from Jane, who balanced on her other hand a tray upon which were glasses, a pitcher of water, and the towel-wrapped scones Joe had earlier forgotten.

"Anything left in that thing?" Joe asked.

"Lez find out," said Boz, striking a match with his thumbnail and drawing on the mouthpiece as he held the flame to the bowl. He swung the hookah around and extended its hose toward Joe.

The pipe made one last trip around the spool and was then forgotten as the party of five sipped their chosen beverages and spread jam and honey on the scones. Jim and Joe lighted cigarettes, Oliver a cigar.

Suddenly Joe lurched forward and, supporting himself

---

* Is it possible to make me a cappuccino with ice, Joe?
  Yes, with pleasure, Jim, as soon as Jane returns.

with his left hand on the spool's surface, gestured with cigarette at Jim and, in a whisper that could barely be made out by those facing him, said, "You haven't heard the latest about the bus."

"Yeah, man," Jim said, "I'm going to get that straightened out right away. I've got all of the purchase papers on that vehicle in order. Shouldn't be a problem to get it back free and clear by tomorrow. As I told you last night, it definitely was not a stolen vehicle—ever. I know that for a fact."

"Jim, I'm trying to tell you!" Joe said excitedly, "If you just let me get a word in here—the bus was *confiscated* by the pigs."

"We didn't learn this until a couple of hours ago," explained Jane. "When we called you yesterday, and when we talked to Oliver on the phone this morning, we only had the version given to us by some police clerk."

"Who, typically, had it all screwed up," Joe added. "Anyway, here's what happened. A friend of Nando's had to move out of his pad and we lent the bus to Nando so he could take his friend's gear over to the cat's new place. According to the lawyer who's handling his bail—they're springing him tonight—the fuzz pulled Nando over on his way back here, *on suspicion,* and took him and our bus downtown. The lawyer told us they didn't find diddly squat in our bus. I knew they wouldn't because I made Nando promise that he'd get his buddy to get his stash over there by some other means, not in our bus, so's there wouldn't be seeds or something spilled. And I never leave anything of an incriminating nature in my blue bus, no way. I knew a cat who had his brand new bus confiscated when they found a roach in the ashtray. And he never saw that rig again. *A god damn roach,* for Jesus Christ's sake!"

Joe slammed his hand on the spool with such force that cups rattled in their saucers.

"When will this nonsense come to an end?" He paused. "Listen, do you want to hear just how ridiculous it can get? A couple of days ago we heard from some folks back east that they put a guy under the death penalty for transporting. He was on his way from California to Baltimore with a U-Haul trailer full of Mexican shit and they stopped him for running a red light on the outskirts of some city."

"Where?" asked Oliver.

"I don't know. My source didn't either."

"Sounds like Mississippi—or *somewhere* down south," Jim suggested. "But why would he be taking a southern route with that load?"

"Who knows, said Joe. "Anyway, he was on speed, hadn't been to bed for two days and nights, was really blotto. His lawyer advised him to waive his right to a jury trial and he went up before a judge. Unfortunately, he didn't get the judge the lawyer had counted on because the dude had had a heart attack and was on sick leave. Instead he got this reactionary sonovabitch and was tried and convicted in about fifteen minutes." Joe sipped his coffee. "But he got away."

"He got away?" Oliver asked. "You're saying he escaped from Death Row? How'd he do that?"

"Let me finish, Oliver. The lawyer delayed the sentencing until the next day, using some legal maneuver or other, and the cat faked convulsions that night in his cell—just a regular cell there in the city jail—and they put him in the hospital with a cop on the door of his room. As to how he made it out of there, I can't say. More than that I was not made privy to—oh, except that the very next day this Neanderthal judge sentenced him, *in absentia,* to death. But I think the whole stinking affair will be thrown out of court once it reaches the appeals process, which is where this lawyer is determined to take it. If he can ever find the crazy cat! It's really a farce."

"So where is he now, Joe?" Jim asked.

"He went underground. My guess is he split for Canada."

"An' the cops an' the judge iz *divyin' up the shit!*"

"No doubt, Boz!" said Joe, laughing.

Joe accepted a Gauloises from the leather case Jim was extending across the spool and leaned forward into the flame of the Zippo lighter in Jim's other hand.

"So what do they have on Nando, since I take it he was clean?" Oliver asked.

"Oh, he was clean all right! I'm just thankful they didn't plant some shit in our bus."

"So, what're they charging him with?"

"Oh, you know, resisting arrest, that kind of nonsense. I mean, it's real strange, isn't it? A guy will get out on bail and he has a black eye, a cauliflower ear, maybe a broken nose, and bruises up and down his back—and the pigs claim he *resisted arrest!*"

"Man, you're really doing my head in," said Jim, sighing. "Boz, is the shop clean?"

"Yep, sure is, took everything and buried it inna woods tenth of a mile out back last night."

"My man!"

"Joe, we really should put all of this away," said Jane, laying her hand on his arm. "This whole thing has me on edge. They could deport me, you know." Then, so *sotto voce* that only Joe heard it, "Either for this or adultery, I guess."

"Righto. Got a hiding place they'll never find, even with their bloody hounds. Somebody turn that exhaust fan on, would you please." He took the hookah in one hand and the plastic bottle in the other and got to his feet. "I'll be back in a minute, and then I'd like to get down to the city slammer. I left a message with that lawyer's secretary I'd be there by six to pay him the ten per cent of the bail bond."

"Do they really use bloodhounds?" asked Oliver.

"I think they use police dogs, Oliver. You know, German Shedders," Joe replied, chuckling. "Say, anybody want to chip in. You'll get it back. It leaves us a little short. I hate to give it to a thief of a bail bondsman, but we have to spring Nando before he gets his head busted or falls down the stairs—or out of a window or something, what they call 'defenestration'." He paused, as though recalling something, and started to speak again. "You know—."

"*Joe!*" Jane interrupted him, urgency in her voice. "*Hurry!*"

"How much you need, Joe?" Jim asked, reaching for his wallet, which was attached to a chain from his belt.

"A couple of century notes would be nice."

"I'll go halves on that," Oliver offered.

Five minutes later the VW Beetle, with Oliver at the wheel, Jim beside him, and Joe and Boz in the back, was turning right onto Guadalupe.

"Open it up, Oliver," Jim urged. "She'll just purr like a kitten at sixty."

"I think I'd like to hold it at fifty if it's all the same to you. I really don't need a speeding ticket today. I have to say, so far it feels real good."

"Wouldn't that be a gas, man, getting busted on the way to the city jail?" Jim said, slapping his knee. "We could say, 'Shit, man, we was *on our way there anyhow!*'" He swung around and looked at Joe, who did not seem amused.

"I just hope I can get my bus away from them without a lot of god damned hassle. Dealing with the bloody bureaucracy in this town can really be one big pain in the ass. It's almost as bad *as Napoli!* I do believe career civil servants take enormous pleasure in making life difficult for the likes of us."

"Shit, Joe, did you just wake up to that fact?" asked Jim, turning around again. "You've been here for almost two fuckin' years now. Boz and I were hipped to that shit an hour after we rolled into this burg. Right, Boz?"

"That is fer god damn sure, Jimbo, and I'll never ferget that day, long as I draw breath!"

"Spare me the details, gentlemen, please. I really have to keep my mind straight until we get Nando out of there and get our bus back."

The blue Greenbrier was at the curb in front of the police station. Oliver parked behind it and Jim got out and held the door open for Joe, who pushed the back of the bucket seat forward and stepped onto the sidewalk in a crouched position. He stood up straight and arched his back, did several neck rolls, and motioned for Jim to resume his place in the front seat.

"I'll never understand how Germans get along with these! And I've owned *two* of the damn things! In Germany I'd often see a family pile out of one, and it was like at the circus when one of those midget cars disgorges an interminable procession of clowns." When Jim had settled back into the seat Joe closed the door and bent over. "I'll either be out in fifteen minutes or so or—*shit*, I hope this doesn't take the *whole god damned night!*"

"Okay, man, if we don't see you or hear something from you by, say," said Jim, pausing to look at his wrist watch, "quarter after six, I'm coming in to see what's coming down. That'll give you a half hour. Meanwhile, we'll take this baby for another little spin, okay, Ollie?"

The process of extracting Hernando from the bowels of the city jail was facilitated by his lawyer's evident familiarity with the system. But when the man, apparently in his mid-sixties, first stood up from a bench against the wall, Joe's heart sank, for he was put in mind of the stock bandito in a third-rate Western, and he prepared himself for the heavily accented sing-song speech pattern and the bumbling incompetence characteristic of the comic personae assigned to the actors in these stereotypic roles. His girth, which lent a rotundity to his five-foot, six-inch frame, his several day's growth of dark beard, and his waddling gate as he approached only served to confirm Joe in his knee-jerk reaction. However, this initial impression was swiftly eradicated when the man introduced himself.

"Professor Lewis, I'm Pepe Feliciano, Hernando's attorney," he said, his delivery evincing no trace of his Hispanic lineage and nothing of the Texas accent Joe had become accustomed to hearing whenever he turned on the radio or ventured out into the community. It was, in fact, the most cultured northeastern accent he had heard since departing Canada a year ago. "I recognized you from the description provided by my client. How are you?"

"Hello," said Joe, grasping the man's extended hand

and vigorously shaking it. "How is it going? Oh, I have the three-hundred right here." He took a folded letter-size envelope from his shirt pocket and handed it to the lawyer.

"Thank you," said Feliciano, returning to the bench, dropping the envelope into a battered briefcase, and again taking a seat. "We should have Hernando out of here in a manner of minutes." He raised his right hand, catching the attention of someone behind Joe, and with index finger pressed to thumb executed a forty-five-degree counter-clockwise motion. "This is all so unnecessary, truly a blot on our judicial system. One day—soon, I do hope—we'll look back on all of this as an aberration."

"I couldn't agree with you more," said Joe. "You seem to really know your way around here."

"Oh, yes, I spend much of my time dealing with just this sort of case. It keeps me from sitting on a bench in the park, and it gives me a feeling that I am serving the people, quite often my own people, you know, something I did not do for many years before I retired last year."

"You're retired?"

"Yes, for almost a year now. We moved here from Connecticut for my wife's health. She suffers terribly from asthma and the dry air here allows her to breath with considerably more comfort than the New England damp."

"Where did you live in Connecticut?" Joe asked. "I spent some time there myself."

"Hartford. I practiced tax law there for forty years, had my own firm, which I turned over to my daughter last September. She had just received her degree from Yale Law School. She'll do well."

"My doctorate in classics is from Yale," Joe said,

smiling.

"Is that so? I knew from Hernando that you had a professorial background, but I didn't know of your Yale connection. Well, we must get together and talk about Connecticut some time. And also about Yale, for I too earned my degree there, my law degree, in 1927, and I have many friends there still."

"The *year of my birth!*" Joe exclaimed, momentarily interpreting Feliciano's smile as inspired by this revelation. The hand on his shoulder told him otherwise.

"*Hey,* man, you *made the scene!*" The gravelly voice and Spanish-American accent sufficed to inform Joe that it was his friend.

He spun around to greet Hernando and was shocked to observe his dirt-smudged face and the disarray of his clothes. There was a horizontal tear in the right knee of his jeans and the left sleeve of his denim shirt was missing. A barrel-chested, crew-cut, red-faced sheriff's deputy stood behind Hernando swinging a pair of handcuffs back and forth.

"He's all yourn, counselor," the deputy hissed and turned to go.

"One moment, please, sir," Feliciano said softly. "I want it part of the record that my client was delivered to me in filthy condition, in rent apparel, and with bruises on his face. You are witness to this, Deputy, as is Dr. Joseph Lewis here."

What then took place was executed with such dispatch that Joe could never quite put it together in terms of its parts. For quite suddenly, Feliciano raised a very small Leica thirty-five millimeter camera to his eyes and the click of the camera's shutter was heard. The deputy was taken completely by surprise and from the neck up he assumed an even redder hue than before, his face contorted in a sneer of such meanness that Joe could hardly keep from laughing. *I'll have to practice that one,* he said to himself, *it's classic W. C. Fields.*

"Thank you, sir," the lawyer said, smiling, to the departing deputy's back. "I'm sure you're quite photogenic."

"Well, how are you, my boy," said Feliciano, motioning Hernando to the bench. "Have a seat and take a minute to tell me if anything more of an ill nature transpired since I had you assigned to a cell by yourself this afternoon."

Joe looked for the camera but it had vanished as unobtrusively as it had appeared, in an act of prestidigitation that his eye had caught not one element of.

"No, man, everything was cool after that," Hernando replied. "Hey, Joe, this cat is the bes' damn lawyer in Austin. I mean, really, man, he's a *god damn saint!*"

"A quaint way of putting it indeed!" said Feliciano, grinning as he got to his feet and snapped the briefcase closed. "I understand Dr. Lewis here has transportation." He turned to Joe and opened his palm to reveal a key lying in it. "I almost forgot. Your vehicle is cleared and ready to go. I suppose you saw it out front." He closed his hand again and re-opened it in a rapid movement. Tucked between the two middle fingers was a card, which Joe took.

"That's my home number. Do call me soon. Matilda and I would like you and your lady to come for dinner. Take care, Hernando."

* * *

Joe was at the spool in the sitting room when the

others arrived. Jim's head had appeared through the VW's sunroof as Oliver pulled away from the jailhouse curb and Joe, standing by his Greenbrier bus, had made out the words, "case of suds!" Boz was carrying a 24-bottle case of Black Horse Ale on his shoulder when he, Jim, and Oliver entered the room. He lowered it onto the spool.

"Man, I just love this Canadian brew!" Jim exclaimed, taking a bottle with one hand and pulling an opener on the end of a chain from the pocket of his cut-offs. "Joe, care for a cold one?"

Joe accepted the opened bottle and examined the label. "Jesus, I haven't seen this since we split Canada. I used to put away a case a week up there. I hadn't tasted it since I was in my teens on the Chesapeake shore. They had state liquor stores in Ontario and you had to buy your beer, or ale, in a separate place from where they sold booze. It was kind of like a warehouse and, boy, did that place ever have the traffic moving in and out of there!" He took a swig of the ale. "Say, that's a very familiar taste! Thanks, Jim!"

"Hey, you're most welcome there, my good man," said Jim, as he handed bottles to Boz and Oliver and reached across the spool to put one at the place next to Joe. "I assume your lady will want one, especially seeing as it's from her homeland. Say, where are they, Jane and Hernando?"

"I put him in the shower," she said , coming through the door from the kitchen.

"I always forget about that back stairway," said Oliver.

"Yes, and I peeked and saw the case of beer—or ale, as I now see. *Black Horse!* My *favorite! Thanks,* guys!"

"You are most welcome, my lady!" said Jim, raising his bottle in toasting fashion.

Joe took a frosted glass from the tray Jane was sliding to the middle of the spool. "I was just telling Jane before you came in that they worked Nando over down there and then threw him into the drunk tank with a couple of rednecks. They were preparing to amuse themselves by breaking his arm when two big black dudes were tossed in there with them. 'Buck niggers,' they would be called by some of the racist types I grew up with in Maryland. Anyway, they knew what the score was, and they just sat down and flexed their biceps and stared at those crackers for a minute or so and after that everything cooled down. But he does have a few bruises here and there, and they tore the shit out of his clothes." Joe got up. "That reminds me, I'm going to go see if the duds I put out for Nando fit him. Back in a minute."

The intricate polyrhythms of sitar and sarod filled the room that Joe and Hernando re-entered. Joe sat down next to Jane and Hernando took the place to the other side of her. His shoulder-length black hair was held in a ponytail with a rubber band and he was barefoot and clad in a white T-shirt and faded jeans that were rolled up above his ankles. Jim held his pack of Gauloises across the spool.

"No, thanks, man, I doan do no tobacco," said Hernando and pointed to the case of ale. "Tell you what though, man, I'd sure like to pull on one o' those." When Jim handed him an opened bottle he held it up and read the label. "Never seen this brand before, but here goes." He held it to his lips and gulped down a third of its contents. "Not bad, not bad at all." He turned his head slightly to the side, cocking his ear. "Ravi and Ali?"

"Yes, just picked it up last week," said Joe.

"*Beautiful!*" said Hernando.

"I saw it there and couldn't resist putting it on the turntable," said Oliver.

"You have good taste," said Joe.

"Thanks, Joe."

"Nando tells me that he expects the charges to be dropped by tomorrow," said Joe.

"Do you really think so, Nando?" Oliver asked.

"Oh, sure, man, no question. This Pepe Feliciano is some kind o' lawyer! No shit, man, he's got more tricks up his sleeve than that Houdini, I'm tellin' you."

"The guy even had a camera in his pocket, or somewhere, a beautiful little Leica, and he shot Hernando and me—with this bull-faced pig right behind us—as we were standing there in the station," Joe said.

"*Bull-faced pig*—!" Jane began, giggling.

Hernando bent forward, laughing.

"Shit, man, he doan have no film in that thing! That's some piece o' junk he picked up in a pawn shop or somewheres. It doan even *work!* He just carries it around with him and pulls it out like that. It *scares* the *shit* outa the pigs. He even brung it to a trial and put it on the table, with all his papers and shit. Like I say, he's got a *shitbag* full o' tricks, like he's kinda a *magician,* man. Then he's a expert on tax law and they knows that he sent some real big shots up the river and that really scares the holy *shit* outa them, he doan even have to *mention that,* man."

"That's rich!" said Joe, chuckling. "So how'll he get the charges dropped?"

"Oh, I doanno, man, he'll think up something, some bullshit or other. He's a funny guy, I really love 'im. You should take 'im up on that *in*-vite and check 'im out, him an' 'is old lady Matilda. She's super, too."

"I'd really like to do that, Joe," said Jane over her

shoulder to him. Her cheek was slightly flushed and it occurred to him that she had had the back of her head to him since he had returned to the room. *They're close to the same age,* he reckoned to himself, *although he's probably a year or two younger, and he's a pretty attractive guy, a little on the delicate side, to be sure. Wouldn't surprise me if she had something going for him.* He felt a sudden surge of desire for her and put his hand on her shoulder. She reached up and squeezed it.

"Joe tells me you have a band, Hernando," said Jim through the thick cloud of smoke from his and Boz's cigarettes and Oliver's cigar.

"Yeah, man, Diverse Muph"—he pronounced it "Die-*verse*", with a heavy emphasis on the ultima, rhyming "Muph" with "tough"—"an' it's a helluva group. I mean, we got some of the baddest cats on the scene here in it."

"What's your style?" Jim asked. "Is it, like, the regular rock sort of sound of today or what?"

"Oh, no, it's a little bit of everything all thrown in together. Like we got this chick on keyboards who writes most of our tunes and she's got classical training—"

"New England Conservatory," Joe interrupted.

"Yeah, she writes—actually, she *tapes* most of our originals and then everybody learns 'em. Then we got another chick on guitar and she's great on rock and hillbilly and shit like that. Our drummer, he's really wild, he can really turn on an audience, and our bass player, he's pretty funky. Then we been rehearsin' with this black dude who really cooks on blues harp."

"And don't forget yourself," Joe added.

"Oh, yeah, I play some guitar and sing a little," Hernando said, looking down at the table shyly.

"*Hey, come on,* Nando!" exclaimed Jane, turning and

catching the eyes of the three across the spool from her. "Nando is too modest to say so, but he's lead vocalist and he's really great!" She turned back to Hernando. "You have a beautiful voice, full of emotion, and Joe tells me he hears all kinds of jazz rhythms in your playing."

"Thanks," he said, raising his gaze and smiling. "I try my best."

"Your best is god damned fine, my friend," said Joe.

"Thanks, Jane, and you too, man." He turned to the others. "These folks here are our two biggest fans. I wish we had a few thousand more like them, but there's just too many bands here in Austin, and then there's all the big-name groups comin' through town. There's just not enough action to support a band. Like, we really want to go on the road, but we don't have no manager to set up a tour and we don't have no wheels. We have a hard enough time even gettin' around here in Austin. Joe's loaned us his van a couple times for gigs, but we need our own big bus or somethin' to go on the road. And, man, we really do have to get outa this city. Too much shit comin' down, like yesterday and last night, and I really doan have no hankerin' to be one o' their patsies."

"I know just what you mean, right, Boz?" said Jim, his companion nodding in affirmation. "Maybe we can come up with some wheels for you. We'll see."

"Hey, that would be cool, man, and then all we'd need is a manager."

"Well, I'm not making any promises, but we'll put some thought to that as well."

"Thinking of pursuing another career there, James," Joe asked, "as you approach your middle years?"

"*Middle years?* Hey, come on, Joe, I've still got my *thirties* to get through, I'm not up there with you and

Bozman here!"

"Just kidding," Joe said, laughing. "Pass me another one of those Horses, would you, please."

"I'll split one with you, Joe," Jane said. "How about you, Nando, would you like another beer?"

"Ale," Joe corrected her, holding up the bottle. "From your homeland."

"No, thanks, man, another one would put me under. Anyway, I gotta split. If I doan get in the sack soon I'll fall over." He got up, nodding to the three males across the spool and touching Jane lightly on the shoulder. "See y'all later."

"I'll walk you over there," Joe said.

"Oh, thanks, man, I can use the company. Been a real bummer, these two days, I ain't shittin' you!"

Chapter 2

This here's fuckin' Tex-ass!

The bus purchased with the thirty hundred-dollar bills was a 1939 REO Speed Wagon. At first, after Jim was told the year over the telephone—the ad had said it was "vintage"—he and Boz had laughed and dismissed it as a joke. But they decided to check it out on their way to look at several other possibilities culled from the Sunday classifieds.

Looking it up on the city map hanging on the wall of the shed, Jim discovered that the address was two streets over from where Joe and Jane lived. On the way over there in Jim's Corvair, Boz expressed the hope that it wasn't "some bum tryin' to sell us the fuckin' Brooklyn Bridge."

"Well, we'll soon find out if it's for real, ol' buddy," said Jim, grinning as he suddenly geared down with a roaring double-clutching action and wrenched the steering wheel hard left onto a side street.

"*Hold on!*" he shouted over the squealing tires.

"Jesus Christ, man, you'll roll this rig yet!"

They pulled up behind the square rear end of an ancient looking vehicle. A metal ladder affixed to its bumper rose to a baggage rack on the roof.

"*Wow,* is *that it?*" exclaimed Jim.

"That's a REO Speed Wagon all right," Boz announced. "I has to see the grille 'fore I kin 'stablish iffin it be a thirty-nine."

They got out and walked slowly along the street side of the bus, looking up and down it as they made their way to the front end. It was painted a gunmetal gray and its bumpers, hubcaps, and chrome trimming shone mirror-like.

"Fer sure it's a thirty-nine," said Boz, reaching up and touching the radiator cap and glancing down at the Michigan license plate. "I done rode in one o' these suckers many a time when I was a kid."

Jim, hanging back a few feet, stood and stared across the hood at Boz, seeming unable to speak, his eyes a little misty, his hand shaking as he raised his Zippo lighter to the Gauloises between his lips.

Boz unlatched and raised the hood on the sidewalk side of the bus.

"*Jesus* in heaven, James, *come 'ere!*"

Jim hurried around to Boz's side and looked into the engine compartment.

"Sonovabitch is like she just come offin the 'sembly line fer chrissakes!" said Boz, whistling through his teeth.

A shadow moved across the glistening engine. Boz looked up and Jim turned his head to see a tall red-bearded man standing on the sidewalk.

"I'm Patterson," he introduced himself, "and one of

you must be Harsh, the other Boswell. I'm the REO's owner."

"Jim Harsh here, Boz there," Jim clarified. "This is quite a beauty you've got here."

"If you're interested in buying it, best thing we could do is take a spin in her."

Patterson closed the hood and took a key from the watch pocket in his jeans and inserted it into a huge padlock that secured the door.

"We had a couple of break-ins a while back so I put this on it." He motioned them into the bus. "After you, gentlemen. Who wants to drive?"

"I'll take her," answered Jim and with a bound up the steps he slipped into the driver's seat. Boz took the window seat by the door and Patterson sat directly behind the driver.

"The starter's down there on the floor," said Patterson, pointing past Jim's arm. "I tried to leave everything authentic as far as the mechanical and operational aspect of the vehicle—in so far as possible, that is. Of course, if you look around you'll see that the interior has been altered quite a bit. But why don't we take her out on the road and then when we get back you can check out the accommodations. By the way, I just learned the other day, the day after I first ran the ad last Sunday, of a source for spare parts. A graveyard over north of town has a thirty-eight REO dump truck. A collector called me and told me he saw it over there a couple months ago and I called the place. If I could understand what the guy was saying over the phone, it's still there."

"That collector guy, he interested in your REO?" asked Jim anxiously.

"Oh, no. He said he had his hands full restoring a chain-drive Mack fire engine, didn't want to take on another big project at the moment." He paused to cough, turning his head and raising his hand to his mouth. "I guess he was interested until I told him what I'd done to the inside here. Collectors are funny types. Some of them would rather start from scratch with some old rusty wreck and take ten years to restore every little detail, than buy something that's been redone like this and have to tear it apart. No, you're the only other folks who've called about Bess here."

Jim and Boz turned around and surveyed the interior of the bus for a few seconds. Directing his eyes again to the control panel, Jim took the gearshift knob in his right hand and tapped the horn with his left palm. It gave off a fat "*BEEP!*" He pointed to the manual choke knob. "Will we need this?"

"No, I had her running after you called."

Jim pushed the clutch down to the floor and depressed the starter pedal. The engine kicked off with a confident roar.

"We're in business!" he said, grinning as he put the bus into the lowest gear and slowly pulled away from the curb. "So, Bess, lessee if you can shake your ass like your sister Kate!"

An almost ecstatic smile spread across his face as he left behind the access ramp to Route 35 and shifted into high, settling into a cruising speed of fifty. Boz leaned forward, listening intently, and nodded to Jim as the latter glanced at him.

"She'll move along right nicely at sixty," said Patterson. "Check out the magnifier there on the outside mirror. See any fuzz back there?"

"Nothing in sight," Jim assured him.

"Take her up to seventy for a quick minute."

It was true, the three-decade-old vehicle climbed to the designated speed without trouble and, except for the higher-pitched sound of the air entering at the top of the driver's side window, the sensation was little different than at the slower speeds. A blast of an air horn startled Jim and he looked across the grass divide of the freeway and saw a Mayflower Moving Company tractor-trailer. The bearded driver's left arm was held high with fingers giving the peace sign. Jim barely caught a glimpse of the cab's passenger, a long-haired blonde leaning forward and flashing a delighted smile at the bus. Jim tapped the horn.

"You'll get a lot of that," said Patterson, smiling for the first time since appearing on the sidewalk. "Truckers, freak or straight, they dig this beautiful old crate."

"Was that a chick with him or a dude?" asked Jim.

"Kind of hard to tell sometimes these days, isn't it?" Patterson replied.

"*Jesus,* this baby is *smoo-o-th!*" Jim enthused. "I'd like to let the Bozman here take her back, okay? I'll cloverleaf it at the next exit."

Upon returning the bus to its original parking space, Boz set the handbrake and killed the engine. Jim turned around to Patterson and nodded.

"Let's see what you've done inside here and then Boz'll check out the undercarriage."

Fifteen minutes was consumed examining the elaborately refashioned interior of the rolling home. Patterson led them through the bus, pointing out detail after detail, sometimes demonstrating the operation of a feature, and displaying throughout the tour a pride of workmanship.

There was, for example, the driver's bucket seat with its adjustable head rest, the console to the right of the steering wheel containing knobs and switches for the ceiling lights, fans, heaters, and sound system, and three bunks lengthwise along each side with back rests that, when lowered on their hinges and secured to the ceiling by chains, served as sleeping accommodations. In the rear of the REO were a two-burner gas range, food preparation counter, sink, and waist-high refrigerator. Across from the kitchen complex was a frosted Plexiglas door.

"In here," Patterson informed them, opening the door, "is the shower. Oh, and a vacuum toilet, like they have on airlines and on some of the long-distance Greyhound and Trailways rigs." He paused and smiled. "Actually, we try to avoid too much use of it for the solid stuff since no one likes to clean it after a dump. We try to hold it until gas stops and roadside park facilities and the like—or behind a bush off the road somewhere. Of course," he added, closing the door and pointing to a sign that said Emergency Exit, "we retained access to the escape hatch, unlike some countries in South America I've traveled in. Bus companies down there often block it with a seat. For that extra revenue, you know." He opened the exit door. "After you, gentlemen."

As Jim and Patterson stood at the rear of the bus talking, Boz went over to the Corvair and opened its trunk in the front and took out a flashlight and a flat dolly about four feet long and fifteen inches wide. He carried it around to the street side of the bus and, leaning over, dropped it gently on its four roller-skate wheels onto the pavement, lay supine upon it and, propelling himself with his heels, disappeared under the REO for five minutes or so. When he emerged, head first and at the feet of Jim and Patterson, Boz gave the thumbs-up sign to his companion.

"I have to hand it to you, Patterson" said Jim, "you have this old baby running like a Swiss watch. "It's a real beauty. Can we shake hands on it? I can give you five bills now and pay the rest this afternoon."

"It'll be a pleasure doing business with you, my friend."

"Know somethin', James," Boz began as Jim headed the Corvair down the street, "Ah do believe my mind were ninety per cent made up that you should buy that beauty soon as ah saw that engine. Course ah was already very favorably impressed soon's we done pulled up behind it. Then when ah took over the wheel—whee-e-ee, *thet* were a *gas*, ah *shit you not!*"

"Looked pretty good underneath, too, I gather."

"Oh, fer sure, fer sure, like as how she been taken real good care of. And the inside clinched it fer the other ten per cent." He paused and looked out the side window absently before continuing. "I reckon that ol' bus'd tell some stories iffin she could talk, Jimbo, a *lotta* stories."

"I suspect so, Boz, I suspect so," said Jim, remotely.

"You figurin' to wrap it up today?"

"Yeah, and I think it'll work out just fine. We'll get the cash out of the bank now and Patterson said he'd make an appointment with a notary for three this afternoon. I guess it's someone he knows down the street. I can do the insurance thing over the phone and we'll get the tags in the morning. Then we'll be *ready to roll!*"

His mind spinning from the brief conversation with Jim late that afternoon, Joe Lewis lay in bed smoking a Camel and wondering if the night would bring him any sleep. The news of Jim's purchase of the REO and his decision to become manager of Diverse Muph would have alone been cause enough to put Joe into a state of excitement, but on top of that, upon Jane falling asleep, he commenced to compile a mental catalogue of the many factors persuading him that he and Jane should "pull up stakes and move on," which phrase he actually said aloud, reaching over and touching his soundly sleeping mate on the arm. Then he sat back and replayed in his mind the conversation with Jim.

"You remember Hernando saying how his band needed wheels to go on the road and how they need a manager and all, right?" Jim had begun. Jane was out grocery shopping and Joe remembered nodding and gesturing to Jim to take a seat across the spool from him. What came next really astonished him, he later told Jane.

"Well, he called me up last night and seriously offered me the gig," Jim continued, fumbling a Gauloises to his lips with a hand that was trembling somewhat more violently than usual. "So I said I'd think about it and Boz and I went out this morning and bought a bus, a 1939 REO Speed Wagon. You got to see it to believe it."

"*Jesus Christ, Jim!*" Joe exclaimed, laughing. "That's going to be a lot of work to get into shape, won't it?"

"No, man, like I said, you got to see this rig. It's been restored—or actually didn't really have to be that much, seeing as how it sat in a shed somewhere for twenty years or so. This dude we bought it from said when he bought it five years ago about all he had to do was replace all the rubber and hoses and put a new battery in it and new tires on and flush out the radiator and engine and so forth. It took him a couple days to get the engine in tune but it runs as smooth as my Corvair now."

"What's it like inside, was it a school bus or what?"

"As far as Patterson could tell—that's the dude we got it from—as far as he could put together from some old ticket stubs and transfers and shit like that he found in it, it was used on an inter-urban line between towns in Michigan, which is where he found it, in Ann Arbor. He's another drop-out from the academic life, like you, Joe."

"And like you, Jim."

"No—well, yeah, but he was a prof like you, Joe, and he split a few years traveling around the country in this REO, see, with his wife and another couple and all their kids. You wouldn't believe how he fixed up the interior with beds and a stove and sink and fridge. Shit, man, it's even got a shower! And a john! Great sound system, too."

"Now let me get this straight," said Joe, raising his hand in a sort of let's-slow-down-now motion. "You said that Nando offered you the gig and you accepted. Are you telling me that you're splitting Austin and going on the road with the Muphs as their manager or something?"

"You got it, that's *exactly* what I'm doing!" Jim answered. "And the *sooner* the *better!* I called Hernando after we looked at the bus and he said, 'Hey, man, let's do it!'"

"What about the shop? What's Boz going to do? You know he can't run your business, he'd go nuts trying to keep the books straight."

"Oh, I'm going to sell it. I already spread the word and I also put an ad in tomorrow's paper. And Boz is coming along, says he wouldn't miss it 'fer all the tea in Tijuana.'"

"*Blows my friggin' mind!*" said Joe, getting to his feet.

"Why don't I get us a couple of those ales left over from last night. We'll drink on it."

After dropping this bombshell on Joe and expatiating on what he envisioned as the Muph's initial tour, Jim finished his ale and left. When Jane returned a half hour later she leaned over to kiss Joe and, surveying the three empties on the spool, said, "Thirsty, are you, honey?"

"Oh, I'm only on my second. Jim was here and had one. Wait'll you hear the latest."

"Tell me while you're giving me a hand with the bags. I got a lot of stuff."

As they carried the groceries into the house he told her of Jim's purchase of the REO and his decision to go on the road with the Muphs. Then, sitting at the kitchen table as she unpacked the groceries, he attempted to convey to her, in as much detail as he could muster, Jim's rambling monologue explaining why he had decided to sell his business and become manager of a band and what his plans for Diverse Muph were.

"One thing he said at the beginning really struck me, babe," Joe began, "and that was that as far as he was concerned it was a 'band', not a 'group'. He said he told Nando that, if he took the gig, he didn't ever want to hear Diverse Muph referred to as a 'group'. Funny that he would make such a point of that little detail."

"It must not be so little to him, honey."

"Yeah, I guess not, must be symbolic in some sense. Oh, I dig what he means. There is a difference, and he rejects that difference, wants the continuity to remain intact, and all that. After all, Jim's from an earlier generation than those kids, even though he's only ten years or so older than some of them, and of course he's playing that down. You know, it's sort of like he's saying,

'Hey, you can trust somebody over thirty, we have some values that you would dig, man,' and he's hanging on to that word 'band' as a sort of symbol of—hey, *all that jazz!*"

"Very good, honey!"

"Yeah, and some of what I just said becomes clearer when I think back over how he said he came to the decision for him and Boz to go on the road with the Muphs. He said he woke up with a helluva hangover from putting away about half a case of that ale last night—they bought a case of Black Horse for themselves—and Boz brought him a cup of coffee. I can see him, lying there on that mattress, the mug of coffee on the floor, lighting up one of those stinking French cigarettes, and listening to those guys next door ball their women."

"I must say, Jim does know how to set a scene," Jane called back over her shoulder from the step stool where she was lining up canned goods on a shelf. "Didn't know he had such a flair for dramatic sequence."

"Yeah. Well, anyway, he lay there trying to plan out his day and he suddenly remembered Nando—he still calls him Hernando, I guess he'll get over that soon enough—talking about wanting to go on the road and asking him to think about becoming their manager. He was trying to put together why Nando would ask him something like that and then it hit him that he had offered to find some wheels for the band. He decided to at least do that much for them and he called to Boz in the kitchen to bring him the morning paper. There was an ad in the classified section that interested him, mainly because it didn't make sense to him. It said something about a REO bus with a rebuilt interior and it being 'ideal for family travel.' But it didn't give any year. So he called the number and the owner, one Patterson—a renegade professor of English, by the way—told him it was a 1939 REO Speedwagon. So he and Boz went over there, more out of curiosity than anything and—. Well, I told you that they bought the rig for three thou. Jim expects to have Texas plates on it tomorrow and he said he'd bring it over as soon as he does."

"So when did he come to this momentous decision." She turned to look at him. "I'm not being sarcastic or anything, but doesn't it truly partake of the momentous, this decision to throw away everything he's built up here and become a rock group—excuse me—a rock *band* manager?"

"Yeah, it is pretty momentous. And, by the way, he doesn't want it described as a *rock* band. 'Cause they're so eclectic, he says."

"So when—?"

"He started thinking about it right there on that mattress, even before he and Boz went to see the REO."

"Despite the distractions from next door!"

"Well, come to think of it, that may well have been a factor in his positive attitude to Nando's offer of the gig, considering the somewhat monastic life he's been living." Joe chuckled as he said this. "Know what I mean?"

"Oh, I think I get your drift, honey." Jane had perched on a high stool at the counter and was chopping vegetables, periodically scraping them off the board into the metal bowl she favored for salads. "Yes, I do know what you mean. Groupies galore and all that."

"Okay, so Jim is lying there on the mattress and he's thinking back over his early ambition to be a musician. I've known for some time how important music is to him, but he never told me until this afternoon that he started on violin at a very young age and took lessons for five or six years."

"Didn't he play bass viol in a band in his teens?"

"He did indeed, stand-up bass in a high school rhythm and blues band, and then he played tuba, and bass too, with the Skull and Cross Stompers when he was an undergraduate at Yale. *Great band!* I used to go hear them when I was working on my doctorate. Jim left for Harvard the same year I got my union card and started my first full-time teaching job, at Davis. So we used to hang out in Cambridge, too, Club 47 and so forth."

"Yes, I know you and Jim go way back."

"Anyway, he got to thinking along musical lines and decided to give serious consideration to Nando's offer. It was interesting to hear Jim talk about his early years. I still can't get over how I've known the cat for more than a decade and I never knew until an hour or so ago that he ever played the violin. Of course, I've heard him bow the big bass many a time, although it's been some years now. I wonder when he last touched the thing. He doesn't even own one any more, hasn't for some years. And he plans to take up the tuba again, too. That's really wild! Jesus, this *whole thing's crazy!*" Joe got up and went over to the refrigerator and took out another bottle of Black Horse Ale. "I see we still have a few of these left. Want one?"

"Why don't you pour me a little glass from yours."

"And that was another thing I never knew about Jim, that before he played tuba with the Stompers, he had played it in his high school marching band," said Joe, again seated at the table and lighting a Camel.

"Sounds like he may be a frustrated musician or something."

"Listen, you should have heard him going on this afternoon about how music was his first love and how he wanted to study piano but had to settle for violin because his parents couldn't afford to get a piano. Then how he switched to the bass when he was about twelve or thirteen and took up the tuba a year or so after that so he could get in the marching band."

"When did the car thing start with him?"

"Oh, yeah, he started on that when he was fifteen, even before he could drive—legally, I mean, because he already knew how to drive. Come to think of it, Jim was a pretty busy guy as a teenager. Playing in the school band for football games and all that, playing for parties and dances in a rhythm and blues combo, tearing down engines and rebuilding them, writing poetry, making damn good grades on top of all that. But it didn't leave much time over for girls. Jim told me he was a virgin until he'd been at Yale for a couple of years and this graduate student seduced him."

"*She* seduced *him*?"

"That's what he said. Invited him over to the apartment she shared with two other grads and stripped—and then *undressed him!* And he soon had the other two girls too! He laughed when he told me this and said, 'Those three chicks took me to graduate sex school!'"

"Is that what guys talk about, the first time you got laid and stuff?"

"Sometimes, yes, if the subject comes up," he admitted. "Something wrong with that? Don't tell me you women don't ever talk about it—and in *graphic detail* on occasion!"

"*Oh, come on!*" she said, turning to look at him with a smile. "What do you mean by that?"

"Okay, here's an example," he said, exuding

confidence that the illustration would make his point. "MacKenzie told me one time about this friend of ours in Napoli whose husband wouldn't go down on her and she couldn't come unless someone did that to her. So, instead of their regular doctor, she went to a Neapolitan gynecologist whom she'd never been to before and told him about it and asked him if there was something wrong with her. And he did it to her *right there in the examining room!* To *show* her there was *nothing wrong with her!"*

"Oh, honey, you come up with the *wildest stories!"*

"It happened just like I told you!"

She chuckled and looked him in the eyes. "Anyway, why would you believe *anything* your ex said? You always say she was a pathological liar."

"Well, she was that, but in this case I am quite certain it was true because this woman who told her that, she would do something like that, no question about it. I believe every word of it!"

"How well did you know this woman?"

"Never mind." Joe poured ale into their glasses.

"Now you've got me really curious, honey." She giggled. "Okay, so if you won't tell me how well you knew her, at least tell me who she was, or how you knew her— or *something, please!"*

"Okay," he said, chuckling, "she was the wife of a British diplomat we got to know there in Napoli. The lady had *really been around*, I assure you. Satisfied?"

"I guess I'll have to be," she said, resignedly.

"Anyway, that's what's happening with our good friend James Clifton Harsh. I'll sure miss him and Boz."

"And Nando, too—and the rest of the Muphers." She sighed. "We're going to miss *all of them*, honey!"

"You know, speaking of MacKenzie and her way with

61

the truth, I should let you read some of the letters she wrote me after she went to Reno for the divorce."

"Why, honey?"

"Because she had become a completely different person. And that's something that has always disturbed me. As a boy, I couldn't understand the change that came over my ol' man when he was drinking. Once every month or two on a Sunday—or on a Saturday, before and after the war, 'cause he worked a six-day week during the war—he'd put a fifth of whiskey and a shot glass on the kitchen counter after breakfast, and by dinner time he had polished it off. He was a different person once he had a few shots in him. *Shit,* he didn't even *eat* dinner, just went to bed about six! And, before the war, he'd do a bottle on Saturday and get up early Sunday morning and start on another bottle. But he'd get up and go to work on Monday—*never failed to do that!*"

"Did MacKenzie get like that when she drank?"

"Come to think of it, we did have some of our worst fights after she had had a drink or two. And usually over nothing, just some stupid argument she would start. But that's not what I'm getting at. It's her letters, how she distorted everything. For instance, she told me that not only did she not love me, she said she had *never* loved me! And all kinds of other nonsense. So it made me question a lot of things she had told me. Like being part Cherokee, from her mother's side. She told me that when I first met her, and over the years she would refer proudly to her 'American Indian ancestry'—to the fascination of some of our friends. So when she was in McLean Hospital I called her grandmother and asked her how far back that was in her family and she *laughed out loud!*"

"Really!"

"Couldn't believe her granddaughter would make up such an 'outlandish story!' She said *her* family was *English* and MacKenzie's *father's* was *Scottish*. And that's what her *granddaughter* was—and she should be *'proud of it!'*" He chuckled.

"My word!"

"And little lies, like how, when I first met her at college, she said she was taking rifle for her phys ed requirement and that they used the M1, the same piece I had trained with in basic training. Very unlikely, to say the least! She wouldn't have been able to *aim* it! Damn things weighed ten pounds! As I look back, I realize that so much of what she told me about herself was *pure bull!* As for the letters, they were just *full* of lies! Oh, yeah, and how she could never again have only one lover at a time, claiming she had several during her six weeks or so in Reno. Well, maybe she did. Anyway, she wrote me almost ever day she was there. Fifty or so letters. I'll pick out some of the best examples for you. It was like she had taken on a completely different personality—and a very unpleasant one, I have to say. I could no longer relate to her as the MacKenzie I had known for a decade or so."

"Well, honey, she certainly did have a problem with the truth."

"I just remembered a good example of her ability to put across a barefaced lie. I don't think I ever told you about this particular episode, although I guess I've banged your ear by the hour with other parts of the saga, and I've appreciated your patience in listening, believe me."

"I'm happy to see you getting it off your mind, honey."

"Thanks. Well, after she checked out of that fancy hotel in Napoli where she ran up an astronomical bill for a month or so she came by the villa to see me and asked me if she could borrow the VW to take her stuff to a less expensive place to stay, said it would save taxi fare, and she wanted to take Rusty along, reminding me how he loved to ride in a car. Like a damn fool I let her take the car and the dog. She was acting pretty normal and I thought, well, maybe she's getting over her delusions and all, you know, just 'snapping out of it,' like my ol' man thought my mother should do when she sank into depression in my early teens. *Silly me!* That was the last I saw of Rusty and the VW for almost a month. And I had *just the week before retrieved the car from Messina!* That's where the *carabinieri* caught the German guy who stole it back in October. Anyway, my new friends at the American Consulate were trying to chase MacKenzie down and they finally located her registered at a downtown *pensione*. They had also found out that she had a bad cold, so they cooked up a plan to get her to this British doctor they had lined up, having clued him to her mental condition. The Italian-speaking American psychiatrist I told you about was also in the picture by now. She was in cahoots with the British doctor and was arranging to get MacKenzie into a clinic for observation. Anyway, I got to the *pensione* first and MacKenzie came out into the lobby. She was blowing her nose and holding a box of Kleenex and I suggested she needed to see this doctor, who would give her some medicine. She was agreeable to this and we were all ready to leave, just waiting for the consulate officers to arrive with their limousine, when a couple standing at the check-in desk suddenly started shouting that their passports had disappeared from the counter. We were on our way out the door and I didn't pay much attention to their problem. I did ask MacKenzie if she had seen anyone else in the lobby and she said no she hadn't. As we were getting on the elevator I said something like, 'Oh, the clerk probably has the passports in the office, taking down their information and so forth,' and MacKenzie nodded and said that was likely the case. So the limousine takes her to the British doctor and Rusty and I follow in our VW, which she had parked around the corner from the *pensione*. We're sitting there in the waiting room, MacKenzie, one of the consulate officers—she was a genuine treasure!—and I. MacKenzie's still blowing her nose. The nurse calls her in to see the doctor and she forgets to take the box of Kleenex with her, just leaves it on the little table. By that time I'm thinking that I'm catching her cold so I reach over to take a tissue and I notice something is strange about the tissues, they're not straight, they're sort of pushed aside and—."

"I think I know what's coming," said Jane, smiling.

"Yeah, I slip my fingers under the tissues and, lo and behold, get hold of *two Australian passports!* Which I hand to the consulate officer."

"You should write about all this, honey."

"Yeah, I guess it's all pretty fascinating. I'll never forget this young intern the night the navy nurse and I delivered MacKenzie to McLean. We sat in the hospital cafeteria swilling coffee for two hours or so while I told him the whole story of MacKenzie's breakdown in Napoli. I'd sure like to have a copy of his notes. He kept urging me on, like I was telling some really interesting story."

"Which you certainly were!"

"Yeah, I guess I was. Speaking of wanting copies, I still kick myself for not making copies of Giovanni's letters to her. They were all written after she got out of

Massachusetts Mental Health Center, during the two months she was in that apartment in Cambridge that I found for her. I told you that they went their separate ways after their fling in Rome for that month or so, evidently because Giovanni couldn't deal with her hallucinations and ramblings on and on about the conspiracy against her. They never saw each other again, although she was in Napoli for another two months. And then, after she was discharged from the hospital, they wrote back and forth a dozen times during those two months she was in Cambridge. She apparently never wrote him while she was in the nut house. And that's not strange since while she was in there she tied him into the conspiracy. By the way, while she was living in that apartment she was hosting parties for some of her fellow patients—I started to say *inmates*—those who had become outpatients, that is. Those must have been some interesting evenings!"

"I'm sure they were! But I'm confused, honey. How did you see his letters?"

"Oh, before I put MacKenzie in a cab to Logan Airport for her Reno flight she left a couple of boxes of clothes and stuff for me to ship to her parents in Baltimore. All of his letters were there, plus a slew of others to her from friends and her family, including a couple from her ridiculous 'lawyer' uncle. And of course I read them all. Pretty interesting, some of the advice she was given how to 'escape' from her 'incarceration'! Our anthropologist friend wrote her a second time, too, with more advice along those lines. He had gotten in touch with the famous Dr. Thomas Szasz, who provided him expert advice to pass on to MacKenzie on how to pull the wool over her psychiatrist's eyes and get out of the 'joint,' as she had begun to call the hospital. And Giovanni's letters were especially fascinating, for instance, how he and MacKenzie had started planning in Rome to get hold of our VW and sell it on the black market and buy plane tickets to the States. And he bragged about all sorts of other deceptions they had conspired in to foil me in one way or another. And there were a lot of references to plans they were making for their future together. Incidentally, his letters really made me wonder about this guy I thought of as a friend—even after he had made a cuckold of me!"

"How so?"

"Well, it was kinda like he was a double agent or something. Here he was, going out with me to those late-night dinners and telling me all these things about MacKenzie, and then a year later writing her and joking about how I had said this and that and the other thing. For instance, I told him I suspected that MacKenzie took the VW because she was short of money and planned to sell it, and in one of his letters to her he said, "He was right!"'"

"Kind of dishonest of him!"

"Well, he was a strange cat, that's for sure. It's sad that at what would turn out to be the end of her two months in Cambridge she heard from Giovanni's lawyer that he had died of a heart attack. Pretty young for that, early forties, but I guess he did have some serious health problems. The last time I ever saw him, when I visited him in this seedy downtown hotel, he was just lying there in bed, sick as a dog. Of what, he couldn't say." He paused as though turning something over in his mind. "You know, I've always believed that the news of his death was what caused MacKenzie to decide to go to

Reno. It just happened overnight! One day she was telling me her plans to find a job and the next day she calls me and says she's going to Reno to get a divorce! She had never even *hinted* to me that she was thinking of doing this. In fact, I was wondering how to bring about a divorce—'cause I had *no intention* of resuming the marriage! *No way* was I *ever* going to live with her again! After she left I found the lawyer's letter about Giovanni dying. I think she received it the day before she called me about going to Reno."

"I'm glad you tell me all this, honey. It helps me understand you better. All you've gone through and so forth."

"Yeah, well, I have paid some dues, babe, no doubt about that!"

Joe spent the evening catching up on magazine articles he had marked for reading and Jane sat across the spool from him working with needle and thread on a dress she had cut from a pattern. He put on a tape of Vivaldi and other chamber music. Every once in a while he remarked on something he was reading about and looked up to gauge her reaction, which was more often than not simply an absent nod, since she was engrossed in the project at hand and, he surmised, the music had apparently carried her far from thoughts of the present. In fact, the subject of Jim and Boz and Nando's band had been by mutual agreement put aside until the morrow. She went to bed about ten and almost immediately fell into deep sleep. Insomnia was one trait she did not share with her mate.

He had come to bed a half hour later but could not sleep. He lay there smoking and thinking. He wondered how much longer he could tolerate the political climate and social confinement of Texas. True, he pointed out to himself, he and his friends did mostly live quite apart from all of that. Still, it had recently reached into their lives, as witness the bust of Nando and several others of his and Jane's circle this past year. He pondered a question that had never before quite so troubled him, namely, Was Joe Lewis's turn with the law on the horizon?

Two weeks ago, as he was rolling a joint at the kitchen table in the middle of the afternoon, a young cop had knocked on the back door of the house. Startled, he looked up and noted the outline of a uniformed officer. Jane, alerted to the potential crisis by his whispered warning, turned from the counter and held the flour canister for Joe to drop film cans and papers into.

As it turned out, the back-door visit by the law only concerned an abandoned car down the alley. But it badly shook him up, and Jane insisted that he find a hiding place in the yard for their stash and paraphernalia. Pointing out that the frequent forays outside that such a location necessarily entailed would likely arouse suspicion, Joe agreed to establish a "Cask of Amontillado" sanctuary in the basement.

Two days after that incident, Jim told Joe that Boz, working on an engine, had looked up to see a suspiciously official-looking sedan driven by a white-shirted man with close-cropped hair cruising slowly by the shop. "Boz swears it was the fuzz," Jim said. "The guy leaned down and talked into a mike just before he gunned it and took off like a 'fuckin' bat outa friggin' hell,' Boz told me when I got there a few minutes after the goon split."

Less than two weeks later, Hernando was arrested. Joe reminded himself that it took only a couple of incidents like these, unconnected though they well might be, to render his characteristically well-balanced outlook into a paranoid state of mind. What was even worse, he would soon lose one of the two most supportive friendships he and Jane had here in Austin, Jim's, the other being Oliver Hanks. "And Boz, too," he said aloud, "Jesus, I'll miss his 'Perfesser' this and 'Perfesser' that. Not to mention the rest of the Muphs."

Suddenly the circumstance of remaining in Austin virtually friendless was, in his mind, so fraught with peril that he wondered what he and Jane were thinking, staying here, "When we can see so clearly the handwriting on the wall," he said softly. That the number of close friends would be reduced to Oliver and several others at the university was cause enough to contemplate moving on to other parts. The recent ill-omened events lent additional motivation to "Getting the hell away from here—*and fast!*" he said, the final two words in so booming a voice that Jane rolled over and opened her eyes wide at him, although the next morning she insisted that she had no memory of any interruption of her slumber.

He counted off on his fingers the few friends who would be left after the departure of the band and, while he could bring into focus the three or four young instructors and teaching assistants Oliver had brought by, two of them women Oliver was sleeping with, he could not remember the names of any of them. Then there were others from the campus, including Asad, an assistant professor in biochemistry, the two graduate students in psychology who shared the house with Jim and Boz, and a former colleague in classics, Melville Hawkins, who was from Cape Town and whom they had known in Canada and occasionally went out and drank beer with of an evening. "If we split Austin I won't miss any of the above," he mumbled, carefully lifting Jane's arm off of his chest and extricating himself from the sheet, "not that they aren't all nice folks and all." *Although I can't say I really know all that well Jim and Boz's house mates,* he mused. *And those guys' girlfriends I hardly know at all. Actually, I wouldn't mind knowing them better, nosiree, not at all! 'Specially that little Mexicana who shakes her behind so nicely.*

Then there were the mere acquaintances, results of a casual encounter here and there, some of them dropouts from the academic life, some political activists, some in the dope trade or other forms of "noble outlawry," as Jim dubbed their pursuits. Some of these last-mentioned types had dropped out of sight of a sudden, not to be heard of until months later, a postcard without return address arriving with a Detroit or Baltimore or Spring Hill, Alabama postmark.

Sitting up and easing his legs off the bed, he reached down for his jeans and pulled them on. Then he cautiously made his way across the room to the door, whispering, "Please, no stubbed toes tonight." His hand felt itself around the jamb and clicked the hall light on. This provided illumination enough for him to go through a stack of file folders on an orange crate in the corner of the bedroom and locate a thick one designated "Teaching Positions, etc." He took the folder downstairs to the kitchen, put it on the table, got himself an ale, and sat down.

"Christ, I'd forgotten I used to write so many people," he said *sotto voce,* leafing through the carbon copies of his letters and replies thereto. Every so often he stopped and read through one, then went on, glancing at the headings, occasionally skimming the first few sentences. *Doesn't seem to be any order to them. I hope it's here because, as I recall, it has his home address on it and he said to always write him there. Must be because there are some snoops in that department, maybe an envelope steamer of talent.*

"Eureka! Here it is!"

He took the letter in one hand and the bottle of ale in the other and went into the front room. On the shelf above the tape recorder he found his fountain pen and some typing paper. Sitting on a cushion in his usual place at the spool, he placed a sheet of paper on a *New York Times Magazine* and began to write with evident determination.

8/2/68
Austin, Texasshole

Dear John,

I have been giving much thought to the offer you outlined in your letter of a week or so ago. God knows how you located me! However, I'm happy that you did, although it causes me to despair that I did not succeed in covering my tracks, always worrying, as I am wont to do, that the bailiffs are closing in.

In a word or two, I have decided to take you up on your offer that, quite coincidentally—and providentially—arrived just as my lady and I began thinking of departing Austin. I just hope that the position has not been filled. Since it only recently came into existence upon the sudden and totally unexpected demise of your colleague and great Latinist Professor Oswald, I am assuming that it may well still be open.

You will have already several days ago received my brief telegram of acceptance that will be on its way tonight and we shall have spoken before you read this. I'm no doubt penning this more to satisfy some need of my own than to communicate much of anything to you. For me it is a sleepless night here in the insufferable heat of this strange city, a stifling city in more ways than one—and certainly the only urban center in this reactionary, racist state in which I could bear residing.

I am both posting this missive Special Delivery from the main downtown p.o. and sending off a few words by Western Union tonight before getting back into the sack with Jane. I shall let her know at breakfast that we crosseth the Rubicon.

Incidentally, it will take us a couple of weeks to get on our way, which means we shall roll onto the campus about the end of the month. I wonder what in the way of housing will be available. What would most satisfy us is a big old rambling house at a reasonable rent. Keep an eye out for us. I'll call you a couple times a week to check in.

I much look forward to seeing you again after—can it be?—five years. You will, I am sure, take to Jane and she to you and Isabelle.

Fondly,
Joseph E. Lewis

He printed the full name, signed "Joe" beneath it, folded the sheets and inserted them into the envelope, addressed it, wrote "Special Delivery" on it in large print and sealed it, counted out sufficient postage and affixed the stamps, put his arms into a denim shirt he found in the hall closet, and went out onto the front porch, stopping by the swing to slip his feet into flip flops. It was a little past midnight and the heat had hardly abated. He walked slowly to the Greenbrier, confident that he was doing the right thing.

Funny, he thought, *I've made some of the most important decisions of my life like this without teasing them half to death, just letting instinct guide me. It will blow Jane's mind that I've decided to go back to teaching, but then, when John's letter came she said no one but I could, or should, make the decision. "And whatever choice you make," I remember her saying, "That'll be fine with me. Go with the writing, put it aside for a year and teach, combine the two, whatever your soul tells you to do."*

Standing with his hand on the bus's door handle, Joe asked himself why he was driving to downtown Austin. *Hell, they pick up the mail two blocks away at 7 A.M. I'll just walk over there and drop it in the box and then I can call in a telegram from the house.*

As he approached the house on the way back from the mailbox, he was flooded with an emotion that took him completely by surprise, a deep affection for the crazy street they had lived on for the better part of two years, and he felt tears welling up in his eyes. It had been their first real home, in that he had moved in with Jane in Canada, whereas in Austin they had found this house together and had decided it was made for them. So he knew that this house would always stand first in his memory of all the many habitations they might over the years occupy and he would often dream of coming back to it, although he knew with certainty that he would never return to Austin to live. For that matter, they might never set foot in this city again, for all it had meant to them.

A bone-deep weariness came over him as he climbed the few stairs to the front porch and stumbled in to the telephone on the kitchen wall. The brief call to Western Union seemed to have given him a second wind and he contemplated having another ale and listening to some John Fahey in the front room. But he had second thoughts, realizing that he would likely fall asleep on the cushions and that Jane would at some point wake up and miss his presence as she always did when he came downstairs and wrote or got blotto drunk on scotch and soda or martinis or sometimes, when he couldn't deal with anything familiar to him, left the house and wandered the campus and its paths for an hour or so.

So he visited the toilet in the hall and struggled up the stairs to the bedroom. Shedding his shirt onto the floor and stepping out of his flip flops, he sat down on the edge of the bed and, with difficulty, slid his jeans off. Then he turned, pulled his legs up onto the bed, and fell back, making a futile effort to get under the sheet. Sleep came over him immediately. Jane reached out and felt him and, reassured, turned and fell back asleep.

After the afternoon conversation with Joe, Jim returned to the shed, where he had left Boz earlier, and the two of them worked until midnight sorting out the tools and gear they intended to take with them on the road and generally putting the shop into order, for the word had rapidly gotten around in the trade that his business was on the market and it was anticipated that interested parties would soon be dropping by to check it out.

He awoke the next morning about nine to the ringing of the telephone on the inverted wooden wine box beside the mattress. He rolled over and reached for it, accidentally knocking it onto the floor. Holding it to his ear, he greeted the caller with a yawn, responded monosyllabically in the affirmative, and returned it to its cradle.

"Hey, Boz," he called, "got any java going?"

"Comin' up, James."

"Say, man, we got a prospective sucker already. Going

to meet us over at the shed at noon."

Then he lay back on the mattress, propping his head on the pillow scrunched up against the book shelf made of more wine boxes. Thoughts came to him of what had greeted them, both of them in a state of zombie-like fatigue, the night before upon their return to the house.

The two graduate students he rented rooms to had brought home girls and the four were "totally wigged out on hash," as Jim described the scene later to Joe. What surprised Jim was that these were not the two steady girl friends of Charlie and Ezra but high school students they had picked up at a concert, and it worried him and Boz that this might be the night the house would be busted. So he took the two men aside and told them in no uncertain terms to take the girls home, or at least to get them out of the house.

"I can understand your not wanting to drop them off at their homes in the state they're in," Jim said to them, "but please remove them from the premises. We don't allow no jail bait here!"

"Shit, guys," Boz added, "this here ain't no Hollywood, this here's fuckin' *Tex-ass,* with a *big fuckin' 'T'!* They'll put yer motherfuckin' asses away fer fuckin' keeps here, *I shit you not!*"

"A useful bit of arithmetic to remember is that sixteen will get you twenty," Jim added.

As they spoke, they could hear from the next room the giggles of one of the girls. The other intermittently sobbed and pealed off into nearly convulsive laughter. Charlie and Ezra were themselves not in very coherent states but they agreed, smiling broadly all the while, to depart the house with the girls. Jim and Boz could hear through the open door of Charlie's room the animated conversation between the girls, who seemed oblivious to the newly announced intentions of the two men to "take us all for a ride in Ezra's station wagon."

One girl was mimicking the speech of their high school biology teacher, who apparently stuttered, and the other girl, the sobbing and laughing one, was saying over and over, "That's *exactly* like him! Oh, my *god,* that's *exactly* like him!" Then she would sob for a few seconds and abruptly break into guffaws that Boz later told Jim had "lak to turn my hair snow white from the gray it have been these ten years and more."

When the four had left a few minutes later Jim collapsed onto his mattress and slept until morning.

"Jesus, man," he told Boz when the older man came in with the percolator to refill Jim's mug, "it was like I got hit from behind with a god damned hundred-pound sack of cement. I don't even remember lying down."

"Well, pour that coffee down, James, we does got us a full day afore us."

Since the appointment to show the shop wasn't until noon, Jim and Boz decided to hook up the trailer to the Corvair and go out to the auto graveyard to check out the REO dump truck Patterson had told them about.

"This collector told me that the owner of the yard is harmless, by the way," Patterson had advised them, "even if a lee-e-tle on the strange side."

They found the proprietor in a dingy office the walls of which were covered with license plates from every state and some foreign nations. Boz did some quick arithmetic and told Jim on the way back to town that there were at least 500 tags displayed and that more filled boxes beneath the desk.

Despite the heat, already in the mid-nineties at ten o'clock in the morning, the man was dressed in a tight-fitting double-breasted blue pinstriped suit, white shirt, and red tie, all covered with dark grease stains. His face and bald head were splotched with oil and his hands were black with filth. They followed him for ten minutes or so as he led the way, the three of them in Indian file threading their way through hundreds and hundreds of automobile and truck hulks in various stages of decrepitude, even decay, some charred beyond recognition, some resting on their axels, many with missing doors, others with open hoods, engineless, gaping like hippos.

"This guy is either nuts or drunk out of his skull," Jim said softly.

"Or an out-an'-out geek!" Boz surmised. "Reminds me of some o' the winos I seen in the yards, James. Tear a head offen a fuckin' live chicken and eat it fer a bottle. *Look* at 'im!"

"Yeah, doesn't look like he's had a shower in recent history, does it?"

The man muttered to himself as he led the way, periodically shouting obscenities over his shoulder and pointing to some vehicle. Jim noticed that two fingers were missing from the man's right hand and he held up his own hand to Boz, folding over the corresponding fingers.

"Yeah, said Boz, nodding, "you can lose a few choppin' up these carcasses, thet's fer goddamn sure!"

When they got to the REO the man turned and gestured to them.

"*Well, come on now!*" he exploded, "what were it you wuz wantin' offen this here peece o' sheet, friends?"

"Oh, maybe the engine and the transmission and a few other things," Jim replied, looking around. "Jeez, how would we get it out of here?"

"Well now, mister, I don't see no sky hooks up there, does you?" he sneered. "But I tells you, they's a road on t'other side o' that Diamond T thar. I kin bring a crane in an' lift the fucker' outa thar. So take a look thar and make up yer fuckin' minds what all y'all want! I ain't got all fuckin' day!" He cleared his throat and spat to the side. "I'll be back in a bit with the crane and a torch. They's a crowbar over thar case thet fucker gives you any trouble!"

He disappeared behind the roofless Diamond T school bus. With the aid of the crowbar Jim and Boz pried open the REO's hood. A large rat dropped to the ground and scurried under the engine and out the opposite side from where they hung over the fender.

"Sorry to disrupt your home there, ol' buddy," Jim muttered. "Looks in pretty good shape. What do you think, Bozzo?"

"Give the lush twenty-five bucks fer the engine and the transmission and another five fer cuttin' 'em outa there." Boz took a screwdriver and vice grips from the side pocket of his overalls. "He won't argue 'bout it, 'cause he need a drink mighty bad—*mighty* bad. I better disconnect the gas line and wires and such afore he rips 'em t' shit."

"Sheet!" Jim corrected.

"Sheet!" said Boz, chuckling, and reached into the engine compartment.

Boz had just completed the disconnecting of wires and line when they heard the deafening roar of the approaching sans-muffler tractor. The man readily agreed to Jim's offer and set about his task. Jim and Boz stood back as he strung chains around the engine and then lowered the crane's hook and joined it to them. Dismounting from the vehicle's saddle-like seat, he deftly applied an acetylene torch to the rusted bolts that secured the engine to its bed. In ten minutes he had succeeded in cutting it loose.

"Sheet and two make aye-yut!" the man cried out as the chain became taut and, with a grating screech, the engine was wrenched from the REO like the humongous tooth of some prehistoric beast. He swung it aside and lowered it to the ground and Boz disengaged the chains. The transmission took a little longer to free, drag out from beneath the truck, and hoist into the air. The man throttled down to an idle and leaned forward.

"I'll meet y'all over to yer rig and you kin show me whar all you want this here peece o' sheet. Then ah'll fetch the injin." He put the tractor into reverse and backed slowly away from them, never turning his head, guiding the vehicle by a side-view mirror.

They made two stops on the way back to Sea Horse Bodies & Innards, first at a self-service car wash to steam-clean the newly acquired engine, transmission, and other parts, then at the office of Jim's insurance agent, where they picked up the REO's new tags and insurance policy. Jim dropped Boz off at Patterson's house so that he could bring the bus over to the shop. The "sucker" who had called earlier was sitting on a nail keg under the oak tree when Jim pulled up to the shop's doors next to a three-wheel Harley Davidson motorcycle with ape-hanger bars.

"Hey, Big John, how's it going?" Jim called out when the Corvair's engine had become quiet.

"Same shit, different day, Harsh," the full-bearded and

three-hundred-pound John Little answered. He was dressed in painter's white overalls that were stained here and there with dark splotches but otherwise looked as though they had been taken from the laundry line minutes before. He wore neither shirt nor undershirt and was barefoot. His jet-black hair fell to his back and the thick hair on his chest curled over the bib of the single piece of apparel. Tattoos of snakes, gargoyles, and grotesque creatures part human, part animal covered his fleshy arms from wrists to shoulders. He flipped his cigarette a full twenty feet off to the side as he shifted his bulk forward and tottered to a standing position.

"Lez talk bizness," said Big John.

Chapter 3

It was in your head.

Joe and Jane were sitting over coffee in the kitchen. The house they had rented for nearly two years was on a dead-end street that had once been called Railroad Avenue but was now simply an east-west numbered street. They learned of its earlier name that spring after the motorized street cleaner brought to light some of the letters on the corner curb and Joe, with a push-broom and a bucket of soapy water, uncovered the rest.

Jane spent most of a morning in Austin's main public library before she came across a turn-of-the-century railroad map that verified the existence at that time of a spur track for a half-mile or so along their street. Since there was no surviving physical evidence, she and Joe concluded that, seven decades and more ago, trains had steamed down the middle of their street on tracks any remains of which lay beneath the asphalt. It seemed reasonable to them that, upon its conversion to horse-

and-buggy and automobile use, the street had assumed a name indicative of its earlier role, and that later, when it was renamed as a numbered street, city planning bureaucrats had erased all reference to its past except the faded letters on the cement.

Joe had Boz, a master metal worker, fashion an official-looking steel plate, upon which Jane painted "RAILROAD AVENUE". Late one night, Joe replaced the official sign on the corner with Boz and Jane's handiwork, thereby honoring the street's long-ago life. Now and then at midnight, Joe would put a speaker on the windowsill of the sitting room, crank up the volume, and play from an LP of sound effects a ten-second-long train whistle.

"How do you like this cappuccino?" he asked Jane.

"Oh, it's delicious with this whipped cream. I really don't care for plain espresso. It's so bitter, even with honey."

"So how do you feel about the teaching thing, now that you've had a day or so to digest it?"

"I'm very excited about it. I think it'll be good for you and I've been thinking maybe I'll take a course or two, something exotic, like anthropology, if they give it. Do you think it'll leave you time to write?"

"I'll find the time, somehow. The courses I'll be teaching shouldn't take all that much time to prepare. Beginning Greek—I can walk into the room and open the primer and that's it for that one. Oh, and I found that box of notes, so the history course won't take too much effort. I'll just have to get my lecture-hall chops up. John said I'll have about a hundred bodies in there. Kind of scary. That senior seminar on Pindar will take quite a bit of work, but it'll be fun trying to figure him out, which no one, to the best of my knowledge, has ever really done—definitively, I mean. I'll brush up on my German and read Wilamowitz's book on him."

"Who?"

"Ulrich von Wilamowitz-Moellendorff, great nineteenth-century classicist. He wrote on all of the major Greek authors except Sophocles."

"Why did he leave him out?"

"Out of respect for his son, who had written on him and was killed in the first world war."

"As for your 'lecture-hall chops,' you'll make it, honey," she reassured him. "I *have* seen you lecture a few times, you know—*more* than a few, actually."

"Yeah, I'll get the hang of it again—but that first day, I'm telling you, looking out into that sea of strange, expectant faces is scary."

"I was there on your first day at Central Ontario and you seemed fine to me. And when you first walked in—well, I'm glad you didn't notice the way some of those little flirts were eyeing you, honey. It would have swelled your head even bigger than it is!"

"Yeah, I remember you telling me. But, really, my leg was shaking so hard that time I didn't know if I could start speaking. The first day is always rough."

"You'll do just fine, don't worry." She touched him lightly on the arm.

"Yeah, sure. I guess I'm not all that worried about it. Just a little stage fright there at the beginning, which is normal and, they say, good. What does worry me, though, is finding a place to live once we get there. John said he'll keep looking—I guess he's got his secretary working on that—but it doesn't look real hopeful, my sweet, not too hopeful."

"Oh, I think something will happen."

"Like what, for instance?"

"Oh, I don't know. But I feel it."

"You and your intuition." He chuckled. "Okay, then *happen us a house!*"

"I promise to concentrate on it for the rest of the day."

"Right. And I'll start that breakfast going."

"Holler when you want me to help," Jane said. "I'll be out back picking some flowers."

About an hour later their guests began to arrive. Jim and Boz first, then Hernando and the Muphs, finally Oliver and Asad. Jim had brought in his dog Oscar and was standing over him in a corner of the kitchen. Most of the others were in the front room, where Jane was serving wine.

"This is a privilege, you know, being asked in like this, my friend, so behave yourself!" Jim advised the dog, whose fierce demeanor and gaunt physique had inspired speculation that he was part Great Dane, part mastiff.

Jim turned to a trim and wiry young woman standing beside him. Her jet-black hair, reaching down onto her back a good ten inches, high cheekbones, and dark complexion made it unmistakable that she was of native-American ancestry, Arapaho in her case.

"Oscar is really not accustomed to this much domesticity," he explained to her. "He's always lived at my shop, that's been his job, guarding the place. And I sold it yesterday, you know, so he's been sleeping in the REO nights and hanging out with Boz and me during the day. But it's too hot today to leave him in the car." He jabbed a finger in the direction of the dog. "Now just *stay* right there, ol' buddy! You've got your water there, and if you're good I'll scare up a second breakfast for you."

"I like the way you talk to him," said Melinda. "Like he's *human!*"

"Well, he is, sort of," said Jim, smiling. "At least that's what he tells me."

"You *heard* the man!" Joe called over to the dog from the table in the middle of the room. "Don't move a *peg!*"

"What an interesting expression, Joe," Melinda said in a very flat western accent. "Rings a bell."

"'Pinetop's Boogie Woogie'," he responded.

"Oh, yeah, sure, Flossie was playin' this old seventy-eight the other day," she said. "That's where I heard it, sure! *Cool!*"

"Now you're Messalina, right?" Jim said, extending his hand to her. "Lead guitar, right? Jim Harsh."

"Hi!" she said, turning to him. "Yeah, but that's just my professional name—which I have Joe here to thank for—but everyone calls me Melinda, which is my Christian name. Although I'm hardly a Christian," she added, smiling. "And, yeah, I play guitar in the Muphs." She took Jim's hand and held it, arresting its trembling. "And you're our new manager. Welcome to the zoo."

"Oh, sure, thanks."

"I'm glad you got your shop all squared away, Jeem," said Hernando. "It would be a drag for you if you hadn't."

"Yeah, Big John Little bought it—for a good price, too," he said. "Know him?"

"Who *don't* know Big John?" said Melinda, smiling. "He's about the biggest dealer in these parts. I'm sure he *did* give you a good price. He's got bread to burn!"

"Yeah, man," Hernando broke in, also betraying amusement, "when I hear B.J. bought your shop I theeng, well, tha's another front for his operation. He'll get somebody t' run it for 'im and he'll run dope out o' there. No shit, man!"

"Yeah, I'm hip to John's history," said Jim, "and I'll be long gone outa there so I could care less. Boz and I finished up the last job we had yesterday, so if he wants any legit business he'll have to put somebody in there who knows something about rebuilding air-cooled engines, and he'll have to hustle, that's all I have to say. If he doesn't, well, the pigs'll catch on real fast."

"Oh, John'll take care o' business," Melinda assured them. "He's not about to get his big ass busted! *No way!*"

"Okay, folks, in the front room with you!" Joe called out. "That's where the action is!"

The trays that Joe and Jane a few minutes later carried in to the front room and placed on the spool were crowded with the entree and side dishes of what Joe called his "British Brunch." It was a specialty of his the preparation of which he would allow no participation in by Jane or anyone else. It had been passed down the generations of his father's side of the family and Joe could remember it being served, as Sunday breakfast, by a butler in his grandmother's row house on Calvert Street in Baltimore three decades ago.

Seated on cushions around the spool were ten people and there were empty places for Joe and Jane. In addition to those mentioned, there were Boz, Oliver, Asad, keyboard player Flossie Black, bassist Tea Squeir, drummer Steeph Hardon, and the youngest member of the band, sixteen-year-old African-American roadie Jessup Lincoln Dorsey III.

"Before I serve my *pièce de résistance*," Joe, still standing, announced, "I wish to offer a toast. Pass the wine around, if you please, and everybody fill up."

"*Hear, hear!*" Oliver cried out, holding his empty wine glass aloft.

"As you know, mah deahs," Joe continued, going deadpan and adopting a W. C. Fields drawl, "this fair city and infamous political whorehouse will imminently be losing some of its most illustrious citizens, to wit, the aggravation known as Diverse Muph, along with God knows how many of its camp followers, groupies, and sundry other support troops. I hereby wish them Godspeed, urge them *non illegitimi carborundum* and to screw 'em all but six and leave them for the polar bears, and, for chrissakes, don't take no wooden nickels! Just remember this, you can cheat on your taxes and you can cheat on your ol' lady or ol' man, but you can't cheat an honest man!"

"*A Pulitzer Prize of a toast, Joe!*" Oliver shouted over the applause and drained his glass.

"Yes indeed, and if they awarded prizes for catalogues of clichés I'd be laughing all the way to the friggin' bank!" said Joe, also finishing off his wine. "Now let's have us some kidney stew on waffles," he said, leaning over the table and starting the huge serving dish on its way around the spool. "Jane, hand me the rhubarb, would you, please, and I'll get it going around the other way. Everybody help themselves to the English muffins and jams and everything. And there's coffee and Irish breakfast tea over on that apple box by Boz."

"Says *'Pears,'* Perfesser," Boz corrected, "'Pears From Oregon.' Think I'll have me some o' thet Oyrish tea."

"Jim, and Mr. Boswell, you, too," Flossie called across the spool as dishes were passed amid "oohs" and "aahs" and other commendations vis-à-vis the food and drink, "the Muphs asked me to speak for all of them and to say that we are all very, very happy that you are joining us! We just know we're on the brink of making it and this is the push we need, getting on the road and all."

"Yeah, Jim and Bozman," Tea called out, "welcome aboard! It's gonna be real cool having you cats at the wheel."

The other band members nodded in agreement. Hernando swallowed his initial mouthful of the main dish and turned to Joe. "Man, you should put this on the market or open a *restaurante* or something. It's *outasight,* mon!" He raised another spoonful halfway to his mouth and held it there. "Hey, Jim and Boz, I want to say that we talk a long time, all of us, about you two goin' on the road and all and bein' manager and everytheeng and the theeng that keep comin' up was that you cats got a repootashun 'round Austin of not rippin' off folks. I theeng that was the main theeng that done convince everybody." He smiled. "We're all real happy 'bout you two joinin' us."

"Jeez, thanks, all of you," said Jim, turning to Boz, who was on the cushion to his right with mug of tea in hand. "How 'bout that, Bozzo, our reputation has preceded us."

"Well, like the Perfesser say, James, ya can't cheat no honest man!" Boz responded, grinning. "Nosiree, can't never cheat no honest man!"

Jessup Dorsey, who was the first to finish his kidney stew-laden waffle and was passing his plate for seconds, turned and whispered to Flossie.

"Oh, right," she said, nodding and raising her hand for Jim's attention. "Jess just reminded me to invite you and Boz over to our last gig at the Armadillo tomorrow night." She swung her gaze around the spool. "*All* of you, in fact!"

"Yeah, man, that's gonna be a blast!" said Steeph. "Our new harp man The Carver is going to be with us for the first time on a gig. He's only sat in at rehearsal with us a couple times so far."

"How's he working out?" Joe asked. "I really dug him out there at that juke joint."

"Oh, man, he's *ba-a-ad, real bad!*" Melinda answered. "I mean, that old cat *cooks his ass off!* I know how you like that old blues, Joe, and you'll dig the band even more, now that he's with us."

"Thees Armadeello—" commenced Asad, who had heretofore not spoken, except in *sotto-voce* asides to Oliver.

"Arma*dil* lo," Oliver corrected, under his breath.

"—would that have sometheeng to do weeth the Armadeello World Headquarters beelding that I pass by on my way to university every day?"

"*That's it, man!*" drummer Steeph called over to him. "Fall by there tomorrow night, man. We're going to peel the paint off them walls!"

"Oh, assuredly, I shall be there. I have long wondered what transpires een that edifeece weeth such eenteresteeng grapheecs. And I have many curiosities to observe thees process of, as you say, to peel ze paint."

Melinda, sitting next to Jim, turned and whispered into his ear. "Can he be real?"

"*Hey, Joe!*" Oliver called out, "Know what would go well with this dish? Some of that stout I know you keep in your fridge."

"I'll get you one, Ollie," said Joe, and a minute or so later was back on his cushion and opening two bottles of the requested beverage. He handed one to Oliver and tilted the other to his lips.

"I developed a taste for this when I was in merry ol' England," said Oliver, smacking his lips. "*Good stuff!*"

"Yes, so did I—in Canada, that is," said Joe, almost under his breath. Then he sat erect and attracted the attention of all at the spool by raising his hand high. "Strictly speaking, this is a going away party for our good friends Jim and Boz and the Muphs, all of whom, for one reason or another, deem it prudent to split this burg."

There were loud cheers, stamping of feet, and loud whistles through the teeth of Hardon and Jessup. Once the laughter had died down Joe continued.

"What you don't know is that it is also the very last convivial gathering of any of us at this spool."

A hush descended upon the room, some of those present looking up from forks poised before mouths.

"Not to over dramatize it," he continued, more than a little surprised at the somber response his introduction had elicited, "but Jane and I shall also be departing Austin."

"Where you all goin'?" Hernando asked.

"I sent off a telegram night before last accepting a teaching position at Hopkins College, in Vista, a few miles from Boulder, Colorado," he replied, directing his answer to the entire party. "We hope to leave three days from now, if we can get our act together and pack up all our gear and so forth and so on."

"I knew you couldn't stay out of the classroom much longer, Joe!" said Oliver, laughing, "I just *knew it!*" He looked around the table. "*Shit,* I'll *miss* all you folks!"

"We'll miss you too, Ollie," said Jane, soothingly, "but you can come and visit, you know—all of you."

"Yeah, my friend," Joe added, "you're always running

back and forth across the country. Just stop by one of those times. We might just settle down in them thar foothills." He turned to Jane. "One never know, do one?"

"One never do, honey," she said, putting her arm in his, "as the sage Fats Waller was wont to say."

Several hours and the consumption of a considerable amount of food, wine, ale, stout, grass, and hash later, the party had dispersed throughout the first floor of the house, some remaining at the spool, others in the kitchen brewing tea and preparing snacks, several sitting on the steps in the hall.

The vintage boogie woogie of Meade Lux Lewis on harpsichord and the Balinese-like stomping rhythms of Cripple Clarence Lofton that had been playing for an hour or so had just given way to the New Orleans heterophony of George Lewis and Big Jim Robinson. Throughout the afternoon at tape's end a voice would come over the speaker, back-announcing the set. At first it was in the broad A's of a jaded BBC newscaster and, as the day wore on, various other personae were heard from, including one who mumbled in a back-from-the-living-dead monotone and another who pleaded in the nasal whine of a southern evangelist, "Doan tech thet daw-wal! Sta-a-ay tuned t' Ga-a-awd's tur-r-n-n-ta-a-ble!"

So convincing was the ruse that none (except Jane, who of course was in on the secret) suspected the source, assuming rather that Joe had given up on tapes and resorted to the FM band. That is, until a rasping whiskey-voiced delivery launched into an extended commercial for "Perfesser Josaiah's Bodacious Health Tonic, gawr-ran-teed to ree-zult in the em-ee-nent dee-par-shurr of all yer fiscal and imazhinary eels." After a minute or so the harangue broke off into convulsed laughter.

Jim and Melinda, sitting on the hall steps, were among the first to catch on, for the small door on the side of the stair well creaked open and Joe furtively eased himself out, unaware of the two who were watching silently from only a few inches above his head. Joe started toward the open door of the front room and realized that he was in the direct line of sight of Boz, who was sitting on the edge of the spool staring at him.

Joe stumbled into the room and collapsed backwards onto two cushions and looked up at Boz, his face contorted in mirth. He seemed unable to get his breath and to be trying to communicate something to Boz, who grinned down at him.

"War that you on the raddyo, Perfesser?"

"I was——," he tried to begin, breaking off into laughter.

"I thought the preacher man was a gonna start speakin' in tongues thar fer a minute. He was *somethin' else!*"

The others in the room, Tea Squeir, Oliver, and Asad, sat up from their semi-reclined positions on the other side of the spool.

"Hey, Bozman," Tea drawled, "what's happenin', man? You talkin' to yerself or what the fuck?"

"The Perfesser's here," Boz said, turning halfway and gesturing toward the floor. "He's layin' here on the floor laughin' hisself silly."

"That was you on the radio, I mean, the speakers there, right, Joe? That commercial at the end there, right?" Oliver called out, rising to his knees and hobbling around the spool to Joe.

In the kitchen Jane and Flossie were joined by Jim and Melinda.

"Hi, honey, whatcha been up to?" Flossie asked putting her arm around Melinda's waist and squeezing her. "We're making some great tea here for everybody. Figure it's tea time, doncha, Jim ?"

"Oh, yeah, and that's a great collection Jane has up there," he replied, nodding upward at a shelf above the counter.

"It needs another minute or two," Jane said. "Herbal takes a mite longer than black tea. I'll get the cups and mugs."

"Lemme help," said Melinda.

"Okay, grab some mugs from that cupboard there on the right. There's some cups in the drying rack. I'll get them."

"Isn't she a doll?" Flossie whispered to Jim, "I mean, Jane. What beautiful hair, and that figure! And such a sweet person. Joe's some lucky guy."

"Oh, yeah, Jane's a beauty all right, no question about that," he answered. "And they don't come any nicer. Yeah, I envy Joe."

"I see you and Melinda have been getting to know each other, Jim. Let me tell you, she is first class! And what a musician! Best guitarist I've heard, period, I don't care who—." She broke off as Jane and Melinda approached the table carrying trays.

"Jim, can you grab those tea pots, please, and then we're all set."

"Tea time!" Flossie cried out as she entered the front room at the head of the procession. Joe was now in an upright position with Boz to his left and Oliver on his right. Boz moved over one cushion and waved Jane to the one he had vacated. Hernando, Steeph, and Jessup had just come in from the back yard, where they had been playing catch with two fielder's gloves and a catcher's mitt, all very worn, and a baseball on which could barely be made out the faded signature of Walter "Big Train" Johnson.

"All those announcers between numbers for the last hour or so," Oliver called out across the table to those taking their seats, "they were all Joe."

"You're kidding," Jane said, winking at Joe. "Honey, you should be ashamed of yourself, duping your friends like that. And no one caught on?"

"I did, Miss Jane," Boz said, "when he done that snake oil bit. I knowed thet warn't fer real, no way, nosiree."

"Joe, you should go on the air," Flossie said.

"That's where he was," Melinda said, "in his little studio. Am I allowed to tell, Joe?"

"Oh, sure, you're most of you long gone anyway, why not?" he said.

"Jim and I were sitting on the steps out in the hall and looked down and there was Joe sneakin' out of a little door underneath us. He didn't see us and it was all we could do to keep from breakin' up."

"So you're all set up with a mike and all under there, Joe," Oliver asked. "Right?"

"Yep, I wired that up last week. I've always had a hankering to be on the radio, so I thought I'd have my own network." He looked around the spool. "Now, I don't reach a lot of folks, of course—just a few who count."

"Hey, right on, my man Joe!" Tea called out, his fist in the air. "*Outasight!* I dug it all the way, man, and I had no idea it was you, man, I just thought you were tunin' in to some weird shit, man—and I mean *weird!* That stoned cat, I mean, I really *dug him,* man!"

The subject abruptly changed to Hernando's arrest when Asad, who had first met him at this gathering, asked him, "On what ground deed the poleese deetain you, Airnando?"

After Hernando had briefly summarized his "bust" Hardon beckoned to Asad.

"I spent a lot of time sittin' around down there last year, when I had a little more spare bread, bailin' out cats. In fact, when I made the scene back here a year and a half ago they had a tail on me as soon as I hit town."

"Reely?"

"No shit, man! I thought I was in the fuckin' movies, man, creepin' around, duckin' in and outa my pad. Then a cat hipped me that they were after this dude from New York that was riding with me on his way to L.A. Anyway, he split and I've never heard from him since, and they took the fuckin' tail off me. I heard after I started springin' cats that they didn't want me, I was just small fry. I heard that from a pig my buddy went to high school with, a narc and a first class asshole if there ever was one. The whole thing is a fuckin' game for those pigs, man. You want to play, they'll be happy to play with you. They don't give a shit if you smoke or drop acid or nothin'. In fact, a lot o' them narcs smoke and do all kinds o' shit. I'd even say that a couple of them are not all that bad dudes. Not when they're out to bust your ass, though! They can turn real mean then, man, and I mean *fuckin' mean!*"

"I still don't understand why they busted Nando," Flossie broke in as Hardon sipped from the mug handed to him. "He's hardly what you'd call 'big fry'."

"Big fry," Melinda repeated, giggling, touching Flossie

on the arm.

"Okay, big *time*," said Flossie.

"Depends on what kind of pressure is on them and what sort of game plan they're into," Jim began, sweeping the spool with his eyes and reaching for his mug with slightly trembling hand. "For them it's like solving equations—or maybe constructing a movie scenario is a better analogy."

Melinda, sitting between him and Flossie, turned to look at his profile and slipped her hand into Flossie's under the spool.

"Honesty, fairness, moral standards, or decency, or any kind of guidelines for behavior that we would respect," he continued, "that doesn't mean diddly shit to them if they need a patsy, someone to take the heat off them. Like the white middle class is all shook up because grass is all over the high schools, even in the *junior* high schools, so what do they do? Why, the fuzz nab the leader of a band that plays the high school circuit. And that's where the scenario comes in. Face it, it's all set up for them. Nando is a suspect from square one. He's a spick—excuse the term—" he interjected, turning to Hernando—"which for them is the next best thing to a nigger—sorry, again, Jess—and he carries on up there on the stage, sending young chicks into ecstasy and all that. So the narcs appeal to the suspicions of the parents, who are already convinced that a dark-skinned dude like Nando is balling their virgin sixteen-year old daughters—"

Flossie let out a whoop. "You'd be hard put to find a sixteen-year-old virgin in this town, let me tell you!" she said, chuckling.

"—so they pick up a guy they think will be an easy bust and who will give them a lot of publicity, take the heat off them, know what I mean?"

"Only they doan figure on Pepe Feliciano!" said Hernando. "Funny, they should have gotten hip to him showin' up for us spicks, eh, Joe?"

"Fortunately, we can depend upon the sluggard nature of their native wits," said Joe. "You know, I had kind of the impression there in the station house that those pigs were saying, 'Damn! That sonovabitch took us again!' I bet whoever composed that particular scenario got his head taken off by the chief."

"Oh, you can depend on it, man," Hardon said, laughing, "that dude got his ass chewed from here to Dallas and back!"

"Joe is playing it smart to split this town," Jim resumed. "Especially since the Man will not feel too kindly about him being a part of springing Nando here. They'll be out to get you, Joe, so you better be real clean from here on out." Jim shook a Gauloises out of the leather case and took it between his lips, held his Zippo lighter to it, and drew deeply. "Know something? They'd love to bust your ass, Joe. You know, ex-professor, corrupter-of-youth sort of thing, runs a den of iniquity. They could really make it messy for you. And especially for Jane. They'd likely get a deportation order on her from the feds and hustle her on a plane for Toronto before you could get your lawyer on the phone."

"No worry, we're going to be out of here within seventy-two hours," said Joe. "I done seen the face on the bar room floor and it done tell me, '*Lewis, get yo' ass in gear!*'"

Silence fell upon the room, broken only by a short phrase *sotto voce* in Spanish from Hernando that Joe, Jane, and Boz nodded in response to but only Melinda responded to, with "*Sí, claro!*"*

Jane, filling cups with tea and passing them along, glanced sideways at Joe. He touched her thigh under the spool.

"We're going to travel clean," Jane announced. "In fact, beginning with tomorrow, we're going to *be* clean."

"Best thing you could do, folks!" said Jim, nodding. "Playing it real smart."

"But today ain't tomorrow," said Joe, "so fill that pipe up again and let's get good and fucked up."

"I thought we already were!" Flossie said, laughing and turning to Melinda. "How about you, keed?"

"I wouldn't mind another hit—especially of that great hash!" said Melinda.

"I envy you," said Oliver, looking across the spool to Joe and Jane, "going to Colorado and all. And I'll sure as hell miss you, that's for sure." He paused and sipped from his mug. "So you'll be there for a year, Joe, that's what your contract is for? And if you behave yourself maybe they'll renew."

"Can you see Joe behaving himself?" said Jim, turning to Boz and winking.

"*He'd better!*" said Jane in mock sternness. "He just *better!*"

"Well, I just can't think of a better place to be," said Flossie. "We used to go skiing in Aspen back when my mom and dad were still together and we always went over to Boulder to visit an old friend of my dad's at the university."

"Do you know anything about Hopkins College?" Jane asked.

---

* Yes, clearly!

"I remember Dad and Moms going over there to have lunch with someone, but I never saw it, that I can recall. I guess they left me back at the lodge. I was only twelve or so. Jeez, that must have been about '56! Doesn't seem that long ago."

"Do you get to ski often now?" Jane asked.

"I haven't for a couple years now, not since I came to Austin." She smiled. "Where would you ski around here? But I plan to take a ski vacation one of these years."

"Come and visit us in Boulder," Jane said.

"Hey, that's a wonderful idea! I'll do that."

"Speaking of water sports," said Joe, "get that hookah going around the table again. And after that I have an idea what we can do, go over to Barton Springs for a late afternoon dip. How's that for a winner?"

"Great idea, Joe, it must be at least one hundred in the shade out there," Oliver said. "Let's take some brew along."

"Okay," Jane agreed, "but let's clear all this away before we go, everybody. One more round for that pipe and it too goes, honey."

"Righto, I'll stow it away in my Amontillado Room."

When the hookah had circled the spool several times Joe collected it, the film cans, cigarette papers, and ashtray and took it all down into the basement. A few minutes later he startled his guests, all of whom were still lounging at the spool, bellowing into the room from the hall,

"*Attènti! 'Diamo, amici!** Come on, you peckerheads, hit the fucking deck! It's a beautiful day in Shee-car-go!" Then he ran up the stairs three at a time and disappeared into the bathroom.

---

* Listen up! Let's go, friends!

"Man, is he ever stoned out of his fuckin' gourd!" said Tea, punching Hardon in the side with his elbow.

"*Shit*, man!" Hardon cried out, doubling over, "I *told* you not to do that!"

"Not necessarily," said Jane. "He's like that sometimes when he hasn't smoked for days."

Returning from Barton Springs, Joe noticed a dark-colored sedan with spring-mounted aerial on the rear bumper pulling out of the alley onto Railroad Avenue as they approached the house.

"*Shit!*" Joe hissed. "I just *know* they're *watching* me."

"Sure looked like a narcmobile to me," said Flossie, who was sitting on a plastic milk crate behind Joe. "Hey, here comes Jim and the rest."

"Bastards were no doubt casing the joint," he added as he pulled the Greenbrier in to the curb. "Yes, sir, I'm definitely going to clean house tonight!"

"You'd be well advised to do just that, Joe," said Flossie as she opened the side door. She stood at Jane's window. "Folks, thanks for the feed and all. Joe, that kidney dish was scrumptious. I'll have to get that recipe from you sometime. And that swim really hit the spot in this heat. I thought I'd die laughing at Jim's dog chasing that ball in the water. The entire day has just been glorious." She leaned forward and kissed Jane on the mouth. "Jane honey, let's get together again before you leave. You take care, you hear. See y'all." She turned and looked at Jim's Corvair pulling up. "Oh, I guess we're driving the two blocks." She hurried across the street and squeezed into the back seat next to Tea, lifting Melinda onto her lap.

"Man let's *move* it!" Hardon cried out. "You should get

a *air* conditoner!"

"This buggy has *natural* air conditioning," Jim replied. "*Hang on!*"

Spotting the unmarked cruiser, Joe revealed to Jane late that evening, was the feather that tipped the scale, convincing him that they should depart Austin as soon as they could set their affairs in order and pack. Oliver had agreed earlier that evening to take over the year's lease they had signed only weeks before and to reimburse them the final month's rent and damage deposit they had paid the owner two years ago.

"It's rather providential, all of this," Joe said as he and Jane sat on the floor sorting out the camping equipment they had pulled out of the hall closet. "I mean, if it weren't for this teaching gig and the four bills Oliver is going to lay on us tomorrow I don't know how we would have made it much longer here in this town. I guess we could've given up the house and lived in the bus. Why, *you would have had to get a job!*"

"Right," Jane said absently. "Honey, can we afford to get another camping stove—the butane kind. I hate the smell of this petrol." She held her middle finger to his nostril. "See, it still stinks and we emptied it last fall."

"The Emperor Augustus had the actor Pylades dragged off the stage when he did that."

"For *what?*" Jane shrieked, doubling over with laughter. "*Asking him for a butane stove?*"

"They didn't use butane back then," he replied, bending over and nuzzling her.

"What did they burn?"

"Bananas!" he replied. "No, I was referring to your giving me the *digitalis infama*."

"So, can we?"

"Sure, I'll get you anything your little heart desires, my sweet, you know that, as long as you give me what I want."

"Right. I'll have a list for you in the morning."

"Say, that was quite a kiss you and Flossie exchanged there."

"Exchanged? Listen, I wasn't prepared for that. I thought she was aiming for my cheek but I couldn't turn it fast enough."

"I'll tell you what *cheek* she had in mind. That young woman is, as they used to say, a little funny that way."

"Do you really think so? I guess I have gotten a little hint of that between her and Melinda—or Messy, as you like to call her."

"I think I laid Messalina on her for keeps. I notice it's on their new poster." He held Jane at arm's length and fixed his eyes on hers. "Tell me, sweetheart, have you ever been made love to by a woman?"

"Well, aren't *we* getting personal?" she said in mock huffiness. "Oh, if you call teenage girls fooling around 'making love', I guess I did that a few times when I was thirteen or fourteen." She paused and looked up above Joe's head. "God, I hadn't thought of that for so long!"

"Did you *enjoy* it?"

"I guess I did—or I wouldn't have done it again after the first time. Girls do know some things to do, you know. But I soon got more interested in boys."

"Come on upstairs with me and I'll show you how much better it is with a man."

"Oh, you've already *shown* me *that, more than few times*, honey!"

They climbed the stairs and went into the bedroom,

shedding their clothes and leaving them where they dropped. He walked her backwards over to the bed, lowering her so that her buttocks rested on its edge, and dropped to his knees, spreading her legs and, as she lay back, placing her feet on his shoulders. She was already a little wet when his lips and tongue engaged her sex. She soon commenced to whimper and Joe cupped her buttocks with his hands and pressed her toward him as she squirmed. When she began a rotating motion and gripped his head with both hands, pulling him up toward her, he stood up and, sliding her a foot or so back on the mattress, positioned himself between her legs and thrust into her, entwining her hair with his spread fingers, looking down at her face. Her irises nearly disappeared behind the upper lids of her eyes and she wrapped her legs about his torso and her arms around his neck, pulled him down upon her breasts, and began to moan as he moved in and out. Just as he was about to go over the top she started thrashing about wildly and sought his mouth with hers and as he came he could feel her nails all but penetrating the flesh of his lower back.

"Jesus Christ on a fucking crutch that was good, baby!" he said in a gravelly voice that he hardly recognized as his own. She muttered two or three syllables that he could not put together in any sensible pattern and then closed her eyes.

As he lay on top of her he sensed that she was relaxing and rapidly dropping off into sleep. So he withdrew carefully from her now tightness, slowly turned her body ninety degrees so that her head was on a pillow, and covered her with the sheet. Then he got up, pulled his jeans on, slipped into his denim shirt, leaving it unbuttoned, took pipe, tobacco pouch, and matches from the top one of four stacked orange crates that served as bookcase and catch-all, and went down to the kitchen.

He found three bottles of Black Horse Ale in the back of the vegetable bin where he had hidden them before the swim, put two of them on the table, opened one, and lifted it to his lips. Four big gulps left only two or three ounces in the bottle. He held the bottle up to the moonlight coming through the window, put it to his mouth again, and drained it. Then he opened the other bottle and flipped the cap across the room. It scraped the rim of the bulk Shaved Dried Seaweed can and disappeared amongst the rubbish. He started to do the same with the cap of the first bottle but, noting that there was no ashtray on the table, slid it over next to the full bottle with his pinkie.

Once he had his pipe going well he tilted the chair back and propped a knee against the table's edge. "Damn, I'm going to miss this old house," he said to the room. "In fact, when all is said and done I'm going to miss this town, even though no little shit has begun to descend upon my head these past couple of weeks."

His thoughts went back to the day they had pulled into Austin a little more than two years ago. Their only contact, and one of the reasons he had chosen the city as their destination upon leaving Canada, was Jim Harsh, who had come there upon dropping out of Harvard graduate school three years before, the same spring that Joe accepted the offer from Central Ontario College. But the few letters Jim wrote Joe were on his business letterhead and so Joe had called him at the shed when he and Jane were making plans to leave Canada, not thinking at the conversation's termination to ask him for his home address. Arriving in Austin on a Sunday, they had found the shed locked and no one answered the emergency telephone number posted by the door. So they had not caught up with Jim until they had been in Austin for several days.

Unfamiliar with the city, they had located the university on the map and cruised the nearby streets. Turning onto the street long ago known as Railroad Avenue, they noted the disarray of the yards, the colorful designs of the houses, and the motley assortment of vehicles.

"What a wonderful street," Jane had remarked. "Look, honey, there's someone in that driveway there."

That was the day of our meeting Nando, Flossie, and Tea, he recalled. *Melinda didn't join the band until late in the fall, right after Hardon replaced that drummer I never can remember the name of. The cat just vanished in early December, left his drum set behind, didn't even take his clothes, Nando told me. In fact, those are the traps Steeph uses to this day.*

Upon Hernando's invitation they had pulled the bus into the driveway and had ended up crashing there for a month or so. They were offered kitchen sink and bathroom facilities and in the back yard there was a picnic table upon which Jane set up their Coleman stove. Joe put the huge cooler under the table and every morning exchanged the nearly melted water-filled plastic soda bottles with those which he had frozen overnight in the house freezer.

Of the ten or so people who resided on the property, all but two lived in the house. Behind the house was a building that Joe soon realized had originally been a carriage house and later had been converted into a garage. There were servants' quarters above and it was in one of these rooms that Emile and Kathy lived. The Father

Time-bearded Emile, whose blond hair reached the middle of his back, appeared to be in his late twenties. Quiet and shy, the sixteen-year-old Kathy had run away from home a year before and settled in with Emile, who had come across her late one rainy night huddled in a sopping-wet sleeping bag by a path on the university campus. Her dark complexion and black hair immediately alerted Joe and Jane to her Mediterranean ancestry.

Nando and Flossie occupied two of the three bedrooms on the second floor of the house, and Melinda later moved into the remaining one. Tea, Jessup, and that drummer guy were in the huge attic-like room on the third floor and, after the drummer split, Steeph moved in with them.

Joe closed his eyes to better focus his inner sight upon the first floor of the Victorian mansion Diverse Muph had eventually completely taken over. "Let's see now," he said aloud, "there are two large rooms, the parlor and the dining room. Then there's a pantry and the kitchen, both in the rear. The two front rooms would have originally been the sitting room and the library. The one on the right—looking toward the street, that is—was where the nudists Gracie and Paul lived." *Well, they weren't really* bonafide *nudists*, he said to himself, *it was just that Paul liked to answer the front door without a stitch on and Gracie would walk around in the yard in her birthday suit.*

He chuckled as he envisioned instances of both circumstances. He was washing the breakfast dishes one morning when Paul answered the door and ushered into the living room the landlord, who had come by to pick up the rent. Joe stood at the sink and watched as the middle-aged man in white suit with panama hat in hand, seemingly oblivious to Paul's lack of attire, simply took a seat on the couch and proceeded to count out the cash

Paul had handed him. Satisfied it was the proper amount, he opened his account book and wrote a receipt, handed it to Paul upon rising, nodded, said, "Good morning, sir," and strode out the door.

There were many occasions when Joe had the opportunity to admire Gracie's handsome body in the raw, for she daily took sunbaths on a large bath towel in the back yard. The first time had been the very first morning he and Jane waked up in their Greenbrier. They were nuzzling up to each other preparatory to making love when they heard footsteps on the gravel beside the bus. Joe lifted the side-curtain an inch or two and they peeked out. "*Some bare-assed bitch!*" he whispered. "*Look* at those *tits* and *dig* that *nifty wiggle, will ya!*"

She giggled. "This is *some crazy neighborhood*, Joe!"

Manuel "Manny" Ortegasso had the front room to the left. *Now there was a candidate for one of those "Strangest Person I Have Ever Known" profiles that used to run in* Reader's Digest *or somewhere*, he mused, and sipped some ale. One afternoon as Joe, in bathing suit, was cooling off with a cold shower under a hose he had rigged up on the side of the house, Manny rushed out the front door and roared off on his Harley 1200. This provided Joe his first opportunity to look into Manny's room and he was astonished at what he saw. He remembered running to get Jane before its occupant returned.

They stood in the room's doorway in stunned silence gazing at the other-world ambience of the room, for Manny had created a temple that, when entered (as they later experienced when invited therein by Manny), transported one into another realm, another time. The first element that struck them a few days later when they joined Manny for tea was the coolness of the room. Joe assumed upon taking a seat on one of the half dozen pastel cushions strewn on the bamboo matting that covered the floor that the room was air conditioned. When he later wondered aloud where the source of the cooling effect was hidden, Jane was quick to answer him.

"It was in your head, honey."

And, in truth, that was exactly wherein it resided, for Manny's room had virtually no movement of air. He had not so much as a single fan and he opened the two windows only at midnight, upon returning from where he spent his days. Nightly, he told them, he practiced yoga for an hour and then meditated until 3 A.M.

Joe reminded himself that the room's sea-green walls and sky-blue ceiling with white clouds that seemed to be drifting by as he lay on his back and looked up at them further enhanced the cooling effect. At one end of the room, he could now see in his mind's eye, was a low shrine with candles and a Buddha figure no larger than one's fist. The shrine's dimensions were such that Joe had suspected that beneath its cloth cover was a milk crate. There was no other furniture in the room, only an inch-thick foam-rubber mattress the width of a single bed against one wall. At the foot of this were carefully arranged stacks of jockey shorts, socks, and handkerchiefs, and the loudly colored, somewhat garish, tank tops, shorts, and pants that Manny favored. Several pairs of brightly colored flip flops were lined up against the wall just beyond the clothes. On the floor beside the bed were paperbacks of *The Autobiography of a Yogi* and the *Bhagavad-Gita*, the only reading matter in the room. There were no pictures on the walls or ornaments of any kind.

They never saw Manny bring anyone by the house during the month that they lived in the driveway. He spent little time in his room during the day, leaving about 10 A.M., including on Sundays. It amused Joe to watch him emerge from the house clad in shorts, tank top, and flip flops—the three items of apparel of shockingly clashing colors—and almost leap onto the Harley, which he parked alongside the front porch, kicking it to a start and revving the engine for a minute or so, and take off down the driveway with a racket as horrendous as nearby thunderclaps.

One Sunday morning this took place as they were making love and they both began shouting endearments and expressions of passion, little of which the other could make out over the din, and came simultaneously, immediately collapsing into hilarity. Their laughter had barely subsided when Jane raised the curtain a little bit, only to peel off into hysterics when she saw Gracie and Paul, both nude, come out the back door and head toward the picnic table. He was carrying a tray laden with mugs, coffee pot, and plate of pastries, she the Sunday paper.

The most anyone in the house knew about Manny was that he held a fellowship in one of the university's science departments and was engaged in some aspect of nutritional research. His diet was apparently connected with this research. He was on a grape regimen for the period Joe and Jane stayed there and would every day pull into the driveway with huge bags of various varieties of the fruit precariously balanced between his legs. He drank only spring water that was delivered several times a week in gallon bottles. They were periodically invited to join the occupants of the house at a communal meal at the kitchen table and, as they sat and ate, Manny would sometimes appear, say hello, fill a large bowl with bunches of grapes from the refrigerator, take in his other hand a gallon of the spring water, and return to his room.

"Once he was on a fast for a month," Paul informed them at one of these gatherings at the picnic table, a sumptuous feast of barbecued chicken that he and Gracie—both attired only in denim cut-offs, she with an apron that more revealed than covered her ample breasts—had prepared on the back-yard grill. "Before that, he was on raw vegetables. I expect to see him keel over in a dead faint one of these days. Strange dude—but a nice man, for all his eccentricities."

"Man, *strange* is not the word for it!" Tea chimed in. "That Manny is one weird cat. I mean, have you ever seen him look at a newspaper or a magazine, or heard a note of music come out of that room? And has you ever eyeballed that room? The only thing that makes the cat even human, man, is that bike." He turned to Joe. "You *dig,* man?"

Joe looked up from the drumstick he was holding down with his fork and to which he had been, with nearly the delicacy of a surgeon, applying a paring knife. He remembered Jane turning to him and, with amused impatience, urging him, "*Oh,* just *pick it up* and *eat it,* honey—like *everyone else is doing!*"

Indeed, all of the others wore the evidence of such an approach to the main course, namely, hands and mouths smeared with the sauce the fowl had been marinated in overnight. Paul's chest and Tea's white T-shirt were splotched with red and Gracie periodically gathered up on a finger little puddles of the sauce that had dripped inside the top edge of her apron and licked it clean. Witnessing this, he recalled with amusement, he had raised his cloth napkin and leaned forward slightly, as though offering to wipe clean the soiled area. It was well that no one else caught his action, so quickly executed was it, for Gracie winked at him and muttered under her breath, "Later, Joe."

"Listen, I studied the fine art of eating everything with knife and fork the two years I was in Italy," he responded to Jane's admonition, "and I ain't about to let those skills deteriorate!"

"Yeah, you should see him peel and slice a banana with knife and fork," she said, as she leaned forward and prepared to sink her teeth into a huge breast that she grasped and which was dripping sauce onto her plate, then hesitated, adding as coda, "or an orange, section by section."

"The etiquette in Italy requires that virtually nothing but bread be touched with the fingers," he continued. "In fact, serve a cultured Italian a BLT and he will take knife and fork to it—which a Neapolitan friend of mine regularly did when I took him to *Ristorante California.*"

"Joe, I have Italian relatives and they doan eat like that," Hernando objected. "They eat sandwiches with their hands and they doan eat no banana like Jane say you do. I doan theeng you got all that right, not when you talkin' 'bout plain ordinary folks."

"Oh, not to condescend," Joe assured him, "but we are not talking about, as you say, 'plain ordinary people'. Oh, yes, many a time I sat on my *terrazzo* overlooking *Il Golfo di Napoli* and observed the table manners of workmen below when they broke for their mid-day meal. They would take out of attaché cases these foot-long loaves of bread split horizontally and filled with combinations of salami, bologna, prosciutto, formaggio, pickles, and cucumbers and spread with *senape*—mustard.

I guess we call them 'subs' here in the States and the Neapolitan term escapes me at the moment. Anyway, at the beginning of the half-hour lunch break they would be like this—" holding his hand open, as though grasping the loaf, a foot out from his mouth "—and at the end of the break like this," concluding his demonstration with his fingers nearly closed and resting on his lips.

"You should fix them for lunch one day soon, honey," Jane said. "We owe these folks one."

"Yeah, I could sure go for that!" Hernando enthused. "My oncle use to feex them when I veesit heem in Freesco."

"*Right on,* man! *How about tomorrow?*" Tea shouted down from the end of the table.

Joe promised to soon do so and then continued his account of the several styles of Italian manners at meal, regaling his audience—or so it had seemed to him at the time—with tales of pieces of apple flying off his plate at "*ristoranti*" and his occasional backsliding, such as the time he found himself holding a stalk of asparagus aloft preparatory to inserting it into his mouth, sword swallower-like, when he became uncomfortably aware that his luncheon companions, two prominent Italian archaeologists on the staff of the *Museo Nazionale,* were staring at him with expressions that combined in equal parts horrified shock and amused indulgence.

"Then there was the time when I first arrived in Napoli and didn't have all that good a handle on the lingo yet and somehow had it in my mind that the Italian for 'too much' was *piu.* We went out to dinner one night a day or two after embarking and I ordered spaghetti with some kind of seafood sauce and the waiter put a platter down in front of me that seemed to me to have enough spaghetti on it for a party of four, so I looked up at him and said, *'Piu.'* He took the plate and returned in a minute with about half again that much on it. Well, I was beginning to suspect that I was saying something wrong so I took out my handy little tourist's conversation guide and looked up *piu* and discovered that it meant 'more' and that the word for 'too much' was *troppo.*"

"Too much, man, *too fuckin' much!"* said Tea, leading off the general high spirits that the gathering began to display for the rest of the evening. "Hey, what say I fetch another couple bottles o' that dago red?"

"And some brews while you're at it, Teaman," Paul called after the lanky bassist, who was already on his way to the house. "How about it, Joe, ready for another there?"

Joe raised the half-empty second bottle of Black Horse Ale to his lips and drained it in three gulps. He looked up at the electric clock on the refrigerator. It was 1 A.M. His thoughts returned briefly to the house down the street. *When the Muphs leave, there will be not one person left who was living there when we crashed in the driveway for that month or so two years ago.*

Several months after Joe and Jane moved into another house on Railroad Avenue, Manny was found comatose in his room one afternoon by Paul, who had noticed the motorcycle by the porch and wondered what could have caused the deviation in Manny's never-varying routine. Joe heard the siren of the ambulance down the street and called the house. That was the last any of them saw of Manny. Suffering from severe malnutrition, he was taken to the University Medical Center Brackenridge in downtown Austin, where he remained in a coma for a day or so. When he regained consciousness he was flown to a hospital in Phoenix, where his parents lived. A shipping firm came by to pick up his belongings, which Gracie had packed up in a single box, and a much-tattooed biker arrived one morning with notarized contract to drive the Harley to Phoenix.

Emile and Kathy came over to the main house one morning and said goodbye to the others, but declined to reveal their destination on the grounds that Kathy's mother and step-father were on her trail and they didn't want to leave any clues behind as to their future whereabouts. Jane had learned, from Gracie, that Kathy had been sexually abused by her step-father several times during the month before she fled.

That drummer—what the hell was his name?—was just there one day and gone the next, said Joe to himself, whistling through his teeth. *Gracie thought she heard a car pull up in front of the house before dawn and leave in a few seconds. He left his clothes, his set, everything behind. Jesus Christ, like in Capone's time. Steeph moved in the next week. Gracie and Paul were the last to leave. Paul decided to go to chiropractic school somewhere in Alabama or one of the Carolinas, somewhere down there, and Gracie was pregnant. Both their families had money, so I guess they'll make it. That "Later, Joe" with Gracie never happened.* "Just as well," Joe said aloud, "else I'd be wondering if she were carrying a little Joe Jr., or Josephina, when they left." By Christmas the house was all Muphs. He stood up, pushing the chair back and stretching with a loud yawn. "I think I'll get me some shuteye."

Chapter 4

*May be the last time you'll ever
lay eyes on Railroad Avenue.*

The day after the going-away party, Jim and Boz presented Joe with a roof rack that they had acquired that afternoon at the automobile graveyard. It was almost midnight when Jim knocked on the front door and Jane, exhausted from sorting through their belongings since that morning, had turned in. Long accustomed to the eccentricities of his friend, Joe assumed that Jim had come over to just pass the time of day—or, rather, night. They sat in the kitchen drinking ale—Jim had arrived with a six-pack of Black Horse in each hand—and talking about their respective experiences in Spain when Joe was startled to hear a rustling sound in the front hall and the slam of the house door. His chair screeched like chalk on a blackboard as he pushed himself away from the table.

"Oh, that's just Boz," Jim said casually, motioning him to resume his seat. "I'll go out in a minute and help him."

"Help him what?" Joe asked. "I didn't even know he came with you."

"Yeah, he was out in the Corvair listening to some sports round-up or something. You know what a baseball nut he is. Something about the World Series coming up and play-off games or some such shit. Never followed the game myself, and I guess you never had exactly an overwhelming interest in such pursuits, did you?"

"No, I never did," he replied, momentarily distracted from the sudden appearance out of the blue of Jim's colleague, "probably because I had a whole family full of baseball nuts, including a grandmother who used to lie on her bed on sweltering Washington summer afternoons—no air conditioning then, of course—and listen to the Washington Senators lose game after game for years. I can still hear that slow cadence and those long pauses of the radio announcers back in the thirties and forties." Joe quickly drained his bottle of the several remaining ounces and, grasping it by its neck, upturned it and held it close to his lips, microphone-like.

"A—a—a—n—nd it's—s a—a fly—y—y ba—a—a—all to—o—o lay—uf—ft fe—e—e—uld," he began in a flat nasal voice, and then, as one imagined the white sphere rapidly descending earthward, the pace of speech quickened and a feverish excitement entered Joe's voice. "And Shoeless Joe iz under it and looks like 'eez got it oh what a beautiful catch oh no 'ee lost it and Big Train Johnson 'eez roundin' second 'eez on 'iz way to third 'eez slidin' into third and third baseman oh I ferget what the fuck 'iz name iz tags him oh no the umpire iz wavin' im safe and the crowd you can 'ear 'em they're goin' wild listen to the motherfuckers oh shit it's pandemonimum 'ere at Griffith Stadium on this boilin' hot July afternoon pure pandemonimum I'm telling ya no shit!"

Jim's face was contorted with laughter as he gasped for breath. He stumbled to his feet and headed for the refrigerator. "Let's go help Boz," he barely managed to get out. "I'll grab one of my sixes here."

"Help him what?" he asked. "Listen to a friggin' ball game?"

"Put that sucker on your roof!" Jim called back over his shoulder as he went through the doorway into the hall.

Boz had run a heavy-duty orange extension cord from a wall socket in the front hall out the front door and had hooked up to it a Black and Decker drill and a wire-cage-enclosed lamp hanging by hook from the open door of the Greenbrier. He was sitting on the bottom rung of a six-foot stepladder fitting the drill with a bit when Jim and Joe came out the door and down onto the lawn. A shining chrome roof rack was leaning against the bus. Jim put the six-pack on the grass and took three bottles from it, removed the cap from each with an opener hanging, along with his keys, from a chain attached to the belt of his cut-offs, and lined them up on the sidewalk.

"Buy you a brew, gentleman," he said. "Here, I'll help you mount that thing, Bozzo."

"Ain't no big thing to do, James," he said through clenched teeth from which half a bit protruded. Holding the drill between his legs, he strained to turn the key on the side of its closed aperture.

"Shit, who the *fuck* used this last, fer chrissakes?" Succeeding in his effort, he took the bit from his mouth, inserted and secured it tightly in place. "Now we's ready fer some action!"

"Okay, guys, but if my neighbors start hollering out their bedroom windows, I'm splitting and I don't know you," said Joe as he started down the walk toward the Greenbrier.

"Oh, don't worry," Jim assured him, "if the drill makes too much racket you can go in and turn the Stones up. That'll drown it out." He turned around to face Boz. "I don't think the folks on this street are exactly early-to-bed-early-to-rise types, do you, Boz?"

"I doan reckon they is, James, doan reckon they is." He climbed half-way up the ladder. "I'll get the holes fer me bolts lined up if you kin heist thet rack up here." His left hand reached into a pocket of the bib of his overalls and withdrew a flat carpenter's pencil.

Jim and Joe lifted the rack up and positioned it on the bus's roof. With the former holding the rack in place, Boz pencilled dots through the six holes of the rack's feet. With the rack again leaning against the vehicle, he drilled, blew the metal dust off, squeezed sealer from a tube into each hole, and placed a rubber washer on it. Then, placing the rack on the roof, he slipped a short carriage bolt into the eye of each leg of the rack and through the roof. Jim got into the bus and began threading the nuts, with lock washers, onto the bolts with a socket wrench that Boz had taken from a loop of his overalls and handed to him.

The roof rack, in near perfect condition, was a going-away gift from Jim and Boz. Jim told Joe that they found it on a late model Oldsmobile station wagon in the same automobile graveyard where they had acquired the spare REO parts. The car had been in a head-on collision in which a family of four—parents and two young children—had "done gone to they's maker," the graveyard owner told them as he watched them remove the rack from the pitifully mangled vehicle.

"As you kin see," the still suit-and-tie-clad and grease-

and-filth-covered man pointed out, "that thar Olds eight war pushed back into them suckers' laps. Them two younguns, they was throwd outen the open windows like two fuckin' soccer balls. Sheet and two make eight thet war a turbal sight t' see. See, I gotten there afore they untangled them bodies from the wreck and gathered up the kids. They put 'em all in bags and taken 'em to th' ice house."

Startled, Jim looked over his shoulder at the man, who was leaning against the fender of a 1950s Buick sedan across the narrow aisle between the rows of metal carcasses.

"Ice house?"

"Thet place whar all they puts corpooses on ice, the whatchamacallit."

"Oh, you mean the morgue."

"Thet's it. Ah has trouble 'membrin' some o' thet fancy talk. Ah never went past the turd grade. Ah ain't like you ejucated folk."

Because the rack's back end had been lined up with the rear edge of the Oldsmobile's roof, it virtually escaped damage. They withheld the account of the car's accident from Joe, not wishing to "jinx" the Greenbrier, as Jim put it to Boz. Jim told Joe that it was during this second visit to the automobile graveyard that he looked hard at the man and saw that beneath all the dirt were wrinkles of such quantity and depth that he decided the man had to be in the neighborhood of eighty.

"I had to laugh at the old man," said Jim. "Boz and I were across from each other getting this rack off the roof and Boz says to me, 'James, I got it done on this side, how you doin'?' I said, 'I got one more screw left, Boz.' The old lush fires back with, 'She-e-et, I ain't even good fer *thet!*'"

Boz had centered it on the Greenbrier's roof so that it began about a foot behind the windshield and its back end stopped a foot short of its rear. It had taken him and Jim only about ten minutes to mount the rack and the whine of the drill on metal had interrupted the night's stillness for less than half that time. During one of the brief pauses, as Boz finished drilling one hole and was positioning the drill for the next, Joe heard a window slam across the street.

"Either your neighbors must all still be up or they're sound sleepers, Joe," Jim called from inside the bus.

"Yeah, I guess so, except for whatshisface over there," Joe said, pointing to the darkened house whence had emanated the crash of the window.

"There you are, my friend!" Jim called to Joe, who was now sitting on the top step of the porch sipping ale and smoking one of Jim's Gauloises. "As good as new!"

"Yeah, James, you can't hardly notice that bend in the front bar," Boz added, "'ceptin' you was *lookin'* fer it."

"I can't make it out and I *am* looking for it," Joe assured him. "Yes, it's a real beauty and I can't thank the both of you enough. Jane is going to really be surprised." He paused. "You know, I'm not going to even tell her or point it out to her tomorrow, just see how long it takes her to notice it."

"That'll be a gas!" said Jim. "Listen, ol' buddy, I'm shot! Been up since five this morning. Can't seem to sleep the last few days."

Sure enough, Jane did not remark upon the addition of the roof rack for the next two days. On the third morning after Boz and Jim had mounted it, Joe and Jane, with a lot of help from their friends, carried their gear out of the house and lined it up around the Greenbrier, which Joe had brought up close to the front steps. Joe and Hardon—who, along with all the other Muphs and Oliver, had been sworn to secrecy about the rack—were lifting a wooden crate of kitchenware onto the roof of the bus when Joe caught a glimpse of Jane, who was standing on the porch. He could barely restrain himself from bursting out in laughter, for the expression on her face was one of bewilderment.

Jim, standing behind her in the doorway of the house, immediately caught on as he saw a grinning Hardon suddenly duck his head behind the box he and Joe were hoisting. A broad smile spread across Jim's face and he put the box he was carrying onto the porch floor, the better to hold back his laughter with hand over mouth. Hearing others come down the stairs inside, he turned and signaled with finger to lips to Flossie and Melinda, who were carrying blankets, sheets, and pillows for the foam rubber mattress and plywood platform that had served as Joe's and Jane's bed the past two years and which Boz had that morning installed in the Greenbrier. By now, Joe had centered the wooden box along the rack's rear bar and was looking at Jane over the bus's roof.

"You know, it's the oddest thing!" Jane called to him. "We've had the Blue Bus all this time and how could I never have noticed that it had a rack on its roof?" She shrugged. "I guess we just never had occasion to load it up like this." She hesitated. "Wait a minute. I remember you tying the tree up there last Christmas and looping the rope through the windows. And you were so worried that it would scratch the paint you put a tarp down first." She heard a snicker from behind and wheeled around to see Jim bent over and on the point of going into convulsive laughter. Flossie began to giggle and Melinda was grinning in an almost tearful way. "*Wait* a minute! *Something* is *going on* here! *Joe!* When did that rack get put on there?"

He had slipped down onto the grass behind the Greenbrier and was rolling over with laughter. Jane ran down the steps and around the bus and threw herself down upon him. "You want to *really laugh!* I'll give you something to laugh about!" Slipping her hand under his T-shirt, she began to mercilessly tickle him. "*Okay!* When did you have that rack put on there—last night after dinner? Why, what's the matter, Joe, can't you answer? Can't you *talk?*"

"*Oh, stop, stop, please stop!*" Joe was pleading breathlessly, choking with laughter. He rolled over out from under her and raised himself to his knees. "It's been on there for *three friggin' days, for chrissakes,* and you just noticed it this minute! And you tell me that *I* have no visual sense!"

"*I don't believe it!*" she said, sitting back on the grass and tossing her hair back, smoothing it out with both hands. "I just don't believe you for a minute! You snuck the bus out last night—I remember you saying you were going to the store for some beer—and had some shop put it on. Why, it's *brand new!*"

"It's a gift from Jim and Boz," Joe said, lowering himself onto his buttocks, hugging his lower legs, and beginning to rock back and forth. They came over at midnight Monday night and put it on."

Jane looked up incredulously at Jim, who was now standing over her.

"He's telling the god's truth, Jane, the absolute god's

124

truth! Boz and I put it on the Greenbrier's roof in the early hours of Tuesday." He looked down at her, smiling.

"Thet there is the truth, Miss Jane," Boz added, "the whole damn truth and nothin' but the whole damn truth, so hep me, God!"

"Well, I never—!" Jane got to her feet and embraced Jim, kissing him lightly on the lips.

"Thanks, Jim." She went over to Boz and gave him a peck on the check. Then she rushed back around to the other side of the bus and threw herself down upon Joe, who was lying on his back, and kissed him, running her tongue in and out of his mouth.

"You really are too much, my dear! How you kept it to yourself for two days, I'll never know. And I must have been in and out of that bus ten times since they put it on there."

"At least," said Joe, "at the very least. But you know, it's like trying to remember whether someone wears glasses or something. Like, I shaved my beard off back in my beatnik days before I went out on an interview at Brown University, and people at Yale I'd been seeing every day for a year and a half with that beard didn't notice that I was clean shaven—for several days, some of them. Then someone would stop me in the hall and look at me closely and say something like, 'Didn't you used to have a mustache—or was it a beard?'"

"Well, honey, I guess we'd better get this old bus loaded while we have all this help. Then we'll feed this crew that stack of roast beef sandwiches you made and be on our way."

"Righto, babe."

It took little more than an hour to pack the gear into

and onto the Greenbrier. A great deal of the contents of the house had been given away. Most of the furniture was left for Oliver, who intended to move in on the morrow. This included the kitchen table and chairs, the spool in the sitting room, dozens of orange crates and apple boxes, and the six cement blocks that had supported the plywood board of their makeshift bed. They also left for Oliver a few of the unmatched dishes that Joe had purchased at Goodwill Industries, where he had routinely shopped dressed only in his blue-ticking overalls and work boots, talking the price down from, say, thirty-five cents a dish to a dollar and a half for a dozen. Joe and Jane had limited themselves to a traveling library of ten books from the hundred or so they had brought with them from Canada and the several dozen they had acquired during their two years in Austin and had packed up the rest and mailed them at the book rate to the classics department at the college. Joe had also written to have his professional collection of more than 500 volumes and a couple of boxes of general literature and history, in storage in Cambridge, shipped there.

Only one item was sold, a huge post office desk Jane had bought for Joe for ten dollars at the bankruptcy sale of a used furniture store. She and Joe had stripped it of its enamel paint, sanded it smooth, and covered it with several coats of clear varnish. It had resided in the front room upstairs where Joe had spent most of his mornings writing the past year. They had dropped over to the attorney Pepe Feliciano's house earlier in the week and extended to the couple an invitation to come over and check out the items they were giving away. The following morning Matilda Feliciano had come alone to look over what they were leaving behind and, upon seeing the desk, had offered them a hundred dollars for it. Within an hour, four tattooed and, all but one, pony-tailed biker types had arrived with a U-Haul van. Joe vaguely recognized them from the evenings he and Jane had spent at Armadillo World Headquarters. There had always been several of their sort perched on the seats of their machines, at least a dozen of which were some nights parked in the loading zone in front of the club. Joe had conjectured that two or three bikers were always left as guards for the small fleet of motorcycles, some of which appeared to be extremely costly. Two of the bikers carried the desk down the narrow stairwell to the U-Haul parked on the grass. As Joe, Jane, and the other two bikers followed, Joe had asked them how they knew the Felicianos.

"Pepe's our main man, man!" one of the two, a muscular blond in leather vest over a hairy chest, had quickly informed him in a delivery appropriate to launching an entertaining anecdote. "Wasn't for him some of our asses'd be doin' serious time, right, Starker?"

"*Fuckin' a, man'!*" the other, a squat and fat, nearly bald, black-bearded man with, Jane later observed, "menacing eyes," had chirped in a falsetto. "Pardon mah language, ma'am!"

"Yeah, watch that shit, Stark!" the other said, chuckling. "Say, mind if I smoke, folks?"

"Be my guest, gentlemen," said Joe. "If we don't smoke here some of us will surely smoke in the hereafter, I always say."

The blond took a cigarette from a vest pocket and held a slender, gold-plated lady's lighter to it. At the first whiff Joe realized it was not tobacco but a joint of especially potent contents. The blond offered it to Jane, who took a drag on it and handed it to Joe, who sniffed its lighted end, drew deeply on it, and handed it to the fat biker. But the blond intercepted it.

"Stark's already fucked up on suds, don't deserve smoke this fine," he said. "Like I always say, mixin' brew and good weed is like *pissin' into the wind!*" He drew on the joint and handed it again to Jane, who declined and passed it on to Joe.

"This must some kind of Colombian," said Joe, then took a hit and handed it to the blond.

"No, indeed, this here's home-grown shit, my man, from down on the farm!" He put the roach into a small clip, held it to his right nostril, and inhaled. "Only thing is, I ain't tellin' you *where* that farm *is!* You *dig*, man, doncha?"

"I would not want to know," said Joe.

Joe and Jane stood on the porch and watched as the desk was loaded into the van, the two bikers who had carried it climbing in with it.

"*Good luck* on your *trip!*" the blond called back to them when he had secured the tailgate. "Wherever you're *trippin'* to!"

"Goodbye, old desk," said Joe, waving, and sighed. "One of these days I'm going to have enough bread to ship my favorite pieces of furniture. I did that once, you know, when I came out west that first time. Ended up selling most of the stuff a couple of months later for about half what it cost me to move it. Funny thing, we passed that Mayflower moving van going up a mountain a couple days before we pulled in to Pullman. It drove through the night and beat us there. Yessiree, *they drive by night!*" He put his arm around her waist. "Ever see that movie?"

"What movie, honey? What are you talking about?"

"*They Drive By Night* with Bogart and George Raft, 1940 or so, where they're a couple of truck drivers."

"I guess I missed that one," she said, turning to look at him. "Honey, I know you'll miss the old post office desk. I loved it, too, you know. Just about rubbed my hand raw sanding it. But I'll find something just as nice for you to write at in Colorado. Anyway, just think of all the legal briefs or whatever that will be written on it, to spring dudes in trouble over nothing." She slipped her arm around him. "You know, I'm really getting excited about Colorado. I've heard so many wonderful things about that state. Just think, you could learn to ski, Joe."

"You'll never catch me on those things! I'd pull another ligament or something. Shit, if I can screw my knee up on the god damned stairs of an East Baltimore row house, just think what I could do on two wood slats sliding down a mountain!"

"Well, maybe I'll take it up again on my own. I'm sure I could find some skiing companion or other. Just think, skiing all day, then snuggling up to the fire in a little cabin with a hot toddy." She looked up at Joe and smiled. "I mean, a female companion, of course, like Flossie, when she comes to visit."

"Yeah, no telling what you two would be up to in a little cabin next to the fire sloshed on cognac."

"Now, Joe, you know that's not my style."

"Jesus Christ on a crutch, how did we get to talking about snow on a mountain in this heat? It's not ten o'clock yet and it must be in the nineties already! Let's go take a shower and see if there's something else we can think of to amuse ourselves."

"Okay, but then we still have a lot of sorting out to do if we're going to get away from here by the end of the week."

And so, on Friday, the fifth of fifteen-hour-long days of sorting, cleaning house, and packing by Joe and Jane and always one or two others, a blue plastic tarp, a gift from Diverse Muph, was thrown up over the closely packed roof rack by Tea Squeir, chosen by Joe for the task by reason of his towering height, and tied down by Jim and Boz with fifty feet of nylon clothesline.

"Thet thar oughten to keep ev'rythin' dry as a desert rat's wit fer ya, Perfesser," said Boz as he stepped back from securing the final knot.

"Now that's one I never heard you give expression to, Mr. Boswell," Joe said, slapping his thigh. "'Dry as a desert rat's wit'! I'll have to file that away with 'sheet and two make eight'!"

"Heerd it years ago in the yards," Boz said. "Jus' never had no 'cassion to use it lately, Perfesser—leastwise not in yer presence."

Jane had disappeared into the house a few minutes before and now emerged with a tray piled high with the two-dozen thick sandwiches Joe had early that morning made from a beef roast he had the night before cooked in the back yard in a covered butane-fired grill that he borrowed from the light-sleeping "whatshisname" across the street.

Jane then sent him in to the kitchen for the cooler of beer and soft drinks, and the dozen or so friends sat on the porch and on the lawn eating, drinking, and talking about some of the times they had shared the past two years.

Early that morning, as he was carving the beef and slicing the bread, preparatory to displaying to her his short-order cook's skills in retaining in memory multiple sandwich orders as to bread type, toasted or not, lettuce, butter, pickle, mustard, and "hold the mayo" specifications, no matter how fast she threw the orders at him, Joe had coached Jane in the correct procedure for a "General George Catlett Marshall Exit." It was essential, he explained, to establish a signal to indicate that the ten minute countdown to departure had commenced so that they could then conclude all their goodbyes, which had to be handled very subtly, of course.

"After which, when I gets up and says, '*Lets go, dear, immediately!*' in an approximation of Neapolitan dialect, you gets your cute little *bee*-hind in gear and heads straight for the Greenbrier, *you heah me*?" The final three words were delivered in a mush-mouth Mississippi Delta accent and as he said them Joe turned to Jane with the carving knife held several inches aloft from the beef and screwed his face up into a hate-filled sneer.

"*Honestly*, honey, did you ever consider posing for a designer of Halloween masks?" she said. "I do think some of your faces would frighten a witch!"

Maintaining the terrifying demeanor he had assumed and rolling his eyes up so that nothing but white showed, his voice dropping to a Wolfman Jack bass, he inquired, "Who give a rat's skinny ass *whad ya thang, sistah?*"

"Okay, *enough*, Joseph Edwards Lewis, *enough!* You're *really* getting *scary!* Now, let's see if I have it straight. You'll give me the high sign by doing a sort of drum roll on your beer bottle with your fingers and that'll mean I have ten minutes to kind of, like, say goodbye to folks. Then you stand up and say, come on, let's go, dear, and—."

"In *Italian*, remember—kind of Neapolitan, actually."

"—and we scoot over to the bus and get in and roar

off, waving."

"Uh huh," said Joe, nodding as he returned his attention to the task at hand.

It was getting on to noon when Joe rose to his feet from his lotus position on the top step and—in so stentorian a manner that several jumped up from where they sat or lay on the grass—announced, "*'Diam', mi' car', 'diam' immediatament'!*" *

There was a tricky moment when Flossie ran over to the bus to again say goodbye to Jane and held on to her hand for several seconds, but Joe gunned the engine, giving a thumbs-up to those looking on, and threw a kiss to Flossie across Jane's torso.

Several were calling goodbyes and Tea shouted, "Take it easy, man! And *don't take no firkin' wooden-dollar bills!*" Then a sudden silence fell upon the scene. Those on their feet began moving slowly toward the bus and those on the ground got to their feet and followed. As if a signal had been given—a church bell ringing in the distance or a blues-drenched train whistle in the middle of the night or a ship's moaning foghorn—it seemed to Joe that all appeared to realize that it would have to be another time and another place when and where they would get together again.

Joe, the pained expression on his face clearly indicating that he was deeply moved, looked past Jane at their friends crowding around Flossie, who had stepped back only a foot or so from Jane's window. Then he glanced at Jane and saw that her eyes had misted over and her mouth was quivering. He slowly eased up on the

---

* Let's go, my dear, let's go, immediately!

clutch, crept across the grass to the driveway, pulled out into the street, and leaned on the horn as he took the Greenbrier up to twenty in first gear. No more than two or three minutes had elapsed since Joe had leapt to his feet and issued the command to Jane in his version of Neapolitan dialect.

"Take a good look, babe," he advised as he braked at Guadalupe before turning right. "May be the last time you'll ever lay eyes on Railroad Avenue."

"Yeah, honey, no telling whether we'll ever have any reason to come back to Austin." She turned and looked backwards over the suitcases and several boxes on the bed. "I guess we'll take a different route from Padre Island to Colorado."

"Yeah, we'll head west and go through New Mexico," said Joe absently as he glanced at the rearview mirror. Then he rounded the corner and headed south, a route he had chosen so that they could, for several blocks after turning left onto First Street, view the Colorado River before picking up Interstate 35, which would take them to San Antonio.

"We left in such a hurry I didn't have a chance to put those suitcases and other stuff under the bed," said Jane. She was scanning the space between the back of their seat and the rear door of the bus. "Jim sure did a good job with those cabinets and shelves. She turned and faced Joe, who was steering with his left hand and filling his pipe from the pouch in his lap with the other. "It'll make it a lot easier to find things. Not like when we came down from Ontario with everything in cardboard boxes. Remember that, honey?"

"How could I forget, babe?" Joe chuckled. "I'm just glad we decided at the last minute not to kidnap—I mean, dognap—little Billie. Might've looked in the mirror on the way to the border and seen one of your Royal Canadian Mounted Police on our tail!"

"Yes, and their horses are pretty fast, too!" she said and chuckled. "Billie was such a sweetie and those people next door treated her just awful. I could've killed them for the way they left her outside in her dog house—even on those sub-zero nights."

"We took her in most of those nights, remember?"

"Not after that horrible woman called up and screamed at you that you were 'a god damn communist professor!' Fortunately, it was almost spring by then."

"Yep, she shore war somethin' else. 'Minded me o' some o' them Eye-*talians* who tie dogs on foot-long chain to they's carts all the day long."

"Well, I guess Boz will be a permanent member of your cast of characters, honey, now that he's not around. And, come to think of it, Boz would have 'seed them Eye-*talians*' when he was over there in the war."

"Yes, Boz did see some action, he did indeed. Walked through most of Southern Italy, he told me, pack on his back and M1 at the ready. Asked him one time if he had killed any Germans and he just looked at me real strange and walked away."

"How did we get on the subject of little Billie?" Jane asked. "Anyway, it makes me think of my cats. I'm so happy your friends there at the college offered to look after them until we arrive."

It had been only a few days since they had made the decision to fit in a week on Padre Island before heading north. Most of the friends they had made in Austin had gone camping there at one time or another, and Jim had even once sent Joe a picture postcard from the island. Joe found the postcard among his papers and had propped it up against the inside of the windshield. It featured a panoramic view of the shoreline, and off in the distant dunes Joe thought he made out the profiles of several head of cattle. But he concluded that the blurred shapes must be shrubs, of which there were several in the foreground.

"We should be on Padre Island by late afternoon," he said. "Hey, put some music on the eight-track there, would you, sweetheart, maybe some Beatles or Stones or CC Revival or somebody—*anybody!*"

"Well, there's the river, honey!"

"Yeah, *so it is!* In a minute or two we'll be on the highway—and then, *Padre Island or bust!*"

"I hope not *bust!*"

"Sorry—unfortunate choice of language," he admitted. He had the filled pipe between his teeth and was holding a wooden match to its bowl.

"Oh, that smells so good," she cooed. "So much better than those awful cigars Oliver smokes—or those stinking French cigarettes of Jim's."

Joe reached into an upper pocket of his overalls and proffered to her a pack of Gauloises, grinning.

"Zigarette, mam'selle?"

A minute or so after they entered the interstate Jane yawned and turned to Joe. "I think I only had about four hours sleep last night. How would it be if I napped for an hour and then I could take over the wheel and spell you so's you could sleep a while. You must be pretty tired yourself."

"Good idea. It hasn't hit me yet but I suspect in a couple of hours I'll be ready for some shuteye. Go ahead. Sweet dreams."

Jane unhooked the belt-shoulder harness that Boz had installed a pair of, climbed over the seat onto the foam-rubber mattress, and pushed the suitcases and boxes aside. Within a few minutes her breathing pattern indicated that she was sound asleep. Joe turned the volume of the music back up.

The word "bust" came back to him and triggered memories of the arrests, trials, and, in several cases, incarcerations of friends and acquaintances the past two years in Austin. Bo Trott, the drummer at the juke joint—he could think of no more appropriate nomenclature for the venue in that cotton field that the Muphs had taken Jane and him to—had been given a speedy trial and sentenced to ten years for possession of a few joints he was caught with behind Armadillo Headquarters. Pepe Feliciano was appealing the sentence. Then there were those two graduate students whose "kitchen" in the chemistry lab had been discovered. *Good thing a couple of professors in the Law School went to bat for them pro bono and they got off with fines,* he reflected. *I have to laugh, though. Those suckers paid their fines with the proceeds from an acid sale handled for them by Big John Little, who took no cut from it—although I'm sure he and his associates sampled the product before dealing it.*

The circumstances of Hernando's arrest were so fresh in his mind that he spent only a few seconds recalling it, wondering in the process what his friend would have pulled in the way of a sentence had he been caught *in flagrante delicto.* He thought for a few seconds. *They probably have a scale of sentences. So many years for white middle class, so many for students, so many for a Mexicano, throw the fucking book at a black—something like that.*

Shit, I hope Pepe springs Bo. Talk about criminal, putting a guy away for that kind of time for having a couple of joints in his shirt pocket! And I know just which one of those dudes he was, too, the one that Messilina was dancing with. Now that was one crazy afternoon. He chuckled. *When Hernando came by that Sunday morning and asked us if we wanted to go out and hear an old blues harmonica player, Jane and I pictured some tavern or roadhouse on the highway. Turned out to be an old farmhouse in the middle of a cotton field.*

The Canned Heat tape had been over for a good half-hour when Joe reached for a match from the box on top of the dashboard, struck it with his thumb nail, and held it to his refilled pipe.

"*Oh, my!*" said Jane, yawning. "I was *out of it* there!"

"Yeah, out like a light from the moment you stretched out back there."

"How long did I sleep?"

"Two hours or so, I guess. I put about a hundred and thirty miles on this baby while you were snoring away back there."

"Joe, do I really snore all that much?"

"Well, actually, I wouldn't have heard you if you had been going on like a wild boar, sweetheart. I had the Heat on at top volume."

"The *heat?* Oh, the *Heat.* Maybe that's why I had such crazy dreams. We were at some concert and the Muphs were all mixed up. Boz was playing harmonica, Jim was on bass, and—. I think it was somebody famous singing, but I can't bring him into focus. And you were dancing with some girl—you know, doing your *Lewis Shuffle.* And everybody was 'stoned out of their friggin' minds,' as you like to say."

"That's interesting. I was pretty high, too, while you were dozing away."

"*Oh?* How'd you get *high?* You promised you weren't going to bring along anything on this trip!"

"No, no, it was a memory-induced high. I got to thinking of that afternoon at the juke joint, out there in that cotton field."

She was sitting up now and running her hands through her hair to untangle it. "Well, you certainly did get pretty high on the drive back to Austin. I remember I took over the wheel so you could get in the back with Melinda and the guys and Flossie got up front with me."

"Yeah, we sure did get wasted a few times in Austin." Joe struck a match with his thumbnail and held it to his pipe.

"I just hope you never try drinking a whole bottle of tequila again. Good thing Tea and Hardon were there to carry you up to bed."

"Yeah, I had just finished reading *Under the Volcano* and was trying to keep up with Geoffrey Firmin, the Consul—actually, he was already an *ex*-Consul by the time the novel commences. Unfortunately, I couldn't come across any mescal. So tequila had to do. Speaking of which, I'd like to pick up a bottle of that before Padre Island."

"Only if you promise to share it with me."

"Of course, babe," he assured her, smiling. "Listen, how about we try to find a place to eat some seafood. I could really dig some clams or shrimp or something, and I'm getting thirsty. A nice cold ale would go down very nicely with some crab and fish."

"How're we doing on gas?" She raised herself so that she could see the gauge. "Kind of low there, honey. We could ask at the gas station where we could get crabs."

"Get crabs," he muttered, chuckling.

"Anyway, we have to find a bathroom—*and soon!*"

"Hope not there!"

"What?"

"Crabs!"

"Yes, we'll look for crabs."

"First place I see we'll stop."

"What about your nap? I guess you'll just have to wait until after we get gas."

"I got a second wind so I'll just skip sleeping. We'll likely turn in early tonight anyway, maybe get up in the morning and see the sun rise. How about that?"

"Sounds good to me. Especially the part about turning in early. These last few days really took a toll." She opened a map. "Where are we?"

"About sixty miles past San Antonio, which leaves us about a hundred from Padre Island, maybe a little less than that. If we stop for dinner, which seems a good idea to me since we're both so bushed and won't want to have to set up the stove and stuff."

"When do you figure we'll get there?"

"Oh, we'll easily be on the island by six or seven. That'll give us time to cruise around a bit, find a good spot to spend the night."

"By your reckoning we must be nearing a little burg called Oakville," Jane said, looking up from the map in her lap and fixing her eyes on the road.

"Oh, we passed that a while back. You were asleep."

"*Joe! Look!* That sign says there's a gas station at the next turn-off."

He left the highway and they found themselves at a blinking red light. A sign stating "GAS" directed them to turn right. A few miles down the narrow country lane they came to a huge billboard announcing "Sam's Station Stop

For Gas, Beer, Bait, Lawn Ornaments, And The Finest Hand Rolled Seegars In Texas." Joe pulled the bus up to the lone pump.

"Jesus, look at that ancient rig, will you? That's right out of the thirties. Wonder if Sam will let me pump the gas. I use to handle one of those things when I was twelve, thirteen years old."

"He looks like he'd be quite willing to, dear." She pointed to a huge oak tree beside the two-story frame building that apparently filled the dual role of housing the business and providing a home for the proprietor. Beneath the spreading branches of the tree was a man reclining on a chaise longue.

They got out of the bus and Jane headed for an outhouse marked "HERN." Joe noted that about twenty feet behind it was another, "HISN." He approached the man. Smoke curled up from the cigar clenched in his teeth and a can of beer, a brand unfamiliar to Joe, rested on the ground among three empty cans of the same lying on their sides. A dog lay on the ground beside the chaise. Neither man nor beast seemed inclined to move. The man pointed to Joe and the dog leapt to his feet and trotted over to him, wagging her short tail. Joe knelt and, holding her by the collar, stroked her back and then examined the dangling tag.

"Well, are you Mister Bowl or is that your master's name? But you're a lady. Hmm." He looked into the dog's eyes. "Your mother was a Dalmatian and your father a basset hound, right? You never knew your parents? Poor gal, orphaned at an early age. Well, let's see if we can talk your friend over there into selling us some petrol."

"Good afternoon, sir," said Joe, standing at the foot of the chaise and hooking his thumbs into the suspenders of his blue-ticking overalls. "We'd like to get our tank filled up."

Joe studied the man as he carefully took the cigar from his mouth and tapped it on the arm of the chaise. When he had ascertained that the long ash it had collected had dropped into the coffee can on the ground he looked up at Joe and winked. *Another old-timer*, said Joe to himself, *seventy if he's a day. And look at that Irish face. He could be part horse, and judging by the red hue, I bet he imbibes something besides those beers he's been putting away this afternoon.*

"Wife allus lak to keep thangs tidy, so I tries to honor thet," the man said, pointing to the can with the cigar and then picking up the cane lying under the chaise and planting it and his work-booted feet firmly in the grass. Using the cane, he slowly pulled himself up to a bent-over standing position. For a moment Joe, looking down upon the man's hunched-over posture, envisioned him hobbling beside him Quasimodo-like. But, pressing down hard upon the cane's knob of a handle, he forced himself, evidently with no little pain, to an erectness that nearly matched Joe's height. They walked slowly toward the pump. The dog bounded ahead of them to greet Jane, who had just emerged from the outhouse.

"Sam Casey," the man said after they had walked a few steps, grasping Joe's hand. "Just call me Sam. Been called thet fer seventy year now, so guess it'll have to do, huh? What be yer moniker?"

"Joe Lewis," Joe responded, "and this is my wife Jane."

"Howdy, ma'am. Beggin' yer pardon fer the rustic facility thar. Wife and I talked 'bout puttin' in a downstairs toilet fer customers, never got 'round to doin' it."

"Oh, it was fine," said Jane, "nicer than some I grew up using."

"Thet so? War all you folks from?"

"I'm from Canada and Joe's from Washington, D.C."

"Never been to neither one."

"Say, think I could pump the gas, Sam? I used to hang out at a gas station when I was a kid and they let me put gas in cars, with a pump just like yours here."

"Be my guest, as the man on the television says. Your missus and me'll go in the office and get acquainted."

Joe could hear the beginning of their conversation as they started toward the house, a question, "Are you going to do any fishing? We got some nice lures . . . ."

After he filled the tank Joe checked the oil, battery water, and, with the gauge he kept in the glove compartment, the tire pressure all around. Then he tightened up the ropes securing the tarp covering the gear on the roof rack and paid a visit to "HISN."

Jane was standing at the counter when Joe entered the station and Sam Casey was leaning on his cane behind it. To one side of the antique cash register were some items she had collected for purchase, including six canisters of butane gas, a chap stick, and a package of waterproof wooden matches.

"Oh, good," Joe said, pointing to the last named item. "I'm almost out."

"Yes, and we forgot to get these, Joe. I'm so happy we got rid of that stinking stove. Now I won't reek of kerosene all the time when we're camping or on the road."

"Yeah, I am too, babe," said Joe. "I prefer you when you don't smell like an oil rigger. Speaking of oil, Sam, I need a quart of thirty weight—in fact, make that two quarts, please."

Sam punched up the amount of each item, added the gas and oil, took the twenty-dollar bill from Jane, cranked the register, made change, and put it in her hand. Then he turned and took a tiny earthenware pot from the window sill behind him and placed it on the counter. Reaching under the counter for it, he laid a cellophane-wrapped cigar beside it.

"This here is fer you, Miz Jane," he said, "and I hope you enjoy this, Joe."

"Why it's a *cactus* plant, honey, *look!*" she said, holding it up. "*Thank you*, Sam. It's *beautiful!*"

"Yer certainly mos' welcome, ma'am."

"Hey, thanks, Sam, I enjoy a good cigar, and this sure smells like a quality smoke. It says 'Sam's Seegars.' Did you make it?"

"Well, I don't roll 'em anymore meself, but it is local product growed by me naybor. But thet thar cactus I dug up meself out back, ma'am."

"Well, thank you so much, Sam. I'll take good care of it. Joe, you were going to ask about a seafood place."

"Oh, yeah. Sam, would there be a good seafood restaurant on the way to Corpus Christi? I really have a hankering for some fish and fried potatoes, maybe some shrimp, too."

"And *crabs*, honey."

"Oh, and a place where we can get crabs too," he said, grinning.

"Oh, indeed there be a fine eatin' place about ten mile down this road. It's called Gully's and they allus has fresh fish right outa the Gulf. I knowed the Gully family fer more'n sixty yahr now. Jake Gully—he been gone now fer some time—we was in grammar school togethern. This here Gully's is ran by his grandson, I fergit what they calls 'im.''

While telling them about the restaurant Sam had hobbled out from behind the counter and was now standing with his back to it and leaning on it with his elbows.

"And it's right on this road?"

"Yeah, Joe, y' can't miss it, ain't too fer, and you kin get back on the highway a little ways past it. I knows thet 'cause I allus stops for a feed there when I goes in to the city, then I takes the big road the rest o' the way.''

"You like to go to Corpus Christi, huh?"

"Yep, me and the little lady allus lak to go down the Gulf and fish once or twice a month, and I been tryn' to keep thet up since she passed, but this old leg doan 'llow me to get 'round thet much no more, so I give up fishin'. But I still gets in the Caddy and goes down the Gulf once a month, just fer the smell o' the sea, ya know." At the reference to the car Sam had nodded backwards over the counter.

"Where do you keep your Caddy, Sam?"

"In the shed out back o' the house, Joe."

"What year is it?"

"Oh, we boughten it soon after the wahr, late forty-seven, Joe, an' she be a forty-eight, one o' the first offen the 'sembly line they done tol' us. Had to be on the waitin' list fer a yar afore we got it."

"Oh, I'd sure love to see it, Sam!"

"Wa-a-all, Joe, I'd love to show it to you and your missus. I'se mighty proud o' me Caddy. We kin go out thet back door there."

"What sort of problem do you have with your leg, Sam?" Jane asked as they walked across the back yard to

144

the shed, concern in her voice.

"Oh, thet's a ol' problem, ma'am," Sam replied, his eyes lighting up with evident enthusiasm. "I took some shrapnel in the Argun. Yep, fiftieth anniversary of thet campaign comin' up. They's plannin' a parade and such up San 'tonio come November."

"Will you be participating in the celebration, Sam?"

"Yes'm, they done asken me to ride in a open-air automobile with some other vet'rans, right up the head o' the line." He smiled. "Now ain't thet somethin', after all them yahrs!" He stopped and turned to look at both of them. "You know somethin'? Thet six month over there in France and Germany wahr the biggest adventure o' me life." He looked down at the ground. "Course thet thar foolish thang goin' on over thar in Veetnam, I doan rightly know what to thank o' thet. Seem lak we ought to let them slants fight thar own wahrs, not send our young'ns o'er thar t' die in some swamp 'r other."

"We feel the same way, Sam!" said Jane, reaching out to take Joe's hand.

Joe offered to help with the door of the shed but Sam waved him aside and, leaning on his cane, jerked the handle and stepped back. The door swung open slowly, revealing the twenty-year-old two-door Cadillac. It had been backed into the narrow enclosure and the aisle on either side barely provided space enough for the car's doors to be opened for boarding.

"*Jeez, what* a *beauty!*" Joe exclaimed, looking down at the distorted reflection of his head and torso in the light-blue hood.

"Sam, it looks brand new!"

"Wal, I keeps 'er polished, ma'am, thet's fer sure. An' let me tell ya, Joe, it'll do a hunert mile 'n hour and still no louder'n a hummin' burd."

"*I'll bet!*" said Joe, opening the driver's side door and peering into the car.

"'Cours', unerstan' now, it be a few yar since I taken 'er up to *thet!*"

"I'll bet you could get ten thousand for this baby, Sam!"

"Thas what all they tells me, Joe. I've left 'er in m' will fer m' granddaughter t' go t' college. She's eight yahr ol' now and she'll be the fust in the fambly t' do thet! Wants t' be a *doctor!*"

On the way to Gully's Joe and Jane talked about Sam Casey, his bitch Mister Bowl, HISN and HERN, the cigar and the cactus plant, his Caddy Eliza, his war wounds, and the very last item he had expatiated upon, the ancient oak tree under which they had first laid eyes upon him.

"I'm certainly glad you thought of asking about how Mister Bowl got her name, honey," said Jane. "That's *one* mystery cleared up."

"Oh, yeah, '*Missed* her *bowl,* Grandaddy!'" said Joe, affecting the soprano pitch of a four-year old girl. "But, you know, that oak tree is what fascinates me—."

"Oh, wasn't that just *magisterial!* I've never seen anything like it!"

"Yeah, it was that all right, must cover half an acre at least. But the part that fascinates me is that there's history in that tree. All that stuff about how his great-grandfather used the tree for target practice, and the Alamo, and all that. All this year we've been in Texas and that's the first time we met anyone like that—I mean, with that kind of family history and all."

"But, honey, we lived in a university community and

they're always like that. Almost everybody we know here is from somewhere else. Don't you remember how it was at Central Ontario? Same thing—only the faculty was from all over the *world*, not just the States, like here."

"How true. I'm not sure we ever met anyone who was even born here, babe." He took the cigar from the pocket in the bib of his overalls and ran it under his nostrils. "Ummmm, sure look forward to this after dinner tonight. Or maybe I'll fire it up after some Gulf fish here in a bit."

"That's likely to *be* our dinner, honey—except maybe for a snack later, some cheese and crackers with beer." She looked at him. "Going back to what you were just saying, about not knowing anyone who was born here in Texas, aren't you forgetting the folks we met that afternoon in the juke joint?"

"*Hey, right!*" he quickly agreed. "Good point, too. They would be the kind who grew up here, who really own the land—in a symbolic way, that is, 'cause they sure as shittin' don't own much at all 'ceptin' mayhaps they's shirts offen they's backs." He had put the cellophane-wrapped cigar between his teeth and slipped into a Texas drawl for the final clause, squinting his eyes and hunching over the steering wheel.

She looked over at him. "You really missed your calling, darling. You should have gone into acting—comedy or something, although I guess you do evil villains pretty well, too."

"I *am* in acting, my sweet," Joe replied. "Most teachers, like most trial lawyers, are actors, some of them hardly more than hams, but still, acting out some part or other. Hey, I think I spots our fish house up ahead, our spotted fish house, a spot of feesh, sir? And, by the way,

147

what's that rolling down the road—a head?" He chuckled as he geared down and made a left turn into the restaurant's parking lot, stopping just inside the pillared gateway.

"Look at the cars, Joe!"

"Yeah, must be a high-priced spread they serve in there," he said, his eyes executing a hundred-and-eighty degree survey of the macadam lot. "Let's see—yeah, there's a space up there next to that pink Caddy. But then, some of these farmer and blue-collar types will go out and buy a five-thousand dollar set of wheels so's they can pretend to be Mr. Moneybags, my dear—then set up housekeeping in a tar-paper shack. Don't they do thet up thar in the Nawth, hon?" For the question he had gone into a syruppy deep-South soprano. He leaned forward and touched his forehead to the top of the steering wheel. "What say I use that voice inside there, babe, and—." His laughter got the best of him and he could not finish.

"*Oh, sure*, honey, that'll *really help!* As if we don't look weird enough, you're going to help matters coming on like Harpo Marx or somebody. Come on, let's go, I'm *literally starving!*" Opening her door, she turned and looked at him. "Now, promise to behave, Joe—*please!*"

"Harpo never talked."

"You know what I mean!"

They entered the restaurant and paused to get their bearings. At first the paneling appeared to Joe to be of some naturally dark wood and until his eyes adjusted to the semi-dark his impression of Gully's interior was of a Victorian living room and he was reminded of the Baltimore row house his grandparents had occupied for almost a half-century. But in less than a minute the blurred lines took on sharpness and he realized that the walls were of stained plywood. There were a half-dozen empty booths along each wall and a row of tables filled a center aisle that led to a door marked Banquet Room.

"This place is really tacky, honey. I do hope the food has better taste than the decor."

"Indeed, the very definition of tacky, my dear. Look at those little plastic lamps along the wall." He raised his arm and pointed to the booths opposite them. "And the mirrors, for chrissakes! Now, *who* the *hell* wants to stare at himself while he's eating? Oh, here we go—Gravel Gertie herself approacheth."

"Who?" Jane asked under her breath.

A busty, blond-bewigged woman in pants and tight sweater teetered toward them on spike heels. It became clear to Joe that she was giving them the once-over as she made her way uncertainly between the tables, every two or three of which she would touch lightly with the tips of her pink-painted nails.

"Five will get you ten that it's her Caddy we're parked next to," he muttered.

"Good evenin', what can I do for y'all, are y'all lost or somethin'?" the woman asked in a drawl. She came to a halt about six feet short of them.

"No, indeed, madam, we're on our way to Padre Island and thought it would be appropriate to sample some of the local fare. Sam Casey, gas station proprietor about ten miles up the pike, recommended your establishment for having the best seafood hereabouts. So we thought we'd stop here and have dinner."

"Well, I'm sorry, sir, but we ain't open to the gen'ral public today. They's a private party in the Banquet Room there and all our gals is a'waitin' on the guests."

"Do you mean to tell me that you can't spare a single

waitress to serve us some fish and shrimp?"

"No, sir, I jest caint spare a single girl nohow. Now y'all jest hev to be on your way effin you please." She began to move slowly toward them. "An' you know somethin'?"

"What say?" he said, grinning in anticipation.

"You should oughta git yerself a haircut—and a *shave!*"

"Well, thank you, ma'am, that's real nice of you to remind me, and in return I'd like to pass on a bit of advice to you."

"Yeah, and what's that, buddy?" The question was delivered with a hiss and a change came over her demeanor that he later described as "from a classic shit-eating smile to a hard-bitten sneer."

"Get rid of that silly rug on your bean!"

Jane had quickly stepped behind him when the conversation took this unpleasant turn. Upon his riposte, the woman lurched forward, tripping and falling at his feet. As she raised herself—somewhat as though she were doing a push-up—to her knees, Joe reached down to help her get to her feet, but she hit his hand away and looked up at him.

"You done that, you cause me to fall, you *fag sonovabich!* Now *get the fugg outa here* 'fore I call my brother'n-law the *sheriff!*"

Jane hooked her fingers over the top of his overalls from behind and gently pulled him backwards on the red carpet that led to the door.

They had been on their way for a couple of minutes, all the while giving expression to their anger over the treatment they had been accorded and vowing to stop at Sam's on the return trip to give him a full report of the incident, when Jane, looking up from the map she had unfolded, remarked, "Joe, doesn't this look awfully familiar to you?"

"*What?*" He glanced to one side, then to the other. "*Oh, shit!* We're going back over the same ground! I forgot I made a left into Gully's." He slowed and pulled over onto the shoulder. "Now I'll probably get a ticket from her brother-in-law for making a u-turn. Oh, well, here goes nothing."

"Honey, it seems we can take thirty-seven right on into Corpus Christi," she began after he had corrected his mistake, her eyes on the map in her lap, "and then turn right at two-eighty-six for a few blocks and left on three-fifty-eight. That'll take us right onto the bridge to Padre Island."

"Actually, it's a causeway, babe. I read somewhere about how they built it."

"I'm still *furious* over that scene in that *awful place!*" She shuddered as she tucked the map under some others on the dashboard ledge. "People can be so mean spirited sometimes."

"Grist for the mill, my dear, greest fer de mill, I allus says." He chuckled before he went on. "Actually, that scene was priceless, *just priceless!* Couldn't have planned it better if I'd tried. *Her falling down like that!* At that moment, I expected the door of that Banquet Room to fly open and a hoard of rednecks in double-breasted suits to come rushing out shouting obscenities at us. I would *really have enjoyed that!*"

"Well, you would have enjoyed it by your lonesome, honey! I was frightened enough by that awful woman. I really thought the next thing would be she would come after me."

"I do think we're approaching the big city, sweetheart. Keep an eye out for an eatery." He leaned forward to look at his pocket watch, which was resting on a neatly folded engine cloth on the dashboard. "Jesus, no wonder I'm famished—*it's almost five!*"

"Well, we haven't exactly been pushing it, Joe. All that time we spent talking to Sam Casey, and—. Hey, you're right, we're coming into Corpus Christi! See the sign?"

"Okay now, keep your eyes peeled for a likely seafood house. There have to be some soon."

A few blocks before the access ramp to the Crosstown Freeway, Jane spotted the Fish Tank, a big warehouse-like building on the side of which were painted caricatures of sea creatures fleeing nets and hooks and even an octopus, its tentacles tangled in a grappling iron. The scene depicted was underwater and only the bottom of the boat—whence these threats emanated—was visible at the very top of this colorful comic-book-like illustration.

"I like the lobster behind bars in the trap there, don't you?"

"Yeah, babe, he bears a striking resemblance to Edward G. Robinson."

Inside, it became clear that the art on the outer wall of the building was only the first frame of a comic strip that circled the periphery of the restaurant. The scenes were of varied modes of the capture and incarceration of the creatures, all of whom wore the exaggerated features of Hollywood personalities and other public figures, including a moll-faced Bette Davis shrimp and a catfish whose demoniacal visage immediately brought to mind the Republican candidate for president in the upcoming election.

"That must be Tricky Dick there, but who's that, Joe, the one beside him with the bloodshot eyes. He looks like he hasn't shaved for a couple of days."

"Fish don't shave, my dear." He directed his eyes to where she pointed. "Oh, yeah, Joe McCarthy."

"That doesn't look like him. I saw him on the tube just the other night giving a speech."

"Joe McCarthy, not Gene."

"I don't know who that is."

"I'll tell you about him some time." He scanned the spacious high-ceilinged room. "A veritable barn, what? I guess we just grab a table anywhere. Looks kinda informal, wouldn't you say?"

"I feel like I'm in the nineteenth century. Just look at those kerosene lamps. My grandad still used some like that when I was a kid."

"Right. I like the keg tables, too." He took her hand and proceeded to one of them across the room near the bar. "Look," he said, pointing to the far end of the bar.

"Oh, there's someone there. I can just see the top of a head."

"I'm going to mosey over there and see what's what."

A minute later he returned, following a girl in her late-teens. Her dark brown hair fell loosely nearly to her waist and she wore denim overalls that had so many patches the effect was one of a multi-colored quilt. She wore no upper garment and the bib of the overalls fell forward as she leaned over the table to empty the ashtray onto the sawdust-covered floor.

"Howdy, sister, your ol' man here says y'all is hankerin' fer some frash fish. Well, Man Mountain just got back with some flounder and mackerel. I'll go fetch 'im so's ya kin tell 'im hows ya wants it cooked up." As she left she called back over her shoulder, "An' I'll be back in a secon' with yer pitcher, mate!"

"I wonder if I can get her to empty the ashtray again," he said, smiling.

"Oh, I'm sure she'll provide you more opportunities to check her anatomy out, dear. She's *not exactly bashful!*" She put her hand on his on the table. "You do have an eye for young babes, don't you? And she certainly is adorable. But she can't be more than eighteen, Joe."

"San Quentin quail, maybe. Although down here in poontang land, I don't know. I meant to ask Pepe what the age of consent is in Tex-ass."

"Oh, sure, Joe, and what kind of an impression would that have made?" She laughed. "Professor in his forties worried about statutory rape!"

"Purely out of academic interest, my dear."

"Uh huh, sure."

The girl returned with a large tinted green plastic pitcher of foaming beer in one hand and in the other two glass mugs that were white with frost.

"Ah-a-ah! Just what I need, Susie," he said, taking the pitcher from her as she placed the mugs on the keg.

"Mountain will be out in a secon', folks," she informed them before returning to her seat behind the bar.

"Susie, huh?" She sipped from her mug. "Oh, this hits the spot, honey! It's just what I need!"

"Yeah, this is some nice cold suds, ain't it?" He had drained half his mug and now filled it again to the top, raising it quickly to lick the overflowing foam. "Yeah, Susie—but not much like my Cambridge Susie."

"My guess is your 'Cambridge Susie' is somebody else's Susie by now—and probably has been for quite some time now. *Oh, Joe, look!*"

He spun around on his keg-chair to see what had startled her. Coming from the far end of the bar was a dark-bearded man of immense proportions. He was easily two or three inches over six feet and he moved in a sort of rolling motion that produced the effect of one of those huge beach balls coming to rest as it approached you on the sand. He was in khaki cut-offs and tennis shoes through the fronts of which his bare toes protruded. A spanking clean white apron fell from his chest to his knees and also served as his lone upper garment. A large fish dangled on a line from each hand, their tails nearly scraping the floor.

"Jesus, a Bluebeard if there ever was one!" Joe muttered.

"*Hear tell from Suze you folks wants a seafood dinner!*" the man called in a deep, booming voice from halfway across the room.

Joe waited until the man was at their side before replying. "That's right. And I take it you're Mr. Mountain?"

"Man Mountain Deene at your service, folks. Just call me Mountain. How'd y'all like these? Lak I should broil these beauties fer y'all?" He swung the two fish around so that they rested on his overhanging belly. "They's *right outa the Gulf!*"

"Oh, they're so fresh looking, honey! Let's have them!"

"Okay, we'll go for that. Can you fix us up with some shrimp as a sort of antipasto? We're really famished after a long drive. And some fried spuds, too. I could eat a bucket full."

"You got it, mate! I'll send Q right out with the

shrimp. I got some taters on the stove. And a house salad comes with the entrée."

"By the way, I'm Joe Lewis and this is my ol' lady Jane."

"Pleasure, folks."

As Deene lumbered across the room, the fish swung back and forth a little and the floor creaked.

"Yes, just call me Lil' Ol' Lady Jane," she said, mild annoyance in her tone.

"Sorry, babe, but it seemed to fit the context better—if you catch my drift." He leaned across the table and kissed her on the mouth. "Jeez, that Mountain must weigh in at about three-hundred!"

The girl brought dishes, utensils, napkins, and condiments to the table and a minute later returned with a platter of shrimp.

"So you're Susie Q," said Joe, smiling. "That's a nice nickname."

"Wal-l-l, it's only part nickname, sir," she said, a slight giggle in her delivery. "Mah man there made it up from mah real name Cosuisky accounta it was a drag gettin' it out and he says ma Christian name doan fit me nohow—it's Irene."

"Why, Irene is a *beautiful name!*" Jane objected.

"Wal-l-l, 'roun' here ahze stuck with Susie Q," she said, leaning across the table and refilling Joe's mug. "You gonna want 'nother o' these?"

"Here, would you just give me a little head there, please," he said, pointing to the mug.

"Oh, sure," she said, leaning forward and topping it off with foam. "So does y'all wan' anotha pitcha?"

"Maybe we'll just do a couple of bottles with the meal. Do you have any ale?"

"*You* are *so awful!*" said Jane once the girl had departed. She laughed and shook her head. "*Give you a little head!*"

"Polish, huh. I knew there was a reason why she appealed to me. My very first—although totally unrequited—serious, very serious, love was a girl of Polish ancestry, one Wanda Pulaski, when I was fourteen."

"Well then, honey, you've probably seen more of Irene's anatomy than you did of your adolescent infatuation. Was she right off the farm too? *Oh, this shrimp is great!*"

"*Isn't it!* No, she was an army brat and lived on—or right next to, I was never quite sure of that—Ft. Meade. I remember how the guys used to tease me about how she was bowlegged from—I can still hear Mutt Wolfe whispering it in my ear when we were stealing cokes from Ol' Man Harrison's ice house—'ridin' those soldiers over Ft. Meade.' *Shit*, she was *only fourteen!*"

"Oh, honey, you're *too much!* You sound like you're *still in love with her!*"

"That Polack bitch just about drove me out of my friggin' mind, I'm telling you! I wanted her *bad!*"

"Joe, cut it out! You're getting me all horny!"

"Yeah, it's been a while, hasn't it, babe?" he said, reaching under the table and patting her thigh.

"Oh, sure—like about eighteen hours!"

"We'll sack in early, babe," he said absently, turning from one side to the other as he took in more of the details of the room. "It'll be the first time in the Greenbrier since that month in the driveway two years ago. Remember that?"

"*How could I forget?*" She speared a shrimp with a toothpick, dipped it in the Hot Sauce, raised it to her mouth, and paused. "You know, I think I liked that time better than any other in Austin." With the shrimp now in her mouth she closed her eyes, chewed, and swallowed. "*Um-m-m-m!* Just *love* these *shrimp!*"

"They are good!"

"Not that the rest of our two years there didn't have its moments, but there was something real special about just finding new friends without even trying. It was all so natural—know what I mean?"

"Yeah, know what you mean, babe, sure do." His head was tilted back. "Look at all the beer cans and stuff up there. Say, they must have music here. I just noticed that piano over against the wall and those speakers behind the bench there. Must get pretty wild in here if people start throwing shit up there into those fish nets."

"There's a bamboo rod up there, too," she added, "or part of one."

"Yeah, they're all around the room, see, in those kegs." He leaned forward. "And I just noticed the taxidermy and photo gallery behind the bar. This place must be a hang-out for fisherman types."

"How about fisher-*women* types, dear, like Sam's 'missus,' how about them?"

The jibe went unanswered, for a rumbling sound distracted both of them. It was Man Mountain Deene approaching from the far end of the bar. A large tray was balanced on the fingertips of his left hand above his shoulder. In his right hand, its edge resting on his "tire," was a smaller one. Susie Q was abreast of him to his right.

"What a pair they make!" Jane whispered behind cupped hand.

"Here you be, my friends!" the deep voice of Man Mountain announced from halfway across the room.

"Croaker and flounder broiled to perfection, if I does say so meself." He lowered the larger tray onto the keg next to them. "And here's your taters and salads," he added, placing two bowls heaped with lettuce and cut vegetables and a napkin-lined basket of potatoes on their keg. Susie put down bottles of oil and vinegar and two ales, opened the latter with a wooden-handled tool she slipped out of a side pocket of her overalls, and made room in the table's center, which Mountain filled with a platter occupied by the flounder.

"Makes my mouth water just to look at them!" said Joe, reaching for the serving tools.

"Ummm!" Jane enthused. "*Smells scrumptious!*"

"*Buon appetito!*" said Mountain, bowing to them.

"*Grazie mille!*" said Joe, smiling up at him.

"*Prego!*"

It was dusk when they pulled away from the curb. Mountain Man had seen them to the door and remained standing there, giving them the peace sign with right hand raised shoulder-high. Jane caught a glimpse of Susie Q waving to them from a window.

Joe patted his overall pocket as he shifted into second gear. "Sure glad to have these. That was very generous of Man Mountain."

"Well, I guess it's all right. But you better be ready to toss them if we run into the law."

"Don't worry," he assured her. "And when we get set up I'll bury them in the sand. You know, what you said before about meeting up with people and suddenly realizing we have new friends. That knack seems to still be with us. I mean, I'm kind of sad that we'll only see Man Mountain and Susie Q when we pass through

Corpus Christi again a week or so from now—then maybe never again."

"Yes, we certainly do leave a lot of friends behind, honey. Seems to be a pattern with us. Not just Texas but back home—I mean, back in *my* home."

"Yeah, I got to like a lot of those folks there. In fact, I never really had that experience of being a part of both 'town' and 'gown' before. And I never was in such a cosmopolitan mix either. Jeez, you never knew when you took a coffee break up in the faculty lounge—or in the cafeteria with students, for that matter—whether you'd be sitting next to somebody in a turban or a sari or a beret or someone striking up a conversation in a brogue or a thick Eastern Europe accent or broken Japanese-English. I had some problems understanding some of my colleagues, I'll say that. Then down in the town I'd find myself talking politics or the war or something with some guy running for a local office who'd come over from Scotland or maybe New Zealand a few years before. Maybe hadn't been there much longer than I had."

"That's Canada for you! Kind of like your country was a hundred or so years ago." She had the map folded to reveal only Corpus Christi and its environs spread across her lap and was examining it with a pen flashlight. "Joe, remember, we just stay on 358 until that bridge—."

"Causeway, my dear."

"Okay, causeway. And then it changes to 22 and goes right onto Padre Island. After that, I don't know what all we do."

"Find a parkin' space, crack a couple o' them thar brews thet big feller laid on us'n, get stoned, and sheck up, *tha's what, hon!*" He had gone into his New England cracker-barrel-philosopher mode for this, his voice taking on a high-pitched Pa Kettle-like quaver.

"You sound like you're about ninety years old, honey. Think you can still get it up?"

"Wa-a-a-l-ll, miss, ah may not be able to cut the mustard, but I can *still lick the jar!*" He finished with a cackle and turned to her, leering with his lips pulled tight as though toothless.

In a few minutes they were crossing Laguna Madre on the causeway.

"Jesus Christ smell that sea air!"

"It's like the Fish Tank, honey, only fresher. Did you notice that?"

"Yeah, those nets, I guess. So what do we do after we leave this pond behind us, babe?"

"Oh, let's see," she said, looking down at the map. "Well, we bear right for the Padre Island National Seashore, then there's a state park to the left. Oh, I just noticed, we'll actually be on Mustang Island first, and then we have to cross a bridge, and *then* we'll be on Padre Island. It's a little confusing. Just bear right. There's a Park Headquarters pretty soon after we cross the bridge to actual Padre Island. Maybe we can get some information and maps and stuff there."

"In the morning, babe, it'll be closed now."

They followed the narrow road until they came to a sign directing them to the beach. Neither had spoken for several minutes, their attention being given to seeking out a suitable place to stop. It was a clear night with full moon and they had seen no cars or other indication of human presence since passing the small cluster of stores and gas station shortly after crossing the causeway. He put the gear shift in neutral and coasted down onto the beach. Tire tracks in the sand were visible in the beams of the headlights.

"I was beginning to think we were in a kind of no man's land," he said softly.

"It's so quiet, honey," she whispered. "Eerie."

He pointed the bus toward the Gulf and cut the engine.

"This sand is really packed tight," he said. "Good thing it is or we'd be dug in to the axels."

"It says in the triple-A book that driving on the beach is allowed."

"Well, I guess that's what we'll be doing. Wonder if the tide comes up this far."

"If you're thinking we'll just stay here for the night, *forget it!*"

"No, no, you're quite right, my dear, that would be a little chancy. Tide might come in and get the engine wet. Be hell to pay, I shit you not! We'll go back up on the road, find some higher ground. Say, can you reach that bottle of hooch that Oliver gave us?"

"That's not *hooch*, Joe, that's *quality cognac!*" On her knees and reaching down into a box on the bed behind her, she found the Courvoisier and handed it to Joe.

"*Brava, signora, grazie mille.*" He had his pocket knife ready and in an instant was ready to pour into the two plastic cups Jane was holding. But first he took a swig from the bottle.

"Boy, that's good stuff! Puts hair on your chest!"

"Well, I really don't think I need any of that. It's hard enough keeping my legs shaved. And you certainly have enough as it is."

"Steve Ford called me Hairy Truman back in my mail carrying days." He poured a couple of ounces of the cognac into each of the plastic cups Jane was holding out to him and took one.

"Oliver would be offended to see you treating his gift in such a shameful manner," she said, giggling.

"Bull *shit* he would! He'd be *swilling it right along with us* were he here. Bottoms up, here's mud in yer friggin' eye!"

She sipped from her cup. "Oh, this is so smooth!"

"Let's get out and walk down to the water."

"Give me a couple of minutes to finish this, honey. You know I'm not a gulper like you."

"Right," he said, relaxing back onto the seat back and fixing his eyes on the sea. "There's something about the sea that has always frightened me. Even though I grew up by it and used to do a lot of sailing. Especially at night."

"You used to go sailing a lot at night?"

"No, I meant it *frightens* me at night. Like I can't imagine anything more terrifying than being out in a lifeboat on the ocean at night and having a huge ship come by." He replenished his cup and took another swallow. "God, it gives me a chill just to think about it! I don't need a shrink to tell me that my fears vis-à-vis the sea derive from some of my late father's idiocies on weekends at the shore when he would pile Sissie and me into that eighteen-foot Maine Coaster and point it up-river with a storm looming on the horizon. One time when I was about eight a squall caught us out in the middle of the Magothy and I was catatonic with terror. *Shit!*"

"Why didn't your mother stop him from such craziness?"

"Oh, she wouldn't set foot in that boat! And she couldn't do anything with my ol' man when he was in the bag! He was very impulsive and if she tried to stop him from doing something his mind was set on, shit, he'd cuss a blue streak and *do it anyway!*" Joe laughed. "*Crazy sonovabich!*"

"You didn't finish the story. What happened in the storm?"

"Oh, yeah. Well, of course we had to lower the sails and furl them and proceed by means of outboard motor. The rain was so heavy we could barely see our way into the harbor. When we tied up to our mooring and the tender was on its way out to fetch us—it had stopped raining by then and the wind had died down—*I suddenly burst into tears!*"

"Why ever?" she said, chuckling.

"The tension was over, of course, and I felt such relief. I guess I was crying as much from joy as from the fright of the whole thing. Cap'n Fields ran the harbor—now there was a legendary beer drinker if ever there was one and we called him 'W. C.' 'cause he made such frequent visits to the head—and he told us that the winds had topped off at seventy-five knots at the height of the storm. That would have been when we were out there in the middle of that river."

"I don't *wonder* you were *traumatized!*"

"Another time my ol' man and a drinking buddy of his named Red Erikson decided to sail out around the Baltimore Lighthouse, about five miles out in the Bay, and took Sissie and me along. I'll never forget the *size* of that structure, and the *huge rocks* all around it, *as long as I live!* It was like a *bloody skyscraper,* out there in the middle of the drink. Motherfucker *scared* the *livin' shit* outa my sister and me!"

Neither spoke for a minute as they stared at the surf in the moonlight. Then Joe raised his cup in a toasting gesture. "Well, *here's* to the *bloody sea!*" he said, and finished his cognac. "Let's go down to the Gulf. I plan to take a dip in it at dawn's early light."

"Okay, but let's go barefoot so we can feel the sand. It looks so clean."

Hand-in-hand they ran down to the water's edge. A sudden swell caught them by surprise and they quickly retreated, nearly stumbling. As they held onto each other the water rose to Joe's knees and soaked Jane nearly to her crotch. Laughing, they ran hop-scotch back onto the beach.

"Dat ol' debbil sea lak to got us dat time!" he cried out over the crashing surf, pulling her to him and kissing her on the mouth.

Sitting in the Greenbrier again over cups of the cognac, they decided to explore the terrain, hoping to find a less threatening place to spend the night. He confessed that he had a deep, albeit irrational, fear that, should they remain where they were, they would awake in the middle of the night to find the bus awash in several feet of pounding surf. His first thought was that they should park further back in the dunes, but she cautioned him, pointing out the possibility of digging in.

"You're right, the last thing I need is to have to go find a tow-truck somewhere this time of night. Let's go back on the road and see if we can find a likely spot."

A sign indicated a picnic area. Following the arrow, they soon found themselves on a strip of concrete about two-hundred feet long with wooden tables and garbage cans along one side. Dunes formed a backdrop to this island in the sand. At the far end of the strip they could barely make out the shape of a walk-in camper, a dim light visible through the curtains of one of its windows.

He cut the engine and turned to her.

"This is more like it. I just couldn't hack it out there on the beach. Too lonely!"

"Yes, honey, I know what you mean. Just seeing these tables and that camper up there and knowing we're on cement gives me the feeling of touching civilization again."

"The sea does strange things to you. Hits you deep. Makes you see the impermanence of things. Say, why don't we hit the sack?"

"I want to visit that little house up there first."

"Oh, right, come to think of it, I do, too. I'll go with you." He took a flashlight from the glove compartment and flicked it on.

Sitting on the edge of the foam-rubber mattress, his legs hanging down in the space between it and the side door, he rolled a cigarette and lighted it with a wooden match. He poured cognac into a cup and handed it to her. She took a sip, handed it back to him, and rolled onto her side, her buttocks resting against his thighs. He sipped the cognac and smoked.

"I can hear the sea, honey, but it's so dark out there I can't see anything."

"Yeah, it's nice, babe, sort of a slow, rolling rhythm to it, kind of like a press roll and then a crash cymbal, then the same thing a split second later. I could really get into that." He stuck his hand out the door and flipped the butt fifteen or twenty feet out onto the dune. "Not going to find much to set on fire out there." He put the cup to his lips and tilted it. "Jeez, I do think I'm a little bombed, babe!"

He lay on his side and pulled her to him so that her

rear was pressing his sex, his hands cupping her bare breasts.

"How's about a little spooning, babe? You in the mood?"

Although both were bone weary their desire for each other surged as if with morning energy and they made love violently, lying on their sides, Joe entering her from behind, she emitting little whimpering sounds as his thrust accelerated to its climax. The love-making gave them a second wind and Joe suggested they smoke one of the joints Mountain had given them.

"Do you think it was in the cards that we find the Fish Tank, honey? I mean, what could have been more perfect after that awful place on the road—what was it called?"

"Oh, yeah, what was the name of that place? Funny, I can't remember." He drew on the joint, causing it to glow brightly in the dark.

"Don't set us on fire."

"I don't know. I've never really figured out how all that works, whether what happens was supposed to happen or what. I mean, things *do* happen only *one way*, you have to admit *that*, don't you." He chuckled. "Well, isn't *this* some kind of *brilliant shit* I'm talking?"

"It just seems they were our kind of folks, honey, Man Mountain and Susie Q, as though to make up for that awful woman at Gully's."

"Oh, Gully's, yeah."

"Yes, Gully's, that was the name." She shuddered and then laughed. "Joe, you were *really something!* You really should be a comedian. That was such a perfect retort to that woman's snide remark about your hair—and your beautiful beard." She touched his beard and giggled. "Your pussy tickler."

"I think you're right about Mountain and Susie. They definitely were our kind of folks. I really dug them both."

"Especially Susie, huh?" she said, turning on her side and pulling close to him, her hand on his thigh. "You know, not only did she have no bra on, honey, Susie Q did not wear *any underclothes at all!*"

He laughed. "*How* in *hell* would you know *that,* for chrissakes?"

"When I went to the bathroom the door was partly open and she was sitting there reading a comic book and her overalls were down around her ankles and she didn't have another stitch on. *What* do you *think* about *that?*" She reached for his crotch. "*Oh, Joe,* you're such a *dirty old man!*"

He pulled her on top of him, closed his eyes, and imagined that it was Susie Q he was entering. He lay still as she assumed the active role. The motion she fell into, upward and slightly forward, seemed to him in synch with the rhythm of the surf and he soon felt himself approaching an orgasm that was longer in coming but considerably more intense than the earlier one.

"Oh, Jesus, baby, you're something else!" he moaned. "You're the best!"

She eased up and off of him and collapsed on her side, sighing.

In each other's arms and lulled by the sound of the sea, they fell asleep.

Chapter 5

We'll just play it by ear, like you always say.

Joe awoke at the crack of dawn and rolled over onto his back, rubbing his eyes. His head ached so badly that he didn't want to sit up, but he decided that, as painful as it would be, his best choice was to get up and make some "industrial strength" coffee. Through the windshield—the Greenbrier's only uncurtained glass—he saw that the camper was gone. He looked down at Jane.

"*Nothing* could wake *her!*" he said *sotto voce*, and naked though he was, crawled up into the driver's seat, his head pounding. "Jesus, I can feel that god damn surf in my cranium!" he mumbled.

In a couple of minutes he had the bus back on the beach in what he judged to be more or less the spot where they had stopped the night before. There was now enough light for him to see that the tide had destroyed all the tire tracks. He got out, quietly opened the rear hatch, rummaged in the duffel bag under the bed, found a pair of white cut-offs and a T-shirt, and pulled them on.

After he returned from peeing back in the dunes he stood looking at the Greenbrier for a moment. Ordinarily, as on road trips, he would lower the door-mounted table. However, with Jane still asleep, that was out of the question. So he quietly opened the hatch and slowly slid two wooden apple boxes and the cooler out of the back of the bus and placed them on the sand in front of the vehicle. It wasn't long before he had the new two-burner Coleman stove, atop its upturned box, heating a battered percolator. A rectangular metal tray rested atop the other box and two mugs, a small pitcher, a sugar bowl, and spoons were neatly lined up on it. Then he loosened the ropes at the rear of the roof rack and, lifting the tarp with one hand, he eased out two folding beach chairs and placed them across from each other at the improvised tables, with their sides to the sea. He sat down in the chair facing the direction from which they had entered the island, placed two aspirins on his tongue, and took a swallow of water from his mug. He drank the remaining nearly full mug of water and stared at the percolator, the steady rhythm of which had slowed to a hiccup every five seconds. Waiting until it stopped, he filled his mug and added a teaspoon of brown sugar and a generous helping of milk.

"That should cool it down," he said and took a large swallow. "Ah-h-h-h, *nothing like that first hit of joe!*"

The rising sun had turned the surface of the water into a glistening mirror. "This calls for shades!" he said, adding, *"Puttin' 'em on, boss!"* as he donned his sun glasses and scanned the horizon. "Well, what have we here? I wonder if that's last night's camper." He went over to the driver's side of the bus, opened the door, and reached under the seat.

Holding the Krauss binoculars to his eyes, he determined, "Sure enough, it's the same rig." He returned to his chair, replenished his coffee, rolled a cigarette, lighted it with his Zippo, drew on it deeply, and put it down on the edge of the apple box. "What say we just check the folks out and see what kind of neighbors they'll make?" he said, directing this rhetorical question to the chair opposite him and raising the binoculars to his eyes.

"Shit if they ain't fixin' to skinny-dip! And she's got some nice bod', too!"

Upon waking, Jane had gone directly to the latrine by the parking lot and now sat across from Joe.

"This coffee is *pure mud,* honey!" she said. "Try to keep count next time, would you please!" She took another sip and grimaced. "Oh, well, at least it wipes out the stench of that awful outhouse."

"The delicious aroma of this bacon will help on that score, too, m' deah. And I'll fix some fresh joe for you."

"*Oh, yes,* nothing like cooking out in the open! And just smell that sea air! Gee, *I'm starving!*" She put her mug down, picked up the binoculars, and directed them seaward. "So what have you been looking at? See any boats out there?"

"I'll tell you what I seed, I seed a lady down thar, I shore did, an' she war *nekid as a jaybird,* she war!"

Jane swiveled and directed the binoculars over the back of her chair. "Oh, that's the truck that was up there where we were. Did you see anyone? Are they up yet?"

"I'm telling you! I saw two people in their birthday suits taking a dip about a half hour ago. The sun had just come up. They look like an interesting couple. She's built like the proverbial brick shithouse and he looks old enough to be her father."

"You're *kidding!*" Jane was focusing the glasses. "Oh, *there* they are! Well, they have clothes on now. Yes, I see what you mean, he reminds me of my Gramps—in a way. She's leaning back on the steps of that thing and gesturing to him. *Sit still, lady!* You're right, she's about your age is my guess and she *really is a knockout!* She's standing now. *Wow! What a figure!*"

Joe, kneeling beside the Coleman, announced, "These eggs will be ready as soon as I flip 'em. Get some paper plates out of the box there, will ya, please."

Again in their chairs after a swim, they made vague plans for the day. Jane's immediate objective, she announced, was to apply sun tan lotion.

"But first, I want to get out of these wet clothes."

"I rather like you in that T-shirt, babe. Sometimes I forget how well stacked you are!"

She looked down at herself. "Yes, well, I'm not sure I want to be seen in public like this. You should put some lotion on, too, honey, or you'll be as red as a lobster by this evening."

"Yeah, I'll do that. But first I want to mosey down yonder and say hello to our neighbors." He got up. "See you in a bit."

By the time he returned from his visit to the camper, Jane had changed into shorts and a halter and was brushing her hair. Her body glistened.

"Here, I'll do that," he said, taking the brush from her. He talked as he leaned over her, stroking her hair. "You won't believe this. I know—. Well. I don't actually *know*

172

him but I've known *of* him for quite a few years. The guy is Professor Henry Pettibone, formerly of Harvard, where he occupied a chair of English Literature and History. He was famous on campus as one of the best lecturers they had. His undergraduate courses were always full. Many students were turned down and had to get on a waiting list for the next year."

"Did you say you *knew* him?"

"No, no, I never met him, but Jim Harsh knew him and took several seminars from him. He said he worked his ass off in those courses—philosophy of history and Irish history, both of which are specialties of Pettibone's. Oh, yeah, and he took one from him on Dr. Johnson. Pettibone's a leading authority on Johnson and Boswell, that whole period—Swift, Congreve, people like that."

"Is he still at Harvard?"

"No, he's been retired for five years or so. *Christ,* he has to be in his mid-seventies—at *least!*"

"Who's the lady?"

"His wife, Margery. She's a real dish. A very handsome woman, a little on the voluptuous side. You're right on her age. She would be four or five years older than I am is my guess. He must be at least thirty years her senior."

"So did you ask them by?"

"They want to meet you, said we should drop by later on. They don't plan on doing much, just sit around and read most of the time. They said they're going to go in to Corpus Christi for dinner. I recommended the Fish Tank."

"You didn't!"

"*Why the hell not?* Listen, their kind of people are hip to scenes like that. After all, they live in Cambridge, right? She teaches American lit at Boston University. She's on sabbatical this year. They're going to Europe in a couple of weeks. Very cosmopolitan folks—as indeed they should be, living the life they do. I mean, shit, they're not exactly a couple of hayseeds, you know."

"Like *me*, you mean!"

"Oh, sure, babe, you're the classic farmer's daughter, straw sticking out of your ears, dung on your boots!"

"Farmer's *granddaughter,* dear." She got to her feet.

He handed the brush to her and sat down in the other chair.

"Guess I should clean this mess up." He looked up at her. "Sweetheart, you can hold your own with the best of them! Just because you didn't grow up in a big city or come from an academic family doesn't mean you're not sophisticated. 'Sides, what kind of a judge of intellect do you think *I* am? Do you think I'd have abducted you if you were some dumb blonde type?"

"*Abducted* me, huh?"

"Manner of speaking, mah deah. Seduced you and carried you off, whatever."

"Anyway, I'm not exactly *blond*, am I?" She stood in front of him running her hands through her dark hair.

"Oh, you always do such a good job brushing it!"

"I'm well practiced on my own locks, babe. And I *love* your hair—you *know* that. Don't *ever* cut it off—*please!*"

"So you think—. What's her name—Margie?"

"Margery. He calls her Maggie."

"So you think Margery has a voluptuous figure, huh?"

"Yeah, she's all right. Too old for me though. I wouldn't know what to do with a women her age."

She burst out laughing. "Honey, you really are too much! She's *your* age, more or less."

"True, but I've never made love to a woman beyond

her thirties. They say women get pretty horny in their forties. Might be more than ol' Joe here could handle."

"Oh, I think you could handle her, honey!" Jane reached over and took his hand. "But I *better not catch you trying, mister!*"

"No worry, my dear, no worry at all." He stretched and yawned. "Jesus, I do feel relaxed. It's nice to have no worries—for the moment, anyway."

"Don't think about anything beyond today, my darling," she said as she sat in his lap. "We're here to enjoy ourselves—and nothing *but* enjoy ourselves! We can eat and drink and swim and wander around—and *make love!*"

"I'm for all of that—*especially* that *last item!*"

"When do you want to drop by the Pettibones?"

"Right after I clean up here and visit the head."

The visit with the Pettibones was brief, in that the couple had decided to drive in to Corpus Christi for breakfast, make flight reservations for the next week, and do some shopping. Henry wanted to acquire a book recently published by a former colleague and Margery added that they were critically low on wine and spirits. So, while little transpired beyond the introduction of Jane and a few minutes of small talk, the Pettibones invited them for a mid-morning brunch on the morrow.

They spent most of the rest of the morning in the water. He blew up a truck inner tube that Boz had given them and, with her astride it and him clinging to it, they drifted out beyond the breaking surf and lazily bobbed on the swell.

"Look, Joe, they're fishing up there." She pointed

toward the southwest.

"Oh, yeah, surf fishing. Wonder what they catch here. Maybe we could buy a couple of fish from them, cook them over a wood fire for supper."

"Let's do that! You could bake some potatoes and I'll make a salad."

The sun was high in the sky when, famished, they came out of the water and Joe rigged a crude lean-to on the side of the bus out of a tarp and tent poles, while Jane made sandwiches, added pickles and olives, and opened two beers. They sat on large beach towels and ate ravenously.

"Jesus, that water made me hungry!" he said.

"It's nice here in the shade, isn't it? And I think a little breeze is coming up."

The swim and the lunch and the beer and the heat combined to bring heavy-eyed drowsiness over them and they stretched out and dozed. Always a light sleeper, Joe was awake before a half-hour had passed. He spread his towel over Jane and filled a mug from the bottle of sauterne lying in the cooler beside the tiny piece of ice left over from the small block Man Mountain had given them. He sat in the passenger seat of the bus sipping the wine and smoking a curved-stem meerschaum. It pleased him that Jane would usually sleep on for an hour or so longer than he, whether in the morning or after lovemaking, for he enjoyed sitting and thinking by himself, over wine as now, coffee or a pot of tea following an afternoon nap, and cognac late at night.

"Well, this is *vacation*, for chrissakes!" he said aloud. "So there's no friggin' need to wait for the sun to be under the bloody yardarm. If I feel like a glass of wine in the afternoon, then I'll *damn well have one!* Should've had a bloody eye opener with the aspirin, some hair of the dog."

The novel he had been working on for the past couple of years suddenly cropped up in his thoughts.

"A lot of folks think that sitting over a drink and just thinking is weird," he continued, still talking to the air, "but I do get some of my best ideas this way."

And after a day or two of germination, he said to himself, *they can result in an episode or a scene or a character. Or maybe just a thought or a phrase or something. Course, if I don't make a note of it, it will often fly right out the fuckin' window! Yeah, even some of my best friends think I'm peculiar, maybe even a bit daft.* He chuckled. *Well, my novel, if ever it sees print, will confirm them in their worst suspicions! Fact is, I don't give a shit what they think! I'd rather—indeed must—be apart from the madding crowd, if I am to retain what little sanity I have left. Anyway, it is they who are nuts, not I.*

His thoughts then turned to Boulder and the small college town a few miles from it where they would soon be living, neither of which he had ever seen, the closest he had come being an academic meeting he attended in Denver nearly a decade ago. And then he saw little but the hotel. Friends had told him of the beauty of Boulder and its surroundings and he had known several who had taught at the university there. Of Hopkins College he had heard little other than that his friend of Yale days John Chalmers Brown had constituted half its Department of Classics for the past five years.

"Well, it will be different, that's for sure."

"Are you talking to yourself again?" she called to him, her sleepy query segueing into a yawn.

"Yes, I'm sitting here talking up a chapter," he said out the window, "and you know how that is with me. Wish we had a tape recorder with a battery. Then I could play it back. Might be something I could use. Say, how's this for an idea for a play? A guy sitting in a mock-up of a Greenbrier, or a VW bus, on the stage talking to himself."

"Why don't you bring me a glass of that wine you're drinking and I'll try to get myself going here. Then we could walk up the beach and collect sea shells and things."

"How did you know I'm drinking wine?"

"I'm clairvoyant—as you well know, sweetheart! Better watch out or I'll read your mind!"

The next morning they slept in. When Joe awoke he reached for his pocket watch.

"Hey, babe, it's after nine," he said, nuzzling up to Jane's back and pulling her toward him. "We have just time for a little morning exercise and a swim before our brunch with the Pettibones."

After they made love and swam for ten minutes or so, they got dressed and strolled, bare of foot, along the sea for the hundred and fifty yards to the older couple's camper, she in a granny dress of patchwork design and he in a short-sleeve khaki shirt and faded jeans held up by a rope-belt. Jane frequently bent down to examine a shell. Most she discarded, but now and then she exclaimed, "Oh, a *real gem!*" and gently lowered it into a coffee can.

Turning up toward the dunes, they approached the Pettibones' camper. Beneath its rather more elaborate shelter than the tarp and tent poles improvised by Joe, Henry Pettibone sat in a canvas chair with a *New York Times* on his lap. Joe caught the headline, "Czechoslovakia Invaded By Russians," as Henry folded the paper and dropped it into a cardboard box between his feet.

"Well, good morning there!" he said as he pushed the

box under his chair with his heel. "I saw you out there in the water a little while ago. It looks quite rough this morning."

"And good morning to you, sir."

"Yes, g'morning," Jane followed up. "How are you?"

"Oh, can't complain—and who would listen if I did?" He chuckled.

Margery, whose back was to them as she stood at the shelf on the side of the camper, turned and smiled, a paring knife in one hand. "Oh, good morning! It's such a beautiful morning, although a little too windy for our usual swim."

"Yeah, we skipped it this morning," Henry added. "So I've been sitting here reading the paper and enjoying my second cup of coffee."

"I love your dress, Jane," Margery began. "And you really need something like that on a morning like this."

"Yes, I was blue when we came out of the water. That breeze has a real chill to it."

"Have you had coffee?" Margery asked.

"No, and we'd *love* some *coffee!*"

While Margery and Jane stood at the shelf preparing food, Henry and Joe sat talking about the Democratic Convention taking place in Chicago.

"We'll tune in on it later," said Henry, having concluded his summary of what had so far transpired.

"Hank is such a political animal," said Margery to Jane as they joined the men. "I've not been able to get him away from the radio all week, and he was just as involved with the Republican convention last month—although he of course has *no use for Republicans!*" She smiled. "Nor do I, for that matter."

"Well, they're the party of *business,* and I do *detest* that

179

world," Henry interrupted, overhearing his wife's remarks. "That fool political party actually believes what that idiot Calvin Coolidge said about this country, a slander upon all that this great nation represents."

"Yes, dear, you certainly do," Margery continued, taking a seat and handing Joe and Jane mugs of coffee from the tray on her lap. "Hank comes from a long line of New England bankers, you see, and he was the first to break out of that family tradition. He long ago convinced me how important it is to know what is going on, and to participate, at least to the extent one has time for. Life can be so busy for an academic. I remember my favorite professor telling me when I was a graduate student that I would have even *less* free time once I finished my dissertation and started teaching. And *he was so right!*"

"Now who could that have been, I wonder?" Henry said, chuckling. "Yes, I do believe in a citizen fulfilling his responsibilities to the state—to the *polis*, in terms of your field, Joe."

"That's right, Henry. In fact, the Greeks had a disparaging word for the person who did not involve himself in public affairs and statecraft. They called him an ἰδιώτης,* a private person—an *idiot!*"

"So you folks are on your way to Colorado after your vacation here," said Henry to Jane, who had taken the chair next to him.

"Yes, and I'm really looking forward to it. I've never been there and I hear it's just beautiful. But we just had to see Padre Island before we left Texas. Isn't this fantastic?" Jane's arm made a sweep that took in much of the horizon. "I could just stay here for a month. But we have

---

* idiótes

to push on next week, I guess. And I think we need a change of scene—from Texas, that is."

"Padre Island is a charming place, my dear," said Margery. "It's the last stop on our summer trip. We rented this thing in Atlanta and have been living in it since the beginning of July. Oh, we have stayed in a few motels along the way. It's nice to have hot showers and all every couple of days."

"How long will you stay here?"

"We turn the truck in Sunday in Corpus Christi and fly to Boston the next day, Joe," Henry chimed in. "Three days after that we'll be in my favorite city, Paris."

"Yes, we just love Paris. We've been going there every year or two since we were married. And we've taken other sabbaticals there." Margery turned to Jane. "You're going to love Colorado, and Boulder, too. It's so beautiful there, with those mountains above the town—the Flatirons. We were there at a meeting a few years ago. Remember that, Hank?"

"Sure do, Maggie."

"So where all have you have been in your travels this summer?" Jane asked.

Late that afternoon, as they strolled far up the beach, sometimes hand-in-hand, Joe and Jane reflected upon the circumstances that had brought them together with the Pettibones, Joe remarking upon the coincidence that Jim Harsh (whom Henry well remembered as one of his best, and favorite, graduate students) had taken courses from him.

"Put that sort of meeting, out of the blue, in a work of fiction, you'd be accused of *stretching credibility*," he said. "Yet it *do happen!*"

Jane said that the casual meeting of the two couples on the previous morning and Margery's invitation to join them at brunch had almost seemed to have been guided by some unseen force, so natural was the friendship that immediately established itself, in that Joe found himself in as deep discussion of literature and life with Margery as with Henry, although the subject inevitably came around to politics with the latter, its topicality being the determining factor.

As for Jane and Margery, they hit it off from the very beginning. It turned out that the Pettibones spoke French as fluently as natives and this inspired Jane to make use of her college minor as she helped their hostess with the preparation of the meal. Joe, whose French was only in terms of reading ability, got even by conversing with Henry in Italian, which neither of the women could understand.

"What did you and Margery talk about, babe? You were going on like a couple of old friends there while Henry and I were listening to the news from Chicago."

"Mostly about her and Henry and how they met and things. You know, I think she really needed to talk about all that stuff, honey. You were right about their ages, more or less. Hank—I mean, Henry—will be seventy-one in October and Margery was forty-four in May. They met in 1946 when Henry came back to Harvard from the war and she was just beginning graduate school. He became her adviser and they began an affair. He was forty-eight, she was twenty-one. Gee, isn't the mid-forties pretty old for combat?"

"Henry told me that he spent the war in England as a cryptologist, with the rank of major." He paused. "So *that's* how it happened. I didn't want to ask but he said something like, 'That's when Maggie and I got together.' It seems he left his wife to marry her."

"Yes, a year after he came back from the war."

"Yeah, he was a code-breaker. All those languages he knows got him a commission—French, Italian, German, Spanish, Russian, even Latin. But *I've got him on Greek!*"

"It must have been strange for her. Henry's daughters were nearly her age, seventeen and twenty."

"You really got the family history out of Margery." He stopped and stared out into gulf. "A very vague memory just came to me, babe."

"What's that, honey?"

"Remember that weekend classics meeting I went to a couple months before we split Canada?"

"The one you came back from so hung over?"

"Yeah, I tied one on that last night there, that's for sure."

"You were a *wreck* when you got home!"

"The Pettibones came up in a conversation I had with someone there. I forgot all about it until just now!"

"And what was it about?"

"Don't have a clue! I was blotto!"

"Well *that's* a big help!" She laughed. "Anyway, honey, it was kind of like she had wanted to talk about all that stuff for a long time." A contemplative look came over Jane's face. "You know, it's funny, but I really didn't hardly ask her anything—I just listened." She stooped to pick up a tiny shell. "Look, honey, isn't it beautiful? So delicate. Maybe I could have a bracelet made of my collection of these real little ones."

"Well, I can't say I gleaned very much personal history from Henry. Mostly we talked about the convention and—." In angry voice Joe continued, "You wouldn't

believe what's coming down there! *Talk about a police state!
Shit!*"

"Tell me about it later, Joe, *please!* Oh, I know it's awful but it's too beautiful here to spoil it with all of that." She held her hand still so that Joe could examine the shell.

"Okay. Say, there is another fine little specimen there. Look how it kind of reflects the light." He scooped up the shell and handed it to her.

"Shall we head back?"

"Sure. I have to get a fire going and clean those fish. That's going to be a feed, I'm tellin' ya!" He took her hand and turned back toward the Greenbrier and their camp. "So, learn anything else about our new friends the Pettibones?"

"You old gossip you!" she said, laughing. "Like what they did in bed back when she was a grad student*?*"

"Yeah, the good stuff!"

"I'll try to remember some of the really personal stuff she told me. I was pretty surprised at how she opened up to me, like she hadn't talked about it before and needed to tell someone." She smiled at him. "Come to think of it, she did say Henry used to go down on her and then ball her on his office desk! And that their affair was a departmental scandal and some took Henry's side and some took his wife's side. Henry and his wife didn't get divorced for something like two years and here they were—Henry and Margery—living together in an apartment a couple of blocks from the family home there in Cambridge. Margery says Henry's ex still lives there. She remarried a few years after all that." Jane stopped and looked at him. "Joe, she married a classicist. Isn't that something? But I can't remember his name!"

"Now I wonder who that could be. The plot thickens."

On Saturday Joe and Jane joined the Pettibones for dinner. It was the older couple's final night on the island. They were dropping the camper off the next day and spending the night in a hotel.

"We thought we'd have dinner at that restaurant you gave us the name of, Joe," Margery said. "We drove by it that morning we went into town but it was closed."

"Yeah, the Fish Tank," Henry added. "Looks something like a place some New York friends—former students of mine—took us to in Lower Manhattan a couple of years ago. You know, one of those lofts that artists have their studios in, a warehouse, actually. You go up in a huge freight elevator. Is it like that inside?"

"Well, come to think of it, it is in an old warehouse," said Joe, directing his gaze up to the clouds. "I'm trying to remember if there was an elevator. 'Cause we were only on the ground floor. I don't know, maybe they live upstairs."

"Well, we thought we'd have dinner there after we drop the camper off and get settled in the hotel, not have so much of a rush on Monday," Margery said and turned to Jane. "Well, what have you been doing since yesterday, my dear?"

"Oh, just lazing around," Jane said. "I just *love* walking this wonderful beach, and the swimming is *just glorious! I don't want to leave!*"

"We had an interesting experience last night," Joe began.

"What was that, Joe?" Henry said, placing a small plastic cup in Joe's hand. "Try this on for size."

185

Joe sipped from the cup. "Hey, you build a mean martini, Henry! You should try one of these, Jane."

"Thanks, I'll stay with this wine, honey. You know gin is not one of my favorites."

"So tell us about your 'interesting experience,' my friend," Henry resumed.

"Oh, yeah. Well, we went up into the dunes and built a little fire from some wood I had gathered and we heated up some canned beans and hot dogs for dinner and we're sitting there talking and drinking our last bottle of wine." Joe hesitated and shifted his eyes from Henry to Margery and then back again to Henry.

Henry leaned forward slightly. "Yes, go on."

"Well, there was this rustling behind us. At first I thought it was the wind, you know, moving a bit of tumbleweed or something, and I didn't pay much attention, but then I sensed something was moving behind me and I looked around." Joe raised the cup to his lips and drained it. "I just about jumped out of my skin! I can't think of anything that ever scared me the way the sudden sight of that damn herd of cattle did! There must have been a dozen or so of them."

Henry and Margery laughed delightedly.

"*That's rich!*" Henry said, doubling over. "I meant to warn you about them. They haven't been around for about a week."

"It was really frightening," Jane said. "Although they didn't do anything and just went on their way."

"Oh, they're quite harmless," Margery explained. "Of course, we knew about them from the guide book. They're free roaming. But I can understand how they startled you—especially if you didn't know about them."

"You tell a good story, Joe," said Henry, getting to his

feet. "Save that one for your first lecture at Hopkins College. It'll break the ice. Always difficult, that opening day." He shuffled over to the camper's shelf. "Speaking of ice, we're just about out of it. Say, 'bout time to throw these steaks on the coals, Magpie."

"One of Hank's more endearing nicknames for me," Margery said, smiling. "Yes, dear, it's time to put them on. And bring the wine over, please."

Joe took the plastic cup from the small tray Henry was extending to him. "Thanks." A thoughtful expression was on his face. "You know," he said slowly, "Jane is right both ways. I mean, I love this island and—. You know, I think I told you, I grew up near the water, in fact near a body of water that this kind of reminds me of, the Chesapeake Bay, and I used to walk that beach with my dog, who was, quite appropriately, a Chesapeake Bay Retriever. Then I spent a couple of winters—fall and spring, too, but we had to vacate summers—in a beach house on Long Island Sound in East Haven. So I have a strong attachment to the water."

"It's so *perfect here!*" Jane interrupted. "*Just glorious!* I haven't had shoes on *for a week!*"

"But Jane's right that we have to move on, to the next act, so to speak."

As they sat eating the steak, canned white potatoes, and salad, Joe turned to Henry. "I suddenly remembered this afternoon that I used to read passages from an article of yours on Defoe's *Journal of the Plague Year* to my Greek history classes."

"Oh, yes, from back before the war. I got very interested in plagues there for a while. Read up on them in medical journals."

"And you made comparisons to Thucydides' account

of the plague in Athens."

"Yes, and Boccaccio, too, you'll remember. Plus later writers, some from the Orient and other places." Henry shifted restlessly in his chair. "Yes, that almost seems like it was in another life."

"It was, Hank," Margery said, taking his hand, "it was indeed."

"So what will you be teaching at Hopkins College, Joe, what sort of schedule are they giving you?" Henry asked, holding onto Margery's hand. "I hope they're not loading you down with twenty hours a week, as they do at some of these small institutions."

"First thing I told my friend John Chalmers Brown was that I wouldn't do more than four courses and two of them would have to be in the languages. So I'm giving Beginning Greek, Pindar, an Honors seminar for seniors on the Roman Republic, and the big Ancient History survey, all year long courses except the Honors one. I'll be doing The Age of Pericles in its second semester."

"Interesting program," said Henry. "That history survey, what will it cover?"

"You know, one of those year-long deals that begins with the Sumerians and ends—if you move fast enough!—with the Visigoths sacking Rome." He took his tobacco patch from the pocket of his shirt, unzipped it, and plucked a packet of cigarette papers from it.

"Now that's something I haven't seen for a spell, Joe," Henry said. "Of course, you see it a lot in Europe, especially the Netherlands. Say, you have that down pretty damn well! That looks like a factory-made job! Would you roll me one of them, please?"

"Here, take this and I'll do another one." He handed the cigarette to Henry and held his Zippo lighter to it. "So

I have to spend the first couple of weeks spieling about Mesopotamia and Egypt, not that I know balls about either of them—and not much in between either."

"Your wit is Rabelaisian, my friend," said Henry, to Joe's and Jane's bewilderment, but evidently not to Margery's, for a broad smile greeted her husband's observation. "So you're kind of a generalist, in a way, right? I mean, you're at home in both the history and the literature. Which is the way I've always seen the picture, and that's the approach I've always taken to my own special period."

"Hank is not a narrow specialist though, understand. Don't sell yourself short, dear."

"Well, yes, I'm grounded in the eighteenth century but, as Maggie indicates, I've roamed around here and there in other periods and I've often given big survey courses like the one you describe. Now, mine were necessarily of a somewhat later period, of course, since my competence doesn't reach into your period." He drew on the cigarette with obvious enjoyment. "And I liked that very much. Back there in the early years I was only a step or two ahead of my students the first time I would work up one of those courses." A far-away look came over Henry's face. "You know, Maggie, as I've said many times, those hours up there behind the lectern with two or three hundred faces out there to talk to were some of the best times I've ever had."

"The significant word there is 'talk', Hank. That was your way, talking to those faces, not lecturing them. Don't forget, I was there in the back of the room." Margery turned to Joe. "I was Hank's grader for two years after he came back to Harvard after the war."

"Yes, I saw you back there," he said, smiling at her as

she reached over and took his hand. "How about you, Joe, do you enjoy giving those lecture courses?"

"I do, Henry, I really do, and I know what you mean about keeping ahead of the students. My first time with a big survey, Greek and Latin Literature in English translation, was pure hell, I tell you. I put ten, twelve hours of preparation into every one of those fifty-minute lectures. Course I don't claim to be the spellbinder you are behind the lectern. Actually, the way I heard it from Jim Harsh, you didn't spend much time behind the lectern. He said you were in non-stop motion back and forth from the blackboard to the front of the stage."

Margery burst out laughing.

"That's perfect, that's really perfect! That captures you *perfectly*, Hank!" She turned to Joe, then to Jane, as she went on. "It would drive me crazy the way he would bound around up there! Hank *never* stopped moving. The students had a name for him. Now what was that? Oh, yes, Perpetual Motion Pettibone."

Henry joined the others in the laughter that ensued.

"I had never given one of those surveys until six or seven years ago," Joe continued, "but since then it's clung to me like a leech. I guess having that on my résumé got me this next job. The senior professor who had taught it for years had a fatal heart attack a few weeks ago and John, an old friend from Yale, somehow tracked me down in Austin and asked if I could take the job. Pretty short notice, what? But I don't mind. Fortunately, I've still got my notes from the last time I gave a lecture course, on Greek and Roman history. And I guess, like you, I do enjoy being up there in front of a couple hundred bodies, maybe shaping something about their thinking. And, over the years, I've become quite a ham." Joe got to his feet.

"I'll tell you this, though, Henry, the scene has changed the last few years since you were there. I think it's important that students be exposed to some of the great authorities in their fields, to teachers like you who have pulled it all together and who can talk about what they know to a lecture hall filled with hundreds of eager young minds. But that doesn't happen all that often any more." Still talking, Joe walked over to the shelf and deposited his plastic cup on it, then turned, gesturing wildly, Neapolitan-style, his head bobbing up and down, his beard executing arcs. As he returned to his chair his voice rose nearly to a shout. *"It's all such a farce!* Higher education as it exists today is the *biggest shuck of all!"* His face slightly flushed, Joe took his seat.

"What do you mean, Joe?" Henry asked, leaning forward and drawing on the inch-long remains of the cigarette Joe had rolled for him.

"The big universities have become diploma factories," Joe answered as he again took out his tobacco pouch, "nothing more than robot assembly lines. They're *screwing* up society when they should be out there in front helping to *straighten it out!* You know, I really believe that most university presidents are just plant managers. They might as well be putting out shoes or washing machines for all they know about—or *care about, for chrissakes!—educating!"* His hand trembled slightly as he spread tobacco on cigarette paper.

Joe's outburst almost seemed to have had an intimidating effect on the other three for a minute or so. Then Henry let his cigarette butt slip from his fingers. Looking down, he moved sand on top of it with the side of his sandal and fixed his eyes on Joe's.

"Don't get discouraged, Joe," he said. "There are at

least two ways for you to go. If you feel that you can do something about the drift of higher education toward conformity, toward producing automatons instead of questioning minds, then you might want to work within the system. Then again, I hear from your charming lady here, and I assume it is not a secret"—he turned to Jane as if for permission to continue—"that you've been working on a novel for several years. It may be that you should devote yourself to that rather than continue with an academic career. That, too, is a form of education, I don't have to tell you."

"One does have to earn a living, Hank," Margery said softly. "Don't forget that."

"Well, we'll see how it goes," Joe said, sighing. "Fact is, I really enjoy teaching and I'm looking forward to this Hopkins situation, small school and all that. Only had that once before, up in Canada, and that didn't work out very well, although I really liked it up there." He turned to Jane. "So maybe I'll hang around and get tenure—and all that jazz. Then again, I could decide to walk out of the paint factory—for good this time. We'll just have to see. Right, babe?"

"We'll just play it by ear, like you always say, Joe," Jane said, reaching over and taking his hand.

A storm had come in an hour or so before dawn, waking Joe, and so he backed the Greenbrier up close to the dunes. They had determined after their first night on the island that the tide did not reach the higher ground and, since the sand was sufficiently firm there, they did not risk digging the wheels in. He soon fell back asleep and did not wake up until about eight. He sat up and pulled aside the curtain. When he saw that it was drizzling he sighed and looked down at Jane, noting that she was soundly asleep. It took him a few minutes of rooting under the bed to locate his rain gear. He was careful to not wake her, for, upon returning from the evening with the Pettibones, they had talked far into the early hours after making love.

When he emerged from the bus he stood for a moment looking at the sea. The sou'wester, full-length oilskin raincoat, and beard gave him the appearance of a nineteenth century New England seaman. After making a visit to the dunes to relieve his full bladder, Joe dragged the tarp from beneath the bus, unfurled and raised it onto the tent poles, set up the two chairs and apple box, and put the percolator on the Coleman. As he sat waiting for the coffee, Joe heard an engine start up. He looked up to the parking lot, realizing that their new friends had parked there overnight. "Wonder when we'll see *them* again," he said softly. "Funny that we should find ourselves on the same Texas beach with those two. As I said the other day, if you put that in a novel, critics would say it was contrived, not the sort of thing that happens *Yet it definitely do!*"

He thought back on some other meetings that would seem farfetched if used in fiction. *Like that time Jyll and I came out of the ice cream parlor and stood looking at that battered VW parked bumper-to-bumper with our week-old Beetle on the Kurfürstendamm. Turned out to belong to a graduate student friend of hers who was on his way to a study-abroad program he had hired on to. Let's see, where was he headed—Heidelberg or Köln? After he ditched his car he rode with us as far as Nuremberg. That was funny how he took the plates off that wreck and just left it in an alley, burned its papers. Wonder if that ever caught up with him.*

The woman at the pensione there in Nuremberg wanted to put us all in the same room, until I objected that we were on our honeymoon. Of course, because Jyll was so paranoid about anybody even hearing us making love, much less peeking up over the foot of the bed from that pull-out thing Frau whatsername wanted to put him on, it was out of the question. Like that time in Madrid she heard that young British couple we made friends with moving around in the room next door and she wouldn't let me do a thing. Funny she was like that. Maybe she didn't want anyone except me to hear her so totally out of control. I remember her telling me, "I'd feel funny doing it with anyone but you, darling." Guess that came from her being a virgin when we became lovers. She was such a sweetheart in bed, just went out of her head doing sixty-nine. "Now do it a lon-n-ng time all around on the outside first, honey!" she'd say every time, once we were in position with her on top. Didn't want my tongue in her pussy until I had her teased into a state of near hysteria. Then those little sprays of moisture, like an atomizer. Jesus, will I ever get that girl out of my system?

It was still drizzling an hour later when Jane tapped on the window and called to him. He went over and opened the door.

"How long have you been up?" she asked, yawning. "I didn't hear you. I slept like a log."

"Oh, an hour or so, I guess."

"Could you fix me a coffee?"

"Sure, comin' right up."

Joe made fresh coffee and then fixed a breakfast from the bacon, eggs, English muffins, and marmalade the Pettibones had given them. After they had eaten and while he cleaned up Jane puttered around rearranging things in the bus. When the rain ended and the sun came out later that morning they drove ten miles or so along the shore line until they came to a sign, "Four Wheel Drive Vehicles Only Beyond This Point." Joe cut the engine. After a few minutes he turned to Jane.

"Are you thinking what I'm thinking?"

"That we should pack up and be on our way?"

"You read my mind."

"I warned you that I would," said Jane, teasingly continuing with, "Better watch out or I'll be into your deepest thoughts."

"I'm afraid you'd find a tangled mess there, babe, a real snake pit. Seriously though, what say we push on this afternoon. I am really getting restless."

"I'll meet you half-way. I mean, I thought we were going to stay for a couple more days. What say we get an early start in the morning. It's turning out to be a glorious day and we could swim and take another walk and maybe buy a couple of fish and have another supper up in the dunes. This time we could be ready for those cows."

Chapter 6

I think Rufus has been on the lam.

They crossed the causeway to the mainland a little after six the next morning. Joe had the night before spread maps out on the bed and, with the dome light on and a flashlight and magnifying glass for pinpointing detail, plotted their route. He concluded that it added up to about 1200 miles to Hopkins College and he figured it would take three days of driving. They agreed to allow for an extra day or two if anything along the way caught their fancy and needed to be checked out.

"Hell, if we find that commune near Taos that Melinda told you about," said Joe as he studied the maps, "we might just hang out for a couple of days. Classes don't start for almost three weeks."

They pulled into Sam Casey's gas station about seven o'clock.

"We'll just gas up and get on our way," Joe assured

Jane, "maybe buy a couple stogies. No need to hang around."

Joe's mistake—if it indeed was one, for he treasured what Sam told them, he later admitted—was to mention, as he and Jane stood at the counter settling up for the gas and cigars and the picture postcards Jane had picked out, Henry Pettibone and his participation in the very WWI campaign in which Sam had been wounded. This revelation had inspired the recounting of the several days leading up to October 9, 1918, when Sam's "carriers" had been blown up a few feet from him by mortar fire and he had taken shrapnel in the leg.

"We marched all night and done crossed the Mouse River thar 'bout fifteen miles east o' the Argun woods on October 8," Sam began. "You dint git from yer fren' the perfesser what all unit his'n wahr so I can't rightly say if'n he wahr thar when we wuz sloggin' through thet mud and trippin' on bar-bed wahr. But likely as not he wuz comin' up in the rear. They done lay down boards fer the artillery to roll on. I'm tellin' ya we wuz a slippin' an' a slidin' all over God's lil acre an' losin' 'quipment all o'er the place. I los' m' soovneers an' m' Red Cross bag an' my sewin' kit—an' a wrist watch that shined in the dark thet I took offen a dead Kraut." Sam smiled at them. "I hung it on m' back like a tail light to keep fellers from bumpin' inta me inna dark an' it fell off in thet mud. I 'member the platoon sarge haltin' us when it wuz still dark an' I set in m' iron hat in thet mud fer a couple minutes and then all hell broken loose from Kraut howitzers. It wuz jest breakin' daylight and I 'member thinkin' that dawn seem to hold a promise of a new day. French guides and wire cutters led us forward and I can hear some o' our fellers jokin' and such to break the tension, still hear it like it wuz yestiday, know whadamean? Thar wahrn't no let-up from then on. I wahr a automatic rifleman by then, an' corp'ral, not a rifleman an' private like I tol' you when you wuz here afore, an' I had two privates, kids right outa school, fer carriers. They carried pans o' ammo. Only way you could fahr one o' them French-made automatic rifles wahr to lay on yer belly. They wuz on a two-leg-ged stand, a bipod they called it, an' it wunt hold to the target 'less you lay down like I say an' kep' it on thet two-leg-ged stand. I had a helluva time keepin' that damn thang clean thar in the mud, but we done learned to take 'em apart in the dark in trainin' an' put 'em back in one piece in less'n a minute."

Sam took a gulp from the can of beer he had carried in from his chair on the porch after Joe had filled the Greenbrier's tank and checked the oil.

"Want one?" he asked, gesturing with it. Joe shook his head.

"Lessee now, oh, yeah, we wuz soakin' wet an' sloggin' through thet mud all night in the rain, catchin' a few winks layin' inna field on our blankets, an' they wuz soakin' wet too, an' alla time we wuz under heavy fahr, three-inch machine gun fahr, morter fahr, artillery fahr. A feller wuz blown to bits a couple yards from us an' I kin hear our captain sayin' to the leftenint, 'Looks like we uz inna wahr,' an' the leftenint sez, 'Yep, I think we iz.'" Sam put the can to his lips but lowered it before drinking. "They wuz trenches all over the place and most of 'em wuz blowed up pretty bad. We'd—m' carriers an' me—jump down in 'em an' look fer prizners. They wuz nobody much left in 'em and them thet wuz dint have much fight left. I 'member the leftenint runnin' through 'em an' tossin' grenades in dugouts and hollerin' fer

199

Krauts to come out. He could say it in Kraut lingo, as I recollect. I jumped over a wooden box and then I turn back and pry the lid open with my bayonet and seed it was machine gun ammo. Lucky it wahrn't no booby trap!" Sam stopped for a moment and looked back and forth several times from Joe to Jane. "I do go on, doan I?"

"Sam, don't stop now, *for god's sake!*" Joe remonstrated.

"Well, I took some prizners meself, an' I'll tell you hows thet come about. At one point me an' my carriers got trapped in a trench that dint seem to be any way out an' they wuz all bar-bed wahr an' craters from shells and such and ulluva sudden they wuz this here Kraut aroun' this one bend and he seen me an' seem like he wuz all wore out. I had my carriers and me spread out so's if'n a shell hit we wunt all be killed at the same time. So I come 'round this bend an' almost bumped into this 'ere Kraut. He wuz bent over almost double and had more 'quipment hangin' off'n 'im than a Christmas tree. I had m' sidearm at the ready and had the drop on 'im. Shore 'nuff they wuz two more right behind 'im and they all three grabbed fer their belt buckles and everythin' they wuz packin' hit the deck—rifles, packs, canteens, ever' blasted thang they wuz luggin'! Then they begun turnin' their pockets inside out! Buttons, rings, even pieces o' cheese fell down in the mud! M' carriers an' me took 'em out o' the trench an' the leftenint said send 'em to the rear. Last I saw of 'em they wuz runnin' back toward our advancin' troops with they hands up behine they necks. Wahrn't long after thet m' carriers were blowed up and I took shrapnel in m' leg." He dropped his left hand to his side and patted his thigh. "Funny thang, I dint know I was hit at fust and I lays there in the mud an' tried to set m' rifle up. We wuz on this ridge and we wuz bein' swept by heavy machine gun fire. But one o' the bipod legs of my rifle had broke off, or been shot off, and the ammo pan wahr all caked with mud. I 'member lookin' up and seein' the cap'n runnin' 'long the edge o' this 'ere ridge with some of the men an' he had a pistol in 'is han' an' it wuz like they wuz rabbit huntin'."

Sam tilted the can, drained it, put it on the counter, and, staring at it as though into a crystal ball, continued. "One o' t'other man saw me a layin' there in the mud and hepped me get up on m' feet. Somehow he got me back to the rear to the stretcher-bearers and they took me to a field horspital, a big tent behine the lines. From there I wuz shipped back to a base horspital. A nurse—she wuz a right purty thang—tol' me later that I wuz kinda outa m' mind and had been bleedin' pretty bad and I wuz worried more about bringin' m' rifle back than enny thang and kep' sayin' how it was charged to me. I guess that feller couldn't carry my rifle and hisn too an' help me on top o' that so he lef' it layin' thar in the mud. He went back to the front an' I never saw 'im agin. I dint come home till after Christmas. Course the wahr ended while I wuz in horspital." Sam paused and, again staring at the beer can, added very softly, "Thet wahr wuz the most excitin' time o' m' life."

Joe pushed it that first day, keeping the needle on seventy, except on some stretches of two-lane blacktop, and declining Jane's offer to take over the wheel. They made only two bathroom stops, refueling at one of these, and ate sandwiches on the run. Jane napped for an hour in the mid-afternoon and when she awoke she poured two coffees from the thermos she had filled that morning. He took the mug from her.

"I do needs that, I'm tellin' ya, Pops," he said in a gravelly Louis Armstrong voice. "Just lak I laks ma womens, too—*hot an' black!*"

"Haven't heard that one in a while. How much longer you planning to keep on driving?"

He looked at the pocket watch dangling from the mirror. "We should be in Lubbock in another hour or so. Find us a motel there." He glanced over at her. "Ever see such a wretched landscape? Parched, scrubby, *utterly unredeeming!* What a horror it must have been living out here before civilization arrived! *Especially* before *trains!* Can you imagine traveling across this stretch of hell in a fuckin' *stagecoach? Shit!*" He paused to light his pipe. "Knew this girl in Seattle whose ancestors came to San Francisco that way, from Boston. Alice Livingston. Hadn't thought of her for a while. She gave me the copy of *Goodwin's Greek Moods and Tenses* that her great-grandfather had used. Has his name, "Harvard," and "1868" on the flyleaf. After she and my friend Elliston Richards got divorced almost a decade ago, Alice moved to Montana and opened a restaurant. What do you think she called it?"

"Alice's Restaurant?"

"Pretty sharp there, lady!" He carefully sipped coffee. "Did I ever tell you about Elliston?"

"I don't recognize the name, honey, so I guess not."

"He was a funny guy, always had a comeback. One time I was bragging about knowing Greek and quoted Dr. Johnson's dictum, 'Greek, sir, is like lace, every man gets as much of it as he can.' And he said the saying would have to be changed to fit into today's tastes. I said, 'How so?' and he said, 'For "lace" you'd have to substitute, "*Poontang!*"'." He laughed.

"*You men* and your *jokes!* But that *is* funny! What did this Elliston do?"

"He was a sort of jack of all trades. Spent some time with one of the San Francisco papers writing obituaries, went to Europe as correspondent for one of the wire services, was a ski instructor on Mount Rainier, sold big sail boats in L.A., opened an art gallery there, too. Gave music lessons on several instruments. Talented cat! Never could settle into anything for long. Haven't heard from him for a few years. Or from Alice."

It was about 5:30 when they saw the first signs announcing Lubbock and they slowed and assessed the motels as they approached them.

"To quote our president on another matter, this town is 'the ugliest thing I ever saw!'"

"Look, honey!" she said, pointing across his chest. "That looks like a reasonably acceptable place, and they have a vacancy."

"Oh, great!" he said, grinning, "we're no doubt making it under the wire just before some massive invasion of tourists—or maybe the annual convention of the WCTU!"

"The double what?"

Ignoring her query, he cut across the road and into the driveway under the shade of the portico. Taking off his sunglasses and rubbing his eyes, he looked over at her.

"Glad that's over! We'll get a real early start and beat what's left of the Texas heat. Probably make New Mexico by noon if we get off by seven." He swung the bus door open, got out, and stretched. "*Man!* Terra firma *do feel good!*"

"Want me to go in with you?"

"No, I'll take care of it."

Sitting in a worn armchair watching a large floor model black-and-white television was a rail of a man Joe judged to be in his fifties. His collar was folded inside his faded blue shirt and his several days' growth of beard gave him a disreputable, even criminal cast. A flimsy metal TV table to his right held an ice thermos, a glass pitcher half filled with water, and a pint of Old Grand Dad. Balanced on his right knee, no hand steadying it, was a tall glass containing a couple of ice cubes. Smoke curled up from a cigarette resting on the edge of a large glass ashtray on the chair's arm. Joe noted that it was crowded with a dozen or so butts. The man raised his bloodshot eyes and winked at Joe.

"Lak a whiskey, ma fren'?" he slurred. "This here's mighty fine, jes' 'bout the best." He held up the bottle and gestured with it invitingly, then half filled his glass.

"No thanks, it's not my drink of choice at the moment," said Joe, smiling. "Tell you what, though, I would like a double and some ice, if you can provide me with that. My wife's waiting out in our bus. We drove from Corpus Christi today, actually from Padre Island, and we're really beat."

"Say you'd like a double o'er ice? Here, I'll fetch another glass." The man put his glass on the TV table and started to raise himself. "Would yer missus join us for a lil nip?"

"No, no," said Joe, chuckling. "I mean, could you rent us a room for the night—a double? And we'd like some ice."

"Oh, sure thang!" he said, relaxing back into the chair. "Thought you was goin' join me in a little drinkee."

"Thanks, but not at the moment. Been driving for

almost ten hours and I think a shower is what we need first of all."

"Shoower thang, fren'!" said the man, with some difficulty getting to his feet and weaving over to a counter on the other side of the room. Joe followed him. "We has us a nice room with double bed an' TV in it. Plenty hot water, too, with thet sun out thar today. And it's air cooled, too. Just turn the thang on and it'll be a icebox in thar afore ya knows it. The room'll be six dollar plus tex."

Joe handed him a ten and signed the register. "Now if you could fix me up with a bucket of ice."

"Sure thang, fren'! I'll brang it down inna minute."

"Thanks," he said, picking up his change. "You won't forget our ice, will you? I want to pour some French wine over it in about two minutes."

"Oh, no, in fac', machine's right over thar in the corner," he said, pointing. "Ah kin git it rawht now."

"Oh, good, that'll save you a trip and you can get back to your program there," he said, nodding toward the TV, which he now realized had no sound accompanying the snow-flecked, flickering picture.

A Styrofoam bucket of ice in one hand and key in the other, he returned to the bus.

"Crazy dipsomaniac for a night clerk," he said as he started the engine. "Kind of a poor man's George Raft. All I could do to get a room and ice out of him without joining him in a high ball. Guess there's not much else to do in this town but soak it up and forget about it. Can't say I blame him."

"You don't think we should look at the room first?"

"No, it'll be all right, and I don't have the strength to drive another fifty feet anyway. There it is, on the end there, number nine."

The room turned out to be surprisingly clean and the furniture seemed almost new. Joe put ice into the two bathroom glasses, filled them with wine, and handed one to Jane. She disappeared with hers into the bathroom and the spray of the shower started in seconds. Joe sat in the Naugahyde chair taking long pulls from his drink. He had just poured himself another when Jane appeared with bath towel wrapped around her body and her hair in a hand towel, turban-style.

"You should do the same before you fall asleep, honey. It'll really revive you. And it feels so good to be clean again. There're more towels."

"Yeah, you're right," he agreed, standing up and dropping his cut-offs to the floor and pulling his T-shirt over his head.

She draped the damp towels over a straight-back chair and donned a terry-cloth burnoose that Margery had bought in Corpus Christi and given her as a parting gift. Consulting the Yellow Pages, she found a Corporal Sands Chicken Palace and called in an order of a basket of white and dark, fries, coleslaw, biscuits, apple pie, and coffee. She smiled upon hearing Joe's voice singing the Beatles' "With A Little Help From My Friends." Abruptly, both shower and song came to an end. She fixed herself another wine and, piling pillows up against the headboard, leaned back against them and began running a comb through her hair, humming the Beatles tune.

"You know, honey——," she began, as he emerged nude from the bathroom.

"What're we going to do about supper?" he broke in. "I'm suddenly ravenous, and there's nothing much left in the cooler."

"I sent out for barbecued chicken. It's on its way.

Better put some clothes on. You'll need something on anyway, it's so nice and cool in here already."

"Oy sai-ee, 'at's bul-l-ly, mite!" he said as he scooped up ice with his glass and filled it to its brim with wine. "Good thing Henry gave us four bottles of this 'cause this one is almost a dead soldier. Must have cost him an arm and a leg, what?"

"They were very generous, weren't they, honey? I just love this." She pulled the garment tighter. "I think I'll improvise a belt for when I answer the door. Don't want to appear *disreputable!*"

"Especially not in such a high-class hostelry as this. Our lush of a landlord would be *shamed!*"

"I'll have to meet him!"

"I'll arrange a formal introduction, mah deah." He chuckled. "Course, we still have a few bottles of ale. Remind me to put some ice in the cooler."

"Yes, an ale would be nice. I'm so parched from that dust. I started to say that it'll be nice to be away from the heat and all. I didn't realize how *tired* I was of *Texas!* It's so exciting to think of being near the mountains—and *trees!* There just doesn't seem to be anywhere to go to get away from the heat here—except Padre Island, and that was *just glorious!*"

"Yep, I do think I've had enough of this state," he said, rummaging in his duffel bag. "And in less than three-hundred miles we'll have seen the last of it." Pulling on a fresh pair of cut-offs and a clean T-shirt, he sat in the chair and put his feet up on the edge of the bed and yawned. "Yes, indeed, it shore were an experience, babe. Its unrelieved monotony of landscape and hellish climate were bad enough—not that we didn't learn how to deal with the heat—."

"*We had no choice!*" exclaimed Jane, laughing. "It was either that or just *dry up and blow away!*"

"Yeah, that house was a godsend—and there was always Barton Springs to cool off evenings," he said, restlessly shifting in his chair, then getting to his feet.

"And Hippie Hollow where we used to skinny dip, remember?"

"Yeah, that was great!" He smiled and then his expression turned serious. "I'll tell you, though, I'm glad I had the experience. 'Cause along with the Texas types— and you'll have to admit we encountered some strange folks—we made some of the best friends we'll ever have."

"Oh, sure, I agree," she said and then sighed. "I just hope we see some of them again."

"I'm sure we will," he assured her, then continued, clearly in a reflective mood, "but apart from the good friends we made and all the good times we had, what most interested me about it here—and remember that it was a first for me, too—was how totally different it is from anything I'd ever experienced before. 'Cause, remember, I'd only lived in the East, in Seattle, and in Canada before this."

"And Italy," she interrupted. "And Korea."

"Yeah, right. But I'm thinking in American terms. And I'd never really lived in the South before, leastwise not the *deep* South. And Texas is not even the South. In a sense, it's more like the West, and almost a different country— which it was for a spell, you know. Shit, I never lived anywhere people get shot at from passing cars! I thought that went out with Prohibition Chicago! Remember what Nando was telling us about those friends of his?"

"Oh, honey, I think our dinner has arrived!" She grabbed her wallet from the bed table and hurried to the door.

From where he was sitting, he could not see the delivery person and the hum of the window unit drowned out the minute or so of conversation.

"I got to try out a little of my Spanish, honey," she said, lowering the cardboard beer-case shell onto the coffee table and sitting on the floor.

"Your *Tex-Mex,* you mean!" he said, chuckling. "Don't think it would go over real well in Barcelona!"

"Oh, are you going to take me to Barcelona?" she said, removing items from the crowded box. "Oh, *what a feast!* Come over and get some of this."

Seated on the floor, he continued in the same vein as before as he alternately gestured with drumstick, French-fry, or bottle of ale across the foot-high table. "Like, your average man—or woman—on the street was friendly enough on the surface, but you never really knew what was lurking beneath that smile. Know what I mean?"

"Umm, this chicken is *scrumptious,* honey! I didn't realize how *famished* I was."

"Yeah, so am I, and this *is* delicious!"

"Why, thank you, sir! I know how to pick my take-aways, don't I?"

"You sure do, babe!" He took a bit from the drumstick. "You know, you wouldn't get away with eating like this in Italy! But I am just too bloody beat to go out to the bus and get us silverware."

Smiling with her mouth full, she waved a breast at him and swallowed.

"Joe, you'll never get over your genteel background, will you? *Silverware!* Honey, *no one* uses *silverware* anymore! We don't even *have any!* Don't you remember, you gave all your family silverware to your ex-wives!"

"Yes, I did, unfortunately—and some of it went back a couple of generations!"

"You were too generous!"

"Anyway, you never quite knew what they were really thinking as they stood there mouthing their 'Good mawnin's' and all those pleasantries about the weather and so forth and so on. But read the papers and they're *murdering* each other—*all the time!* Did you know that Texas is in first or second place in executions?" He selected a thigh, took a biscuit, and spooned coleslaw onto his paper plate. "You know, seeing Texas up close is something like finally seeing Joe McCarthy in person and realizing that he *really does* look like Herblock drew him— *maybe even more so!*"

"Well, as I told you at the Fish Tank, I don't know who he is, so I'll have to take your word for it, honey. But I agree with you that Texas was something else. And if you think it was a shock for you, what do you think it was for me, a farm girl from Ontario?"

"Gee, you got apple pie, too—and *java*. Think I'll just have me a piece of that."

Joe scooped up one of the slices of pie onto the flat of his hand.

"Guess they only provide plastic for coffee here."

"Honey, don't you think it was strange that we met up with the Pettibones?" she asked, as she placed her bone-filled paper plate into the beer case lid. "I mean, aside from your knowing—or knowing *of*—Henry, of all the people we could have shared that beach with, isn't it kind of weird that it would be a couple like that?"

"Yeah, you mentioned the coincidence of that before, my knowing of him through Jim and all and, yeah, that *was* kind of strange, to say the least." He slid the pointed end of the pie into his mouth, chewed briefly, and swallowed. "Even stranger was his knowing Milman Parry in the nineteen-twenties, when they were both at the Sorbonne and Parry was working on his dissertation on Homer. Of course, they would naturally have met up at Harvard after that." He sipped his coffee. "He asked me if I had found out why Parry shot himself in that Los Angeles hotel room in 1935 at the age of thirty-three. I said, 'Nope, I've read everything he wrote and everything about him I could get my hands on but still don't know the answer to that one.' And that I don't believe it was an accident, as some say."

"No, you don't get what I mean at all. Sure, that part was strange, very strange, but like you said, coincidences like that do happen, even stranger ones than that." She paused while she carefully cut off a small piece of pie with her plastic spoon. "No, what I meant was that we have so many things in common with them. I mean, look at us and then look at them. Margery's twenty-five or so years younger than Henry. They met at a college where he was teaching and she was a student and he left his wife to marry her. And then they didn't get married right away but lived together anyway for a couple of years. Don't you think all that is pretty strange?"

"Yeah, I guess I hadn't thought through all of that—although it may have been working on a subliminal level for me." He paused. "One or two details there don't match."

"Like?"

"I didn't leave my wife. Jyll split."

"Well, that's splitting hairs, honey, no pun intended. I really think it was mutual, you and Jyll breaking up. You have said you're still not sure who decided first, you know. Something like the chicken and egg conundrum."

"*Conundrum!* I like that!" He looked reflective for a moment. "Anyway, I still haven't figured out what went wrong with Jyll and me, except that I put her in a situation there in Napoli that made her feel like an old married woman with nothing to do except shop and keep house and be a faculty wife instead of the career professional woman she had grown up wanting to be—on the model of her mother, of course."

"I understand that part of it, honey. I'm a lot like her in that respect, as you know, despite our different backgrounds. In fact, we'd probably *like* each other—or *have* liked each other, under different circumstances." A smile flickered on her face, perhaps arising out of the irony of her observation. "Guess there's not much chance of that now!"

"Hardly!"

"But we're different, too, you know," she said, reaching out and touching his cheek. "I wouldn't treat you the way she did. I hope you know that."

With his mouth full of pie he could only nod in assent.

"She seems to have a sort of wild streak that gets in the way of her judgment sometimes, don't you think?"

"Yeah, she did, she sure did, one of the things that attracted me to her, I guess."

"To your undoing, sir!"

He laughed. "*You can say that again!* Good thing I didn't learn about it those couple of months I stayed in Napoli after she went back in the middle of the year. I'd have *really* gone over the deep end!"

"Oh, I think you did a pretty good job of that as it was, honey!"

"Yeah, *I sure did!*" He paused. "You know, I can deal

with all that now, even laugh about some aspects of it."

"Like the man with the bomb on the plane?" She smiled in a sympathetic way.

"*Ha!* You know, I was never so certain of anything in my life!"

"A bomb disguised as a sandwich!"

"Well, I think when he finally pulled it out of his bag I realized it was no bomb." He chuckled at the memory. "But if I'd known about her and Francesco——."

"You know, one of these days I'll piece all of that together, but so far it's like a jigsaw puzzle with missing pieces—quite a few missing pieces, actually."

"I guess I've suppressed a lot of that." He finished his coffee. "Maybe I should get it off my chest once and for all."

"Maybe you should, honey."

"I guess I had hints enough of what was going on but couldn't admit to myself that she would do that a couple months after we got married, especially considering how she always said how she wouldn't feel right doing it with anybody but me. In a way, I think she was making up for still being a virgin at twenty when we became lovers."

"She was curious, honey, wanted to know what it was like with someone else. And, after all, the guy was a *practiced seducer!*"

"*Indeed he was!* He knew all the moves! And talked about it a lot, all his affairs, one-night stands, and so forth."

"To Jyll, too?"

"*Oh, yes indeed!* How when he was teaching Italian at this girls' school he '*went right through that class!*' Jyll was *all ears* to *that!*"

"So he was on his way back here from Greece when

213

he stayed with you?"

"Yeah, for a week, in November. He'd been at the American School in Athens for a year. Brilliant young man, only nineteen, bilingual in Italian and French, could read German. *Quadra*-lingual, actually 'cause the sonovabitch even learned Modern Greek that year, to my envy!"

"I think you told me Jyll had known him for a while?"

"Yeah, for three years. They were in one of my summer classes together, in 1960. He was sixteen at the time, Jyll was eighteen. Also, she took a summer course on Aeschylus at Harvard a year before we went to Italy and he was in it, too. I remember meeting her in the Square for lunch one time and they came walking down the street together. I hadn't seen him for a couple of years and I was pretty surprised to see them together, had no idea he was in that seminar with her."

"I think I'm actually getting you to tell this story from the beginning for the first time. So how come he knew all these languages and was in graduate school so young?"

"His mother was Italian, married an American soldier who later was one of the early Fulbright scholars and eventually became a professor of art. Anyway, his father met his mother in Napoli when the Allies entered the city in October of 1943, got her pregnant, married her, brought her, and him, back here in 1945, and was back over there in 1946 on a Fulbright studying Italian painting. He had graduated from Harvard and finished all his course work for his doctorate just before the war. And his son, Francesco, followed in his ol' man's footsteps, enrolled at Harvard—*at the age of fifteen! In Classics.*"

"A real Whiz Kid!"

"Yep, he was that all right!"

"And a charmer from the word go!"

"Yep, a *cocksman* from the word go!" He smiled. "You know, I think I'd like another brew."

"I'd like one, too."

He got up and brought back two bottles of ale from the cooler, handing one to her.

"Would you be a sweetheart and get rid of the ice in my glass, please?" she asked him, smiling.

When he returned he uncapped the bottles with the opener on his pocketknife and filled her glass.

"Honey, I just love it when we sit and talk like this!"

"You mean *I* talk and *you* listen is more like it, babe." He took a swing from the bottle.

"Well, you have a lot to talk about, honey, not like my couple of boyfriends and—."

"And *girl*-friends?"

"Well, we won't talk about *that!*"

"Some day I'll get you plastered and get all that out of you—*in detail!*"

"We'll just *see* about *that!*"

"Where was I?"

"He was a charmer—a *cocksman*, as you so delicately put it."

"Oh, yeah—and *beautiful*, too."

"Beautiful?"

"He was very slender, had a figure like a teenage girl, and jet-black hair." He took another swig. "And, you know, he was the first guy I knew personally who let his hair grow long."

"This was 1963?"

"Right."

"Inspired by the Beatles, no doubt."

"Yeah, they hadn't made it to the States yet, not till

February the next year, but he'd seen them in England."

"So he had this mop of ebony black hair and a figure like a girl. Handsome?"

"You better believe it! Those Italian features from his mother and a lighter complexion than hers from his Wasp ol' man. Very effeminate cast to his features—as well as his whole way of handling himself. I thought at first he was queer, but he soon straightened me out on that with his tales of conquest and so forth. You know, the way I figure it, he appealed to women's mothering instinct, that was his secret. They would take him to their bosom, baby him."

"So Jyll told you about their little affair on the phone a week or so after the Susie thing, after she split?"

"*Sure did!*" He tilted the bottle up, drained it in two swallows, and belched. "*Ah-h-h!*"

"Getting even!"

"Yep, getting even."

"What'd she say?"

"She said," he began, his voice rising in volume, "that she '*beat me to it.!*' She said that she and Frankie—I'd never heard anybody call him that before, he was always 'Francesco', so maybe that was her pet name for him. Well, that they had become lovers during that week he stayed with us in Napoli, that they had spent every morning in bed while I was teaching." He finished off his ale. "*Seven fucking mornings!* Couple of afternoons, too, when I had my seminars. *Right under my nose and I didn't see it!* Or *did* I?"

"Oh, honey!" she said soothingly.

"At this point it's difficult for me to separate the details of what she told me from my own creative imagination."

"You and your *creative imagination!*" she exclaimed and sipped some ale. "Try to concentrate on *what she actually said!*"

"Well, I do recall that she made a point of describing how the first time happened. She reminded me how I always brought a cup of coffee in to her in bed before I left and how I didn't that morning. She also reminded me that she had been saying the night before, as we were all finishing off a bottle of wine, how she liked to sleep in sometimes and would probably do so in the morning since it was so late. And that I shouldn't bring her coffee like I usually did. We had been talking about what she could show Francesco around Napoli and I recall something about how they wouldn't have time for the Museo Archeologico if they were going to meet me for lunch so they'd just take a drive and check out the Museo in the afternoon. I walked to school so she always had the car. In case you forgot, the guy was born there, so naturally just about anywhere you turned there was something he wanted to see. He hadn't been back there since he was a year old."

"I did forget that."

"So anyway, she told me that he took the hint and brought her a cup of *caffè con latte* soon after I left. She said when he woke her she sat up and pulled the sheet up to cover her tits."

"She was *nude?*"

"*Nekkid as a jaybird!* We had made love that morning and then she went back to sleep."

"Your Jyll was one horny little girl!"

"*Sure was!*" He got up and went over to the cooler and took out the last bottle of ale, returned to his seat on the floor, and opened it. "So he sits on the edge of the bed and watches her drink the *caffè con latte*. She's holding the cup in one hand and the sheet up to her neck with the other."

"I'm assuming this is part creative imagination and part what she told you?"

"I couldn't say. It's all very real to me." He began rolling a cigarette. "Actually, I think I'm being pretty accurate. She went into a lot of detail in that phone call." He held the flame of the Zippo to the cigarette and drew deeply. "When she finishes the *caffè con latte* he takes the cup from her and puts it on the table beside the bed. Then he leans forward and kisses her. At first, she doesn't respond, but as he works his tongue in between her lips she puts her arms around his neck and lets the sheet drop. He begins sucking the nipples of her breasts and works his tongue down to her belly button and then her pussy. When he has her wet enough he doffs his knee-length bathrobe and enters her and she wraps her legs around him and—."

"Joe, stop! You're getting carried away! Jesus! And you're making me horny as hell!"

He exploded in laughter, his face flushed.

"You expect me to believe she told you all that?"

"Actually, most of that she did. I think she stopped about there, but I know how it went from then on. I was married to the girl, after all. So I was rather familiar with her style. And most of that style I taught her, virgin that she was. Want me to go on, supplementing it with—?"

"*No*, I *don't* want you to go on!" She smiled. "But I think it does you good to talk about it—*up* to a *point,* that is."

"You're a good listener, babe. You know, I couldn't hardly mention MacKenzie's name to her, she was so jealous. She'd say something like, 'Oh, isn't this *romantic*, Joe, hearing all about your *ex-wife*—your *second* ex-wife!' *Sarcastical as hell!* Not that I ever went into any detail like what I've told you."

"I have no reason to be jealous, honey, 'cause *I've got you*—and *I'm* gonna *keep you!*' She winked at him.

"Well, I ain't goin' nowheres, babe, you can *depend on that!*" He was silent for a moment as he strove to regain the course of his narrative. "So that's how it went that week, every morning, couple of afternoons. Oh, I forgot, she told me she even snuck down the hall one night *after I was asleep!*"

"She really took a chance there!"

"I think she went a little out of her mind over that guy. I mean, look at it. She's twenty-one, he's nineteen, *looks* like he's *sixteen*, he's her second ever lover. The girl's *hot to trot!*" He drew on the cigarette and blew three perfect smoke rings toward the ceiling. "And you know something? She claimed to be squeaky clean that whole time up until she caught Susie and me and split. A year or so later Linda told me that Jyll started seeing 'Frankie' as soon as she got back to Cambridge from Napoli!"

"Really!"

"In her letters to me those two months I stayed in Napoli before going out of my skull she mentioned bumping into him in Widener and having lunch with him. Every few letters his name would turn up. Just innocent-sounding little mentions, you know, but it was like she just had to say his name. And since I was blind to what had gone down in Napoli, I didn't think anything of it."

"Well, honey, I just hope Jyll has found happiness." Walking on her knees, she came around to his side of the coffee table and sat on his lap. "I know how much you and Jyll loved each other, honey, and I think it was a very special kind of love for both of you. I think you had a lot of things in common and I think you both brought things to the relationship, good things, different things, for each other. It was just the wrong time for both of you and, as you've admitted, the circumstances were wrong, for both of you. They should never have sent you back to Italy so soon after what happened the first time, especially with a brand new wife, and her just beginning on her dissertation and all. And when you really come down to it, honey, neither of you was ready for marriage. You were still suffering from the awful break-up with MacKenzie and I think Jyll really needed to live some before she got herself tied down. She was so bookish, so intellectual, so involved in her studies, she doesn't seem to me to have ever taken much time to go out and have a good time and—."

"Get laid!"

"Yes, get laid!"

"It still puzzles me that she got so upset when she saw Susie and me that night. I mean, look what *she'd* been doing! She fucked him twenty or so times that week." He sighed. "She claimed they did it *three times* most mornings."

"Oh, once was not enough for Jyll either—like me?"

"Evidently! And she and I *never* did it a *third* time! It *really* upset me when she told me that! Oh, they did it all—everything we did and *then some!*"

"Well, I've never done it more than once with anyone else, honey." She snuggled up to him. "Anyway, it wouldn't have mattered to her that she had already been unfaithful to you. She'd *still* be furious. Men and women both practice double standards. You know that, honey."

"How true!"

"And the way you flaunted it, taking Susie for drinks in the Square and all, how can you blame her for being upset?" She pulled herself closer to him and kissed him on the mouth. "But, you know, Joe, the part you never seem to be able to admit and the thing you should stop torturing yourself about is that your affair with Susie that Jyll caught onto was your way of splitting, too. It wasn't just Jyll splitting, it was *both* of you."

"Yeah, I guess if I had thought we had a chance, I wouldn't have been screwing around like that."

"Well, what can I say except that I'm *glad you got caught!*"

He kissed her.

"You know, honey," she began in a summing-up tone, "Jyll would never have gone along with the drop-out scene. She wanted her career too much. And even though she asked you later to come to California and try again, would she really have gone along with you, and supported you, while you tried to find yourself? For that matter, how long would post doctoral research in jazz history, or photography school, or whatever have *satisfied* you? You were too close to dropping out of *everything*, honey! I would have given you two, three months, at most, and Jyll would have kicked you out—or you would have split. One or the other."

It impressed him that she was able to see so clearly into the circumstances of Jyll's and his demise.

"You're pretty insightful there, babe."

"I know!" she said, smiling.

"It still upsets me that Francesco did that. You know, guest in my house and all. And it *surprised* me, *too!* At first, you know, I didn't believe Jyll—or didn't *want* to believe her. But she soon convinced me it was all true." He paused. "I mean, the guy *deferred* to me, he *respected* me. After all, I had even been his *teacher,* for *chrissakes!* At a summer school session, a Homer seminar. Jeez, he was *sixteen* at the time! And reading Greek better than any of my graduate students!"

"I would suppose that just added to his appeal for Jyll. I mean, he had quite a mind, right?"

"Yeah, she did admire brains, no doubt about that. I mean, that was a big part of *our* relationship." He picked up the empty bottle and examined the label. "You know, I think that may have been one of my longer Plutarchian digressions. How did I get going on Jyll and all that?"

"We were talking about the Pettibones," she reminded him, returning to the subject. "It's pretty weird when you think about it. Like, remember when we were over there having dinner with them and you and Henry were in their camper listening to the radio? Well, Margery told me a lot of things about when they first met and how they started living together, how Henry used to visit her afternoons in this tiny little attic room she lived in and then how he left his wife and moved out and they eventually got a bigger apartment together. And things like that. I told you how she said it was a big scandal and all and how some of his friends took his wife's side and others his? Well, doesn't all of that kind of remind you of something?"

"Oh, sure, I can't hardly think of one friend of Jyll and me who's kept in touch with both of us—except Linda, oddly. But it's often like that when a couple breaks up."

"I don't see why you think it's so strange that Linda keeps in touch with both of you"

"She was Jyll's best friend, babe!"

"But you and Linda were very close, honey, don't

forget that." She hesitated, seeming to ponder what she had just said. "A little *too* close, in fact—but I guess that sort of thing does sometimes happen, even with best friends."

"So what it really comes down to is that we met up with a couple who fit some of the pattern of our getting together when I left my wife—or she left me or we left each other—and so forth and so on. Doesn't strike me as especially coincidental."

"No, listen, it was more than that, honey. You still don't see what I'm getting at about how weird it was listening to Margery. It was like she was trying to tell me something. It was like she had to talk to someone about all that ancient history of her and Henry's years together, but also that she was trying to tell me something."

"You mean the difference in their ages and all that, sure. Actually, Henry's twenty-seven years older than Margery. It's only seventeen between us, babe. Does that bother you?"

"You know it doesn't, honey. I've made that clear already—*many* times, for God's sake!" Jane reached over and took his hand. "No, it was just so strange that we should meet up with a pair like them who are, well, *kinda* like us, if you know what I mean."

"Yeah, I see what you mean, like a mirror image in a way. Funny."

"In a way, I think Margery was trying to reassure me. I think they've had a really good life together. They seem to spend most of their time reading and writing, from what I gather—and traveling. I mean, when Margery's not teaching. They love to travel. I guess they've been all over the world."

"Yeah, Henry told me a little about how they visited

the battlefields where he saw action in the First World War, and some visits they made to England. They even went to Japan a few years ago for a month or so. Yeah, they do get around. We'll have to do that, too. I really want to take you to Italy and Greece. I'd like to see Scotland, too, where my earliest roots are, I guess."

"And France, don't forget France. I want to see Paris. And Barcelona. And Japan, honey. I want to see that bartop entertainment you saw there." She chuckled. "Makes me horny *just to think about it!*" She sipped coffee. "That's right, Margery told me Henry was in that war, that awful war, and that he saw some terrible things."

"I couldn't get much out of him about that. And I guess we wouldn't even have gotten on the subject except I was telling him about Sam Casey and the fiftieth anniversary of the Argonne campaign coming up and the Armistice celebration in Corpus Christi and all that. Henry was very interested 'cause he was actually in that campaign. He was an artillery battery captain. Battlefield commission from first sergeant after all the battery's officers had met their maker. I told him about Sam, that he was a combat rifleman. Course, I didn't yet have all the details that Sam filled in for us this morning."

"*Chilling!*" She shuddered.

"About all Henry would say was that it was '*hell five times over!*' and that he still has the occasional nightmare about it." He had gotten to his feet to carry the box of trash to the can in the corner and as he resumed his seat in the chair and began rolling a cigarette he looked over at Jane, who was leaning on her elbows on the coffee table.

"He was twenty, four years younger than you are right now," he said, taking out his tobacco pouch and papers. "And Sam Casey was not yet out of his teens. I figure

Sam was nineteen when he took that shrapnel. And still eighteen when he rushed that hill and took that machine gun nest. Shot two Germans in the face and put his bayonet through the third's neck. Nice, huh? It's funny he wouldn't tell me any more than that when we stopped there on our way to Padre Island. And only that little bit because I spotted the bayonet on the wall of the barn after you were already in the bus waiting to go. Then when we stopped there this morning he left that out—but he really opened up! *What a story!*"

"You didn't tell me about the machine gun nest."

"Didn't want to spoil the rest of the drive for you."

"Thanks," she said, blowing him a kiss. "But *how horrible!* Putting a bayonet into someone's neck! How can someone *do that?*"

"*Kill or be killed!* Yeah, it's pretty horrible, that's for sure. I put bayonets into sand bags in basic but never had to into a person. Course I was mostly behind the lines in my kitchen."

"Why do people have to fight wars?"

"It's been going on for a while," he said, striking a wooden match with his thumbnail and holding it to the cigarette. He drew deeply and allowed the smoke to slowly drift out as he leaned back, staring at the ceiling for a moment, then turned to her. "Read your Homer if you want to learn what hand-to-hand combat is all about."

"Did you know that Margery is taping Henry's life story?"

"No, I didn't know that."

"Yes, Margery said she has almost enough for a book but she has to listen to it and take it down and then she said she has to check a lot of stuff. Not the personal stuff but dates and titles of books and articles Henry's written, and stuff like that." She began to laugh. "That's going to be quite a book!"

"Why's that, babe?"

"Oh, because Henry doesn't seem to want to hold anything back. Margery says it's going to be worse—or *bette*r—than the autobiography of somebody Harris or other."

"*My Life and Loves*, the autobiography of Frank Harris," he supplied. "Well, he'll have to go some to match Frank Harris." He chuckled.

"Margery said Henry stayed over in France for six months after World War I and used cigar coupons to travel all over the country. She said he'd just get on a train—and of course he was still in uniform with medals on his jacket and all—and salute the conductor and sign a cigar coupon and hand it to him and take a seat in the first class section."

"*That's rich!*" he said, laughing.

"Margery said he balled so many French women the other officers called him Henry Petergash," she said, flushing slightly.

"*That old rascal!*" he said, slapping his thigh. "And they're putting stuff like *that* in the book?"

"Oh, yes! She said Henry wants it to be a sort of modern-day Rabelais. He told her, 'What do I have to lose at this time of life?' She said she's only being careful about hurting people and libel and things like that."

"That is gonna be *one helluva book*, I'll say that!"

"I know some things that aren't going to make it into that book."

"What would that be, babe?"

"Oh, some things Marge told me about her own life."

"Frinstance?"

"Like when Henry lost interest in sex for a while about five years ago after he had an operation, she had an affair." She was now on the bed leaning back against the pillows, her legs curled up beneath her. "And, you know, honey, I think she's had some others since then."

"The plot thickens again! Did she go into any details? I'm all ears."

"Not much—except that that first affair was with one of her graduate students, a guy about ten years younger than her. And he was married. But he got a teaching post somewhere in another state and she doesn't see him anymore. That's why I think she's still having affairs."

"Why's that?"

"Because she said something like she didn't want that part of her life to come to an end. She said something like, 'Hank was a hell-raiser from his teens through his forties so it's not right that I have to have a half-life.' And she said something about how women last longer that way than men, anyway, and that it's *women* who need younger men, not *men* needing younger women." She paused abruptly and looked him in the eyes. "You know something, I think she was still a virgin when they met. Something she said gave me that impression. Would you believe?"

"Sounds like you two really hit it off, babe."

"Well, like I said, she seemed like she had to have somebody to tell all that stuff to—and I was there. And I guess the wine loosened her up a bit. But there was something else, honey. I mean, I really think they both kinda thought of me like a daughter or something. She never had any children and I guess she was too close in age to Henry's daughters to think of them as daughters. The younger one is in her late thirties now and the other

227

in her forties, a year younger then Margery. The younger one is on her third husband and the other one never got married—the professor of law, the one they visited in Chicago on their way here. I forget where she said the one with all the kids lives." She snickered. "I have to laugh at Marge and her sense of humor, honey. She said her step-daughter should write her autobiography and call it *Life Under Three Husbands!*"

"*Ha!* That's a good one! And it sounds like *you* could just about write their family history."

"Well, she didn't tell me much more. At least I can't think of anything else." She drummed her fingers absently on his kneecap, for he was still seated in the chair and his legs were pressed against the bed. "Oh, wait, there was something about a French girl Henry had an affair with, in the 1920s when he was over there with his first wife—her name was Simone. He started seeing her again when he was in England during the war, the one I was born during. She was Jewish and she came to England around 1939. But she went back to France after the war and Henry was never able to find out anything about where she was. Her whole family just disappeared. Isn't that awful? I knew folks like that back home. I mean, where only one person survived and could never trace any relatives. One of my best girl friends—she was adopted—was like that. So sad."

Neither spoke for a minute or so. She rested her hand on his thigh and he cupped her hand with his.

"Yes sir, they are two individuals, they are!" he said. "You know, when you stop to think of it, their time together, plus Henry's history before they ever met, is a real slice of American social and intellectual history. Henry would have been riding in a horse and carriage in his early years and now they get on an airplane and they're in Paris in a few hours. Then look at how Henry was raised in that Victorian New England world. No wonder he finds it hard to deal with some of the things happening today. Like, remember him grumbling about how—. What was that he said? Oh, yeah, 'You women have it better than we men do now! *What the hell else do you want?*' Remember that?"

"Oh, yeah. Well, Margery says that's mostly him being 'his curmudgeonly self.' She says he's always had a reputation for that and for saying what he thinks. I guess he's not exactly the diplomatic type. But she said he really believes it's right that women have started to get their due and all. She told me that in some ways he was ahead of her in believing in women's rights—and still is, in some ways. She said he took stands at some college in Iowa—or maybe it was Ohio, I still get them mixed up—where he was a visiting professor and he was supporting tenure for women and things like that and it didn't make him too popular with the other professors."

She fell asleep an hour later while they were watching a movie and he turned the TV off and went out to check the bus. Then he noticed that the office light was on and remembered that he had sort of promised to join the clerk in a nightcap when he got more ice for the cooler. Curious what shape the man would be in, he decided to wander down that way and take a look.

The sun was high in the sky as they crossed the line into New Mexico and it was late afternoon when Jane alerted Joe to keep an eye out for 285, which would take them north toward Santa Fe. From there it was only an hour to the commune near Taos that Melinda had told her about. She suggested that once they got past Santa Fe they begin to look for a place to camp overnight. She had bought cans of corn beef hash and beef stew, bread, butter, jam, cheese, milk, and eggs at a store across the street from where they had gassed up in Lubbock, and a very hung-over Eddie the motel clerk had sold him a case of beer and given him a huge Styrofoam cooler half full of ice to keep it in. She pointed out that it would be better to see the commune in daylight and then decide whether they wanted to stay the night there. He agreed, adding that by the time they pulled over today he wouldn't be fit company for anyone.

Two hours later found the Greenbrier beneath a tree in a grove a mile or so from the highway. She had come back from a visit to the woods. He had opened the double doors and was bent over and reaching under the bed. He pulled a box out and placed it on the ground, then lowered the door-mounted table.

"We are definitely gonna have to bundle up before the cool air moves in!" he said, handing a bulky sweater to Jane. "We are in the foothills of the Sangre De Cristo Range—and the river will bring the temperature down some, too."

It was dusk when he dipped the soapy dishes, utensils, and frying pan in boiling water, wiped them dry, and packed them neatly into the apple box. He poured the half a cup of still-warm water from the coffee pot over his hands, rubbed them together, shook the water off, and dried his hands on his jeans.

"Aren't you finished yet, honey?" she called to him from the bus.

"Be right there, babe."

He stepped up into the bus and sat on the edge of the bed.

"I don't think I'll have any trouble sleeping tonight," he said, sighing.

"Shhh," she said, pointing out the open door. They both froze and listened.

"Some animal or other. Shit, hope it's not a grizzly or a cougar or something," he whispered and leaned forward. "Hell, it's a *dog* and he's sniffing around where I buried the trash."

He ceased his pawing of the ground and looked up. His tail commenced to wag tentatively. Joe slowly let himself down onto the ground and patted himself on the thigh. The dog cautiously moved forward and came to a stop a couple of feet from the bus. Joe bent over and let his hand hang down to knee-height. The dog edged forward, sniffed the hand, licked it gently, and looked up into his eyes.

"It's okay there, boy," he said softly and very slowly raised his hand and caressed the top of the dog's head. "Good boy, good boy."

"He's so thin, honey," she whispered, lying on her side. "What is he, some kind of hunting dog?"

"Some breed or other of spaniel—or maybe hound," he replied as he scratched behind the dog's ears with both hands. "He looks half-starved to death. I suppose if we feed him we'll never get rid of him!"

"Well, we can hardly chase him away! Why don't you see if he'll eat some of that hash, honey. I got six cans of it."

The dog spent the night stretched out on the front

seat of the bus. It was in the morning while they were sitting on a log waiting for the water to heat for their instant coffee that he named him.

"He's very pretty," she said, "or perhaps I should say handsome, since he's a boy dog."

"A boy dog!" he said, chuckling.

"I just love his color," she continued, ignoring his jibe, "and the pattern of his coat. It's sort of a speckled red."

"Then we'll call him Rufus Perryman."

"I'm not going to ask where in the world you found that name for him," she said, looking at him quizzically, "because then I'd have to explain to people why we call our dog—what was it?"

"Rufus Perryman."

"Okay, I'll call him Rufe."

A half-hour later they were on their way, eating bread and jam and sipping second mugs of coffee. She had the road map on her lap and Rufus was lying on a tarp she had spread out on the bed.

"Where do you suppose he came from, honey, some farm or ranch or what?" She turned and glanced back at the dog. "They certainly didn't take very good care of him, poor dear."

"I think Rufus has been on the lam a while, my dear. My guess is he got in the way of some hunters. He's got some scars."

"I don't understand. You think he was killing sheep?"

"No, no!" he said, amusement in his voice. "On the lam—el, aye, em—is an expression, means running from the law, a fugitive. I think Rufus here has been on his own for a while, maybe months." He tilted the rearview mirror down and glanced at it. "He looks pretty worn down to me. But he seems willing enough to adapt to the good life—don't you, boy?"

"Oh, look, Joe, he knows you're talking about him," she said, studying the dog's image in the mirror on the back of the now lowered visor. "You know, if what you say is true—and from the looks of him you're probably right—I think the only thing we could rightfully do was take him with us. I mean, even if he did belong to someone, they surely don't deserve to have him, far as I'm concerned. We always had dogs around at home and even if they slept in the barn they were well fed and everything." She studied the dog. "Why, he's just *gaunt!* How can people *treat* animals like that? *Honestly!* Did you see how he wolfed his breakfast?"

"Yeah, he would have finished off another couple of cans if we'd offered them to him, no doubt about it." He yawned. "I really needed that ten hours last night, babe, really needed it."

Melinda had told Jane the commune was a couple of miles off 522 about twenty miles north of Taos. About halfway there they came upon a hitchhiker. His crew cut and clean-shaven face inspired Joe to remark, "Pretty straight looking cat, what?"

"Straight or crooked, honey, we have no room for another passenger, especially with that huge backpack he's carrying."

"Right," he said as, hands raised from the steering wheel, he gestured to the hitchhiker their inability to help him. He smiled and nodded in return, turned, and continued walking.

"'Deep Gully'," he said as they approached the sign announcing Arroyo Hondo. "We'll have to find that bridge before we leave here."

"I just love these little towns, Joe. It's like being in Mexico."

"Si, an' you lahwv the-e-eze stee-ee-en-kink ombrays who lee-e-ve he-e-er?" he said very slowly, "you la-ah-wv them, too, señorita?"

"Melinda said there'll be a sign about a mile from here," she said, pointing to notes in the map's margin, "a peace sign, honey—see?"

"You want me to eyeball the map before or after we land in the ditch, babe?"

"No, keep your eyes on the road, dear."

"Could that be it there on the tree?" he said, gearing down into second.

"Oh, yes! How clever—and *artistic,* too," Jane enthused. "You almost don't notice it, it's so natural like."

Indeed, thirty or so feet from the ground the tree's trunk and two limbs that hung down like arms were framed in a wreath of a yard's diameter.

"Nice," he agreed, "very nice. Now all we have to do is negotiate that Indian path there." He turned the bus into the dirt road and stopped.

"Do you think we'll fit, honey? It's so narrow."

"Oh, sure, we'll make it just fine. Looks like someone has done a little trimming of branches—which is nice 'cause it'll keep us from losing any gear topside." He put the Greenbrier in low gear and let the idle move it forward. "We'll just take it slo-o-w-w and ea-ea-s-sy."

Rufus was standing directly behind them and looking intently through the windshield. The road was bumpy but well maintained and he was even able to cruise in second gear for stretches. About twenty minutes had passed when they came to an open field. Vehicles—several vans, a Cadillac hearse of 1940s vintage, an ancient milk delivery truck, two VW Beetles, three VW buses, and a huge many-hued school bus that appeared to have been splattered from one end to the other with buckets of paint—were parked to the left and right.

The field rose a hundred yards to a circular, domed structure of wood. The building had a balcony-like walkway just below its roof and large windows, spaced ten feet or so apart, beneath this catwalk. Atop a flagpole that jutted from the center of the dome was a weather vane in the shape of the peace symbol. Of stainless steel and flashing in the morning sun, it caught their eyes as they alighted from the Greenbrier. They stood transfixed.

"I swear to Christ, babe, that thing is sending a message. I wish I knew Morse code. Then again, maybe it has its own language."

"It's hypnotizing, isn't it?" she said, slinging her shoulder bag behind her. "Well, shall we see what gives up there?"

*"Diamo, carina!"**

---

* Lets go, dearest!

Chapter 7

WHERE THE REET MEET TO EAT

"Oh, that air is so nice," she sighed, "after that awful Texas heat, isn't it?"

"Sure is, babe, sure is."

"I think I'm going to like Colorado. According to the book here, we'll be a little more than a mile above sea level. So it should be nice, summers."

"What's the elevation here, can you find that?"

"Let's see now," she said, leaning down over the map on her lap. "Oh, here it is, seven-thousand, eight-hundred, and thirty-four feet. And, Joe, we're almost in Colorado! Isn't that *exciting?*" She took up the AAA book again and studied it for a minute or so. "We'll have to come back this way some time and visit the town, honey, it looks really interesting, this whole area, in fact."

"Yeah, we'll do that. Plenty of time for trips after we get settled in, babe, plenty of time."

Determined to arrive at the college by mid-afternoon,

they had pushed off from the commune after breakfast and now, an hour before noon, were already at Raton Pass. She unwrapped the two peanut butter and jelly sandwiches she had made that morning, handed one to him, and filled their mugs with mint tea from the thermos.

"Ever consider becoming a vegetarian like the Peaceful Folk, Joe?"

"I really think I'd miss my steaks and southern fried chicken too much to do that. Anyway, they aren't strict vegetarians, they talked about catching fish in the stream and cooking them over a campfire."

"Yes, but they don't eat anything that's slaughtered and I kind of like that idea, don't you? Doesn't it bother you at all to think of that?"

"I tell you, I have a simple solution to that problem."

"What?"

"I don't think about it," he said, smiling.

They were silent for a moment and then he glanced at her.

"Tell me, did you find those people just a little odd or something?" he said.

"Well, they were a lee-e-tle stra-a-ange, I do admit that—but in a nice sort of way, don't you think?"

"Yeah, there were some interesting types there, but I'm not at all sure I could stand being around them on a steady basis."

"You didn't seem to mind watching them massage each other out in the sun, did you, honey?" she said, smirking.

"Now wasn't that something? And nobody seemed to mind being eyeballed, did they?"

"I think they were showing off, that's what I think!

Course, I do have to say, some of them had something to show off!"

"I'll go along with that, babe, I'll certainly go along with that!"

"I thought you would," she said, chuckling. "I don't think wild horses could have dragged you away!"

"One thing that puzzles me is what the hell do they live on? I mean, they do have a garden and some laying hens and some of the women make necklaces and leather stuff that they sell to some tourist shop, but that sure can't amount to much. You saw the load of stuff that station wagon brought from town, right? You know what I think? I bet they're subsidized by their families or someone—or someone there has a nice bank account. How else could they pay the rent and the grocery bill? No one there has a job."

"I know what I forgot to ask you, honey, what were you and that guy who lived down at the end of the hall talking about, the one with all the books in his room? He seemed kind of interesting."

"Oh, yeah, the writer. Another ex-professor. You know, he made me want to read some of D. H. Lawrence's novels again. Did you know that Lawrence lived around there for a couple of years back in the early twenties. And I'd liked to read that woman's memoir about Lawrence when he was there, too. I can't remember her name—something Plymouth or other? And there's a sort of shrine to Lawrence not far from the commune. That guy I was talking to is convinced that Lawrence was into peyote, that he was tripping. He and Aldous Huxley were close friends—Lawrence and Huxley, I mean—and Huxley visited Lawrence in Taos. He thinks Huxley tried peyote with Lawrence. Or maybe that was after Lawrence died. I actually can't remember whether he said Huxley came to Taos to see Lawrence or what. We were both pretty zonked on that hash. It was a pretty funny conversation, when you come right down to it. Of course, Huxley got into all kinds of dope in the fifties, I already knew that, and I read somewhere that his wife gave him—at his request, I mean—gave him acid on his deathbed. I think he died about a decade ago, something like that. *Hey*, are your ears popping?"

His query meeting with silence, he looked aside at her. "Hey, ya done drop off there, hon," he said, his delivery taking on the thick speech of the "mush-mouthed hillbilly," as he had designated it in his mental catalogue of voices.

"Well, that doesn't portend too well for my looming lecture hall presence, do it?" he said. Gulping air, he found his thoughts returning to the two days and nights and brief morning they had spent with the two-dozen or so Peaceful Folk who resided in the handsomely designed structure on the hill. There had been plenty of fine grass and some, as Tea and Hardon would say, "outasight!" hash around, and he and Jane had joined in on a hookah that had been fired up after supper both evenings. Mescaline had been offered them but they declined, neither feeling that they wanted to risk a downer on the eve of their arrival at the college.

And I sure wasn't going to drop anything and go up on that bridge with them, Rio Grande or no Rio Grande. From what Jane read me about the thing I think that could be pretty scary, I do. Sorry to have missed the sights, folks, but that can wait until we take a trip down thisaway.

He glanced at her again, noting that she was still asleep. Pulling up to a pump at a gas station on the outskirts of Trinidad, he picked up the map from her lap and mumbled to himself as he estimated that they had about 225 miles to go.

"They got coffee to go in there?" he inquired of the attendant, nodding toward the diner across the road.

"Shore do, pardner, shore do, best coffee these parts!" the man answered, turning his head aside and letting go with a stream of dark tobacco juice. "Counter girl's name's Mabel, we calls her Able Mabel. You tell her The Cowboy sent you, she'll treat ya *real nice,* she will." He leered at Joe from beneath his wide-brimmed hat, took the bill from him, and made change from a wad he pulled from his shirt pocket.

Returning to the van with two Styrofoam cups of steaming coffee, he discovered that she had crawled back onto the mattress and was sound asleep. He finished his coffee before continuing on the interstate that would take them to Denver, he figured, in about three hours. From there it would be less than an hour to the little college town a few miles from Boulder.

Watching the needle climb to seventy, he suddenly remembered the dream he had awakened from in the middle of the night, a recurring one over the years but one that he could not recall having had for several years, perhaps not since he had left Canada.

The details differed but the dream was the same in its general outline. That is, its essential pattern was consistent even though the location, point in time, and *dramatis personae* varied from dream to dream. For instance, it sometimes took place during his childhood or teens at one of the rural or small-town schools he had attended in Anne Arundel County, Maryland, sometimes when he was at one or another of the three universities of his undergraduate and graduate years, and sometimes seemed to be happening at some indeterminate time over the course of his teaching career. Location was often a blend of early and later life, rendering him confused, upon waking, as to whether, in the dream, he had been student or instructor.

The basic pattern of the dream had him standing at the front of a classroom, unprepared. Often it was a case of simply having forgotten his notes or, as in one recurring nightmare, his carefully rehearsed oral report on *Oliver Twist* had vanished from his memory. His riveting account of the book had in 1938 held rapt his sixth grade classmates, but in the terrifying nocturnal scenario he rose from his desk and, realizing that his mind was a blank, stumbled forward to the front of the room, tears welling up in his eyes, his fellow students smiling up at him in expectation, the teacher (never recognizable) withdrawing to a desk at the back of the room. It was at this point, when he turned and faced the class, that he routinely awoke, sometimes sobbing.

The dream of the night before had him in the role of professor entering a large class room as the clock clicked onto the hour, stepping up to the lectern, opening his file folder, and discovering to his horror that he was staring at a blank sheet of paper. Red faced and stuttering an apology that he had forgotten his notes, he was greeted with uproarious laughter, ostensibly arising from his admission that he needed notes from which to lecture on a subject that was his specialty.

"*Jesus God!* How many more times will I have to go through *that?*" he said aloud. "What a relief it is to wake up and realize it was only a dream! I wonder if it'll really happen some day."

"What's that, dear?" she said, half sitting up from the mattress, then dropping back down onto the pillow she was hugging and falling back asleep.

It was a little after three when they pulled into Vista, the small Colorado town where Hopkins College was located. Joe had gotten a second wind and Jane, who had had a good long sleep from which she awoke only after they had left Denver behind, was fresh and alert.

"Let's take a few minutes and check out this burg," he suggested, "and then find that motel John recommended."

" Good idea, and after we get a room let's go out to eat. I'm sick of peanut butter sandwiches and corn beef hash."

"Sure, we'll have ourselves a feed, we will, maybe a porterhouse and baked spuds, nice salad, bottle of wine, shoot the works. After all, I'm on salary as of this week."

"Stop it, honey, you're making my mouth water! I'm starving! But it is a nice thought that we'll have a regular income for a change, instead of constantly dipping into our rapidly depleting savings."

There was little activity on the campus except on a couple of streets given over to fraternity houses, and even here it was evident that the main body of students had not yet arrived. The groups of three or four sitting on the steps of the houses, or the odd loner walking along the sidewalk or crossing the street, clearly represented that vanguard of student organizers sent ahead to prepare the houses and plan the first parties of the season, he conjectured. So, following John Chalmers Brown's advice, they headed out the road along the creek to the motel.

A small restaurant a few blocks from the campus that billed itself above its door as "FRITZ'S GRILL—WHERE THE REET MEET TO EAT" attracted his eye.

"Say, that seems a possibility. Want to check it out?"

"Sure, I could eat a cow! Let's do it, you can park right in front there."

As they were crossing the sidewalk, a thickly-bearded man of compact build and shoulder-length dark hair dressed in jeans, denim shirt, and cowboy boots and sitting on the low brick ledge beneath the restaurant's wide plate-glass window nodded at them and raised his hand in the peace sign. They returned the greeting with smiles.

Listening carefully and jotting down their order on a small pad as Joe cautioned her not to bring their steaks "burnt black, Texas fashion," the waitress assured them she would "keep an eye on Cook" and return soon with a bottle of "real Italian red."

To his evident delight, the waitress proudly presented them with a four-year-old Bolla. As she expertly removed the cork with a lever corkscrew and poured a taster's portion into his glass they learned that her name was Cassie Kelso and that she was a student. She added that "the guy out front is a local character they call The Whittler" and that students would be arriving "in droves" over the weekend.

"If someone had told me a month ago that we would be sitting here, I in the role of newly arrived member of the Department of Classics and you as a faculty wife, I would not have even remotely considered it in the realm of the possible," he observed after Cassie had removed the dishes and promised to return "in a jiffy" with Jane's tea and his coffee.

"Well, dear, let's just agree right now to enjoy it and not take it too seriously," was her response, an admonition that he readily seconded, raising his wine glass to hers and touching it lightly. "By the way, I'm happy you are getting into the habit of referring to me as your wife, which of course I'm on your records here as being. Keep it up!"

"Of course, babe. It's actually how I think of you anyway," he assured her. "Speaking of college records and such, tomorrow morning I'll check in at administration and get my hands on our moving allowance that John promised, and then we can check out the campus."

"And start looking for a place to live."

"Yeah, I wonder if John has any leads for us."

She squeezed the plastic honey bear over her tea and stirred it and then looked up at him.

"You know, honey, I've been wondering since we arrived here today what I can find to do in this town. I'm really a little bored at playing *haus frau,* as I think you know. Remember how restless I started to get in the spring."

"Yes, and don't think that hasn't been on my mind as well, babe. Maybe something at the college, maybe the library is a possibility. And you said you might take a course or two. That would be a good idea."

"Then there's the university, too, and Boulder is so close. I could be there in minutes. Remember how soon we got here after we passed the sign back there?"

"Sure, you could maybe find something over there."

"I really think I need something to do every day, something to kind of build my day around, know what I mean? It won't be easy having you occupied all the time with classes, with your writing—you have to find time for your novel, Joe, you just can't let that slip away from you, you know that, don't you?"

"Oh, I have no intention of letting that happen."

"I hope not, because you'll be impossible to live with if you do."

"Something flashed across my mind a minute ago, now what was that? Oh, yeah, I have to at least call John tonight, let him know we're here."

"Right. You can do that from the motel."

He held his napkin to his mouth and muffled a belch. "Maybe I'll be lucky and pull some days with mornings off. That's when I do my best writing." He gestured to Cassie and pointed to his cup.

As she was replenishing his coffee there was the sound of a motorcycle out front and they all turned toward the wide front window. A couple were astride the Harley and The Whittler was at the curb handing a small packet to them.

"*God damn it!* I *wish* he would not do that right out front like that!" Cassie exclaimed, her extreme annoyance quite apparent in her flushed face.

The cyclist sat gunning the engine for a moment as he dropped the packet into a sidesaddle and reached out and slipped something into The Whittler's hand. Then he and his female companion leaned far into the u-turn that he expertly executed with tires squealing and, with a deafening roar, the machine took off up the street.

The next day, at about ten in the morning, they sat in the Greenbrier across from Fritz's supplied with one rental lead, provided him earlier that morning over the telephone by John Brown's—now also his—secretary. He stared at the pad in his hand and realized that, without a map, he didn't have a clue where the address was. He had forgotten to ask Cassie for directions as she served them pancakes, bacon, scrambled eggs, and coffee. Then he noted that, across the street, The Whittler had just arrived and now occupied his customary perch by the eatery's window.

"Howdy, fren'," the man greeted him, looking up from the block of wood and the knife he held poised over it, "kin I help you in some fashion?"

"Well, yes, I was wondering if you might know where Walnut Street is."

"Sure do, fren', know this ol' town like the back o' my hand."

Deftly clasping the wood between his knees, he pointed to the higher part of the town with his right hand and then turned his left hand over and began tracing lines on it with his knife, indicating to Joe several intersections he should look out for in order to reach the desired destination.

"Jist point yerself up to the hill thar and follow yer nose. Thet there will get you thar the quickest and it'll also get you thar sooner than any other way, fren'."

"Did you ask him if he lives there on that ledge?" she inquired as they pulled away from the curb.

"No, and frankly I'd be afraid what kind of answer I'd likely get. Pleasant enough chap," he continued, slipping into Cockney, "but jist a leetle awd, ly-dee, a leetle stry-inge, 'e wuz."

The Greenbrier made its way down the main street to the first intersection he had been advised to look out for and then another and then up a steep hill at the crest of which they found Walnut Street. He geared down and began looking for house numbers.

"It should be along here somewhere. You know, I grew up on a street a lot like this, Victorian sort of architecture, big trees, and so forth and so on. Look at those houses, will you, some of them must be fifty, seventy-five years old. See any numbers?"

"Yes, it must be in the next block," she said, glancing at the pad in her hand.

He parked behind a VW bus. A three-story wooden-frame house sat back a good fifty feet from the dirt path that served as a sidewalk. A porch ran along the front of the building and around one side.

"Right out of Charles Addams, isn't it?"

"I should say so!" she said, looking it up and down. "I *love* that *tower!* Let's see if we can find anyone. And, oh, look, an old fashioned swing on the veranda! Didn't you say some house you grew up in had one?"

"Several of them, actually."

The front door was not locked so they entered and found themselves in a dark hallway. He called out, "*Hallo! Anyone at home?*" and the only response was a brief creaking of floorboards above. She suggested they look outside and led the way out onto the porch and around its corner to steps leading down into the back yard.

Seated cross-legged on the ground in the shade of a tall oak was a young man whose full black beard and steel-rimmed glasses lent to him a rabbinical cast. He leaned forward over a book in his lap, oblivious to the approach of the two strangers until Joe's foot cracked a twig and he looked up, his austere expression suddenly replaced with a crinkling smile. Jane was the first to speak.

"Excuse me," she said, flushing slightly. "We were told

that this house is for rent. Would you know anything about that?" She pointed to Joe. "I'm Jane Lewis and this is my husband Joe."

"Oh, sure, I've been helping to get it ready. We—that's my friend Lesbeth up there, see, in the bay window. I'm Saul."

They turned to look up and saw blond hair for a fleeting moment and then it was gone.

"She's finishing up the second floor. You want to take a look? It's my job to show it."

By late-afternoon the Greenbrier had been unloaded, the kitchen put in enough order to contemplate the preparation of an evening meal, and grocery shopping done by Jane while Joe took Rufus on a long walk. A casserole in the oven, they relaxed on the front-porch swing drinking beer from bottles. Familiar figures were sighted by Jane.

"Look, there's our new friends Saul and Lesbeth!" she said, brimming over with pleasure. "They can be our first guests! Why don't we ask them to have supper with us. We can eat out here."

"We'll have to since there's not much to sit on or eat at in there." Getting to his feet and waving to the newcomers, he laughed. "Now that you've made your nest, you want to fill it with playmates."

"Of course—and when we've rounded up some furniture from Good Will, and you said your professor friend offered a table and some chairs and things, then we can have a fancy ball."

"We can have that later on the mattress, baby."

"Hi, what you have done all day?" Lesbeth, an exchange student from the Netherlands, asked.

"Hello, hello," Saul said.

"Oh, unpacking, shopping, you know, first things first," she answered.

"Oh, how pretty cats," said Lesbeth. "I didn't see them yet. May I hold one?"

"You mean '*what* pretty cats' and '*before*', not '*yet*', sweet," Saul corrected. "You're getting your idioms mixed up again."

"I don't wonder," said Jane, handing one of the cats to her, "with all the languages you have to keep straight. Yes, we went over to the Browns right after breakfast and got Tom and Jerry here. Our family was separated long enough. They flew here from Austin."

"Yes," Joe said, "you've heard of flying squirrels. Jane, take them up to the tower and launch them into flight. Our friends here have probably never seen wingéd cats in action." He burst out laughing at Lesbeth's wide-eyed expression of wonder as she examined closely the cat in her arms.

"Oh, you are joking me!" she said, giggling.

"Yes, Joe has to have his silly little jests. No, we had them flown up here just before we left Austin. We took a little vacation first. And that's when Mr. Perryman over there joined our clan. We found him—."

"Or he found us."

"—by the side of the road in New Mexico."

"You mean he never knew the cats before? He doesn't seem to even *notice* them!" said Saul, incredulity in his tone.

"Jane figures Rufus grew up on a farm or a ranch," said Joe, "and must have had cats around him since day one. Anyway, nothing much bothers ol' Rufe there. "

"Amazing!" said Saul.

"We'd like you to have supper with us if you don't have other plans," said Jane.

After the meal, while Jane and Lesbeth washed the dishes, the two men sat on the porch steps, Joe leaning back against the banister post, his legs stretched out. He was slowly twirling a snifter of Fundador and Saul held a mug of coffee.

"So you came at quite late notice to replace Professor Oswald. He was a very nice man. A friend of mine took a lot of Latin from him and he just loved him. He said the old man had been reading Latin and Greek for almost six decades, can you imagine? He could write in both languages, even poetry, and could *speak* in Latin. *Imagine!*"

"You'd have to go live in a monastery to learn to do that today," said Joe, "and you might have to look a ways to find one at that, I mean, one that still used Latin on a day-to-day basis. I had a friend a while back who was a renegade priest, got married and had several children, and he gave me a pile of psychology textbooks, all of them in Latin. Said his professor, a priest of course, was a nut on sex and used to read case histories to them, in Latin, from Kraft-Ebbing." He chuckled at the memory and raised the snifter and took a whiff of its contents. "Ahh, this Spanish brandy is nice. I used to put away a bottle of this every couple of days when I was in Italy a few years ago. Until my liver acted up on me. Yeah, I came on very short notice indeed, kind of a combination of being at slightly loose ends with not much else on the docket and helping out a friend in need. John Chalmers Brown and I go back a ways, and seems like he was up the proverbial creek without a paddle." He sipped from the snifter. "And of course there was also a slight need of an income, a steady income, for a change."

"So will you be taking over all of Professor Oswald's courses?"

"Yes, I'll be doing his Great Ages of Ancient Times lecture course and his first year Greek, plus his Honors seminar on the Roman Republic," said Joe. "Oh, and I got to choose the author for the senior seminar in Greek, Pindar."

"How do you feel about all of this? You said you've been away from teaching for a while."

"I rather look forward to it, actually, although when I quit the racket two years ago I vowed never to set foot in a classroom ever again." He paused and looked up at Saul. "Don't misunderstand me, I really enjoy teaching. It's the bloody *system* that I have problems with."

"Like what? Excuse me for asking but I'm planning on going into the profession and I'd like to know what to expect."

"Well, you just have to accept that some aspects of the system are pretty silly and then you do what you can. Like, for example, the big lecture is pretty absurd, unless you have a guy up there who has something approaching charisma. And I say that as one who looks back on his undergraduate years with a lingering—and *considerable* in several cases—respect for the professors whom he sat there taking notes from three times a week. The absurdity residing, of course, in the regurgitating of said notes every six weeks or so in a Blue Book. But if the guy up there can be inspirational, as several of my teachers certainly were, then I guess it justifies the system. I don't know, I'll just have to give it my best effort and hope it succeeds in inspiring a few young minds."

"You're fortunate to have had some inspirational

teachers," said Saul, "I mean, for lecture courses. I've taken a lot of those big lectures—before I transferred here, I mean—and I can only think of two professors who inspired me."

"Yes, I guess that's par for the course. That's about how many I had, both in history. One gave a string of courses on Greece and Rome, even Byzantium, and then there was this fantastic guy, considered by all to be the most powerful lecturer in the entire university—."

"Where was that? And who—?"

"University of Washington," Joe interrupted, "and his name was Giovanni Costigan, whose field was English and Irish history. Somebody wrote a magazine profile of him one time and said he might be 'the best history teacher in the *world*'!"

"Wow!"

"Yeah, he really turned me on to that stuff, to history, I mean, when I was a freshman. In fact, I changed majors because of him, from architecture to history."

"I thought you were in classics."

"I started Greek and Latin when I was a sophomore and I switched to classics in graduate school." He looked up at Jane and Lesbeth, who had returned to the swing.

"Have you been getting your lecture voice in shape, Joe?" said Jane. "We could hear you way back in the kitchen."

"Yes, I thought I'd let the neighbors know that I am *heah, deah!*"

"Well, I'm sure they now know that *somebody* is *heah!*"

"You have such a great big house and no bed or table or chair or anything," Lesbeth said.

"We have a mattress!" he corrected.

"Oh, Joe, Lesbeth has been telling me about the Thrift

Palace in Boulder. It's owned by one of the churches and has all kinds of stuff at really great prices. She and Saul furnished their apartment from there."

"Well, why don't we drive over there in the morning, babe, see what we can pick up." He turned back to Saul. "So Professor Giovanni Costigan—."

"What an odd name!" said Saul.

"Wondered when you'd notice that. His father was Irish and his mother Italian." He glanced aside at Jane and Lesbeth, who had broken off their conversation and were listening. "He would stride into the lecture hall right on the hour, sometimes a little out of breath because he rode his bicycle from his house a half mile from the university, and just start talking, no notes or anything, except maybe sometimes a book with a marker in it so he could find the passage he wanted to read to the class—and then he'd hardly look at the page, just reel it off! He could quote poetry, ten or twenty lines or more, or prose by the paragraph. And unlike your run-of-the-mill historian who too often knows only politics and military affairs or whatever, he would tell us students about social conditions and so forth, and the culture and the arts of the period he was lecturing on. And he was one of the most well read people I've ever come across. In that profile I mentioned, he said he didn't know everything about the First World War, that tens of thousands of books had been written about it, and he said he'd only read *500 of them!* And he had been *everywhere.* When he went on sabbatical or got a grant and took leave, he wouldn't go and hole up in some library or archive and write a book, he'd go out and *talk* to people. Like, one place he'd go every couple of years or so was Africa. I remember he went there one summer—*in a hundred-and-ten degree heat, for chrissakes!*—and he came back and gave public lectures on conditions there, and warned that the situation was *'explosive'!* This was in the *1950s,* mind you! He had more information on everyday life there, what the people were thinking, what the future was likely to bring, you name it!"

"How lucky you have been to have him as teacher," said Lesbeth.

"Yes—" Seth agreed and, before he could complete his sentence, Joe continued.

"He gave public lectures on historical figures and writers, too, sometimes in a local Unitarian Church, sometimes on campus. I never missed one of these and they were always packed, standing room only. For example, I remember him giving talks on Blanco White and Alfred Dreyfus and Roger Casement. And Freud. And Einstein and Oppenheimer, he did them together in one talk. Or he might pick some writer to expatiate on. He did one on Ford Maddox Ford, and the next day I went to my favorite used book store to find a copy of *Parade's End.*"

"He still has that copy," said Jane. "I read it in Austin. *Great book!*"

"Yes, one of my all-time favorite novels. And he had this sort of apology he always said as he was winding up his talk. After holding his audience spellbound for an hour or so—and they were hoping he would go on for *another* hour—he would say, 'Well, I don't want to go on interminably—'." He chuckled. "I can see him in my mind's eye right now saying that."

His monologue was terminated by the arrival of Rufus, who came trotting across the lawn. The dog had clearly exhausted himself and now went straight for the pail of water by the faucet beneath the porch. Drinking his fill, he staggered over to a large oak and collapsed in a heap at its foot. Tom and Jerry, lying on the porch railing, stared at him impassively.

"Mr. Perryman, you okay?" Jane called over to him. "Joe, he looks like he's ready to have a heart attack!"

"Vat a comic name you have give him," said Lesbeth.

"He'll be all right, babe, that panting will cool his engine down in a minute or so."

Later, having made love on the mattress in the second floor room they had chosen for their bedroom, Jane surprised Joe by not immediately falling asleep.

"You're still awake," he said, putting his arm under her and pulling her toward him. "That's a change."

"I'm just so keyed up, honey, there's so much to be excited about. I really like our first friends, don't you?"

"Yes, they're an interesting pair, very intelligent, both of them."

"I'll say. Did you know that Lesbeth speaks seven or eight languages? She said nobody else speaks Dutch so they have to learn everybody else's."

"Well, she'd be nice to have around, wouldn't she now?"

"Don't get any ideas, mister, just watch yourself!"

"I mean as an interpreter. Though she does have her good points."

She was astride him now and had, to his astonishment, slipped him into herself again.

"We never did it so soon again!" he said, almost moaning. "Oh, baby, this is even better than before!"

"It's always best the second time around, honey, isn't it? *Oh, isn't it!*"

* * *

The next week was taken up with furnishing the house, first the main floor, then their bedroom, and finally, his study, a back room on the second floor. On a hunch, he stopped one evening at the telephone repair building in Boulder and left with a huge cable spool and a door, sold to him for five dollars each by the night watchman. A college maintenance truck dropped off the items promised by the Browns, a kitchen table with four chairs and a dresser, the last of which Jane claimed for her own use. The truck then returned to the campus to load up the nearly thirty boxes of books Joe had arranged to be mailed from Cambridge to the college.

For Joe's desk, the door was set up on orange crates, and two-dozen wooden apple boxes, purchased at a fruit distributor on the outskirts of Boulder, became his bookcase and file cabinet. Before they knew it, the house was furnished, albeit sparsely. Only the third floor, which consisted of a sort of efficiency apartment, an attic-like storeroom, and the tower, which Jane had undisclosed plans for, remained empty. They planned to rent out the apartment.

Hardly had Jane returned from submitting the rental announcement to the college housing office when a prospective tenant turned up on their doorstep. Joe was on the porch, his back to the street, sanding down the spool, preparatory to applying a coat or two of varnish to it, and Jane was in the swing reading yesterday's *Denver Post*.

"This is going to be one handsome piece, I tell you."

"I'm sure it will, honey. You've worked hard enough on it. Oh, Joe, please don't forget to oil this thing. It's driving me crazy."

"Why don't you try singing to it, babe, like, 'You're driving me crazy!' Isn't that a nice tune? Louis Armstrong did a wonderful version of it with his big band, around nineteen-thirty, if memory serves."

"Yes, it's nice, and you have a nice voice, honey. You should sing more. But I really prefer that you oil this thing!"

"But I rather like its sound, babe. It do remind me of when I was a teenager and used to sit in the swing and neck with the girl next door. I ever tell you about her? She used to like to sunbathe out on the back roof and I would eyeball her from the bathroom. She would take off her blouse and I was only about ten feet from her—we lived in a three-story side-by-side duplex—and man did that work me up! Then later on we'd—."

"Pardon me, but is this where the room is for rent?"

Joe spun around and Jane looked up from the paper to see standing at the foot of the porch steps a slender and swarthy young man.

"Why, yes, this is the place," she said, alighting from the swing and coming forward. "I'm Jane and this is my husband, Professor Lewis."

"Joe Lewis," he said, descending to the flagstone walk and extending his hand.

"Pleased to meet you," the young man said, shaking the hand and lowering his head a couple of inches in a sort of bow to Jane. "My name is Vincenzo D'Allasorio. I'm a student at the college and I would like to see the room—if it has not been taken."

Joe took a closer look, particularly noting Vincenzo's dark eyes and his height, which nearly came up to his own. His brown hair fell to his shoulders and he wore a long-sleeve khaki shirt, its collar buttoned, and faded and threadbare corduroy pants, their snugness accentuating his lean body. A tattered army knapsack hung from his left hand. His scuffed and worn-at-the-heels Oxfords shifted nervously as he spoke.

"Well, let's go up and have a look," Jane offered, motioning to Vincenzo to follow her, she and Joe having agreed on a division of labor in which the renting of the apartment fell to her. As the two disappeared through the front door, Joe heard her say, "By the way, it's more than a room, it has its own private bath and a little kitchenette."

Having assumed that Vincenzo had learned of the vacancy from the notice she had filed, Jane and Joe were surprised when he turned up the next morning with his gear, mostly books and records, with Saul and Lesbeth. Vincenzo explained that they knew each other from an Honors seminar in philosophy and that they had let him know of the apartment's availability.

"We got you a mattress and a desk and chair," said Jane as she once again led the way up the stairs to the third floor, holding a stack of LP albums against her stomach. The others carried boxes.

"Oh, thanks, that's all I'll need."

"Yes, Vince has been here three year and he still live out of cardboard cartoons," Lesbeth added.

"I do not like to be encumbered," he responded, "I like to be free of possessions."

"Except for books and records," she continued teasingly, "and if you don't be careful he have twice these many before Christmas."

Accepting Jane's invitation to join them for

sandwiches and ice tea, the three sat in the swing awaiting her return from the kitchen. Joe leaned back against the porch railing, facing them, and it struck him as an opportunity to gather some information relevant to his still very unfamiliar situation.

"Can you give me an idea what to expect here at the college?" he asked, scanning their faces by way of indicating that any one of them could respond. "What are the students like, are they serious or what? And how about the faculty? Anyone in particular I should go out of my way to meet—or avoid? What are they like and so on and so forth? Mind you, I'm not prying or anything, it's just that I'm coming at this whole thing cold. I hardly even knew this place existed until a month ago. So far I—Jane too—we really like it. And, listen, be assured that anything you say will be held in the strictest confidence. Except, I have to tell you, I discuss everything with my life mate there," nodding to Jane, who was now standing between them with a tray of sandwiches, glasses, paper plates and napkins, and a pitcher of ice tea.

"And my lips are sealed," she said, lowering the tray onto an apple box.

"Well, you already know Professor Brown—" Saul began.

"Ah, yes, Charmer Brown," Vincenzo interjected, Lesbeth emitting a quickly suppressed sound that Joe assumed was the beginning of a sort of giggle.

"—and you must know that he has a pretty good reputation here and is well liked. I took his lecture course on Greek and Latin authors, in English, I mean, and Vincenzo took some Latin from him."

"I did too," Lesbeth said, "and I liked him, he's a real nice man, and most smart too."

"Yes, he's okay, he likes to practice his Italian on me," Vincenzo added.

"How is his Italian?" Joe asked.

"Not bad, not bad, a little too formal perhaps, bookish, I think one could say."

"Then there is Erik Van Loon," Saul went on. "He teaches math and is somewhat of a character. He usually comes into the room with a newspaper and before he begins the day's lesson he'll take five minutes or so and critique the editorials. It gets pretty hilarious sometimes."

This time Lesbeth openly giggled as Vincenzo, thrusting out his arm in a sweeping gesture and barely missing her hand-held glass, declaimed, "This great benefactor of mankind has been maligned, castigated, and vilified—."

"Oh, yeah, he goes after Dirksen every chance he gets," Saul said, smiling. "That was pretty good, Vince." Saul caught Jane's eye. "He's from Vancouver, by the way, but before that was British, took his degree at Oxford, an Honors, I understand, brilliant man, and very popular with students."

"Oh, how long has he been here, Saul?" she asked.

"I think about ten years."

"Is he married?"

"His wife died five or six years ago. She was killed in an airplane crash, coming back from visiting her family in Scotland."

"How sad," she said, turning to Joe. "We should include him in our first dinner party."

"Don't be surprised if he wants to bring a friend," Saul advised. "He dates students."

"I am thinking if the Professor Van Loon will soon take a new wife from among them, will he?" was

Lesbeth's response to this, whether intended as a question or rhetorically, Joe could not determine.

"Well, we'll certainly have to invite him over for dinner soon, Joe. He sounds interesting, don't you think?"

"Yeah, we'll have to do that, babe. So, how about the students, have anything to say about your fellow students?"

"Students are students wherever you goes, take it from me, folks," said Lesbeth, "here, there, everywheres, you better believe it."

"That's the truth, mostly out for a good time, not very serious," Vincenzo opined somberly and Saul nodded in agreement.

"Present company excepted, of course," said Joe, smiling.

"*Assolutamente, Professore, assolutamente!*" exclaimed Vincenzo in delivery Joe immediately identified as educated Florintine. It amused him to anticipate what the young man's reaction would be to his Neapolitan accent, or to the bits and pieces of that city's dialect that he planned to spring on him later.

Saul got to his feet, taking his, Lesbeth's, and Vincenzo's glasses and placing them on the tray. "We have to go. We've got another house job to finish this afternoon and Vince is helping us with it. Gosh, it's going to be great having you folks here, and thanks for lunch."

"Yes, thank you," Lesbeth said, taking Jane's hands in hers and squeezing them, "I like you folks a lot. I have a meal soon for all of us, a Dutch specialty, a surprise."

"Thanks, see you later," said Vincenzo, turning and waving, as the trio headed down the steps.

Joe gathered up the paper plates and placed them on the tray.

"Think I'll take that dog for a stroll, and then I'm going to mosey over onto campus and feel it out a little."

"You should do that, dear. Won't be long now before you're over there every day. Better start getting used to the place."

Chapter 8

Pindar can wait.

All but fifteen minutes had passed of the office hour Joe had established—immediately after his 10 A.M. lecture—for students to "just drop in and rap about anything that's on your minds." It was now three weeks into the semester and, although he had announced a week before that he would arrange to meet at some other time with any student who had a class right after the lecture, so far only one had requested that and only two others had turned up at his office between 10 A.M. and noon.

A young woman whom he recognized had come at the end of the first week. She sat down and crossed her legs, revealing the tops of her hose and several inches of pale flesh between the straps of her garter belt. He raised his eyes to her face, noticing the pin on her sweater, and then remembered her as one of several rather exhibitionist sorority types who occupied first-row center.

Extending a sheet of paper to him, she said,

"Professor Lewis, could you sign this for me. I'm afraid I have to drop your course."

He took the form, placed it on the desk, and asked how she had come to this decision.

"Oh, the material is so unfamiliar to me," she purred.

"But that's the very reason why you should take the course," he explained, proudly informing Jane at lunch a short while later that he had dissuaded her from dropping, crumpled up the form and dropped it into the trash can, assured her that he was always available for consultation, and ushered her from the room.

A few days later one of the more prominent campus hippies, came in to ask his opinion on the "pass/fail" proposal for Honors courses that was currently in committee. He introduced himself with, "Everyone calls me Pee Wee," adding, with a puzzled expression, "I've forgotten why." The discussion took up the entire hour, during which the youth impressed him with his knowledge of philosophers ancient and modern. As the long-haired and patched-jean twenty-year-old rose to leave he casually mentioned that he regretted that he had not registered for the course but had only, on the recommendation of a friend, come that day to "check you out, man" and concluded that his friend "was right on target about your style not being the usual canned bullshit." He requested permission to audit the class and Joe told him to "Feel free to just drop in whenever you want to."

"Thanks, Professor Lewis."

"Well, I guess nobody else is going to show today," he muttered, looking at his pocket watch on the desk, closing Pee Wee's warn and much-marked copy of an English translation of Plato's *Republic*, handing it to him, and getting to his feet.

With a can of beer resting on the arm of a large rocking chair that he and Jane had bought earlier that week at a yard sale, Joe sat on the front porch on a Friday afternoon a month later. The Oxford text of Propertius lay open to *Elegy IV.8*, which he had been preparing for a weekly individual tutorial with a student who was writing her senior thesis on the poet. Taking the pencil from behind his ear, he jotted several words in the margin. "Have to work up a piece on this poem, send it in to one of the journals," he mumbled. "Haven't published anything since Canada."

The slow movement of the rocker produced, on the backswing, a creak that reminded him of sounds he recalled hearing aboard sailboats on which as a boy he had cruised the Chesapeake Bay. He closed his eyes and the flushed face of a fourteen-year-old appeared before his mind's vision for a mini-second. The backdrop—a cramped cabin, the bunk's disheveled bedclothes, the swell of the sea sighted through the single porthole—was startling in its clarity. *Jesus, haven't thought of that afternoon for an age,* he thought, opening his eyes. *Wonder what he's doing now. Practicing medicine somewhere, I guess. Gynecology, I bet.*

Closing the book and raising the can of beer to his lips, he plucked his watch from his leather vest's pocket and dangled it by its thong. *Jane should be back from Boulder before long and maybe we'll go have a steak or something at Fritz's. Be nice to just sit back over a bottle of wine and listen to her unwind after her seminar.*

Rocking slowly back and forth, the can gripped tightly, he raised his other hand and waved to three students passing by. He suddenly realized that one of them was in his lecture, but he didn't know who her companions were, other than that they apparently shared an apartment in the next block. The notion struck him that he should hold office hours on the porch. *There must be some way of communicating with these people*, he mused. *That room on the third floor of Smith is so inhibiting, deadening, really, it's no wonder no one hardly ever comes around. And* no one *has ever come back!*

Except to contemplate briefly on the front room as the location once the weather turned, his reflection on this matter was terminated by the postman striding across the lawn from his left. Waving a rubber-banded bundle of periodicals and letters, he took the three steps in one bound and handed it to Joe.

"Runnin' a mite late t'day, Professor," he said, dropping his bag on the floor with a thud and removing his pith helmet with his now free hand, with the other mopping his bald head and brow with a large red kerchief.

"May I get you a can of this, Mr. Stephens?" Joe offered.

"No, thankee, lady friend three door down done gimme big glass o' lemonade, but thankee alla same, take a rain check, see ya," he rapid-fired in response, donning his headgear, scooping up the bag, and leaping off the porch, each element of the tripartite action segueing to the next with an almost ballet-like grace.

Reminded of his own Maryland mail-carrying days in his undergraduate years, he watched Fred Stephens as, losing not a scintilla of his urgent momentum, he jabbed a handful of letters into the waist-high mailbox beside the steps of the house next door and then disappeared through the hedge. It occurred to him that it had been nearly an hour since he had out of the corner of his eye seen the postman cross the street at the corner and he wondered what else his "lady friend" had, in addition to the cooling drink, provided him. Then he unfurled the packet, his thoughts returning to the possibility of having students coming to the house. *Hell, we could even have an open house for them. Wouldn't that be a ball, a hundred or so bodies! And what if some of them brought friends? Could turn into quite a bash. Have to have it outside!*

He went into the kitchen for another beer. As he closed the door of the "ice box"—his favored terminology since his Depression-era youth when an iceman, a block of his ware resting on shoulder pad and held by tongs, had twice a week entered the back door of one or another of the rented residences his extended family had occupied—he glanced at the battered and taped electric clock on the wall. It had recently commenced to buzz and hum with such a clatter that Jane would no longer allow it in the bedroom. He paused to contemplate its history. It was a member of that core group of household items that had remained constant throughout two of his three marriages, interregna of bachelorhood, first trip to Europe (where it had remained silent, unwilling to adapt to an attached transformer), wanderings from coast to coast, and current relationship.

The clock's hands had some years ago met with an accident—the details of which he could not recall—that severed them at about two inches from the spindle. But the practiced eye could determine the very slight difference in their shape. The clock's crippled condition endeared it to him, so much so that he could not bear to part with it. He had given Jane a small traveling clock and hung the relic in the kitchen, where it continued to annoy her. "I think your days are numbered, my friend," he said softly.

Hardly had he returned to the rocker when he recognized the Greenbrier's engine, gearing down as it rounded the corner. Jane waved as she closed the van's door, her image through the two sets of glass doubled as though seen through a camera's out-of-focus viewfinder.

Dropping her knapsack on the deck, she leaned over and kissed him on the mouth, then sat on the swing, kicking her loafers off.

"How did your day go?" she asked.

"Oh, fine, but I'm glad it's Friday. How was your seminar?"

"Great, great, we're still doing Fitzgerald and I have to read another one of his novels and some short stories for next time. Then after we finish him we're going to do Hemingway."

"'Bout time ya git lit'rut in 'Murcan writers," he said, smirking.

"*Oh, you!* How many of *our* writers do you know *anything* about, sir?" She tucked her legs up under her. "How about getting me one of your beers, dear, then when you come back I have something to tell you."

After dinner at Fritz's they drove over to Boulder to check out the multi-colored buses she had seen parked on the campus and described to him.

"THE HIGH WIRED GLOBAL HOOTCHY KOOTCHY EXTRAVAGANZA AND SIDESHOW!" he read from a banner stretched high up between two poles, the arrangement serving as an entranceway to the corner of the green occupied by the seven garishly painted school busses. "Shall we see what's going on?"

They approached a foursome gathered around the door of one of the vehicles and introduced themselves.

"You thay thersh another collish here?" lisped a bulbous-nosed man in the garb and make-up of a clown.

"Right, Hopkins College, in the next town, not far from here," said Joe, nodding.

A red-bearded beanpole of a man in top hat, threadbare cutaway, baggy trousers, and tennis shoes out of the fronts of which his toes protruded drew deeply on an ivory cigarette holder, held his breath, and extended it to Joe. Honoring Jane's advice that he not "advertise" his "proclivities" while in the role of faculty member, he waved the offer aside.

"Can you hold him while I go get a bottle of juice?" asked a girl who seemed to Joe no more than sixteen or so. Without waiting for a response she thrust a baby into Jane's arms. "I'll be back in a sec." Barefoot, she hitched up her flowered granny dress and scurried across the open area toward an ancient bus on the roof of which were strapped a number of long galvanized pipes.

"Remindsh me we gosh to gesh the dome up. By the way, jush call me Jeshter and thash Uncle Tham. Thish here ish Beauty," he added, lightly touching the arm of a young woman with close-cropped black hair whose features suggested to Joe that she was of Mediterranean, perhaps Greek, ancestry. She was clad in a brightly colored cotton jumper and nothing else—*Unless she has underpants on*, Joe surmised—and was of such stunning face and figure that he deemed her appellation to be singularly fitting. "And thash Country Gal headin' back thishaway."

"Joe, what a *darling baby!*" Jane cooed, gazing down into the child's eyes as she gently rocked him back and forth.

"He's the pet of the troupe," said Beauty in a contralto

271

so rich and controlled that Joe wondered whether she was a trained singer, *"just spoiled rotten!"* Comically wide-eyed, she leaned forward. "Aren't you, Blue? That's his name," she explained to Jane, "because of his eyes."

"They're like oceans," she agreed, "like the blue of the sea."

"Now, I thought he got that name from his disposition," said Uncle Sam, his accompanying laughter becoming a paroxysm of coughing as he stumbled backward and climbed up into the bus.

"Uncle is really wrecked, I see," the returned mother said and took a seat on the bottom step of the bus with her baby cradled in her lap and sucking on the bottle. The laughter behind her subsided and then recommenced. The baby giggled. "He's so funny, ain't he, my sweet?"

"So, what are your plans, you going to hang around for a while?" Joe asked, directing his query to Jester.

"Yesh indeedy," he answered, his toothless condition revealing to Joe the source of his Elmer Fudd-like speech. "Soonsh we gesh the dome up—thash shedsuled for tomorrow—we'll be putting on showsh. Magic tricksh, tap dansh, freak show in the mornin', beauty contesh every afternoon, and a conshert and light show at night."

"And don't forget the movie tomorrow afternoon," Beauty interrupted.

"Oh, yesh, can't leave thash out. Remindsh me we got to get some poshtersh up around campush."

"What—?" Joe began.

"We're going to show a movie we made of the troupe," Beauty said, anticipating his question. "It's really wild, hope you all can come, it's in a little theater in the Onion, three o'clock tomorrow afternoon. I've been meaning to tell you," she continued, turning to Jester, "I just got back from checking the place out and it's real nice, seats about three-hundred. They said they'd have someone there to set things up and run the projector, and they're spreading the word."

"Cool," he enthused, "real cool, that'll get the newsh out about the conshert tomorrow night."

"Okay, we'll see you there," said Joe.

Back in the Greenbrier he told Jane that he wanted to get Monday's lecture prepared before going to bed.

"I was wondering about that. I know how you hate having it hanging over you until Sunday."

"Yeah, and then tomorrow morning I can go over the Honors seminar stuff. Pindar can wait until Monday."

"And then we can take the rest of the weekend off?"

"Yeah, babe, the way we've been going lately, I do thinks we deserves it."

They looked toward the school bus. Jester, his back to them, was doing a sort of jig, for the benefit of Blue, Joe assumed. Beauty and Country Gal waved goodbye. The beep of the bus's horn alerted them to Uncle Sam, who raised his hand in the peace sign.

About noon the next day they sat in the Greenbrier eating ham and cheese sandwiches and—along with several hundred others, presumably students and town people—watching as a crew of thirty or so unrolled huge sheets of canvas and dragged them over to others who, aloft on the frame of the dome, hoisted them into place and secured them with hooks and rope. Joe wondered how many of the workers were members of the troupe. Some of them appeared to him as unlikely drop-outs. He remarked on this to Jane, singling out a brush-cut youth who had taken his shirt off and tied it around his waist.

"Yes, and that girl there, isn't that Blue she's holding?"

"Yeah, she could be one of my lecture students, straight as they come." he poured more coffee into his mug and proffered the thermos to her. She waved it away. "But look at some of those other characters, will you, right out of a Western—like that guy there, the one on the end of that pipe there in the boots and levi's. Looks like he just came in from the range on a horse."

"There's another type there, the lady in the bonnet, isn't she sort of like those Amish folk?"

"Yeah, and the guy next to her, the one with the mop of hair, he could be Cotton Mather. *Too much!*"

"Oh, Joe, look at the jugglers!"

"Good afternoon," a voice at Joe's window greeted them and they turned to see Beauty beaming a radiant smile. At her side was a neatly combed and strikingly handsome black man whose rolled-up sleeves revealed the biceps of a weight lifter. Behind her stood a short and rotund man with muttonchops and handlebar moustache in an ankle-length white smock and flip flops. A black derby with what appeared to be a foot-long Ostrich feather plume tucked into its ribbon band sat atop his head at a rakish angle and a large Mickey Mouse alarm clock, hanging by a leather thong around his neck, rested against his chest.

"Hi!" Jane called across Joe. "What a beautiful day for your festivities!"

"Yes, we're hoping it stays that way for tonight. I want you to meet some friends of mine. This is Samuel Churchill and this is Tubs."

Joe reached out and shook the hands of both and Jane raised her hand in greeting.

"Helen has been telling me about you, Professor," said Churchill, leaning over to better make eye contact with Jane. "Haven't I seen you over here, Mrs. Lewis?"

"Well, I do take Professor Shapiro's American lit seminar."

"Sure, that's where I saw you, coming out of there. I was waiting to talk to him about Faulkner's stay in Hollywood."

"Sam is writing his dissertation on William Faulkner," Beauty, now Helen, explained.

"Quite an undertaking," said Joe. "I've always found him difficult, although I enjoy him a lot."

"Oh, he's difficult, all right, sometimes downright impenetrable. But I persevere!"

"I admire you," Joe said. "Like to see your work some time."

"Speakin' o' work, we oughta git movin'," said Tubs, holding his timepiece up for them to see.

"Yes, it is getting on, Tubby," Helen agreed and, turning back to the two in the Greenbrier, explained, "We were on our way down to the theater to set things up. "Shall we look for you later? Three o'clock?"

"Yes, we'll be there," Jane assured her. "Wouldn't miss it."

Wandering around the site for the next hour, Joe was struck by the industry that had gone into the encampment. Not only had the assembling of the capacious dome been completed after a morning's labor, there was a canopied shelter containing two long tables and forty or so folding chairs and another smaller one that served as the kitchen. So fully equipped was the latter that Joe was reminded of field messes in which he had worked during his army service in Korea.

One of the buses was serving as a vending center for clothes and jewelry made by members of the troupe. Paintings were hanging from a clothesline strung between two busses and pottery was arranged on squares of canvas on the ground. The onlookers had nearly trebled by now and Joe estimated that at least five hundred were mingling with the forty or so who had arrived in the buses.

Everywhere was activity. A dozen or so, some of them troupe members and others from the university, knelt with paint brushes on both sides of a four-foot-wide, fifty-foot-long strip of canvas. Pied piper-like, a flute-playing clown in dunce's cap led two similarly attired jugglers and an Indian file of fifteen or twenty students and at least that many children, all of them with painted faces, around the periphery of the occupied area.

"Shall we get our faces done?" said Jane teasingly, taking his arm and smiling up at him.

"Maybe later, maybe tonight. *Hey, let's check that out!*" he said, pointing to a crowd circling a war-painted pair in leather Indian garb and moccasins who were in the final stages of pitching a tepee.

Seated in the back row of the tiny movie theater of the Student Union Building with Helen between them, Joe noticed that she was carrying a copy of *The Electric Kool-Aid Acid Test*.

"Interesting reading there," he commented.

"Oh, yeah, it's kind of background reading for me."

"How's that?"

"Well, you know, I'm not really one of them, I'm just along for the ride—and of course to gather material for my research paper."

"Tell us about it," Jane urged.

"Yeah, we took it you were just another freak," he said, leaning forward and winking at Jane, "like the rest of us."

"Oh, I guess there's some of that in me, and who knows what I'll be like in another month or so. I'm not going back to Berkeley until next semester."

"The plot thickens!" he said. "What kind of a research project are you involved in?"

"Well," she replied, smiling, "I guess it is kind of confusing. Okay, this is what I'm doing. I'm writing a master's thesis—I'm a sociology major—on communes, really organized communes, not just fly-by-night outfits like a bunch of kids who dropped out or something. Structured communes that operate with some definite purpose. Like this one is primarily a theatrical troupe and they travel around giving shows, kind of like old-time vaudeville. Hootchy Kootchy has dancers, musicians, jugglers, clowns, a *lot* of clowns, acrobats, magicians, mimes, actors, you name it. They even have a lady who *swallows swords and eats fire!*"

"How do they support themselves?" Jane asked. "Do they make money doing this?"

"And communes go way back in American history," said Helen, ignoring Jane's query and warming to her subject. "In England, too, and then of course there's circuses and carnivals and all that," she continued, the momentum of her monologue evidently carrying her on. "And the gypsy tradition, don't forget that. What did you say?"

"Do they support themselves doing this?"

"Oh, yeah, they do make money doing the shows, but not always. Like here they'll just put on a concert for free, maybe get some leads where to do one for a fee down the road, at another college, I mean, or somewhere. Then they do all kinds of other things too, like they have mechanics—they *have* to, to keep those antique busses running!—and the guys do repair jobs and lawn work and paint houses and all kinds of other stuff. The women make clothes and jewelry. And they sell their paintings and pottery." She broke off suddenly. "Look, there's Sam, I think he means it's going to start." She turned to Jane, whispering, "Isn't he a hunk?"

Joe looked around the now filled theater. Judging by their attire, he assumed that those attending were, without exception, students. He did not see any from the troupe, who would certainly stand out in such a gathering. The lights dimmed and over the sound system came the Beatles singing "With A Little Help From My Friends."

Upon the screen, in color, appeared the familiar buses arriving at a site not unlike the one on the green that he and Jane had earlier made a tour of. On the fender on the driver's side of the lead bus sat Jester in clown costume. In one hand was a toy steering wheel and the other held a large old-fashioned megaphone to his mouth. The buses stopped and each disgorged a dozen or so clowns and outlandishly dressed and made-up individuals, among them those they had met the evening before and several others he thought he recognized, vendors and kitchen help he had seen as they passed their stations that morning.

The scenario on the screen suddenly deteriorated into chaos, with some dashing in this direction, others in another, clowns tripping clowns and then, gape-mouthed, laughing uproariously, Jester climbing onto the hood of the bus and gesticulating frantically and shouting through his device. That is, one assumed that he was shouting and the clowns laughing, for the movie had no soundtrack other than the music providing a sort of film score, some of it familiar tunes by rock groups and some not so familiar, except, clearly, to a few in the youthful audience.

As order was restored and the forty-strong and very motley crew of roustabouts lined up alongside their respective vehicles, the volume of the music was gradually lowered and, superimposed upon the fading-out strains of Bob Dylan's "Rainy Day Women #12 & 35" (to which a few had been executing exaggerated march steps), was Josh White's "John Henry."

Some troupe members climbed atop the buses and handed down lengths of pipe to those on the ground while others dragged bundled canvas from the rear emergency doors. There was Uncle Sam, there was Tubs, there were Country Gal and the flutist. Then, of a sudden, Joe did a double take as he saw Uncle Sam atop a bus handing down a length of pipe to himself while Tubs struggled, alongside his identical twin, to pile canvas upon a high pile. A close-up of Jester was joined by yet another Jester, both with contorted face and both screaming into megaphones. Beside him, with twin Blues' mouths to their breasts' nipples, stood a pair of serene Country Gals. This double image was repeated in the case of others as the camera panned to a wider spectrum of the activity.

It became clear what was happening as members of the troupe descended from the stage into the audience and laughter and applause erupted throughout the packed theater, many rising to their feet in ovation. The dozen or so whose presence on the stage had created the illusion grabbed hands of those on the aisles and of some seated two or three seats into the rows, shaking them vigorously. Only Jester remained on the stage for a moment to urge all to be sure that evening to come and "bring your frendsch to the greatish show on earth, the Hooschy Kooschy Eshravagansha and Shideshow."

As suddenly as they had appeared, the troupe members were gone through the exit at the back of the theater and the film continued, "Lady Madonna" playing during the erecting of the dome on the screen and other tunes accompanying the feeding of the troupe and various skits performed by mimes.

As the audience made its way out of the theater, Sam appeared at their seats and invited them to come along with him and Helen to his office for coffee.

The concert, light show, and other entertainment continued into the early hours of Sunday, attracting an audience of several thousand, and dawn was breaking as Joe and Jane headed home. They slept until late in the afternoon, returning to the Boulder campus after dinner. Every day of the next week, afternoon or evening, sometimes both, found them spending a few hours with the troupe. Jane and Helen had become good friends by mid-week and one evening, at Jane's urging (they had brought her home for supper), she talked about herself as they sat at the kitchen table.

His initial impression had been correct, he learned, for she was the daughter of Greek immigrants, Aristotle and Helena Kavakos, who had settled in Oakland, in 1935.

"They left just before the dictatorship started up," she told them, "and they had just barely enough money to reach California, where they heard the climate was nice, something like home, and they had friends there, too.

They put all their savings—wasn't much, I guess—into a little corner store, a mom and pop grocery store, 'cause that's all they knew, really, what they had grown up doing back home, helping out at the family fruit stand, that sort of life. My mother was pregnant with my oldest brother when they got there and she had five more children. I'm the youngest."

"When were you born, Helen?" Jane asked.

"Forty-four."

"Oh, so was I!"

They looked at each other, smiling with delight.

"Okay, you two, enough of the mutual admiration society and get on with the story, please," Joe said in mock sternness. "Did you grow up speaking Greek?"

"Oh, of course, that's what we spoke at home, always, and with our friends in this little Greek enclave, our neighborhood. I *love* speaking it—only I don't have much chance to now. In high school there was a Greek Club and we used to put on dances and big meals of our family specialties—*that was great!*—and we'd invite all our families and friends. Gee, I really miss that, the old neighborhood, all my friends, the music—I *really* miss the music."

"Yes, Greek music, I'm very fond of Greek music," he said.

"Yes, and I love to dance, just *love* to dance to it. But not just Greek music, gospel and rhythm and blues and all that too."

"When did you get into that?"

"Oh, I was always into it, Joe, it was all around me. You see, we were really only a minority in this part of Oakland. Most of my folks' customers were black, that's what the neighborhood was, mostly black. I went to school with blacks, some of my best girl friends were black, I dated black guys. I even went with a black boy my senior year of high school." She chuckled. "You know, summers I would get so dark lying out in the sun and swimming and stuff that I could pass as black! Jook—that was his name, my boy friend. Jook and I, we'd go downtown, I mean, into San Francisco, and no one would notice us—like how people stare at a mixed couple, you know? But they wouldn't pay any attention to us. That was funny." A cloud seemed to come over her face and she looked down at her hands, then raised her eyes to theirs. "We broke up and he joined the army right after graduation. I hadn't heard from him or anything for a year or so and then just after last Christmas I heard he was killed in Vietnam. He was twenty-three. He had just made sergeant, I heard at the funeral. Such a waste. I cried myself to sleep that night when his sister called me. That war is so stupid!"

"It's insane and criminal!" said Jane, reaching out to touch Helen's arm and squeezing it.

"So that's how I grew up, folks, a crazy mixed-up way of growing up, I guess—but very American, too, wouldn't you say?"

"Indeed it was and I envy you," he said, "I really envy you, seeing as how I'm the quintessential Wasp."

"You hardly strike me as the Wasp type, Joe!"

"He isn't!" said Jane "He just likes to say that."

"But it's true, in terms of the way I grew up!"

"Yes, dear, but people do change and you have certainly changed."

"That's probably the understatement of the century—judging by what I've seen of you!" said Helen. "But let me tell you something interesting. See how this grabs you, since you now know all about how I was shaped growing up in a neighborhood like that." She looked around the kitchen. "You know, I really love being here with you, this is so like how we used to sit around after supper and talk and talk and drink wine. Greek wine, of course, my father used to make his own. I miss all of that so much. It's so strange, I have to tell you, being on the road with these—. Papa would call them 'screwball crazy kids'." She laughed at the thought. "He loved American slang, even if he did get it mixed up a lot. I miss him something awful sometimes."

"When did you lose your father?" Jane asked.

"Three years ago, of a heart attack. He had just turned fifty-five and we gave him a big birthday party, just two weeks before he died."

"I'm so sorry."

"Yes, and we know what that's like, too," Joe added. "Jane lost both her parents at an early age and her grandfather died just before we met. My ol' man left this world five years ago and my mother followed him two years later."

"Do you have brothers or sisters, Jane?"

"No, I'm an only child. You're the lucky one! All those companions while you were growing up! Joe has a sister, an older sister."

"Reminds me, I must write her, see how she's doing over there in London."

"London?"

"Yes, Helen, she's on leave from Johns Hopkins University, doing research at the London School of Economics." He smiled. "Writing a book, her third or fourth now."

"Wow! Very impressive!"

"How is your mother doing?" Jane asked.

"Oh, she's okay, she has a lot of friends there and she's still running the store. I made her promise to get some help and cut down her hours and she did. My brother and one of my sisters live nearby and they're keeping an eye on her. I call her every week."

"So you were going to tell us something," he reminded her.

"Oh, yeah, about Sam and me. You know, I really like him a lot, he's a great guy, really brilliant, we just never run out of things to talk about. I met him less than a week ago and it's like I've known him all my life. Anyway, he took me to a meeting of the Black Student Union last night and it was real weird, I'm telling you. They spent most of the meeting attacking him for acting like a white person and they completely ignored that I was sitting *right next* to him. *It was like I was invisible!* This one dude in an afro kept asking Sam why he was doing his dissertation on Faulkner and told him he should do it on Richard Wright instead of 'some ofay cracker'! Then some of the others jumped all over Sam for hanging out with the troupe. They asked him if he was going to join the Union in some demonstration against Hayakawa next week or if he was going to be sitting in the audience 'next to some white bitch'. I'm telling you, it got pretty nasty!"

"How *awful!*" said Jane, looking across at Joe as though expecting an explanation from him.

"Well, I know where they're coming from even if I don't agree with the way they come on—especially to someone like you and Sam," he offered.

"It's funny, really, knowing how Sam grew up there in those Boston suburbs. The truth is I'm closer to blacks than he is. But they never gave me a chance to open my mouth. Not that it would have done any good, I guess.

They weren't ready to listen to anything rational or anything like that."

The days flew by and before Joe and Jane knew it, the High Wired Global Hootchy Kootchy Extravaganza and Sideshow had departed, taking much of Saturday to decamp, first, dismantling, with the help of dozens of week-long student camp followers, the dome and tents. Then, after breaking for the mid-day meal of brown rice and vegetables, strapping the pipes atop the buses, packing their gear, and lining up abreast and slowly policing the area of every last bottle, can, scrap of paper, and cigarette butt, the buses roared off to the accompanying piercing squeals, laughter, and farewell shouts of hundreds.

Although he had immensely enjoyed the virtual total immersion in the bizarre society of the troupe and often during that week had even contemplated the possibility of joining them at some later time, Joe welcomed the calm that suddenly descended upon their life as they stood there with Sam on the green and watched as the crowd dispersed.

"I'll sure miss that lady!" said Sam.

"We will too, Sam," said Jane, "squeezing his forearm. "But she said she would stop and visit on her way back to Berkeley in January. So you'll see her then."

"Yeah, and we might hook up in Boston when I go home for Christmas—if they're anywhere near there then."

"I guess their itinerary is not too fixed," said Joe, chuckling.

"*Hah!* You can *say that again!*" said Sam. "They strictly play it by ear, don't follow any score at all."

The calm of their lives did not last, however, for both Hopkins College and the university increasingly heated up with political activity. The Boulder campus was a way station for anti-war protesters traveling across country in either direction and it also scheduled a number of public events that attracted large crowds. For instance, San Francisco State College president S. I. "Sam" Hayakawa attempted to speak, as scheduled, in the university's largest hall and was heckled off the stage by two radical contingents who had filled the front rows and raised the standing-room-only audience to fever pitch. An election-eve rally, a reading by eminent San Francisco beat poets, another by the novelist John Barth, a performance of their *Frankenstein* by the Living Theater, a noon-time open-air sing-in by Joan Baez, concerts by John Mayall's Bluesbreakers and others, an SDS national convention, served as additional launching pads for demonstrations against the war.

Then there were the frequent anti-war marches that Joe and Jane found themselves participating in, he initially the lone representative from the faculties of either of the two institutions. In fact, so openly did he wear on his sleeve his distaste for the war, he was called upon to act as unofficial liaison with both his Hopkins colleagues and the faculty-student End the War Coalition at the university. He took great pride in having persuaded a handful of professors from both institutions to attend some of the protest activities.

Far from distracting him from his work, the often hectic days and evenings of protests and meetings, the latter sometimes held in their front room around the spool, had somehow geared up Joe's energies and he told

Jane that he had seldom been so productive.

"I'm on a roll, babe!" he said one Saturday evening as they relaxed after dinner over the remains of a bottle of Italian wine. "I knocked off a good thousand words this morning and this afternoon got most of my preparation for Monday done."

"I'm so glad you're keeping to your Saturday morning writing routine. Think maybe you'll finish your novel by next fall?"

"Maybe," he said. "We'll see."

Chapter 9

Why, it's like Switzerland!

The evening in the late fall of 1969 that Oliver Hanks arrived proved to be the termination of an Indian summer that didn't seem to want to end. Joe had not seen one like it since his early teens in Maryland, relating to Jane how it had been warm enough on Christmas Day when he was twelve to try out, in his shirtsleeves, a soccer ball he had found under the tree that morning.

He had yet to wear any sort of jacket or coat to campus that semester, his third at Hopkins College, protecting himself from the infrequent rain with a huge, tattered, black umbrella, a relic of his first stay in Italy, a beloved accessory that, notwithstanding Jane's and others' importuning, he had resolutely refused to discard and replace (not even with gifts, which he conveniently "lost" on their initial outings), defending its retention on grounds of its "character" and the store of anecdotes it had generated for nearly a decade, his favorite being the time he had been unable to get it closed upon entering the cabin of a funicular in Napoli.

She remarked on how much the season reminded her of autumns on her grandfather's farm, where she had lived from the age of five when her mother died and her father, who often traveled as a salesman, was unable to keep her, he himself dying when she was nine. They grew accustomed that fall to spending many of their late afternoons and evenings, sometimes until midnight, on the porch and had even set up table and chairs there, where they and their ever-widening circle of friends often held potlucks, sometimes at little more than an hour's notice. On this particular evening they sat and awaited Oliver, who had called from Denver to alert them of his imminent arrival.

So settled in as an academic couple were they that Jane had joined several faculty wives organizations and frequently attended public lectures on both campuses with Priscilla Paul, the dean's wife. Her spring term paper on "Flora Symbols in *Howard's End*" had been so well received by both her professor and fellow students that she had registered for another seminar, her third, this semester and was working her way through a hefty reading list that included *Moby Dick*, *Huckleberry Finn*, *The Scarlet Letter*, and *Leaves of Grass*. (Joe was so taken with the title of her term paper that he created a character in his novel and named her Flora Cymbols.)

He had begun to eat lunch Mondays at the faculty dining room in the spring with several colleagues who had joined with him in openly protesting the war, and he dropped by the cafeteria once or twice a week either for lunch immediately after his office hours or coffee and pie in mid-afternoon following class, frequently in the company of a student or two. Insofar as possible, he kept Tuesdays and Thursdays free of classes, appointments, and other distractions, putting in ten or twelve-hour days at his desk in the upstairs back room, the mornings on his novel and afternoons and evenings in preparation for his classes. Because he was repeating the history survey and again giving beginning Greek, about half of his teaching load took little effort beyond reading over lecture notes and reviewing a few pages of the primer in the few minutes he stopped off in his office before class. Thus he had been able this semester to concentrate on his Petronius and Apuleius: The Latin Novel seminar, which he had never before taught and found both fascinating and very demanding, an Honors seminar for Greek majors on Periclean Athens, and a tutorial on Greek Lyric Poetry with Vincenzo.

The summer had been a lazy one, with long walks up into the Flatirons, picnicking alone sometimes, but frequently for a full day's outing with friends, notably Saul, Lesbeth, and Vincenzo, or Erik Van Loon with one or another from his pool of student companions, more often than not the blonde in pageboy who had sat in the front row of Joe's last year's history lecture and whom he had awarded A's to, Dinty Moore. She turned out to be, to Joe's surprise, a philosophy major and, in Erik's estimation, "a crack mathematician."

They also made new friends, acquired at both the college and in Boulder, for example, during the receptions after the experimental film screenings that were held weekly in the little theater in the university's Student Union—the Onion—and at such outdoor events as concerts by the local symphony in Chautauqua Park and the Human Be-In, a three-day celebration and anti-war protest on the grounds of the city's downtown park.

One of the season's high points was the arrival one afternoon in July of a letter from Jyll's lawyer bearing the news that the divorce had been filed (on the grounds of "extreme mental cruelty and unreconcilable differences") and the decree was anticipated early the next year. Other than that and the occasional postcard from Jim or Flossie (one, in late August and postmarked Annandale-on-Hudson, New York, said simply, "Wall-to-wall mud, grass, and music—what a friggin' gas! We love you, Flossie and the Diverse."), the mail dropped off considerably during the hot months, usually amounting to little more than "Occupant" junk, a periodical or two a week, and parcels from Blackwell's or some other mail-order book seller.

Camping up in the foothills soon after the college term had ended, sleeping in a pup tent purchased, along with other equipment, at an army surplus store in Denver, and cooking over an open fire, they had just finished making love one mid-day on an immense flat-topped bolder jutting out of a hillside. He was sitting up on the blanket-covered foam rubber mattress rolling a cigarette when he heard the clang of metal. Looking up, he saw that a van was parked on the road that ran along the crest of the hill across the ravine. A man was moving back and forth at the rear of the vehicle.

"Looks like we have company," he said, reaching for his binoculars. "Better get your rags on, babe." Adjusting the glasses to the two-hundred yards that distanced them from the activity, he studied the scene. Continuing in one of his favorite personae, he adopted the oral guise of some of his more impoverished grade school companions in rural Maryland. "Methinks the feller have some kinda problem thar, Em'ly. In fec', I duz believes he be petchin' uh tahr."

Rolling up their bedding and securing it under a nearby bush, they walked over to the road and introduced themselves. The tire-patching stranger looked up from his task as they neared him, took Joe's hand, bowed his head toward Jane, and told them he was "knowed amung the tribes herebouts as Big Thunder." He was about even with Joe's six-foot-plus frame, gaunt and muscular, cleanshaven, and wore his graying black hair in a ponytail. His buckskin vest, the lone garment of his torso, revealed the thick hair of his chest. His attire, Jane later observed to Joe, was "so authentic, I thought I had met my first real American Indian!"

"Say, think ya could spell me here whilst I catch m' breath?"

Joe took over on the bicycle pump, which fortunately was a heavy-duty one, while the man took a seat next to her on the log that served to buttress the road, which skirted the very edge of the steep hillside.

"Tribes?" she asked.

"Injun tribes, what's left of 'em, I trades with 'em. I allus stops at Koshare Kiva over La Juanta on m' trips to Texas, and they's a Arapaho and Shoshoni reservation up north, an' I gets up thar ever' moon er so on m' runs to the Dakotas. An', oh yeah, they's a pueblo, an' a commune o' freaks, too, near Taos what all I stops at, too." He gestured toward Joe. "We gets 'nuff air in thet thar thang I kin show y'all what all I got in m' truck." He got up to take over again at the pump. "Don't ever travel without no spare tahr," he advised them. "I thunk I'd larned that lesson." He grinned at them. "But I guess I done forgot it."

"That commune near Taos, would that be the Peaceful Folk?" Joe asked, lowering himself to the log and putting his arm around Jane's waste.

"Yeah! You heered o' them?" he said, holding the pump handle still.

"We stopped there for a couple nights on our way here from Austin a year ago."

"No shit! Now ain't that somethin'!" He laughed and slapped his knee. "Crazy bunch o' fuckers, warn't they? Come home in June an' tol' Doe 'bout 'em an' she taken off 'er dress an' had me t' rubbin' 'er back out inna sun, *nekked's a fuckin' jaybird!"*

So congenial ("simpatico fantastico" was Joe's subsequent summation of the encounter) did they find "Big" that they readily accepted his invitation to stop and visit him and his "ol' lady" Doe Eyes on their way home. The next day about noon they arrived at the cabin, high up in the hills at the far end of a three-acre field of tall grass and nestled up against the woods, with the gift of a half-dozen trout they had caught in a stream that morning. Joe offered to help clean them, admitting that he had not done so since his teens, but Doe, as she instructed them to address her, took the bucket from him.

"I'm gonna filet these little beauties and pan-fry 'em for our lunch, folks, along with some spuds we grew ourselves," the somewhat buxom and freckled twenty-year-old with granny glasses announced as she took off at a brisk walk toward the rear of the log cabin, the long ponytail of her red hair bouncing against the strap of the skimpy halter supplementing the cut-off jeans that barely covered half of her buttocks.

"She got a ass on 'er, doan she?" Big casually observed, turning and gesturing to a ring of five up-ended chair-high logs and inviting them to "tek a load off." Disappearing into the cabin, he returned in a couple of minutes with a long-stemmed pipe and took a seat opposite them.

"This here's one of m' prize possessions," he said, cradling it with both hands and holding it up for them to examine.

"That's a beauty, all right!" said Joe, whistling.

Jane leaned forward. "Why it's *made of stone!*"

"Gotten it offen a Sioux chief who claim 'e war hunerd an' fifty yar ol'." He looked from Joe to Jane and then back again to Joe. "And I *blieves 'im!* Ol' fucker war dried up like a ol' proon, had wrinkles y' cud fill with water an' *float a fuckin' canoe in!* Thang cost me ten cartons o' Camels."

"Cheap at half the price, as they used to say," said Joe.

"One for every fifteen years of his life," Jane observed.

"*Damn right!* Glad he warn no two, *three*-hunerd!" The gold caps of his central incisors glinted as he smiled at them. Then, resting the pipe across his legs and securing it with his left hand, he produced from an inside pocket of his vest a leather bag about the size of a fist. Loosening with his teeth the thong that secured its mouth and tucking it between his thighs, he proceeded to pack the pipe's bowl. "Got a couple lids o' fine Mexican on m' last trip south. We can toke up while Doe's cleanin' them purty trout y'all brung us. I laid a joint on 'er so's she wunt hev to play ketch-up once she gits 'em on the fahr." He raised the pipe to his mouth and, with the thumbnail of his right hand striking a wooden match that he plucked from behind his ear, held the flame to the bowl. Once he had it going well he passed the pipe to Jane.

Their intention had been to have lunch, probably be shown around the property, and then head on back to town. But the meal of the trout, an immense frying pan of potatoes, and a green salad of produce fresh from the couple's garden was topped off with a pan of freshly baked brownies that Joe soon realized were laced with the "Mexican." They remained at the rough-cut log table by the windows in the main room of the cabin until late-afternoon as one after another LP spun on the turntable and Big and Doe talked about their backgrounds, their life there the past year, and their plans for the future.

Doe was three months pregnant and hoped it was twins because she wanted to have "a passel of kids and that'd be a good start." The disparate backgrounds of the two made for numerous speculative discussions over the coming months between Joe and Jane and among some of their friends in the college community. Doe had grown up in an upper middle-class family in the suburbs of Indianapolis, where her father owned a large drug store and her mother answered the description of the typical full-time housewife and mother, Doe being the eldest of four girls. She and Big, twice her age and a wanderer since his teens in his native rural Tennessee, had met the year before when she was a sophomore at the university and he had set up shop there the week the Hootchie Kootchie troupe had been on campus.

"He swept me off my feet on that first day when I bought some earrings from him—these right here as a matter of fact—and I spent every night that week in the back of that truck right there," Doe confessed, pointing first to the dangling string of tiny beads that brushed her neck and then out the window to the van.

"Jesus, what is that music?" Joe asked. "It's blowin' my fuckin' mind!"

"Thet thar's *Music In A Doll's House*," Big replied. "Family. Come out a year ago. I'll put *Hair* on next. That'll *waste ya*, man!"

"It's a *god damned symphony, that's* what it is!" Joe exclaimed. "That cat on harp is *wailin' his fuckin' ass off!*" He turned and examined Jane's eyes up close. "Little dilated there, babe, how ya feelin'?"

"*Oh, I feel great!*" she answered, grinning in a somewhat lopsided way. "*So relaxed!* Did I actually hear Big say he's going to put *hair* on? But he already *has* hair on!" She bent forward giggling and rested her forehead on the table. "This has been the *craziest afternoon!*"

By early evening the effects of the brownies had subsided to a mild euphoria and Joe and Jane sat in the Greenbrier exchanging goodbyes with Big, who was at the van's passenger side placing an opened pack of Camels in Jane's palm. They waved to Doe, who stood on the cabin's front stoop, breasts bare.

"You know, those joints were so perfect—I think he made them with that little machine—that I lit one up later that night thinking it was a Camel. That was *sure some surprise!*" he said, as they swung gently back and forth on the porch, waiting for Oliver to arrive.

"I'll never forget the look on your face when you saw Doe there at the front door, tits to the breeze," she said, chuckling. "Thought I'd have to push your eyeballs back in!"

"Now why do you think she did that?"

"Oh, I think she was just showing off. She did have a

rather voluptuous kind of Rubenesque body. And I think she had a thing going for you, honey, not to swell your head, but I did notice quite a few times that she was looking you over."

"*Really!* And Big, I do believe, had *his* eyes on *you!*" He took a swig from the bottle of ale. "Figures, you know. They sure liked to talk about it. I think maybe they wanted us to spend the night."

"I think you're right."

"How would you have reacted to such an invitation? I mean, an actual invitation to switch partners for the night."

"I really don't think I'm ready for that, sweetheart. Although, I can't think of very many couples I might have liked to do it more with, know what I mean?"

"Remember what Big's parting words were?"

"How could I forget?"

"'Now'm gonna go in an' fuck m' ol' lady to a *fare-thee-well!*'" he said, furnishing the line in near perfect mimicry of Big's drawl. "Funny we should be talking about them tonight when Oliver's just about ready to turn the corner up there."

"Why ever?"

"Well, because I was once again thinking back on how different their lives had been before they got together and how Doe said Big couldn't hardly sign his own name a year ago."

"What's that have to do with Ollie?"

"Remember Dinah, the hitchhiker he picked up coming back from Chicago?"

"Yeah, so?"

"That truck driver she married when she was sixteen, he was illiterate, too, and she was teaching him to read while they were on the road." He reached down over the arm of the swing and put his empty bottle on the floor. "And *he* taught *her* to *drive* that rig! A *Kenworth!*"

"Oh, yeah, he only made it to the second grade or something—and she was a pretty bright young thing, according to Ollie. Didn't he get her into the university?"

"Yeah, in some sort of probationary status her first year, as I recall." He took her empty bottle and placed it beside his own. "You wonder what the attraction is, intelligent women like that running off with some character who can just barely read road signs. I guess he'd have to be able to at least do that in order to get a driver's permit. Say! How the hell would he even take the written test?"

"Well, I never even saw a picture of Dinah's trucker, but I can sure tell you what the attraction of Big was, especially for a girl who grew up like Doe did."

"What was that?"

"Remember how she said she hardly ever saw her father, they never did anything together, it was always her and her sisters and her mother?"

"Right, 'retail hours' and all that, home at ten o'clock, he'd drop 'em off at church and go open the store Sundays. I get your drift—Big's her daddy." He burst out laughing. "Sure, he's her *big daddy!*"

"Right, but there's something else he is."

"And what's that, babe?'

"Her *stud*, honey! Are you stupid or something? What do you think they do up there in that loft?" She turned and, swinging her legs over his, encircled his neck with her arms and kissed him. They swung slowly back and forth as she ran her tongue in and out of his mouth. "Anyway, she's teaching him to read. Didn't you see all the comic books in the outhouse?"

"Yeah, that's right. But I thought they were hers."

"Joe, *Doe* was an *English major*, for chrissakes! There were novels and poetry all over the place. *That's* what *she* reads!" She kissed him again. "So what do you think *he's* teaching *her?*" She loosened several of the middle buttons of his shirt and ran her hand around lightly in the hair on his chest. "Know something? You are making me so horny! Let's go upstairs so *you* can teach *me* something."

"You're on, babe! We'll have a *regular seminar!*"

They didn't hear Oliver's VW, or any other indication that he had arrived, so heavy was the rain and so horrendous the thunder of the storm that hit as they were making love.

"Wasn't that *wild?*" Jane, still lying atop him, purred into his ear.

"*Jesus, yeah!* I can't remember us ever doing it in such a storm."

"Sh-h-h—hear that?"

"Someone's on the porch, babe. That's the swing."

"I do believe our guest has arrived, dear."

"Anybody up for some big band jazz of the twenties?" Joe asked, placing on the table a tray, on which were a bottle of Fundador and three snifters, and carefully pouring an ounce or so into each.

"Don't you mean the thirties?" said Oliver, his forward motion to accept the glass from Joe setting the swing into motion, "And isn't it called 'swing'?"

"If you're talking about Basie and Goodman and Artie Shaw and those cats, yeah, but I had in mind some Fletcher Henderson and early Duke." He held the snifter to his nose and then raised it high. "Here's to you, my friend." He went back into the house.

"You sure look great, Jane!" said Oliver, turning and looking directly into her eyes. "You have a kind of *glow* to you. I guess the life here agrees with you."

"Thanks, you look pretty good yourself, Ollie." She studied him for a moment. "You've let your hair grow. I do believe it's nearly as long as mine!"

"Hardly," he said, reaching behind her and touching the ends of her hair. "Jeez, you can almost sit on yours. Maybe almost as long as Joe's, though."

"We've enjoyed it here a lot, Ollie—even if we still don't quite feel that it's really *us*." She looked away for a moment and sighed. "Before I met Joe it was pretty much the kind of life I looked forward to. You know, nice secure job in a university library somewhere, maybe even here in your country. But I'm not so sure any more that I fit all that well into this kind of scene, know what I mean?"

"Oh, we all have our mixed feelings," he said, holding the snifter under his nose. "Hey, this stuff is really smooth, very nice. So how's Joe dealing with it?"

"Okay in some respects, not so well in others." She nodded toward the door behind them.

"'Sugarfoot Stomp'!" Joe announced. "With Pops on the solo coming up soon." He pulled up a chair and sat down, facing them.

"So how's the novel coming along, Joe?"

"I got quite a bit done on it over the summer, but have hardly taken it out of the box since then."

"I'm going to have to find you a bigger box, honey. You can't hardly get the top on it anymore." She turned to Oliver. "Joe passed the thousand-page mark."

"Still writing it out longhand, Joe?"

"Can't do it any other way, Oliver. The words have to flow down my neck across my arm out through my fingers," he said, holding up his arm and wiggling his fingers, "dripping out from these and running down out of that fountain pen onto a yellow legal pad. Won't work any other way, I'm afraid."

"I bought Joe an old desk-model Royal typewriter, huge thing, at the Good Will, Ollie, and he won't use it for anything except copying his articles and book reviews to send to journals, even writes *them* out longhand first."

"John Berryman says he needs a big supply of two liquids in order to write a poem—*ink and whiskey!*" said Joe and sipped the brandy. "Well, I've pretty much put the latter aside these past couple years or so, but I does need the former, yes I does." He sipped again. "You know, I heard him read at Harvard. Rained cats and dogs that night, almost didn't go, but a friend of mine said I'd live to regret it if I didn't and she dragged me out into that storm. Know something? She was probably right. I'd put that reading up there with one that I went to in the fifties of Theodore Roethke, when I was an undergraduate at UW, in Seattle."

"You get around—yes, you *sure do get around,* I'll have to say that about you, Joe! So how does it feel to be back in the saddle?"

"*Comme ci, comme ça,*" he replied, and abruptly changed the subject. "And how's your own work coming along? Wrapped up the diss yet?"

"Expect to finish it next summer, if all goes well, and I don't have to teach more than one section."

"I know how that is, those summer terms can really screw up your head. I made it a condition before we came here that I wouldn't do *anything* at *all* during the summer. And *by God,* I didn't even set foot on campus after the last day of class—after I turned in my grades, I mean. Had the department secretary forward my mail to me here. We had a great time, didn't we, babe?"

"We sure did!" She turned to Oliver. "We camped up in the mountains, went fishing, went into Denver and heard a jazz band, did all kinds of things."

"Now we're back to the grindstone."

"I'd sure like to get a position at a small place like this. You know, this year was the first time I've ever had a really small class, a dozen or so students in a kind of seminar setting, and I really enjoyed that closer contact. Only thing was, it was kind of hard coming up with the grade distribution."

"How's that, Ollie?" she asked, turning and directing a stern look at him.

"Oh, you know, they all wrote really great essays for the final and it was hard ranking them." Clearly uncomfortable in her glare, he glanced over at Joe. "I gave them a take-home exam so's I could get away a week early."

"I wondered about that."

"*Ranking* them?" Jane continued insistently, her forehead furrowing.

"Yeah, like, you know, coming up with a proper distribution, the *curve* thing. I mean, you've got to at least have a spread from A to C, that sort of thing."

"*Oh that's a lot of crap, Ollie!*" she said, more than a little heatedly. "I've been taking seminars down at the university and no one's gotten a grade lower than a B yet! And *why the hell should they?* They're all good students! Probably just like yours are in that class!"

Joe caught Jane's eye, winked, and then turned to Oliver. "I think you caught yourself in a contradiction there, my friend."

"How so?"

"Well, if you want to grade as you just described, seems to me you'd be better off somewhere where they don't have small classes." He got up and poured another ounce or so of the brandy into the others' snifters.

"Or where they don't have grades," Jane added.

"It's a catch twenty-two," said Joe.

Then she, apparently taking a cue from Joe that they should direct the conversation away from its present course, continued with, "Ollie, have you heard anything from Jim and the rest of them? We've gotten a postcard once in a while and that's about it. They were at that Woodstock thing in August and in New Orleans a couple of months ago and we haven't heard a thing since then."

"Oh, I meant to ask—." He broke off, a puzzled expression coming over his features. "Didn't Jim call you?"

"No," Jane answered.

"He called me two weeks ago from Chicago," Oliver continued, "and said they had a gig at the end of December in Denver and they were figuring on hitting there a few days before Christmas. He said Flossie and that Carver guy have friends there—you know, the harmonica player. I thought Jim would've called you by now."

"*Oh, that's exciting!* Joe, we'll have them all out for a Christmas party!"

"Yeah, great, be good to see Jim and the rest of the Muphs. Haven't heard much from them this past year and a half. Like Jane said, a postcard every once in a while.

They were in Boston one time, San Francisco another, then down in one of the Carolinas, all over the place. Say, did they ever make it back to Austin?"

"No, never did. Came to Dallas back in the spring for a one-night stand but I couldn't make it, had a hundred blue books to grade and was up all night. Jim didn't call me till that afternoon! *Crazy sonovabich!*"

"We often talk about Austin and all the great friends we made there, you and Jim and Boz and Flossie—" she began.

"Don't forget Messy," Joe interrupted.

"—and Mell and Nando." Having counted these off on one hand, she looked at Joe quizzically. "You know, I can't remember the names of that pair we took the dark room course from, honey."

Hesitating, Joe closed his eyes, then opened them and said, "Oh, yeah, Sylvester Stilton and Mindy Rinks. I don't think you ever got to know them, Oliver. They had a yawl they were always working on down at Corpus Christi, spending money right and left to equip it with very sophisticated radar gear."

"Yeah, I remember meeting them one time at your place. Weren't they leaving on some trip somewhere or other?"

"They were going to sail around the world—or so they said." She got off the swing. "It was not always very clear what was reality and what was fantasy with those two, was it honey?"

"No, as a matter of fact, it wouldn't have surprised me if we'd found them moored in the harbor there on our way to Padre Island. They sure were two of the most dedicated heads I've ever run into. Don't know if I ever saw them when they weren't stoned out of their skulls!"

"And that guy who drove the student shuttle bus, what was his name?" Oliver asked. "You started to tell me something about him one time, something about—."

"Oh, yeah, Johnny," said Joe. "You know, I never did get his last name. I don't think he ever told us. It's funny how we thought he was a narc when he stopped the bus right in front of the house that time and asked us for a glass of water. *Paranoid!* We had been waving to him once in a while if we happened to be out front for some reason, just getting home or something. So one time he just stops in the middle of the street and pulls the hand brake up and hops out. 'Kin y'all spay-yer a cuppa wahrter?' he says. So Jane went and got him a big glass of ice water and we stood there gabbing about the weather or some bullshit. Then he makes a regular thing of it, stops once or twice a week."

"Of course, he passed the house a half-dozen times a day," Jane pointed out.

"Yeah, he had this morning run, had all his classes in the afternoon."

"What was he studying?"

"Business major."

"Which of course made Joe all the more suspicious."

"*Damn right!*" Joe put his empty snifter on the table and leaned forward. "Then one day the sonovagun asks if he can bring his girl by some evening and 'visit a spell'! *I like to shit in my pants!*"

"I never heard this story," said Oliver, laughing. "So what all'd you do?"

"So I said, 'Sure, bring her by, we'll have a beer,' so forth and so on. House got a cleaning, I *shit you not!*"

"You never saw Joe so busy with the Electrolux, Ollie, and he was spraying everywhere with Airwick—."

"That's when I dug my Amontillado Room in the basement."

"Then?"

"So he and Mary came around, he's in coat and tie, black FBI shoes, she's a right pretty lass, cotton candy blonde, short skirt, sort of a fifties look, had me thinking she should be wearing an 'I Like Ike' button. Conversation is a little slow getting started—."

"Oh, Mary and I, we had a great time talking about clothes!"

"Then I'm out in the kitchen with Johnny getting some beers and he looks like he's real embarrassed and he asks me, 'Joe, izit as good as some o' m' buddies sez'—he had this classic Texas drawl—'ballin' a chick when yer wrecked on mary-wanna?'" Joe rocked back and forth in his chair and guffawed.

"Well, I've heard this one a few times, guys, so what say I go fix us a snack? You must be starved, Ollie, and Joe is always up for cheese and crackers and pickles and stuff. How's that sound?"

"Sounds great, Jane!" answered Oliver, not removing his gaze from Joe. "I am pretty hungry. So then?"

"So I took a chance. You know, sometimes you have a kind of gut feeling about someone, and I suddenly had total trust in this dude, know what I mean? I sent him back into the living room and told him to ask Jane to come out. She went along with it so I went down in the basement and fetched the hookah and some outrageous Texas weed and we turned those virgins on. After we finished the first bowl we asked her how she liked it, assuming, naturally, that she was hip to what we were doing."

"And?"

"She didn't know *what the fuck was going on!* Said something like, 'It has a very different taste.' She thought I just wanted them to try some 'very aromatic tobacco or other'!" He rocked forward and slapped his knee. "*Thought I just liked friends to try out my latest tobacco find!* Of course she was wrecked out of her skull—*but didn't know it!*"

"And Johnny?"

"Oh *he* was *flying*!"

Oliver joined in with Joe's laughter. "Did you ever find out if Johnny's question got answered to his satisfaction?"

"He never said, but from that time on, his appearance—and her's too—changed radically. Didn't see them for a while—he got a different run right around that time—and when we did, he was growing a beard and letting his hair grow, headband, jeans. She had her hair straight and was letting the roots grow out—turned out she was a brunette. Cut-offs, work shirt only buttoned about half-way up, no bra. Both in sandals, the whole bit."

"Crazy!"

"Sure was!"

"Say, that rain is letting up," said Oliver. "My last twenty minutes or so here was pretty rough. Thought I'd have to pull over and sit it out. Would have but I was afraid the car behind me would follow me off the road and rear-end me."

"Yeah, it's hardly even raining."

"Help me get my gear in before it pours again, will ya."

"Let's go!"

They slept in the next morning and had a big breakfast

of scrambled eggs and sausage links, cornbread with jam, and a large pot of coffee. Then, while Jane packed a lunch and Oliver remained at the kitchen table and talked to her, Joe gathered ponchos, walking sticks, and knapsacks for the hike.

When they pulled into the parking lot Rufus jumped over the seat into the space vacated by Joe and almost knocked him over as he leaped out of the Greenbrier. He ran furiously toward the Flatirons and in a few seconds was out of sight.

"*There he goes!*" said Joe, laughing. "Amazing how he always heads in the right direction."

"Well, where else do we go when we come up here with him?"

"Right. Say, with this slight chill in the air, looks like a beautiful day for a stroll up thet thar hill," said Joe.

"Yeah, there's a little dampness from last night's downpour, too," Oliver observed, putting on the poncho Jane handed to him. "What's the building? Looks like some kind of resort or something, all those cabins. What gives?" He walked over and peered into a window.

"I would suppose that William Jennings Bryan stood on that stage sixty or seventy years ago," said Joe, looking over his friend's shoulder, "and held forth in mellifluous voice with, 'I shall not help crucify mankind upon a cross of gold . . . ,' and so forth and so on."

"Oh, right, the Chautauqua circuit. I saw the sign."

"We saw some great Chaplin here last summer— Buster Keaton, too."

"Okay, guys, *time to move!*" She called to them as she swung a knapsack up onto her back and took off at a brisk pace.

They walked two miles, following a path that skirted the Flatirons, until they came upon an Alpine-like meadow, which they crossed. The spot they settled on sloped slightly downward, affording a view of the plain and the near edge of Boulder. They leaned on their walking sticks and gazed at the horizon. Behind them were the mountains. Jane took the last poncho out of her pack, spread it on the ground, took hers off, folded it into cushion size, and sat on it, hugging her knees to her chest and sighing.

"Yeah, I worked up some sweat on that walk," said Oliver, carefully placing his pack on a large flat rock. He pulled his poncho over his head and dropped it at his feet.

Joe did the same after lowering his backpack to the spread poncho. "Yes sir, this is God's country, no doubt about that!" he proclaimed. "*Too bad man found it!*" He reached into the pack and produced three bottles of ale and removed their caps with the opener hanging from a thong around his neck. "Came up here one time and forgot the damn church key!"

"Used your teeth?" said Oliver, taking the bottle proffered him.

"Nope, Jane's belt buckle. But I knew a guy in Baltimore who could do that."

"Well, friends, here's to your everlasting happiness!" toasted Oliver, raising his bottle high.

"Thanks, Ollie. I guess we're doing pretty well so far, aren't we, honey."

"Sure are, babe, sure are!" Joe gulped down a fourth of his bottle. "Thanks to Jane's provision, we are able to partake of this pre-prandial libation."

"And you're carrying the rest of my provision, Ollie, so why don't you swing your pack over here and I'll set the table."

"We come up here at least once a week," said Joe. "And I walk the mile or so from home to college and back every other day."

"You do look in great shape, man."

"Rufus just loves it up here. Honey, why don't you whistle for him." She zipped her windbreaker up. "That rain really cooled it off."

"Yeah, let him know where we are, anyway." He cupped his hands together tightly and blew into the small opening left between his thumbs, emitting a piercing wail.

"*Jesus Christ!*" gasped Oliver. "*Scared* the *shit* outa me!"

Joe laughed. "Steady on, mite, that's me fog 'orn call!"

"We had to leave Mr. Perryman up here one time last summer, Ollie, and a couple of hours later we heard this scratching on the screen door and *there he was!* Of course, we were going to come back for him later—but it *wasn't necessary!*"

"Jane looked up hounds in the library and found out there are documented cases of them wandering as far as seventy-five miles away and finding their way back home. Part homing pigeons, apparently."

The conversation was discontinued for several minutes as they broke off pieces of bread, cut cheese and hard salami, and washed it down with second bottles of ale. Oliver broke the silence.

"You know, I lay awake last night for an hour or so thinking about your situation here and wondering what the hell I'm going to do with my life after next year when, I hope, that god damned dissertation is accepted and I have my bloody union card, finally, after all these years."

"I'm sure it'll all come together, Ollie, it'll all come together," she assured him. "Meanwhile, just enjoy.

311

Voilà!" She threw a kiss to the horizon and then let her arm continue in an upward, all-encompassing arc. "Just look at those mountains! Why *it's like Switzerland!*"

Chapter 10

Let the fuckin' good times roll!

So much snow had been blown up against the front of the house, the banister protruded from the drift barely enough for Joe to locate the stairs to the porch. Ascent thereto was awkward in the extreme because the stairwell was piled so high with snow it was difficult to find individual steps. Joe misjudged about half way up and as his feet went out from beneath him and he began to fall, he dropped his knapsack and flung his hand out instinctively for something to grab onto, but his gloved hand did not connect with anything and he fell forward on his face into the soft snow.

A car was coming down the street, its sounds barely audible above the wind. He rolled over onto his side and squinted into the falling flakes, which were, it seemed to him, the size of silver dollars. It was the Corvair and Jim, Melinda, and Boz were getting out of the car and struggling through the two-foot-high snow that covered the ground. They didn't see him until they were nearly on top of him.

"No, James, I'll come back out an' fetch our gear an' the rest o' the stuff!" he heard Boz call out.

"Hey, man, what're you doing lying out here in the weather?" Harsh shouted over the storm as he nearly tripped over him and he and Melinda struggled to help him up, their own feet slipping and sliding as he came to a standing position. "And how the hell *are* you *anyway,* man?"

"Yeah, Joe," said Melinda, kissing him on the mouth, "it's great t' see ya, man!" She picked up his knapsack.

"*Howdo, Perfesser!*" called Boz, pausing several yards from them and surveying the scene, his characteristically wry smile indicating that he relished, far beyond its intrinsic worth, the "Rescue of The Perfesser Lewis From the Blizzard," as he soon dubbed the episode. Adjusting with a shrug the large gunnysack slung over his right shoulder, Boz followed the others as, arm-in-arm, they slowly made their way up the stairs.

Inside the hallway the four of them stamped their feet, Joe brushed the snow off his clothes and removed his Dart Drug "99 Cent Bargain" work gloves and Sunny Surplus seaman's knitted cap, and all hung their coats on hooks along the wall.

"Sheet, mon," Jim Harsh exclaimed, affecting an "Island" accent and with no little amazement in his voice, "Ah theenk we wud fer shoo-oo-wer nawt mike it oop that heel!"

"Fer shoo-oo-wer ah dint tew!" Melinda parodied him.

"Piece o' cake," Boz interjected as Harsh was about to continue. "Enny time ya got yer engine o'er yer drivin' wheels, izza bloody piece o' cake. I knowed from the word go we'd leave thet hill behind us, with no trouble ay-tall. I done drove in worse'n thet manys the time!"

"In thet caze," said Melinda, "ah shore em glad ya was et da wheel, Meester Boswell!" Boz winked at her in appreciation of her exaggerated mimicry of him.

Anticipation of the companionship, warmth, food, drink, and other amenities that awaited him on the other side of the door at the end of the hallway dominated Joe's emotions, despite the distractions of the banter being provided by his companions. It seemed to him that Jim and Melinda were a little drunk but he really couldn't be sure in the confusion of the last few minutes. He paused at the door to the front room and motioned with his hand behind him for the others to also do so, for the music was at such a volume that he assumed those inside were unaware of their arrival. It was The Band's "I Shall Be Released."

He eased the door open a crack and peered into the room. Jane, Saul, and Oliver were facing the fireplace, wherein flames licked up around a large, charred log. The hound Rufus Perryman lay close to the hearth. All their backs were to the newcomers and their gazes were transfixed, he conjectured, on a combination of inner and outer visions.

"God only knows what they see in that fire," he whispered, turning to Melinda, who was beside him. Euphoria surged over him and he put his arm around her waist and squeezed her to him. She shook her head inquiringly, starting to speak, and Joe put his finger to his lips, shushing her.

On the surface of the great spool that served as a general purpose table and at which the three, seated on cushions made of wholesale-size legume and nut sacks, stared into the fire, were the paraphernalia of cannabis indulgence, in particular the water pipe, a large box of wooden matches, several packs of cigarette paper, a package of pipe cleaners, a half dozen thirty-five millimeter film cans (with masking-tape labels identifying one as "Col.," another as "Mex.," still another as "Calif.", etc.), a Swiss Army pocket knife, and a half-moon-shaped piece of wood (from an apple cider keg) that served as a cutting board for hashish.

This is one of those situations, he reflected as he sniffed the tell-tale aroma, *where one has to avoid scaring the shit out of people, especially in view of the fact that what they've been smoking no doubt has them a million miles from here. A sudden shock could tip them over the edge into hysteria. But how to do it? If we descend upon them without warning it'll freak 'em out of their gourds.*

Sensing that one of the three hovering behind him was on the point of vocalizing their presence, he glanced back over his shoulder and again held his finger to his lips. Melinda stared into the room with a look of fright, almost terror, afterwards confessing that she had thought Joe was planning some practical joke with the intent of startling those gazing into the fire. But he simply lifted his heel a couple of inches from the floor and stamped the bare board in a quick, but not violent, motion. Jane turned and looked back, her casual movement indicating nothing of shock, little enough even of surprise, her greeting a smile of pure pleasure.

In turning, and then rising to her knees, she conveyed to Saul and Oliver that something was afoot. The former reacted immediately, leaping to his feet. Oliver merely turned, staring across the fire-lighted room, and then waved to Joe, who was heading off to the left in the direction of the sound equipment. Oliver appeared vague and uncertain, not even seeming to recognize the others until they were well into the room, almost atop him. Then, slowly rising to a kneeling position, he suddenly broke into a broad grin, embracing the legs of Melinda and Jim, and grasping the outstretched hand of Boz, over whose shoulder the sack was still slung.

The decibel level abruptly dropped by at least half as Joe reached the wall filled with the many components of the sound system. Conversation instantly ensued, Boz leading off with, "Found Joe out thar buried in the snow. Near fruz, I'd say. No tellin' how long he bin there." He seemed to be looking around for a likely resting place for the sack. Joe, gathering from Boz's scanning of the room that he wished to be rid of it, relieved him of it, nestled it on his own shoulder, and started off in the direction of a door on the opposite side of the room.

"Hey, where you goin' with that, Santa Claus?" Harsh cried out and rushed over to him. "There's a couple o' things I wants out o' there." Joe stood patiently, his back to the room, while Jim gently took hold of the sack, lowered it to the floor with care, and extricated two bottles of ale and a cake tin from it. Joe turned and approached Jane, who was embracing Melinda, having similarly greeted Jim and Boz.

"Honey, you are *almost blue!*" she called to him from across the spool, where she had once again taken up her position on a cushion. "Why don't you sit by the fire and I'll fix some coffee for you."

"Rather have tea," he replied, dropping to his knees and hugging and kissing her.

Saul took a pewter pot from amidst the cups on the spool. "I'll take care of that," he announced, heading for the kitchen. "Be right back."

"Oh, hey, everybody!" said Jane, this is Saul!"

"*Hi, everybody!*" he called over his shoulder, raising his free hand in a wave to the three newcomers. "I'll be back in a minute with some fresh tea."

"Here, come over by the fire," Jane addressed the others. "You must all be frozen!"

"Sure do look invitin', and I do love a fahr," Boz observed, approaching the fireplace and studying its contents for a moment. "Appear it could use a little pokin' up." He already had the tool in hand as he began the last sentence and was on his haunches stirring up the embers. "Maybe needs a couple pieces o' thet kindlin'," he muttered, pointing with his free hand. "Hand me that thar slat, James—no, no, thet *long* one thar. Right, now you got it! And thet other'n under it, too. Oh, *we're cookin' now!*"

Joe, Jane, Melinda, and Oliver, all now seated on cushions, watched as Boz and Jim refueled the fire. The telephone rang and Jane began to rise, but relaxed back onto the cushion when she heard Saul answer it. Her attention was distributed among the conversation between Oliver and Melinda, who was recounting the harrowing climb up the hill in the Corvair and praising the expertise of Boz in negotiating it, the firebuilding of Jim and Boz, whose efforts had by this time created a veritable roaring inferno in the huge hearth, and Joe's meticulous sorting and arranging of the motley, and jumbled, assortment of odds and ends scattered on the spool. Lost in contemplation of these three scenarios, she appeared to have forgotten that the telephone had rung. She was startled out of her reverie by Saul calling from the doorway. "*Hey, Jane, telephone!*" As she hurried to the kitchen, Saul emerged with teapot in hand.

Tea and cake were being served several minutes later when Jane resumed her place at table. The water pipe, its bowl replenished with a mixture of pot and hash, stood in the middle of the spool.

"That was the Pettibones, Joe," said Jane, as she squeezed in between him and Oliver. *"They're in Denver!"*

Joe was preparing to fill the cup at her place but, as she announced this, he arrested the teapot in mid-course.

"Incredibile! Are they coming out?" His tone indicated surprise, almost shock, at this turn of events, and his response to her news was infectious. Oliver's hand seemed seized by a spasm and he nearly tipped over his full cup of tea. In reaction to the rattling of cup and saucer, Melinda lurched away from him, bumping Jim and knocking the lighted Gauloises from his fingers. Boz deftly snatched up the cigarette, which had rolled halfway across the spool, and held it out to its owner. Maintaining the lone comprehensive view of this scene of near chaos, Saul, standing on the other side of the table, broke out in wild, all but hysterical, laughter, as precipitately terminated as it had commenced.

"What the hell's going on here?" a grinning Joe inquired. "I simply asked if the people were coming out from Denver and you'd think a god damned poltergeist had landed in the middle of the spool."

"It's all right, dear," Jane soothed him, adding, "Why don't we do that pipe Oliver packed?"

"What makes you assume that Oliver packed it?"

"Well, I guess because he fixed the one we did before you came. Why, did *you* pack it?"

"That's the trouble with you, Oliver, man leaves you alone with his ol' lady for a few hours and no telling what's going on." Toward the end of this he had dropped into the speech pattern he had adopted earlier that day at the mirror in the men's room in college engineer John Staples' "home" building, his idea of a "Georgia cracker" accent.

"But *Saul* was here," Jane interrupted, primly, seemingly more than satisfied with the impeccable logic implied in her declaration.

"So you were in on it, too, there, young man." This was said by Joe in an almost matter of fact manner, little or nothing of interrogation attaching to it, as he leaned forward, examining the contents of the water pipe's bowl. "*I* packed this," he said insistently. "No one except yours truly had a thing to do with this masterpiece."

"I can't *stand* the *suspense,* for chrissakes!" Melinda cried out. "Are the whatserfaces coming over or not?"

"Yeah," Joe said, turning to Jane, "you never answered my question."

"Oh, no, they said the roads are too bad to go out tonight. They'll be here tomorrow. Anyway, how could they find this place in this storm."

"Where the hell are they?"

"Oh, they're staying in a downtown hotel, honey."

"I'm happy to hear that!" he exclaimed. "Had a vision for an instant there of them sleeping in that camper—*on a night like this!*" He shivered. "Funny, I guess I'll always think of them as living in that thing. Far as finding this place, I don't think that would actually present much of a problem to Henry Pettibone. He has been known to get himself out of—after, of course, he'd already gotten himself into—some very tight places." He turned and leered toward Jim and Oliver and Melinda. "If you gets my point." Oliver looked puzzled but Melinda grinned and punched Jim in his side.

"Joe, they flew into Denver today," said Jane, chuckling. "Did you think they were traveling the country in a camper in the middle of winter? *Honestly!*" She sighed. "It's too bad we couldn't have them here, but I just can't see them on the floor in sleeping bags. We could get a room for them in that nice little motel we stayed at, remember?"

"Don't see why not—," he began but was cut off by Saul.

"Why not Vince's room? He's got that couch now—plus his mattress."

"After all, Henry was over there in France in the first one, all that trench warfare, all that horror. Told me some folks said it had made him 'peculiar,' said, '*God damn right it did!*'"

"Joe, were you listening to what Saul just said?" Jane was trying to get his attention by tapping him on the knee with her middle finger, each time raising her finger to an almost vertical position. All but Oliver, who was seated on the other side of her, were oblivious to the action of the finger, and he was, it would seem, hypnotized by it.

Joe peered over the tip of his nose down his greying unkempt beard at Jane's wagging finger. "What you doing down there, woman, giving me the *digitalis infama* again? Didn't I already tell you that when a member of the audience showed a finger to Nero, the emperor had him removed from the theater?"

"Are you saying this man wahr in the First World War, Perfesser?"

"That is correct, Boz, he commanded an artillery battery, got gassed, went through hell, if you know what I mean."

"Oh, yes, I do know 'cause I done me a bit o' readin'

up on thet subject. Thet was some kind o' mess in them thar mud holes. And you say he got *gassed*? *Whew!* Yes indeed, I do think he deserve somethin' more than a floor to sleep on!"

As the foregoing observations were in progress Joe had been slowly sliding the water pipe across the spool toward his interlocutor. When it was directly in front of its apparent destination, he tossed the box of matches so that they landed by the hookah's glass base.

"I gets the honor of fahrin' it up tonight?" Boz inquired, clearly not a little incredulous. "That's a real heavy honor, thet is, indeed it is, it bein' the first pipe fer all us together fer Christmas an' all!"

"Hey, I never thought of that, Bozzo," Jim offered, "but that's right!"

"Well, I guess Joe done," said Boz under his breath, at the same time striking with his thumbnail a wooden match tightly encircled by his four fingers and holding its flame to the bowl of the hookah, drawing all the while on the mouthpiece at the end of the eighteen-inch tube. When it was well fired up he pushed the hookah back to the hub of the spool, where it had been when he and the others had arrived.

The water pipe remained there, turning a little as each of the party leaned forward to receive the mouthpiece, inhale, and pass it on to the person to his or her left. In this manner the consumption of the bowl's contents traveled its silent (except for the bubbling sound) and clockwise course around the spool several times. The bowl glowed each time inhalation took place, and to Joe, who had stood up intending to add a log to the fire, this had the appearance of a slowly blinking red light, sort of a slow motion version of a late-night traffic signal, the kind of thing, it occurred to him, that an underground film maker would use, perhaps blending it from the one scene into the next.

"*Joe!*" Saul called up to him. "*Hey, Joe!*" And still not getting his attention, "*Hey, Joe, come out of it!*"

"Oh, yeah, what's happenin', man?" He looked down at Saul.

"Joe, the Pettibones can stay up in Vince's room!"

"Hey, that's right, Vince is away until after New Year's," he said, leaning down and supporting himself by the tips of his fingers on the very edge of the spool. "Hey, Jane, did you hear that? Henry and Margery can stay upstairs in Vince's room."

"*Really!*" she said, winking at Saul.

"I guess I won't get a chance to meet that guy who lives in the attic," said Oliver, "if he won't be back until then. Looks like an interesting dude, judging by his digs. I see he's a painter."

"What kind of painter?" Jim asked, rising to his feet and continuing his query in pantomime, broadly stroking up and down from midriff to forehead and with clenched left hand at thigh holding an imaginary pail. Then, index finger and thumb delicately touching, hardly moving, and poised at eye level no more than a foot from his face, he squinted in concentration at some point eight or ten inches beyond his hand.

"Both, actually," Saul replied, breaking into a smile. "And right there in his pad, sometimes at the same time."

"This whole conversation is really spacing me out," Oliver announced, his hands shaking as he reached for a tin of tobacco and papers in the center of the spool, somewhat in the manner of Jim Harsh, whose hands were uncharacteristically still on this occasion.

"Why's that, Oliver?" Joe asked, chuckling, "I don't have any trouble following it."

"Honey, I haven't seen you so stoned for months," Jane broke in. "Anyway, shall we call the Pettibones and ask them to stay here?"

"Sure, sure, I think that would be really fine. Have a real old-fashioned Christmas." He beckoned for her to follow him as he turned toward the kitchen. "Say, why don't we rustle up some grub."

"Joe," she called, remaining seated, "there's a casserole in the oven and a salad in the fridge. That's how Ollie and Saul and I were carrying on while you were on your trek over to the campus."

"Don't you want another hit on this," Saul turned and asked her, offering her the hookah's mouthpiece.

"God, no, or I'll never manage to get dinner together! As a matter of fact, why don't you come out and help me. I think time has gotten away from me and my ability to organize seems to be rather minimal at the moment."

The two of them disappeared into the kitchen. Their voices could be heard intermittently for several minutes while Joe was rewinding and removing the tape preparatory to programming the next portion of the evening. He knelt beside a milk crate and took out of it a flat box labeled "Grateful Dead Live" and "Stones Bleed." With the aid of a huge pair of headphones he proceeded to cue up the tape, his expression displaying, at first, incomprehension, then amusement.

"Is that the Doors playing backwards over Dr. John?" he said.

"Say what?" asked Melinda, evidently the only one to hear him.

His ears covered by the headphones, he did not

respond, but stopped the tape, rewound it, removed it from the machine's spindle, and glanced at its label, which said, "For Joe." He leaned it against the crate.

Now where did that come from? he said to himself. *Oh, yeah, someone back in Austin laid it on me. Who the hell was that? Different machine, I guess, four-track or something.* Rummaging around in the milk crate, he found the tape whose label matched that of the box and threaded it onto the take-up reel. He then cued it, manually rolled it back several revolutions, set the volume back up to where it had been upon his entry into the room from the snow-drift experience, pushed the "Play" button, looked back over his shoulder at the four remaining at the spool, a rather fiendish grin on his countenance, and returned to his place. As he settled into the cushion, awaiting the take-up of the leader, the firelight accented his eerie expression somewhat in the manner of a flashlight held beneath the chin in the darkness, the sort of effect one strove for when telling ghost stories on Halloween.

When the Dead hit at a nearly deafening volume, Oliver and Jim started as though punched in their sides. But neither Boz nor Melinda flinched a muscle. Jim, who was seated between them, now seemed to have lapsed into a trance, staring straight ahead blankly, and Oliver was tapping on the spool with the extended index finger of his right hand. Joe held the picture in his eyes for several seconds, pretending that he was listening to the music on headphones by himself as he stared at them sitting there in silence. Then he got up and went over to the controls, adjusting the volume to a level at which conversation could resume. Returning to the spool, he took a place beside Boz, calling across it to Oliver.

"That the way you s'pose t' dig the Dead, daddy," he

advised.

"*Yeah, man!*" said Boz, his voice taking on a hoarseness that bordered on mimicry of Louis Armstrong's gravelly speech.

"The only way to really dig those cats is to *be* there *with* them!" Oliver chimed in.

"Why'd you turn it down, Joe?" Melinda asked. "That's nothing compared to our practice sessions." She paused, then went on, cutting off Joe, who was on the brink of an opening syllable. "Even if you put cotton in your ears it almost blows your head apart. Just before we left today we practised two new numbers and Jim listened with dead headphones on."

Jim was shaking his head from side to side, smiling. "Dead headphones, dead headphones," he was saying, repeating it several more times.

"Who're these people coming over tomorrow, Joe?" asked Oliver. "Anybody I know?"

Joe was lighting, by a candle Jane had placed in the center of the spool, one of Jim's Gauloises. Until he sat back it was not clear whether he had heard Oliver's question. After inhaling deeply and releasing the smoke, he coughed several times from deep in his lungs and caught Oliver's eye.

"Probably not this incarnation, Ollie, but who knows? Maybe one time, somewhere, in an earlier life, you did run into Henry Pettibone and his wife Margery." He drew again on the cigarette. "But I'd rather let them speak for themselves."

"*Henry Pettibone!*" Jim exclaimed. "*Thought* I recognized that name! I took seminars from him!" He laughed. "Brilliant man! He's coming here?"

"I know you did, Jim, and Henry sure is brilliant—and

Margery is, too," he answered. "They'll be here tomorrow."

"*Crazy,* man, *crazy!* I seem to remember you writing me a year or so ago that you met up with my old Harvard professor. How did that come about now?"

"They were up the beach from us on Padre Island, Jim, right after all of us split from Austin a year ago August, and we became great friends, hung out at their camper. Henry and I talked politics, Margery let Jane know about their skeletons in the closet and so forth."

"Yeah, they have a few of them, I heard," said Jim. "I had him in the late fifties and early sixties and he did love to talk politics. He definitely did not like Ike and was overjoyed when Kennedy beat Nixon."

"You should hear him on the Republicans now, Jim!"

"I bet!"

The music took over for the next few minutes. Joe sat silently gazing at the fire. *I ought to go out in the kitchen and tell Jane to call them back tonight,* he said to himself. *No, I could do it in the morning. Maybe I'll run in there and get them. Probably catch them at their morning coffee. Sometimes Henry had brandy with it, Margery said, sometimes in it.* Thinking back on it, he wondered if she had meant he always had it, either the one way or the other, or just sometimes and then one way or the other. *Kind of thing they argue about by the hour in the philosophy department,* he thought, with amusement, *except it's made to sound 'high falutin', as Boz would say in his down home way.*

"Oliver," he called over the music and leaned forward across the spool. "Why don't you get that bottle of tequila?"

"It's right there," Oliver said, pointing to the corner by the door where were a very worn, belted leather suitcase with "Paris," "Berlin," and other stickers, a battered army footlocker, a rolled sleeping bag with patches here and there, and several cardboard boxes, their flaps tucked in to each other in alternating, locking pattern. Joe rose and went over to the assembled baggage, turned, and looked quizzically back at Oliver.

"It's in the box on top," Oliver informed him.

Flipping open the box's lid, Joe plucked out the bottle of tequila and, pausing to peer out the window, returned to the spool.

"Christ, I wouldn't want to go out there!" he exclaimed.

"No, tha's a bad un out thar t'night, Perfesser," Boz confided from his humped-over-forward position, not lifting his eyes from the disassembled hookah that he was busy cleaning. "By the way, Perfesser, where the hell wuz y' comin' from when we come on you thar on the steps?"

Boz presented the question with an almost studied casualness, Joe remembered the next day when he was recalling for Jane how the news had first come out. For, so certain was she that he would not have introduced the subject, she made him probe the depths of his mind until he could convincingly cite what had initiated the revelation. She made him go over it on subsequent occasions, too, long after the circumstances of that afternoon had dominated their waking hours, changed their lives, taken the time of their friends and others, infuriated many, earned the respect of a few, and, for the most part, delighted his students.

Of course, among the last named there were the dissenters, who—in a phrase that would become a cliche within a few weeks—"deserved it in the first place." Of particular delight to him was the statement to the press by the college dean, a professor of German and a bilingual first-generation American, that he was "fairly incensed" by Joe's action. He found it a curious expression in the context and wondered what idiom in the man's alternate tongue could have suggested it. Henry Pettibone, commenting on it, and on some of the other clippings Joe sent him, in a letter that Joe deeply valued, observed, "Joe, did this statement come from someone with even a modicum of wit, I would have thought it intentionally equivocal, even rife with double meaning, but well knowing your esteemed colleague, a certified Boobus Americanus and attested member of the Booboisie, it was more likely a futile attempt at profundity."

"I was up to school posting my grades, Boz."

"*In this weather?* I dint think they'd even be open over thar. Don't they lock up fer Christmas?" He was still bent over the parts of the hookah, a pipe cleaner in one hand, a piece of brass tubing in the other, and apparently about to resume his inquiry when Melinda entered the conversation.

"So you finally got all your exams graded, Joe?"

"Yes, I did, Mess, I read every one of those hundred and thirty three blue books," he answered her. "Took me three days and nearly drove me crazy. And I gave every last one of my students an A for the semester grade."

A hubbub sounded in the butler's pantry. Jane and Saul emerged, both carrying a tray, his laden with a large casserole dish and an immense earthenware bowl of salad, hers with two loaves of bread on a cutting board, plates, wooden bowls, stem glasses, utensils, and linen napkins. A couple of paces behind them came Jim, an unlighted cigar clamped in the left corner of his mouth and in each hand a bottle of wine grasped by the neck. Those seated at the spool were quickly clearing aside cups, ashtrays, hookah, and paraphernalia.

Joe took one of the bottles from Jim and studied the label. He nodded to him. "Thanks. Appreciate it."

"Thought you'd like it. Got a case of it in Denver yesterday. It's out on the porch." He handed him a corkscrew.

"That'll keep it nice and cool," Jane observed, sliding to Joe the tray, on which were seven crystal wine glasses.

Having levered the cork from one of the bottles, Joe poured an ounce of the white wine into a glass, lifted it to his lips, sipped it, nodded in affirmation to Jim, and filled each glass almost to its brim. The glasses were passed around the table and each of the party sat silently for a half minute or so, Jane, Melinda, and Boz with eyes closed and leaning slightly forward as though in prayer, Jim studying the still cold cigar now held in his hand a few inches above the spool's surface, Oliver and Saul catching one another's eyes and smiling somewhat sheepishly, Joe turning his head slowly from side to side and surveying the faces of his companions. All then leaned forward and lightly touched glasses.

Breaking the silence, Joe announced in Cockney, "*'Ere's bloody mud in yer friggin' eye!*" and raised his glass to his mouth, downing its contents at one gulp and then pouring himself another.

Jane and Boz were serving onto plates from the casserole as Melinda and Saul heaped bowls high with salad. The uncut loaves of dark bread with serrated knife at its side rested upon a crude cutting board that could well have been a companion of the slats Boz had earlier been feeding to the fire. Oliver took the knife in hand and began converting a loaf into wafer-thin slices.

Food and drink took up the attention of all for several minutes. Except for grunts, several single-syllable compliments, and appreciative smiles in eulogy to the food cast in the direction of Jane, attention remained fixed upon the plates, until Oliver looked up and, catching Joe's eye, signaled to him with his hand.

"Of course, you were joking before when you said you gave all A's, right, Joe?"

Jane looked at Joe, puzzled.

Although the music was still at the reasonable level at which Joe had reset it, still, no one heard the door to the outer hall open and close. It was the atmospheric alteration, the almost indiscernible drop in temperature that occurred as the cooler air from the hall mixed with the heat of the big front room in which the meal was being enjoyed, that distracted Joe from responding to Oliver's question. He glanced over his right shoulder toward the door to the hall.

It wasn't so much that he didn't recognize the snow-covered figure in buckskin standing there, scarf obscuring the lower half of his face, a back pack suspended from his right hand, a guitar case from the other. That limitation to his knowledge did not disturb him in the least. What nagged him was that the figure fitted to a pattern somewhere in his subconscious and he couldn't bring it up. It was something like trying to work something—a whisker from his moustache, say—out of the very top of the throat, Joe reflected, and indeed, the movement of his head simulated the nodding forward and up and swallowing that accompanies this kind of distressful effort.

The scant ten seconds before anyone else became aware of the intruder allowed Joe to almost, but not quite, bring into focus in his mind's viewer the image he required in order to dispel his present mental unease. But it just would not come up. He turned back to the table, seeking help or advice on the practical level of how to deal with the circumstance of a newcomer, a stranger (to all in the room, he assumed), arriving in the first few minutes of a meal. Inspired by the sudden recollection that he was the host of the gathering, Joe began to rise from the cushion. One leg supported him by foot, the other by knee, when he noted that Oliver was no longer looking at him as before, when putting the question to him, but was gazing off to the right of Joe with a questioning smile. Joe looked quickly back to the door, and then spun his head again toward the table for help.

By this time Oliver had leapt up and, with a lunge that almost had him tripping over his own boots, reached the intruder and, lifting him off his feet in a bear hug, swung him around several times.

"Where the hell did you get the Daniel Boone outfit?" Oliver asked his nephew, but the others had by now been alerted to his presence and the question went by the wayside for the moment.

"Oh, it's Orson!" Joe exclaimed. "Why I thought you were a complete stranger! I thought you were in Denver!"

"You said you wuz gonna come out tomorrow," Boz interjected. "An' we wuz gonna come git ya."

"Well, I got restless, so I hitched out."

"In this weather?" said Jane. "You certainly have a sense of adventure!"

"It was a gas!" said Orson, grinning.

"Was everything all right back at the REO?" Melinda asked.

"Sure, sure," Orson replied, his delivery carrying,

slightly, the force of dismissal of the query. Then he turned back to his uncle. "Bought it off a dude from Montana in Denver this morning."

"How have you been?" Oliver asked and, in the absence of an extended hand to meet his outstretched one, he grasped Orson's arm above the elbow.

"Fine."

"You look half frozen, Orson! Go over by the fire and get thawed out," Jane urged.

"Yeah, it's really blowin' out there, and I had to walk up here from downtown with all my gear. *What a drag!* Oh, I better get that back pack over here and make sure it's not soaked through from the snow!" He took long strides to the door where he had dropped his backpack and guitar case and dragged the pack over to the hearth, on the edge of which he took a seat and began to unlace his boots, which were of G.I. combat style. He pulled them off and placed them on the hearth and the snow began melting and running down them, forming little puddles on the bricks.

Boz came over from the other side of the spool and knelt in front of him. "Better not leave them boots up agin the fahr, Orson," he cautioned. "Here, I'll stuff some newspaper in 'em fer ya."

"Thanks, man." Satisfied that his pack was dry inside, he turned toward those at the spool. "Sure were a lot of people stranded and gone off the road. This truck driver I got a ride with had to stop a couple of times or he'd have hit someone. There were pigs all over the place." Legs pulled up against his chest, arms embracing them, Orson shivered. "The dude driving that rig must have weighed three-hundred pounds. He stopped in town for gas and then he invited me to have coffee and pie with him. So I had a piece of pie and hot chocolate with him in this place where we was the only customers and the help was this cute chick and a freak with hair down almost to his butt. That was real cool. This dude said he was heading over the mountains and if he didn't make it he'd just pull over on the shoulder and put the flashers on and sleep. He said he had blankets and food and everything he needed in his sleeper. *'Everything I need 'cept a broad!'"* Orson grinned sheepishly. "He talked like some character in an old movie. Like—who's that fat guy with the high-pitched voice?"

"Andy Devine," Boz said, supplying the answer that was on the tip of Joe's tongue.

"And he had a two-way radio in the cab. That was real cool, how he was talking like he was on the radio, or a cop or something. *It was a gas!"* He laughed and then felt his socks and pulled them off and laid them on the hearth. "Anyway, he was having a third piece of pie and more coffee when I split and started walkin' up here."

"What make o' rig wahr he drivin'?" Boz asked, having finished to his satisfaction the stuffing of Orson's boots.

"I didn't notice."

Saul placed a plate heaped with the cheese, vegetable, and macaroni casserole and a bowl filled with salad next to Orson and Joe handed him a glass of wine.

"See how you like that, Orson."

The young man sipped from the glass and nodded his approval. Then he looked up at Saul. "Say, man, where's that French chick I heard you was shackin' up with?"

"She's Dutch, she's from Holland," Saul corrected, "and she flew home for the holidays. If you stick around, you'll meet her. She'll be back right after New Year's. Anyway, we're engaged."

"That's no chick, that's his fiancée," said Joe *sotto voce.*

"*Really!* When's the big day?"

"Next summer. We're going to get married over there."

"Outasight, man!"

"Orson," Jim called over to him from across the spool, a cigarette bobbing up and down in the corner of his mouth, "when did you split from the Muphs?" His hand shook as he applied a Zippo lighter to the Gauloises. "I mean, they had their shit together, didn't they?"

"I don't know, Jim." This was said hesitantly and, following Harsh's drawl, almost mimicked it. But anyone there who took it as having intent of ridicule would have been soon "disabused of the notion," to use an expression dear to both Jim and Boz. For Orson continued with pained look and began to stutter, as was his wont in circumstances of stress.

"I j - just d - d - didn't know w - w - what w - was c — comin' down," he barely managed to get out. "It w - was p- pretty w- weird."

"*What the fuck was going on for chrissakes?*" Jim asked excitedly, clearly affected by Orson's unsettled state of emotion.

"Is Floss okay?" Melinda asked.

"Oh, yeah, she and Nando went to see some friends she knew from college. But Lard was kind of drunk, I guess. You know how he drinks those quarts of beer and you never know how many he's put away." Orson seemed less tense now and had stopped stuttering. "And Dorsey never hardly says anything, just laughs."

"What're G. W. and his lady doin'?" Boz interjected. "Ain't they s'pose to be kinda keepin' the rest together?"

"They went to see a movie in town, took a cab about an hour before I split."

"*Shit, Boz!*" Harsh said, a worried frown spreading across his face, "I just hope they keep it together!"

"Oh, I think they will," Boz reassured him. "Tea an' Steeph has pretty much been keepin' their heads straight—up to now, anyhow."

"Tea, yeah," said Orson, "but Hardon, I don't know what to make of that guy. He can get kinda crazy and you don't know what he's thinkin'."

"Yeah, he's unpredictable," said Jim.

"Say, anybody got any grass?" Orson asked, getting to his bare feet and fixing his gaze on something in a far corner of the room. "*Hey, that's my sleeping bag!* I wondered what happened to it."

"It got mixed up with the others and got brung along," Boz said, approaching Orson and handing him a dark-papered joint, which Orson put to his lips. "Good thing it did, too, or you'd be crashin' wrapped up in a rug."

"That's another thing I left—I mean, back there on the bus," said Orson, leaning forward into the match held in Boz's grease-stained and calloused hand. "I think maybe I forgot to get my weed back from Hardon." He drew deeply on the joint and held it in for several seconds. "Hey, Jim, I think Hardon is speeding."

Jim's initial reaction to this was to nod to Melinda. Then he turned back to Orson. "That really puts me up tight, Orson. You're not just saying that, are you?"

"Are you sure?" said Melinda.

"Listen, man," Orson shot back defensively, "I saw him popping some pills in the back of the bus. He thought everybody was gone out of there but I was layin' down up in front, and I could see him in the mirror, you know, that big wide mirror over the windshield. Then I got up and—. He wasn't hip that I seen him and I didn't let on none, so I went back and we smoked a joint and then I split and got on the road out to here." He felt his breast pockets involuntarily. "Yeah, that's where my shit is! Steeph has it." He paused and glanced up at the ceiling. "Unless it fell out somewhere—hey, maybe in the truck!"

"Well, if that jockey have it you shore did make a friend thar. Those guys on those long hauls are catchin' on to it, I do hear," Boz observed, then turned to Jim. "No use frettin' 'bout it, James. Hell, if it doan work out, then it doan work out, that's all. Put it away, man. Whole idea of us comin' out here was to ferget the hassles." He had lighted another joint and passed it across the spool to Jane. "Best thing is to just enjoy ourselves whiles we can. All this good grub Jane and Saul fixed and plenty of good wine. I hear tell Oliver even brought a bottle of Mexican fahr water. Three or four different brands o' dope in the house. And it's almost Christmas and all that. I say we oughta jes sit back and *let the fuckin' good times roll!*"

"*Hear ye, hear ye!*" Joe shouted, and then, in a lowered voice, he continued. "Now I don't know much about what's going on with your band, but if it's anything like as heavy as it's beginning to sound like, I suggest we drop the subject and move on to something considerably lighter, if you dig what I mean. As Boz says, *it's Christmas!*"

"Maybe we could sing carols," Saul suggested. "I could get my Autoharp and Orson has his guitar."

"*What a wonderful idea!*" said Jane, her voice joyous.

"*Yeah, great idea!*" Joe agreed and began to get to his feet. His upward motion was suddenly arrested by a hand on his shoulder. It was Oliver, who was now kneeling beside him.

"Joe, you never answered my question," he said.

It seemed to Joe that he was hearing a replay. Indeed, earlier in the day he had failed to provide an actual answer to a question put to him by Oliver, something about Orson. He had recommended to Oliver that he direct the question to Orson himself, Joe recalled, because he didn't feel that he had sufficient information. Something about Orson's plans, that's what it was.

"I think I suggested that you ask Orson about that when you caught up with him, Oliver. After all, he's right over there," said Joe, pointing, then looking around the room. "Well, he was a minute ago."

"How was Orson involved?" Noticing that his glass had been refilled, Oliver raised and drained it in two gulps, his eyes misting over slightly as he lowered the glass and reached for the bottle in the center of the spool, filled the glass to its brim, and offered the bottle to Joe. "No, Joe, I think we're talking at cross purposes."

"Thanks, don't mind if I do," said Joe, winking at Oliver as he put it to his lips and drained it of its remaining few ounces. "The only question I recall you asking me was—and that was before I went over to the college—was about what Orson's plans were, was he going to hang out here or what the hell's he's going to do, and I suggested that you ask the young man himself. I recall saying something like, 'He'll be out here later today, I understand. Then you can do an inquisition on the lad.'"

A providential twang of guitar from across the room served to establish the location of Oliver's nephew and Joe made as if to get to his feet.

"No, no, Joe, it's got nothing to do with Orson. It's got to do with you and what you said you did when you disappeared for a couple of hours this afternoon," said Oliver, attempting to rectify the misunderstanding.

"Was you gone thet long, Perfesser?" Unbeknownst to Joe and Oliver, Boz had been kneeling behind them and following their conversation for the past several minutes. "How long was you layin' there in thet snow bank?"

"Only a minute or so," Joe replied, revealing his surprise at Boz's presence by the manner in which he suddenly turned to respond. "Or maybe two hours," he added, chuckling.

Exasperation in his voice, Oliver rasped, "Either I'm going insane or we all are." His effort to continue was aborted by a wracking cough and, unable to go on, he gestured futilely at Joe and Boz.

"What's he trying to say, Boz?"

"I think he be disrememberin', Perfesser. I been eavesdroppin' and couldn't help hearin'—."

"I think there might be a contradiction there," Joe interrupted.

"—him sayin' somethin' about a question he ask you before."

"That's right," Oliver offered, having regained the faculty of speech.

"And I think he thunk you never tol' us what you was doin' fer thet couple o' hours you was gone. But I 'member you sayin' you went up thar to turn yer grades in—."

"To post them," Joe corrected.

"—and that you done give all A's," Boz concluded.

"And then I asked you if you really did do that, Joe, give all A's." Apparently in an effort to impress Joe with the urgency of this revelation, Oliver gestured widely with his left hand and sent a half-full wine glass rolling across the spool towards Jane, its contents spreading in a stream toward Melinda, who reached out with one of the cloth napkins provided earlier and began mopping it up.

"What in the world are you people talking about over there?" Jane called. "And why are you throwing glasses of wine at me?" She had blocked the passage of the glass at spool's edge and was now examining it closely, running a finger tip lightly along its rim.

"Sorry, Jane," Oliver apologized, smiling. "I'm known to do worse than that." He paused and continued slowly, unsmiling, a suggestion of condescension in his tone, utilizing a mode of delivery perhaps honed in the classroom. "What I'm trying to find out is whether Joe *actually*"—he repeated the word with even greater emphasis—"*actually* gave the final grade of A to *every single one of his students!*" He brought his hands together in conclusion.

"Why *of course he did!*" Jane remonstrated. "What else *could* he do?" She caught Joe's attention with her eyes and said, "I didn't know you told anyone what you did, honey."

"It slipped out while you were in the kitchen, babe."

Oliver turned back to Joe, containing Boz in his view as he addressed the former. "Joe, this is really incredible. In fact, it's hard to believe."

"*Why,* Oliver?" said Joe, raising his eyes in amusement in the direction of Jane.

"Because they'll *sack* you, *that's* why!"

Joe turned to Oliver, amusement no longer in his demeanor. "Don't you think I've taken that into consideration, my friend?"

"*Oh, sure, sure, I'm sure you have!*" Oliver looked away from Joe toward Jane and Melinda, who had now taken a seat beside Jane. Jim stood behind them, his left hand holding a cigarette and trembling slightly, his right cradling a square clear-glass ashtray.

"They won't let it stand, Joe!" Oliver continued. "They'll appoint a committee to read the exams and then they'll assign legitimate grades."

"Do you feel that the grades Joe gave are illegitimate?" inquired Jane, a trace of hostility in her tone.

"Now wait a minute. Just hold on," said Oliver. "I'm very sympathetic to why—I assume why—Joe did it. I'm merely pointing out some of the potential consequences—the *likely* consequences, when you really come down to it." Oliver scanned the faces of those seated at the spool. Saul, having finished clearing the dishes, had taken a seat on a cushion between Boz and Orson, whose guitar lay across his lap. Only Jim was left standing, "I suppose it's final. I mean, you're not going to withdraw—."

"I never withdraw in the middle of an act, Oliver!" came the reply. "It's unhealthy, and very hard on the nerves—and messy, too."

"You don't seem to take it very seriously, Joe," Oliver scolded. "Which doesn't surprise me, I guess, knowing you as I do." He looked around the table as though for confirmation.

"Oliver, you're really taking this from the wrong end," Jane began, patience and firmness in about equal balance in her unhurried, measured cadence. "Joe takes his action *very* seriously. Don't be misled by his foolishness. Believe me, it wasn't something he thought up this afternoon—"

"Oh, I'm certain of that!"

"—and to him it's not a joke. A lot of people are going to take it that way, I'm sure, but it's not the way he feels about it." Jane looked at Joe. "But I should let him speak for himself."

"Well, frankly, folks, I just don't feel like making a speech or delivering a lecture," said Joe, an open pocket knife in his right hand, the bottle of tequila in the other. "Saul, think you could fetch that set of shot glasses from the butler's pantry? Not even sure if I want to talk about it tonight. It's done and I'm glad that part of it is over. Oh, I know the shit's going to hit the proverbial fan— maybe sooner than you think. Sure, school's closed for the next week and a half, but someone will notice that my grades are up and not be able to resist eyeballing them." Joe had peeled the plastic covering from the top of the bottle and was working the cork out. It made a squeaking sound and he looked up to see if others were enjoying it as he was. "Hear the little mousey? Of course, mine will be the earliest ones posted. No one will get them up until classes commence on the fifth of January. In fact, no one is expected to post them before then because no one can get in to check them out, anyway. I mean, none of the students. But you can be damn sure that one of my esteemed colleagues will notice them and spread the word. Some of those people can't stay away from that place. I wouldn't be surprised if some of them are in their offices on Christmas Day." He looked up and nodded thanks to Saul, who had placed a small tray of an assortment of whiskey glasses on the spool in front of him. Joe picked one up and held it for all to see then put it down and selected another for display. "One size fits all," he said incongruously and smiled. "You know, Jane's right—I've been thinking on this for a long time. And maybe I'm still not even sure myself of the total meaning of it. But I know this much—it's the only time I've felt satisfied with myself after turning in my grades."

In the brief silence that followed—no more than ten or fifteen seconds—an unspoken agreement seemed to be in force, namely, that Joe retained the floor. Having placed the bottle of tequila on the tray with the glasses and then tucked the knife's blade into its handle, Joe ran his hand through his beard and got to his feet, announcing to those at the spool and to Saul and Orson, who were now over in the corner tuning their instruments, "Well, anywho, the shit's not likely to come down for a day or two or three, at the very earliest, so let's enjoy ourselves. Jim, why don't you fetch a couple more bottles of that fine wine. I think everybody's getting a little dry, and this firewater, as Boz so appropriately dubbed it, may not be to everyone's taste."

Expressions of support came from all present, excepting Oliver, who for the moment seemed withdrawn into himself as he sat twirling one end of his drooping moustache and staring at the shot glass of tequila Joe had poured for him. The subject of the grades Joe had posted late that afternoon was effectively dropped as he and Jane left the room to investigate Vincenzo's quarters on the third floor and assure themselves that their tenant had left them in good enough order for the Pettibones to be comfortable there. Letting themselves into the tiny apartment, they looked around. The strains of "We Three Kings" reached them from below.

"I think they'll really like it up here, Joe," said Jane, putting her arms around his torso and resting her head against his chest. "I just love that French window, don't you?"

"*Ah, si, la finestra a due battenti.*"

"It makes me feel like I want to be laid. Isn't that

strange?"

"*Sì, certo! Molto strano!*" said Joe, kissing the crown of her head. "Yes, I had them in one of the flats I lived in, right in downtown Napoli, as a matter of fact. Yes, this room has a very European look to it—it even *feels* Continental." Joe shifted slightly, turning Jane with him, so that both could look out the nearly floor-to-ceiling window. "It'll be a trip down Memory Lane for Henry and Margery. Wouldn't be at all surprised if they come down to breakfast speaking French."

"Ummm, it's such a beautiful night, Joe." She snuggled close to him. "Reminds me of when I was a little girl and it would snow for days on end."

They disengaged and walked over to the window, holding hands. Jane looked up at him. He was staring out into what had become a white maelstrom.

"Joe, I want you to know that I'm really proud of you for what you did today." She hesitated for several seconds before going on. "And I want you to know that it doesn't matter what happens. I respect you for it and I think it was a very courageous act."

His eyes now on hers, Joe took her face in his hands and kissed her on the mouth. "You're pretty wonderful," he mouthed into her ear, his hands now holding, and slightly lifting her by her buttocks.

Her arms around his neck, Jane stepped out of her ankle-high boots and pulled Joe down with her onto a pallet made of a couple of foam rubber cushions with a blanket thrown over them. It had a temporary look, as though it had been hastily improvised the night before, but Joe knew that the disarray actually dated from sixteen months ago, when his then soon-to-be student had taken the apartment. *Vince does most of his studying on those very cushions*, Joe mused, picturing in his mind's eye the lexicons, grammars, and commentaries that the young scholar always had spread around him on the makeshift bed and the floor.

His hands underneath her denim skirt, Joe worked Jane's cotton panties down her thighs, provided assistance by her shifting her weight from side to side. The removal of her panties, and then her skirt, accomplished, Joe rolled a half turn to his side and unbuttoned and pushed to his knees his levi's, hooking his thumbs onto his jockey shorts and carrying them along with the jeans. Jane was unbuttoning his shirt as he executed these procedures and, having done this, she slipped her sweatshirt over her head, revealing her firm, very full breasts. Now she watched with amusement as Joe, his furled pants hampering the effort, struggled to unlace his boots. Finally free of foot gear, Joe kicked the levi's off, allowed Jane to divest him of his shirt, and then pulled his black tank top over his head. They both retained their nearly knee-high socks.

The love they made was not of their usual style, Joe later remarked, and the intensity of his climax was of a degree he wasn't sure he had very often experienced, Jane adding that, for her, "the floor moved—or *maybe the god damn foundation of this old house!*"

What constituted the difference, he later explained to her, was her handling of his genitalia, her cradling of his testes in one hand while she lightly stroked the shaft of his member with the other, at the same time taking the very tip of it in her mouth and delicately working her lips on its ridge. He had barely touched her *mons veneris*, yet her own aggressiveness had aroused her to a pitch of passion that he had seldom observed in her. She had abruptly mounted him, maintaining a sitting position at first. The angle of approach for him was nearly that of entry from behind ("*Modo Italiano*," a guide at Pompeii had informed him, pointing to a painting in one of the brothels.), so high did she ride him. She began to whinny after a couple of minutes and he came a few seconds later, pulling her down onto him and burying his face between her breasts, inhaling deeply of her very ripe erotic bouquet.

It had quite exhausted them and several minutes passed before she raised herself just enough for Joe to slip out of her. She stretched out alongside him and he pulled the blanket over them.

"That was something else!"

"It sure was!" Jane purred into his ear.

They dozed off in each other's arms for a minute and were startled out of this brief sleep by a thump against the window. Sitting up, he pulled her up with him and, easing her back down and disengaging himself from her embrace, rolled out from beneath the blanket, tucking it around her. She turned onto her side and settled back into sleep.

They must have put the ladder on the porch roof, he reasoned. *That's what I did back in the fall when I was clearing the leaves out of the gutters. I almost lost my grip! And I was cold sober! Wonder who is crazy enough to try that on a night like this! Just to bang on the window while we made love. That's like some dumb army joke!* With no light on in the room, he felt, if not invulnerable, at the very least protected enough to face which of his friends had managed the ascent. He edged up to the window from one side and, leaning a little to the left, peered out into the blizzard. Frost had collected on the inside of the panes, making it very difficult to see, and his breath upon the glass did not help. He moved on to another pane, holding his breath this time. Yet visibility was still minimal. He wrenched open the window—it hung on side hinges like a door—and thrust his head out through the opening, squinting into the white-flecked dark. Shivering, he folded his arms across his chest, hugging himself. A swish above his head was followed in a mini-second by a thud. Alerted by the first sound, he had quickly moved aside to the very edge of the window. *Oh, snowballs!* he concluded, and this was confirmed by the sensation of damp on his right shoulder. The missile had apparently met its terminus on the thick oak lintel several feet above his head, he realized.

Laughter erupted from three figures below in the deep snow. Patches of white on their clothes lent to them a comic rag doll effect. A newcomer, approaching from behind them, was almost completely clad in winter white. *What a night it would be to drop some acid*, he reflected. *Then again, tomorrow could be heavy, what with all the shit that's likely to come at me because of the grades. Better stick to the milder stuff, maybe even get bombed on tequila.* He looked over his shoulder at Jane. Only her long black tresses protruded from the blanket. When he again looked out into the snow he saw that the scene was bereft of people. There was stomping of feet, mingled with boisterous laughter, on the porch below, and a voice, which Joe could barely make out as Oliver's, cried out, "*Just the thing to warm you up, sir!*"

Another voice, gravelly and indistinct, replied. A door opened and slammed closed and he shut the window. Then there was only the sound of muffled merriment two floors below Vince's apartment. He was suddenly aware that the singing had discontinued. "Probably while we were making love," he said under his breath, shivering and reaching down for his tank top and pulling it on.

"Did you have a nice time at the ball, dear?" He smiled as he quoted this query from the film *Rachel, Rachel,* seen by them a year ago, then decided that he would let her sleep a bit longer while he checked out Vince's kitchen for some refreshment, a decided thirst having overcome him.

Between the big room and the tiny kitchenette was an inter-passage about ten feet long and lined with shelves filled with several hundred books, a foot-high stack of LPs, piles of underclothes, socks, sweaters, shirts, and jeans, lidless shoeboxes of three-by-five cards, stacks of spiral notebooks, empty wine bottles, jars crammed full of pencils and ball point pens, a large grapefruit juice can containing paint brushes, an electric typewriter, shoes, boots, a Rolleiflex camera in a leather case with strap, a package of Trojans, canned goods, boxes of Wheaties, pancake mix, Twinings tea bags of several varieties, and other foodstuffs, and a motley assortment of dishes and glassware. On the top shelf on one side of the passage lay a pair of skis and an easel.

He reached up and plucked off of a shelf two blue-tinted glasses he had acquired from a trattoria he had frequently dined at in Napoli and which he had added to the dinnerware provided to Vince when he moved in. He thought briefly of the many times he and Vince had sat in the crowded kitchenette drinking from these very glasses.

Entering the kitchenette, which was not much larger than the passageway leading to it, he spotted a bottle of red wine on top of the refrigerator. Grasping it with his free hand, he re-entered the passageway and, seemingly unconscious of the bizarre sight he presented clad in nothing but a sleeveless undershirt (or "East Baltimore sport shirt," as he had long ago dubbed the style) and knee-high socks and holding at his sides the bottle and glasses, paused to skim some of the books' titles.

There was a five-volume boxed set of Mommsen's *History Of Rome*, the Modern Library Gibbon, Paul Cauer's *Grundfragen der Homerkritik*, Boswell's *The Life of Samuel Johnson*, thirty or so other histories, biographies, and critical works, fifty or sixty Greek and Latin texts, most of Oxford publication but several each of Budé and Teubner, many novels, including *War and Peace*, *Lolita*, *Lady Chatterley's Lover*, *Tropic Of Cancer*, and *The Life and Opinions of Tristram Shandy Gentleman* (from which Vince was fond of reading aloud, in British accent, absurdist passages), collections of essays and short stories, and a half dozen cook books. Joe, determining to, at some later date, compile a catalogue of Vince's literary and scholarly tastes, continued on his way back into the apartment's main room.

She had not moved from the position he had left her in. He went down on his knees and, placing the glasses and wine on the floor beside her, touched her lightly on the shoulder. "Hey, sweetheart, are you asleep?" he whispered.

"What?" She tried to sit up, discovered that she was snared in the blanket, and fell back, freeing herself. "Oh, honey, I must have fallen asleep. How long have I been out?" She yawned, displaying the perfectly lined and glistening teeth that one sees in the mouths of Hollywood starlets, the difference being that hers were not capped. She pulled the blanket around her.

"Not long," he answered, uncorking the bottle and pouring wine into the glasses. "Maybe ten minutes. Better keep that around you, it's a little chilly in here."

"Oh, this is nice," she said, sipping the wine. She

shivered. "Although I wouldn't have turned down a hot toddy! How in the world does Vince survive up here?"

"Oh it's not usually this bad. I forgot to light the space heater over there," he said pointing to a far corner. "And the kitchen stove has a heater feature, too. It's no problem getting this place toasty warm. And, after all, it's down near zero out there. And with that wind it's like ten below!" He sipped the wine. "Besides, I had the window open for a while."

"*What?*" She burst out laughing. "*Why on earth*—?"

"They were bombarding us with snowballs, that's why!" he said, rising, "and I wanted to have meself a look-see. Come on, put your clothes on and let's get downstairs—unless you want another lay."

"I love that idea!"

When they had finished their third (they had begun the morning thus) act of lovemaking of the day, this time with him on top, they lay side by side in tight embrace for a few minutes. He kissed her one final time and began searching for his clothes again. Unable to locate his jockey shorts, he pulled on his jeans and shirt, put on his boots and laced them, and stood up. He noted that she was already dressed.

She raised her eyebrows with parodied haughtiness: "Well! As usual, I'm ready and waiting on you! Oh," she giggled, pointing to the foot of the mattress, "you forgot to put on your shorts."

He stuffed them into a hip pocket and reached down to the floor for the now empty bottle and glasses. "Better get rid of the evidence or Henry and Margery will think we run a house of debauchery."

"I hardly think they would care," she said, chuckling.

"They are not exactly what you would call bluenoses, honey."

"Have to agree with you on that!" he said, laughing.

"Who was snowballing us?" she asked when he returned from the kitchenette.

"Oh, Oliver, for one. Couldn't make out who his accomplices were. And I had the impression that someone arrived, on foot, just as they ran for cover."

"Oh, did you retaliate?"

"No," he sighed. "They didn't give me a chance."

Assuring himself that the window was securely closed, he opened the door, reminding himself in the dim light from a bare bulb at the foot of the stairs that egress from the apartment was treacherous, in that one took no more than two steps before meeting the edge of the narrow landing.

"Watch yourself," he cautioned and offered his arm to the rear. "Guy who built this place must have been lopsided, like a side-hill badger."

They descended the two flights to the first floor.

Labored guitar chording, practice-like, was the only indication of the presence of anyone in the big front room, he realized, as he reached for the knob. For a moment he pretended that it was Jane inside, picturing her in his mind's eye knitting at the spool, and that he was alone in the hall. A touch of her hand on his elbow erased the illusion and he turned and kissed her on the mouth. After their lips had disengaged she held him briefly, her arms around his neck. "I bet they know what we were doing," she whispered. "And we probably *reek* of sex!"

"Sure. That's no doubt why the music stopped. Remember? They were singing carols." He winked at her.

Melinda, alone, sat on the edge of the spool, Orson's

guitar cradled in her lap. Startled, she looked up from the instrument, her fretting fingers held stiffly in place.

"Oh, there you are," she said. "I think I finally have this thing in tune. God knows what kind of shit Orson plays on it, considering the shape it was in. No wonder he was only doing percussion on it just now!" She carefully laid the guitar beside her. "So how did Vince's pad check out?"

"Just fine," he answered, somewhat nonplussed at her choice of the term "pad." Regaining his composure, he continued, "Fine, just fine! I think the Pettibone's will be very comfortable up there."

"Where is everyone, Mel?" No sooner had she asked this than laughter from the kitchen provided the answer.

"There's some friend of yours in there," she informed them, rolling her eyes teasingly at Jane, as he recalled her doing to Flossie in Austin. "Kinda cute dude."

"Better check it out," was his response, turning on his heel and beckoning to Jane to join him.

Facing Joe as he entered the kitchen were Oliver and Jim. Boz, at the sink washing dishes, glanced back over his shoulder, smiling. They were listening in respectful attention to a man whose back was to Joe and Jane. The Astrakhan that covered his ears added an inch or two to his five-foot-six-inch height and his fur coat fell to his ankles. Jane confessed later that she had not a clue as to his identity until he turned around to greet them, but Joe recognized him immediately upon entering the kitchen by virtue of his nervous shifting of balance from one foot to the other. He took hold of his elbow from behind, nearly causing the man to lose his grip on the quart of tequila.

"Hello, hello," he mumbled and, unable to reciprocate the elbow shake pressed on him by Joe, instead gestured with the half lemon his other hand cupped. Joe's first impression was that he was drunk, so slurred was his speech. But even a cursory examination of the man's features revealed that his face was nearly numb from the cold. "And how are you, my dear?" he greeted Jane, leaning forward to kiss her on the cheek.

"*Oh!*" she squealed, "you're like *ice*, Erik, how long have you been here?"

"A few minutes, my dear, merely a few minutes, several, one might say. I arrived as your guests here were directing artillery at the upper reaches of the fortress." He turned slightly to again address his silent audience, now augmented by Boz. "Telling your friends here of days in old May-hee-co." Van Loon extended his lemon-holding hand for a sprinkle from the salt shaker Boz was offering him, licked the back of his hand, turned it over and sucked the lemon, and took a swig from the bottle. He handed the bottle to Oliver, who, with considerably less finesse than Erik had displayed, performed the same ritual and offered the bottle to Boz, who declined, indicating that his hands were occupied, one with the salt, the other with a bottle of Black Horse Ale. "And recommending that they not miss Sam Peckinpah's latest, which deals rather well with the early-century scene there."

"I'd like just a little, in a glass, honey," said Jane, taking the bottle from Oliver and handing it to Joe. "With a slice of lemon, please."

He was relieved at the distraction and went over to the cabinets built into the wall over the sink and the counter, where Boz had neatly lined up in the drainer the dishes used at dinner. No one spoke as he studied the selection of glasses. Noting that the shot glasses had been returned to the cabinet, he opened the glass door, took one out, and placed it on the counter, found a fresh lemon in the refrigerator's vegetable bin, cut a slice, notched it, tucked it onto the lip of the glass, poured an ounce of tequila into it, and took it over to Jane. He returned the uncorked bottle to Van Loon.

Jim had left the room and was just now returning with the case of wine he had left on the porch. He took up a kneeling position at the refrigerator and was laying the bottles on their sides on a lower shelf.

"Really packing in the supplies there, Jim," Oliver remarked absently, his attention now on Joe's back, now on Van Loon, who had again partaken of the tequila and was now moving slowly backward toward the kitchen counter.

"Anybody care for some wine?" Jim asked. His question went unnoticed, no one responding to his offer.

A bubbling, hissing sound alerted Boz. who rushed over to the gas range.

"I never can get used to how long it takes to get a kettle goin' up here in this altitude!" he said, shutting off the gas and pouring from the huge metal kettle into two teapots that awaited on a work shelf to one side. He turned and addressed Van Loon, who had placed the bottle of tequila and the lemon on the counter next to the saltshaker and was standing at his side rubbing his hands. "Would you like a cup of tea, Perfesser? Hot out o' the kettle!"

"Oh, thank you, sir, I would indeed!" he responded with evident enthusiasm.

"I'll bring it over to you, Perfesser. What do you take in it?"

"Some of that would go very well with it, don't you think?" he said, pointing to the tequila, and returning to the group standing in the middle of the kitchen.

Oliver was standing a little to one side, an expectant look spreading across his face. "You said you walked over here from the college, Professor Van Loon?" he asked.

"Yes, Oliver, and it was a delightful nocturnal stroll, I do say!" the scholar replied, smiling. "And please call me Erik," he pleaded. "Far too much formality is foisted upon us by the strictures of our profession. Let us not carry it over into our social intercourse."

"Are you thawing out, Erik?" Joe asked solicitously. "It must be five below out there by now—*and that wind!*" He went over to the double set of windows that looked onto the back yard and scraped at the frost that covered the panes. "Can't see much out there, it's so dark."

"My body heat does seem to have replenished itself," he replied, "with the aid of your stimulant here." He nodded a thank-you in the direction of Oliver and, taking in his hand the mug Boz was extending to him, raised it and gently massaged his chin with it. "Had that sensation of local narcosis a visit to the dentist leaves one with, but the feeling has largely returned, I'm happy to say. Happy to be *able* to say," he added, smiling."

"I think we should all go back into the front room," Oliver announced with a sort of urgency and then, as though the matter were settled, he turned toward the door. "Joe still has some explaining to do, as far as I'm concerned. And could someone bring the tequila, please? I'd like another taste."

Joe reached out to intercept the familiar blue pack being offered to Erik, for Jim, his hand trembling, seemed only with difficulty able to hold on to the pack. The direction in which Oliver was trying to take the conversation annoyed him and he caught Oliver's eyes and frowned sternly at him, indicating, he hoped, that he resented his attempt to reshape the scenario. Serving— but certainly not intended—to dispel the tension apparent in Joe's sudden change of mood, Jane's glass slipped from her fingers and smashed at her feet. She had taken no more than a sip of the tequila, and several shoes, including Erik's, were splattered with drops of the liquid. He looked down.

"Oh, I say!" he said, but did not move. The others stepped back almost in unison, Joe lagging a split second.

"*Oh, damn!*" Jane blurted out, her now empty hand slashing the air in a descending motion. "I liked that glass."

"I'll clean this up and fix you a replacement, my sweet," said Joe, gesturing toward the floor with his palms in a calming gesture. "Why doesn't everyone go into the front room, as Oliver suggested. We can put some music on. Might even come up with something that you can tolerate, Erik."

"Oh, don't worry about that," he insisted. "My children have rendered me quite catholic in my tastes, converted me, so to speak." He smiled. "Just the other day my youngest daughter paid me the ultimate compliment, assuring me that I was the 'hippest father around, not a square, like most dads.'"

"Nicer praise than that you can't hope for, Erik," said Jane and, with a fresh shot glass of tequila in hand, led the way through the butler's pantry to the big front room, the four males following Indian-file, Erik directly behind her, the bottle of tequila in one hand, mug of tea in the other, then Oliver, a tea pot suspended by handle along each thigh, next Jim with a tray of glasses and mugs, and finally Boz, balancing on the flat of his hand a shoulder-high tray on which were an uncut lemon, the salt shaker, a box of Ritz crackers, a cutting board occupied by several varieties of cheese and wurst, a stack of small plates, and a large kitchen knife.

Left to himself, Joe got down on his knees and, spreading a square of paper towel on the floor, gingerly picked up the shards of glass and placed them on it, carefully folded the towel to its center by its corners, and deposited it in a trash can under the sink. He wetted two more towels and wiped up the sticky residue of the tequila. Then he took a stemmed wine glass from the cabinet, one of a set he had bought in Florence on the Ponte Vecchio, and examined it with evident affection, recalling the very occasion upon which he had acquired it. *It was our trip to the city with the students and my colleagues and Jyll and I ducked out of the hotel as soon as we had taken our suitcases to our room. She bought me a leather case for my cigarettes and I got her a handmade Florentine Spoon Heart Necklace. Which, by God, she was wearing the last time I ever saw her!*

Removing from the refrigerator a bottle of the white wine, he searched among the many utensils hanging on hooks screwed into the bottom of the cabinets, located a wooden-handled corkscrew, applied its point to the neck of the bottle and rotated the bottle until a nickel-shaped piece of foil fell to the counter. Expertly extracting the cork, he checked inside the neck of the bottle with his little finger for fragments of cork, found several and flicked them into the sink.

Filling his glass to the brim, he worked the cork back into the bottle, placed it on the table, and sat down in one of the straight-back chairs. He struck a match with his thumb and held it to the Gauloises he had taken from Jim's pack. As he sat sipping the wine and drawing on the cigarette he became aware of a scraping sound out on the back porch. He opened the door and hurried across the small porch to the screen door, pushing it open with some difficulty into the closely packed snow. It finally opened enough and he nearly lost his balance as Rufus squeezed by him, tail wagging, and darted into the kitchen. Making a beeline to his bowl beneath the work board and finding it empty, he bounded across the kitchen, shaking snow off along the way, and disappeared through the butler's pantry.

He secured the inner door and returned to the table. *Jesus, I wonder where he has been? Probably up in the mountains, if I know him.* He shivered. *And I wonder where Saul and Orson are. They certainly wouldn't have gone very far in this weather, I hope. Then again, Erik, twice their age, didn't think anything of hiking over here. Course, when I took my trip earlier it wasn't anything like as bitter out there. That wind must be gusting at thirty. Never heard this house creak like this before.*

"Well, up and at 'em!" he said to the room and stood up, the chair scraping the floor loudly as he rose. For about a half-minute he paused, stroking his beard. Then he took the glass and the bottle and, more than a little curious what was going on in the other room, left the kitchen.

He entered the room to the eclectic strains of John Fahey's guitar. A dog barked. Startled, Rufus looked up from his basket bed toward the speakers. Erik was standing to one side of the fireplace watching a crouched Boz feed kindling to the fire. A heated discussion was taking place at the spool between Oliver and Jim Harsh. Jane was seated between them and Melinda was across from this trio, Orson's guitar propped beside her. Oliver extended the bottle of tequila across Jane to Jim, who waved it away.

"Man, I used to swill that firewater by the gallon," said Jim. "I'd still do a little taste now and then if I thought I could stop with that, but I know better. Hard enough to control the suds and vino without getting back into that shit!" Noticing that Joe had entered the room, he beckoned to him. "Hey, Joe, com' 'ere. We've been talking about you." He stood and whispered into his ear. Joe listened intently and, stepping back, smiled, and looked down at Oliver.

"Always the *provocateur*, Ollie," he said. "Go ahead and ask him, if you want to. It's no big secret."

Jane turned and looked up at him. "Why don't *you* ask him, Joe? That would seem more appropriate."

"You're probably right. It's just that one doesn't know the proper way in such a matter. Never done this before." He approached the fireplace and stood at Erik's side. Apparently unaware that he had entered the room, Erik turned quickly and nodded to him.

"Oh, *there* you are, Joe!" he said. "Meant to say, colleague, that was a fine thing that you did."

Joe studied his austere features for clues to his position on the matter, for he was well aware that his friend was wont to employ irony when he deemed the argument called for it. *Is he preparing groundwork for tripping me up?* he wondered, and hastily commenced a mental search for the justifications he had gone over and over on the walk in the snow back to the house. *Then again, maybe he was not even referring to the posting of the grades—he hadn't, after all, said, "this afternoon"—but to some trivial aspect of the evening.* Joe reminded himself that the man's sense of humor sometimes struck him as having the subtlety of a lead balloon. *Could he be commending me for staying behind to clean up broken glass?*

"I've been on the horn to the dean about it," Erik continued in clarification, seeming to read Joe's mind, and leaned forward with his mug clasped in both hands. It seemed to Joe that he was on the verge of coughing or perhaps even preparing to throw up into the container. Neither was the case, it became clear, for Van Loon suddenly tossed his head back and laughed, his eyes watering, his lips quivering. "*My boy—!*" he tried to go on, and lurched in the direction of the spool.

Already on his feet when Joe had approached the mathematician, Oliver reached out to offer support to him and took the mug from him, beckoning him to take the cushion beside Jane.

"Are you all right, Erik?" Jane asked, for he had begun a hacking cough.

"Let me have a little of that mescal—in a glass, if you please," he answered, and upon it being poured and handed to him by Jim he threw it down in a gulp. "One of the bad habits of my generation, and one which I must confess I have had little success disposing of. Don't know if my cells would understand if they were deprived of it 'cold duck.' As I believe the expression is."

"Turkey," said Jim, so softly that only Melinda, now beside him with her head on his shoulder, heard him and stifled a laugh.

Joe took a seat beside Jane.

"I probably should have been more open and above board when I first arrived, Joe, but I was carried away with the hospitality of your friends here and the wonderful atmosphere of festivity prevailing," Erik explained, now fully recovered. "I had the impression that you had retired for the evening, and when you and Jane appeared, it seemed a shame to besmirch the convivial ambience." He paused. "Now be assured that I support your action, and I think I understand the motivation at its source. But to discuss, not superficially, but rather in terms of its wider implications, so weighty a matter necessarily alters the mood of a social gathering, and that was a responsibility I wasn't sure that I was prepared to assume upon arriving here this evening. Although, as I think it is obvious now, that is why I walked over here on this terrible—beautiful, actually—night in the first place. Now that it is out in the open I suppose that I have no alternative but to explore the entire matter. So, with apologies to all present, I would propose that we do just that."

Chapter 11

Just let it happen.

It was, Joe reflected, odd, though perhaps meaningful, that in the same batch of mail (not yet forwarded to him and picked up at the classics department and dropped off at the house that morning by Erik) that brought the dean's letter, an especially virulent postcard arrived. Seated at the kitchen table, he read it before opening the envelope identified as from The Office of the Dean.

The typewritten card—inspired by a letter to the editor that Joe had written to the *Denver Post* more than a month ago—was addressed to "Joe Lewis, the great." It began, "Well, well, well: So you don't like the way the D.P. carried the story about the recent commie demonstration on the campus. You screwball professors are what's back of all this hoodlum rot. Putting screwy ideas in the kids heads."

The mid-section of the text featured a blanket description of his colleagues in his and other departments as "filthy scum," as well as individual references to several of them as, for example, a "filthy scummy son of a bitch" and an "old whore." It continued with the warning, "Better be cutting your vacation short kid and we mean short. Having two boys on their way to Vietnam with the chances of never coming back, don't be surprised if you get a .30-06 stuck in your ribs if something does happen to them. Think it over you commie bastard. Mad." The card was unsigned.

The dean's letter, dated the 30th, informed him that the semester grades of all of his students (Joe had assigned blanket A's to all four of his classes) had been temporarily held back, "until this grievous and irresponsible action on your part has been rectified." He offered to "wipe the slate clean of the entire matter if you will agree to waive your professional prerogatives and submit the blue books to an impartial board of readers so that proper letter grades can be recorded." In the event of rejecting this "generous offer," the dean concluded his brief missive, "your contract will be revoked, suspension effective at 5pm a week from the date of this letter."

Ironically, Joe noted, the suspension would not begin until the end of the second day of class of the winter term, on Tuesday, January 6th.

"One of those oversights a bureaucracy is so prone to," he said, chuckling, after verifying this circumstance by consultation with the kitchen calendar. "That will give me a chance to explain my position to all four of my classes," he pointed out to Jane, who had brought two mugs of coffee to the table and was studying the postcard. "And say goodbye."

"If you live that long," she wryly observed. "Honey, are you going to do anything about this postcard? It worries me that your picture has been in the school paper a couple of times."

"Watch my back, I guess," he said, smiling, and raised the mug to his lips. "I don't take that sort of rubbish seriously. Some nut case or other. What, me worry?" He grinned and reached for a tin of Prince Albert that was rubber banded with cigarette papers. While he was occupied rolling a nearly perfect cylinder, she again read the dean's letter.

"You're right, honey, they screwed up the date. If you're lucky, they won't notice that. That'll be wild, you just showing up for your first classes! Of course, you might not make it to the second day."

"Yeah, they may call out security." He chuckled, smoke curling around his beard, which, already flecked with gray, now suddenly appeared almost white.

"Joe, did you write that letter to Texaco yet?" Her reference was to their recent encounter with a gas station manager who had addressed Joe as "Santa Claus" and demanded that he "Get that heap off my property."

"I've been composing it in my mind, sweetheart."

They sat silently for several minutes, both sipping coffee, he sending smoke rings across the kitchen.

"So after that where do we go, honey?"

"For the moment, babe, I'd like to just play it by ear. Anyway, the dean may not get away with firing me. I'll get on the horn—funny, Erik using that term—and see what sort of support he has turned up, find out who's on my side."

Because of the holidays, word of the A's had moved slowly among the students concerned, although this was not the case with the faculty, what with emergency sessions of the Regents as well as of at least two faculty committees. Erik had attended a meeting of the committee on Appropriate Standards of Faculty Conduct (which Joe dubbed the "ASSFUCK") and delivered a stinging rebuttal of the dean's position, lacing his defense of Joe with quotations from Cicero, Shakespeare, Clarence Darrow, Thomas Hobbes, John Stuart Mill, and Bob Dylan (this last provided him by his daughters). He concluded with Eleanor Roosevelt's "A woman is like a tea bag—you never know how strong she is until she gets in hot water," adding, "Likewise a brave and principled man!"

A reporter from the student newspaper had come to the house and taken a statement from Joe, which she promised would be published verbatim in the January 5 issue, putting it into the hands of students on Monday, the opening day of the term. The young woman had come equipped with an expensive Japanese camera and, using available light reflected into the kitchen from the glistening snow, shot him in standing and sitting poses, Joe insisting that Jane be included in some of the photographs.

In one of a number of telephone calls from Erik updating him on the progress of the university's response to his posting of the A's, Joe learned that his grade sheets had actually been stripped from his office door by the furious dean on the very morning after being affixed there. That news of the grades had, within three or for days after his posting of them, reached most of his students was due, he later was told, to the efforts of the waitress Cassie Kelso at Fritz's Grill, where he had stopped for coffee and cigarettes on his way home that afternoon.

Puzzled by Joe's cryptic remarks in response to her query where had he been in such a blizzard and, after he had departed, exceedingly curious as to her favorite teacher's mysterious "mission" (which was the word that he had chosen to describe his outing), Cassie followed a hunch, left the Grill in the care of the dishwasher—who had been taking his break in a front booth when Joe arrived—trudged through the snow to Smith, let herself into the building by a basement door that she knew was generally unlocked, and discovered the blanket A's. Upon reaching her apartment later, she had made calls to two fellow students. By the night before classes recommenced, except for a few who were late returning from their vacations, his students knew of the grades.

Upon one matter Joe was inflexible and Jane in full support of, to wit, that the grades would remain unchanged. As for the suspension, he spent two or three days turning over in his mind the game plan recommended by Miles Satherwaite, a tenured member of the biology department and a noted authority on genetics, who had taken up Joe's cause with enthusiasm and had enlisted a small body of faculty support for him. An ardent civil libertarian who had marched along with Joe on student protests, Miles felt that Joe had a valid case for the courts, although he held out little hope that his contract would be reinstated.

"A leak came to me almost immediately after that meeting of the Regents to the effect that two Neanderthal board members sat on the dean's head when he started to back off of his suspension of you," Miles related. He cautioned Joe not to bring in "the peripheral issue of students' rights," expressing the fear that "it could backfire on us."

"In other words," Joe surmised, "I am not to encourage, or become a participant in, a student demonstration."

"Correct!"

"Too bloody cold for that shit anyway, Miles!" he assured him, adding, with a malicious grin, "Of course, we could do a sit-in. The dean's got a wet bar and a kitchen and everything in that office suite he occupies."

Shortly after Erik had delivered Joe's mail on the morning of New Year's Eve and then hurried off, Miles had turned up on their doorstep. The eminent biologist sat with them over tea and scones at their kitchen table and assured them that he had lined up more than adequate pro bono legal support among some young alumni ("and alumnae," he added, smiling) and, based upon a conversation that he had had the evening before with the dean, he warned him that he likely would be all but barred from the campus if he attempted to meet with his classes after the second day of the term. Miles' legal team had threatened the dean with an injunction if he attempted to keep Joe from his classes on the opening two days of the term.

After that half-hour discussion in the kitchen, Joe sat at the table and pecked out on his forty-year-old desk model Royal a three page single-spaced rough draft of his position, the final paragraph focusing upon his conviction that the dean's suspension of his contract constituted "a dangerous threat to faculty prerogative, faculty autonomy, and faculty freedom."

By noon, after he had taped the dean's ultimatum to the refrigerator door and put the postcard in a little glass frame and propped it up against the hookah on the spool, they were convinced that Miles's proposal that they take the matter of his firing to the appropriate professional organizations and then into court was their best option.

"Let the liberals take up your fight, honey," was Jane's advice. "Give them something to do. And remember, you had qualms about accepting this job in the first place. Looks like the decision whether to stay is being made for you."

"You are so right, my dear," he replied with conviction. "It's time for us to split."

That afternoon he sat over coffee at the kitchen table while she baked bread and a cake, jotting down on a yellow legal pad various courses of action, presenting to her now this plan, now another. Discarded by them and crossed off his list almost as quickly as conceived were: that they visit the Pettibones in Chicago, where Margery was, for the spring semester, a visiting professor at DePaul University and Henry was using the city's libraries for research; that they become "camp followers" of Diverse Muph (who were already on the road to St. Louis and other points south); that they emigrate to Canada and become farmers; that they get jobs in a Seattle vegetarian restaurant.

After supper he was in the front room reading a two-week-old Sunday *New York Times*, while a tape of two-piano boogie woogie by Albert Ammons and Pete Johnson played, when she came in with a pot of herbal tea, mugs, a basket of muffins she had just taken out of the oven, and a jar of blueberry jam. She placed the tray on the spool.

"What do you say we pull out next week and head for Cambridge?"

"That's near Boston isn't it?"

"Right across the Charles River from it."

"Of course—and Harvard's there. Well, *I've* never been there, so I guess that's *one* good reason for going there. You got any others?" she asked, taking a seat and pouring the tea.

"Oh, you know, find out what's going on in that part of the country. I've been reading here about some of the action in those parts. Makes me kind of homesick. We could check out Cambridge for a month or two. You know that I lived there for a spell, both before and after my times in Italy—and I do miss that burg. And then maybe we could mosey on up north when the weather breaks up there." He sipped his tea and began spreading jam on a muffin.

She chuckled. "Honey, the weather doesn't break up there until May. Remember, I'm from Canada. Not that I mind the cold. I grew up in it, and look what we've had here this past week or so." She sipped tea and stared briefly out the window. "Well, it's worth thinking about."

"That's right, that storm blew in on the afternoon I tacked my grades up."

The occasion suddenly rushed back to him. Much of the evening was crystal clear. He could remember with clarity Jim and Melinda helping him to his feet and struggling up the stairs with him, Boz following with the gunnysack. Making love to Jane on the foam rubber in Vince's quarters was especially vivid, and he could recall much of the conversation that had transpired in the kitchen and in the big front room, at least up to the time of Erik's departure. Boz had insisted on driving him home, and did so, without mishap, returning in twenty minutes with Orson and Saul, who had hours earlier walked into town, "to see what the fuck was happenin', man," the former had explained. There was some talk

370

about who was going to bed down where. Jane had led this discussion and had assigned beds and floor space in the front room to the various parties, and Boz had brought in some wood from the porch and stacked it on the hearth to dry.

It was about what happened after that—about midnight, according to Jane—that his memory became murky, eventually fading altogether. He had no recollection of going to bed that night. The next morning, after he had consumed three cups of coffee and swallowed four aspirins, only then rising from their bed where he had lain for an hour reading *Vanity Fair*, had Jane told him that he and Oliver had finished off the bottle of tequila and a full bottle of wine before Oliver had passed out on the cushions and been covered with a couple of blankets.

"And that's where I found him this morning when I went down about eight," Jane told him. "He got right up and put on his coat and boots and headed for the front door, like the house was on fire or something. When I looked out the window he was standing in two feet of snow taking a pee, for the longest time, right under the big oak." She had giggled. "Steam was coming up from the snow."

"Were you there while Oliver and I polished off all that booze?" He remembered asking her.

"Who do you think put you to bed? With the help of Boz, that is. He carried you upstairs over his shoulder. Then he went back down and slept by the fire. He was up before me this morning. That was the coffee he made that you lay abed swilling." She had paused then, watching him pull his jeans on. "I have to tell you, honey, that the conversation between you and Oliver for that last hour was all but incomprehensible. After that, *Finnegans Wake* would be a piece of cake."

"Hey, you're a poet and don't even know it," he had responded, yawning and rubbing his eyes. "Say, why don't you crawl back in here with me. I'm pretty horny, and it's the best remedy in the whole fuckin' world for a headache."

"I guess we have just about enough time for that and for some breakfast. And remember that we have to pick out a Christmas tree and be back here when the Pettibones arrive for lunch," had been her response as he commenced to unbutton her jeans. "I called them a little while ago. They rented a car, a jeep. *Oh, you! Horny* is hardly the word for the state you're in! *What gets into you?*"

"I'm going to show you what I have on my mind for a pre-breakfast *hors d'oeuvre*," he had replied, pulling her to him.

A proverbial million miles away, he became aware that she was addressing him. "What was that?"

"*God,* Joe, *where were you?*" She poured him more tea and handed him a muffin. "I said, don't you know someone who went up into Maine or Vermont or somewhere to start a free school on a farm or something a couple of years ago?"

"*Oh, yeah,*" he said, his tone revealing interest in, even enthusiasm for, the possibilities implied in her inquiry. "Dewey Coolidge went up to Vermont right after he got married. Beebee—everybody called him Beebee, don't ask me why. Never did get to the bottom of that. Lessee, that was about five years ago, that summer I was living in Cambridge, and I went to his wedding on this little island that her family owned—or owned part of, I forget—and, man, was that a drunken bash!"

"Yes, Joe, you told me all about that," she quickly cut him off. "Please don't drift off again. Do you have an address for him?"

"I could probably get one, babe."

"Then you could write him and see if he has anything going, something that might have a place for us. You know that we both want to teach in some way or other and that might be a possibility. Of course, he may not even still be there. But there would be other free schools. I've read about them and seen ads for them in underground papers."

"Yeah, I could get a letter off to somebody in Boston who used to know Dewey and the musicians he hung out with, somebody who was at his wedding, maybe. Jeez, what *was* her name? Oh, Winston! That was the girl he married. Maybe her family, if I can find that invitation."

"What an odd name for a girl."

"Actually, that was her last name, but everybody called her that."

"You could write and use General Delivery in Cambridge for a return address. Then when we get there in a couple of weeks or so, maybe there'd be a letter for you. Anyway, honey, the idea of teaching kids is much more appealing to me than slinging hash in some restaurant—."

"Speaking of hash," he interrupted, reaching for a small paper sack nestled up against the base of the hookah.

"I just think we should keep our options open, that's all I'm saying," she reassured him. "We don't have to make any definite plans right now. There'll be plenty of time to decide what we want to do, once we get on the road."

They were in bed soon after midnight. There had been some banging of pots and pans, shouting, and brief fireworks from across the street. Over breakfast at the spool the following morning he remarked that it had been the most "uneventful" New Year's Eve he had "enjoyed" for some years, "Maybe since that solitary one I spent in Napoli a decade ago putting away a bottle of Fundador, and freezing my ass off in that villa with its marble floors." *And wondering where in the* hell *MacKenzie was!* he said to himself. *My students told me it sounded like the city was under bombardment when the church bells rang out midnight! And I was so bloody blotto I never heard a thing!*

"It was nice doing it in front of the fire last night, wasn't it, honey," she said, putting her arm around him.

"That's for sure, sweetheart. You were, as they say, *hot to trot!*"

The telephone rang only once that day. It was Miles asking if he had finished writing his statement and could he bring it by his office "on the morrow." He agreed to do so.

She spent much of the morning sorting through clothes, bedding, and linens, while he lay on their bed reading from a stack of articles he had for months been clipping from magazines and papers. The subjects included the cinema, politics, social issues, music, and European travel. Except for the barely heard jazz violin (Joe Venuti, Steffan Grappelli, Stuff Smith, and Eddie South) from the speakers below, the room was all but silent except for the occasional rustle of paper as he finished an article and dropped it into a trash can fashioned from a bulk-nut tin.

After he returned from taking his statement over to

Miles' house, they had a lunch of black bean soup, dark bread, cheese, and ale, and returned to the bedroom and made love, afterwards sleeping for an hour or so. The rest of New Year's Day was occupied as had been the morning. The evening found them in bed by ten o'clock, and, having again made love, soon asleep.

Seated at the spool with his back to a roaring fire after breakfast the next morning, Friday, over a third cup of coffee, he could see the postman Stephens approaching. Gloveless and hatless and wearing only an Ike jacket over a plaid shirt for upper garments, he seemed impervious to the bitter cold that Joe had experienced earlier for only a few seconds when the morning paper had landed with a thud on the outer edge of the porch and Rufus would not budge from his bed, although he was trained to fetch it. Stephens swung his bag around and checked for magazines, deftly plucked out several, folded them around the letter mail, took the porch steps in a single bound, shot the bundle into the rural-style box, and leaped down the steps and across the lawn through the foot-high snow.

"There's old Fred," he said, looking down at his pocket watch on the spool and getting up, "right on the minute, for a change. Guess he didn't stop for coffee and you know what at his lady friend's down the street."

She reached over for the watch, which was behind Joe's cup, and shook her head in wonderment at the mail carrier's uncanny adherence, for the most part morning after morning, to his Kantian schedule. She heard the outer door slam and then Joe burst into the room.

"Still cold as a witch's tit out there!" he wheezed, dropping the bundle of mail on the wheel and rubbing his hands.

"Oh, honey, this one's from the Pettibones," she exclaimed, slitting the envelope open with a teaspoon handle. It took her only half a minute to read Margery's one-page handwritten note. "They're in Chicago and Henry is back to work on his memoirs and his new book on Dr. Johnson and Boswell. Margery likes it at DePaul."

"We'll have to get a letter off to them before we leave," he said absently as he riffled through the other letters and picked out a postcard. "What's this? Oh, I remember this young woman, from last year. She used to come up after the lecture and ask me about some of the sources I read quotes from. Yeah, she was pretty bright. Says here that she heard some rumor about me giving everybody A's." He picked up an envelope and examined the return address. "Now here's a name I don't recognize. Oh, it's from Denver." He tore the letter open with his index finger.

"Who—?"

"She says she sent my letter to the editor about the 'Hayawaka'—little transposition there—incident to Spokane, Chicago, Kansas City, and Escondido. She says, 'I consider it the best evaluation of the episode I've read. Thank you for writing it.' Well, that's nice to hear." He handed the postcard and the letter to her.

"Here's something from the registrar." He ripped the envelope open and read the enclosed letter intently. "*You won't believe this—!*" he began.

"What?"

"Those SOBs are not entering my grades on my students' report cards!"

"Honey, remember what Miles said when he warned you about some of the scenarios you should be prepared for. That was one of them, that they would put pressure on you through the students."

"Yeah, but I never thought they'd actually withhold the grades," he sighed. "How could they seriously believe I'd give in, for chrissakes." He crumpled the letter up and threw it into the center of the wheel and picked up another envelope. "Now what's this? Oh, I wondered why my check didn't come the day before yesterday. Guess the holiday mail held it up." He carefully inserted the spoon handle into the envelope, slit it open, removed a sheet of paper, unfolded it, and read. "*Oh, shit!* Would you *believe this?* Those assholes are *holding up my month's pay!*"

"*Oh, no!*" She took the letter from his extended hand. "They're really playing dirty, honey! You should call Miles right away and tell him."

"First I'm going to call up that idiot of a dean and give him a piece of my mind!"

"Now, honey, remember what Miles said—and you agreed to go along with it—to let him and the lawyers handle all communications with the university. Except for the students, that is."

"Yeah, yeah—."

"And you're not very good on the telephone, you know, especially when you're worked up like this."

"You're right," Joe agreed, leafing through the *Realist*, which he had selected from the mail after glancing at the covers of the *The Nation, Rolling Stone, Arion, Blues Unlimited*, and *down beat*. "Hey, here's an article about our friends the Peaceful Folk. Like to meet up with them again some time."

"Here, you haven't read Margery's letter."

"Oh, yeah, forgot all about it. What's she have to say?"

"Read it."

The imperative was gratuitous, for he was well into the second paragraph as she spoke. He looked up from the letter. "Makes me wonder if maybe we should head west instead of to New England, babe. They'll be in San Francisco in the summer. Of course, they're going there for different reasons—museums, galleries, the library at Berkeley, theater, all that cultural jazz."

"Now, honey, you know that we like those things, too."

"Sure, sure, I know that." The volume level of his delivery had abruptly dropped almost to a whisper, his focus of attention seemingly concentrating on something in the street. He stared across the spool out the front window. "I'm just saying that there could be a lot going on there that we should know about, be a part of," he continued in halting speech, evidently distracted. "It all happens first in California. Remember how Kesey set Tom Wolfe straight." He leaned forward, propping himself up a half foot or so with the flats of his hands on the spool. "I wonder what Fred finds so interesting about the bus."

She looked up from the magazines she had been desultorily examining. "Oh, he's probably going to ask you again if you want to sell it." She relaxed back into her cushion. "I want to read this article on the Weathermen. I heard over the radio this morning that someone stole an ROTC plane in Wisconsin and tried to bomb a munitions factory, but the bombs were duds. They didn't say whether it was Weathermen. If it was, that's just one more reason for me to think they're all nut cases."

"It just makes me wonder whether the East is the right place for us right now. After all, we've only been out here for a year and a half—not counting Austin, that is." He also had settled back into his cushion and his voice had returned to its customary mode. The distraction provided by Fred Stephens seemed to have had a calming effect on him. "I seem to be going through some very heavy changes and it's very hard for me to make decisions. Like, I've had a tremendous sense of relief ever since I turned my grades in—it's been almost two weeks now—and part of that has to do with the fact that I won't have to stand up there and play that role anymore. But the much greater part of that feeling of relief is that I feel that I have cleansed myself." He sought her eyes. "I'm not sure if any of that makes any sense at all. Probably not."

"It makes a whole lot of sense to me, honey. Don't forget, I've had to live through all of this with you. You coming home from class distraught over students—kids, really—crying in your office because they were terrified they would lose their deferments." She looked at him, tears welling in her eyes. "That sort of thing." They leaned toward each other and embraced.

"I hope I don't go all mauldin—I mean maudlin, funny slip of the tongue there!—up there in front of my classes next week." He smiled, stroking his beard. "I'm already Mauldin, with this rat's nest. Hey, did I tell you that somebody—I have to remember to bring those student evaluations of me home—put down that my 'appearance has deteriorated over the course of the term'? *Hah!*"

"*That's rich!*" She laughed. "Oh, I'm sure you'll be able to control yourself, honey. After all, you're a pro. And, yes, you are a sight to behold, my dear." She looked up from the magazine. "I think there's someone at the door."

Walking to the college later that morning, he found it

hard to keep from his mind the image of the four flat tires. Fred Stephens had promised to return with his brother-in-law's tow truck as soon as he finished his route, explaining to them how he would put the bus on axel supports and take all four wheels off and have the inner tubes patched.

"Have 'em back on your Greenbrier before supper time!" he had assured them. "Wonder who the sonovabitch was who did that to you, Professor! Like to catch up with that sucker! If I do, *he's gonna need more than patches, I shit you not!*"

Arriving at the building, Joe climbed the three flights to his office. The thumbtacks that had secured his lists of grades were still in place, tiny shreds of paper peaking out from beneath their heads.

"Guess my esteemed colleague lost his cool," he muttered to himself. He entered the tiny office and dropped his battered G.I. knapsack onto the desk, opened its middle drawer, took out about half of the inch-high stack of departmental stationery and slipped it into the knapsack ("Might want to write myself some letters of recommendation," he later explained to Jane.), scooped up some number 2 pencils and inserted them into the side pocket of his pea jacket, and turned toward the shelves opposite the room's lone window. A small Liddell and Scott *Greek Lexicon* and Cassell's *Latin Dictionary* (he kept the bulky unabridged ones on his desk at home) occupied a waist-high shelf and on the one below were spread out a half-dozen professional journals. He put the two volumes and the periodicals into the knapsack.

"Guess that's about it," he said, looking around the starkly empty room. "Never did use this office very much—except for the odd student conference. *Very* odd, *some of them!"* He chuckled, swung the knapsack over his left shoulder, and closed the door behind him.

On the way down the back stairs of the building his thoughts turned to the upcoming week. He found himself both keenly anticipating yet dreading the farewell classes with his students, especially the lecture course. Equally disturbing, yet exciting, was his and Jane's imminent departure from the college, the town, and their third home together, the rambling frame house they had rented since arriving on campus a year and a half ago. He wondered for a brief moment how best to get out from under the remaining months on the lease, a problem that he and Jane had not yet discussed. As to the direction in which to head the bus when they pulled out of the driveway, they had agreed to "just let it happen." ("Whichever way," he had remarked, "it sure will be good to get back to civilization. I've *had it* with the provinces!")

Can't seem to settle on very much of anything, he reflected, putting his shoulder against the heavy door that opened onto the parking lot. As he approached the end of the lane adjacent to the building his attention was suddenly arrested by a detail of the third-to-the last parking space. Its nameplate, which had read, "Prof. J. Lewis," was missing. *"Goddamn,* these fuckers *mean business!"* He laughed and slapped his thigh. *Damn, and I was planning to cop that thing the night before my last day on campus!*

Resolving to stop worrying about what the next few days would bring in the way of further aggravation, he turned his thoughts to Jane and their plans for the final two days of the holiday. *Get wrecked on that Moroccan that Oliver left for us—or was it Turkish? No, Jim had the Turkish.*

He headed up the driveway toward the library, intending to return the copy of *Vanity Fair* he had taken out months before and had reached the final page of on New Year's Day. He paused every now and then and fixed his gaze upon one or another of the buildings. It was not the first time he had seen the campus's Spanish American architecture in snow and, as before, it made him want to again see Arizona and New Mexico in winter.

As he turned up the path to the library, another figure hurried along a hundred yards or so to his rear and, as Joe reached the night drop, executed the same turn. It was Miles Satherwaite and he waved to Joe, having shifted a foot-high stack of books to a precarious perch under his left arm. Several of them escaped his grasp and landed on the ice-covered path, their impact followed by a snap of echo. Miles almost lost his balance, his feet slipping and sliding as the heavy man reached down to retrieve the fallen volumes. Joe rushed down the path, reaching him just as he had again secured the books to his chest with a bear hug, and noticed that one of the volumes was the first of the Modern Library set of Gibbon.

"Well, I didn't expect to run into you over here, Joe," he said as they made their way up the path to the drop. Joe held the hinged drop open as Miles fed the books in one by one and then he inserted his own lone volume. "You said you were going to stay away until your status was clarified."

"Miles, I really don't think there's much left that officialdom needs to say in the way of clarification," he replied. "After all, the registrar has held back my grades, they're sitting on my pay check, and I no longer even have a parking space."

"When did all this happen?" said Miles, clearly taken aback by the threefold news update.

"The letter from the registrar and another from the

payroll office arrived in this morning's mail—I tried to call you and you weren't home—and I just saw the handiwork of maintenance as I ducked out the back door of Smith on the way up here. I was cleaning out my office." He nodded in the direction of his knapsack. "It's all in here."

"What do you mean, maintenance—?"

"They took my parking space name plate off the wall. Then again, maybe our dear dean himself was out there with a screw driver." He laughed at the image.

"I don't like the sound of this, don't like the sound of it at all!" said Miles somberly. "I must get on the phone right away to our legal team and bring them up to date about this turn of events. Very serious, very serious indeed."

"Yeah, and while you're at it, Miles, be sure to tell them that some asshole ice-picked my tires last night, all four of them."

They were halfway back down the side-path to the main walkway when he made this announcement. Miles abruptly stopped, his Slavic-Nordic features all but in seizure, and looked Joe in the eyes, evidently seeking assurance that he was joking.

"What? You're not serious!"

"I shit you not, Miles!" said Joe, grinning. "My mailman is getting them fixed as we speak. His brother-in-law owns a gas station. My friend Boz would have taken care of it, but he's in St. Louis by now—if that old REO didn't break down again."

"Who would do a thing like that, Joe? Why, your grades are only known among the faculty, so far, and surely—."

"Come on, Miles, this has nothing to do with the

grades, this is a town and gown thing. Listen, I get hate mail all the time—and even a few rabid phone calls. I should show you some of that garbage. One nut even threatened to waste me with his hunting rifle. You know the positions I've taken since being here. I've made no secret about where I stand on this bloody war. I've written pieces in the school paper and even had a couple of letters printed in the *Denver Post*. You can see my hairy visage in photo after photo of the protest marches on campus." He motioned for his colleague to join him in proceeding toward the wider path. "By the way, Miles, I'm sure that word has gotten around to a lot of my students by now about the A's. They have ways of finding out things." He thought of Cassie and determined to stop for pie and coffee on the way home.

"So, you are still firm in your resolve to go through with this, Joe? You've had no thoughts of changing your mind?"

"About letting the A's stand?" There was incredulity in his voice. "Not a chance, Miles. Shit, I wouldn't miss this party for all the tea in China—or in California!"

Miles looked puzzled for a moment.

"Oh, I think I understand, yes," he said after a moment, smiling. "That's a novel way of putting it."

The two contrasting figures stood at the paths' point of convergence, Miles in his camel's hair, knee-length overcoat, Cossack's fur hat, and oxfords, Joe in his patched jeans, navy knit cap, and ankle-high work boots. The biologist was clean shaven and what little hair he had around his ears did not protrude from his head gear, whereas the classicist's beard reached to his chest and his hair, in a pony-tail, rested upon the back of his jacket. They turned and looked at each other.

"Wonder if you and your wife—I mean—," Miles hesitated, clearly uncomfortable.

"It's all right, Miles," Joe reassured him. "In a manner of speaking Jane *is* my wife—common-law style that is—and soon will be even legally so, now that my third ex finally got around to filing for divorce."

"Oh, I'm sorry, I didn't know—."

"What's to be sorry? Fact of life. Decree should be in the mail down the road a piece."

"Anyway, I wondered if you and Jane could come over for a drink some night soon. Martha would love to see both of you and—." He took his fur hat off and was running his hand over the crown of his head as though brushing aside strands of hair. "I mean, there wouldn't be anyone else there."

Taken by surprise, he hesitated before responding, wondering whether he should gracefully decline, perhaps pleading, *"Because of the stress of recent days, Jane and I like to get wasted on hash and go to bed early and mess around."* He suppressed a smile. *Could be a drag, sitting around gassing about civil liberties and academic politics, playing the tiresome academic game of "people and places," listening to Mozart. Don't know if I could deal with an evening of that kind of a travesty of social intercourse. And I sure don't want to find myself on one side of the room trying to hip Miles on why I gave all those A's while Jane and—. Jeez, I don't even know his wife's—oh, yeah, Martha—while Jane tries to make conversation with Martha. Wonder what she's really like. Could be another stifled faculty wife. Sometimes that's the type who's ready to break out of the cage. Maybe he's on the verge, too. They'd probably find it interesting to be in the company of some of the local freaks for an evening.*

"I'll tell you, Miles," he said, realizing that he had to wrest control of the situation, else a potentially excruciatingly dull evening loomed for Jane and him, "sorting and packing is taking up most of our spare time these last days here. So we left it open for people to fall around to our place tonight. Why don't you and Martha drop around, anytime after seven."

"Say, that's very nice of you," said Miles, accepting with apparent delight. "I don't see why we couldn't do that. Why don't I call you later, say, about six, to confirm."

"Fine. Hope you can make it."

Taking a short cut home from Fritz's Grill, which he had found to be closed until the morrow, he noticed that the path through the woods had been cleared and sanded. The air was cold but bright sun burst through the bare, skeletal trees and here and there were moist patches on the flagstone steps that led down to the next level of the path. It put him in mind of New England in March or early April—especially that spring when he had returned from Napoli so shaken—when the gray had left the sky and fallen snow didn't stand a chance against the early afternoon sun.

Too bad Fritz's was closed, he mused, *but I guess not too many students have returned and business would be slow. I should give Cassie a call and see if she's picked up any scuttlebutt. Oh, wait, she said she'd drop by tonight with her brother. Really pisses me off those SOBs holding back my grades. Now I'll have to announce it in class in order to make it official. That'll sure take them by surprise. But then the Bugle should be out before eleven. That'll get the news around. And maybe the Campus Press over at the university will run an article. I'll get Jane to call up one of the students in the seminar she took this semester. Anyway, I'll make sure to be about five minutes late, give 'em a chance to spread the word. Shit, somebody'll probably get up and make the announcement for me.*